BLOOD AND WATER

SIOBHÁIN BUNNI

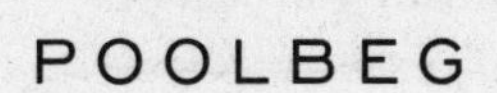

This novel is entirely a work of fiction. The names, characters and incidents portrayed in it are the work of the author's imagination. Any resemblance to actual persons, living or dead, events or localities is entirely coincidental.

Published 2016
by Poolbeg Press Ltd.
123 Grange Hill, Baldoyle,
Dublin 13, Ireland
Email: poolbeg@poolbeg.com

1

A catalogue record for this book is available from the British Library.

ISBN 9781781999905

Printed and bound by CPI Group (UK) Ltd, Croydon, CR0 4YY

www.poolbeg.com

About the Author

Born in 1968 in Baghdad, Iraq, Siobháin is one of six children born to her Irish mother and Iraqi father. Educated in Kylemore Abbey in Connemara, she then graduated from the College of Marketing & Design in Dublin. She lives in Malahide with her three children, Daniel, Lara and Lulu.

Also by Siobháin Bunni

Dark Mirrors

Published by Poolbeg

Acknowledgements

I don't for one minute take for granted the honour of having a publishing contract, but writing with a real deadline is a totally different experience to writing with only myself to answer to. *Blood & Water* should have taken a year to deliver but life got in the way and it has taken almost three. And it's been an incredibly rewarding but strangely focused experience, so when it comes to those I need to thank, this time around, there is only a handful of amazing people on my list.

Thank you so much, Paula Campbell, Poolbeg's fine publisher, for having the patience to stick with me.

No nonsense and straight to the point Gaye Shortland, my enduring editor, gentle but firm, I am very grateful for your keen eye and for recognising the thread that made the story.

Outside of writing but ever present in the background are my parents, Nael and Anne Bunni to whom this book is dedicated, for their continued advice and support.

For my brother Layth and his fiancée SarahJane for constantly checking in and making sure I'm on track.

Once again I have to thank my sister Lara. What can I say? You're a mad yoke, but you keep me smiling and make me feel loved!

For my sister Nadia and brother-in-law Paul who

pleaded to read a draft – not sure if they've actually read it, but thanks anyway for being curious!

On the lighter side, literally, for Aidan and the Gym Bunnies (!) at Just Classes in Malahide for the brief, very energetic and utterly fatiguing moments of fun in my week – thanks a million.

And finally for my three children, Daniel, Lara and Lulu. You make me proud habitually, you make me laugh loudly, you make me happy daily and are the reason I get up each day glad to be alive and honoured to be your mum.

Dedication

For my Mum and Dad, Anne & Nael, with infinite love and gratitude.

Prologue

They carried the coffin into the crammed church, two abreast and three deep, their footsteps falling in time to the sombre drone of the organ. In silence they offered up the polished rosewood casket at the front of the altar. A long display of white lilies was placed on its top, then one by one they genuflected and turned to take their places in the pews reserved for the family at the top of the church. The three brothers stepped into the first pew beside their sisters and mother. From behind they were a unified force, standing tall, shoulder to shoulder, all dressed in black for the occasion.

Here the siblings were in familiar territory: this was where they had come as children to pray each week. It was where their parents had married and where they were each christened, all five of them. However, on this day they were burying one of their own earlier than they could ever have expected, and under less than usual circumstances.

An enormously well-respected family with almost celebrity status, this deference was evident in the numbers that gathered to mourn alongside them, with sympathisers spilling out the doors onto the gravel square outside.

Government ministers standing side by side with local dignitaries, friends and neighbours. To the outside world, spectators to the event, they were solid. This, they reflected quietly in their seats, was a close-knit family that didn't need the emotion of grief to be united. They were the family that was referenced around other folks' dinner tables, the '*Why can't you be more like Sebastian Bertram, so polite, so smart?*' or '*Cormac Bertram, he's handsome, so entertaining*'. The tactless statements that every other child dreads to hear: the comparison and the disappointment. Today that admiration and respect was amplified.

Together they stood tall, heads bowed: a fine and imposing example of family unity. A family any parent would be proud of.

Detective Inspector Milford stood at the end of his carefully chosen pew in the west transept and watched them standing together. The opening hymn ended and they took their seats, heads down, eyes focused on the floor, each lost in his or her own grief.

From the pulpit, one of the celebrating priests welcomed the congregation, calling it a day of great sadness, a day of enormous loss not just for the family but also for the community and the county – the loss of a true statesman and long-serving politician who gave his service to the county and the cause he so obviously loved. He bowed his head in sorrow as he extended his sympathies to Barbara, the grieving widow, who without lifting her gaze from the floor shook her head as if to deny the reality of what was happening. Poignantly then he invited them to join him in prayer for the repose of a soul that was taken so prematurely, so violently, from them.

Milford didn't take his eyes off the front pew, noting their every move, every nod of their heads and shift in body pressure. He didn't miss a budge or nudge or a single word, their incantations and their hymns, their participation and their expressions. He watched them from start to finish and admired their staunch, stoic performance. And when they spoke from the rostrum their voices boomed through the vaulted church, the readings and prayers delivered so beautifully and with such perfect pitch and diction. And, like the rest of the congregation, he found himself thinking how extraordinary they were but for reasons different to those of the grieving onlookers.

As funerals go it was almost perfect. It had mood and humility; it spoke of greatness in this life and rewards reaped in the next. Extolling the life lived and celebrating great achievements, the priest rejoiced not just in the deceased, but also in those that he had influenced around him. And the music: what an impressive arrangement – sentimental when required yet uplifting as the words declared a welcome into heaven.

Heaven: do we really still believe in that concept, Milford wondered while he watched and listened. He was more of a live-for-today kind of a guy – Carpe Diem and all that – happy to leave the caretaking of heaven to God, if one existed. And while he wasn't so sure about heaven he was certain of a final judgment, and not in heaven but here on earth, in the here and the now. Sceptically he scoffed as the creed warned: *"From thence He shall come to judge the living and the dead."*

Yes, apart from his own heathen wonderings, the service was almost faultless and that, for Milford, was the quandary. If the priest hadn't regularly mentioned the name of the deceased throughout, it could have been anyone's funeral. It was textbook stuff. Definitely not his preference.

Curiously, for someone who died so suddenly there were no tears, like it was a relief or a long time coming, Milford surmised, then silently admonished himself for stepping ahead of the investigation, a classic error he often had to reprimand his overly eager juniors for. But his instinct wasn't often wrong.

As the service reached an end, again the men took up their positions at the elaborate casket to lift and bear its weight on their shoulders. Slowly, arms bracing each other, they followed the three celebrating ministers down the aisle, passing through the heady scent of burning oils and incense. The church bell tolled loudly, once for every year of his life, its ring sounding a bleak and sorrowful pulse into the crisp autumn morning.

Barbara, dressed elegantly in an expensive fur coat and hat ensemble, flanked on either side by the girls, stood to take up her position as chief mourner behind the coffin. Someone, she wasn't sure who, handed her a single long-stemmed lily which she held loosely in her hand. Why, she wasn't sure. He always hated lilies, she thought as they paraded down the red carpet towards the glaring brightness of the open doors. She did her utmost to ignore the well-meaning but, in her mind, patronising stares that honed in and watched them like hawks as they moved. She felt exposed, on display. Not sure what to do or how to behave she kept her eyes, like raging fireballs in their sockets, focused forward. She wished she'd had the foresight to take her sunglasses from her bag before leaving her seat. There should be tears. Why are there no tears, she asked herself. Taking assurance from the hand that gently squeezed her arm, she briefly entertained the urge to wring one out, for show if for nothing else. What must they think of us? But she simply didn't have the energy and instead did her best to ignore the audience. The stinging sun assaulted her eyes as slowly they stepped into the sunshine. Shielding herself from the burning rays, she let Ciara take her bag and dig out her glasses for her. Putting them on, she smiled and nodded politely, relieved by the privacy they afforded.

Reverently the coffin-bearers navigated the steps into the crowds outside: the late arrivals and the ones that couldn't squeeze into the packed church. Parting biblically, heads lowered, the gathering made way for the procession that snaked around and alongside the old majestic granite church, then headed up the gently sloping path to the graveyard where the open grave and an unsettling pile of freshly dug clay awaited. Perfectly timed, the last toll sounded as they reached the graveside where the coffin was awkwardly lowered on to the banded pulleys that would drop William Bertram's rigid bulk into the ground.

How had it come to this, Barbara asked herself, hardly able to remember the past few days, never mind the last few decades. Was there a point in time that she could actually mark, a point from which it had all spiralled so wildly out of control? This wasn't a spontaneous thing, she knew that. Things like this didn't *just happen*. It had been building for a very long time. Our finest hour, she mocked silently. She wished she could say it wasn't, wished she could say that it had been an impetuous act of frustration that just got out of hand, went too far. But that would be a lie. This, she acknowledged rationally, was a culmination of years of actions. No one was more cognisant of that than she.

Hilarious, she thought, watching as the coffin was lowered and somehow one of the inexperienced pallbearers managed to almost let slip his end of the pulley into the hole. She imagined William standing beside them, glaring at them, infuriated by their inability to co-ordinate and get it right. '*Why do you insist on being such idiots?*' she imagined him roar, always the perfectionist. Always himself imperfect.

"Our family," she said aloud. She hadn't meant to, but it had come out involuntarily, quiet but audible nonetheless. If the girls were surprised they didn't show it. She knew they had heard: she felt them flinch. But they looked neither up nor at her.

She stole a glance at each of her children standing to her left, her right and directly in front of her across the grave. Silently this time she spoke to her dead husband. *Look at them,* she told him. *Our family, connected by blood, but divided by personalities. We were supposed to nurture them, to teach them how to experience each other, to tolerate and care for each other.* Outwardly she shook her head. This was the conversation she didn't have the chance to have with him in person. These were the words she needed him to hear. *Look what we have done to them. Look what you have done to me.* Now she felt the tears that had been so obviously absent freefall down her cheeks. But they weren't tears of grief, rather they were tears of frustration and shame. She had watched it happen and did nothing to stop it. She let it happen. Her body shook.

Ciara, of all people, put an arm around her shoulders and let her head rest against her shoulder. How ironic, Barbara mused, that this child should be the one to offer her comfort, their roles reversed, their lives changed. She felt the strangely welcome pressure of her fingers on her upper arm. She was free now to feel, as she should, waking finally from years of inertia, the sensation of Ciara's embrace peculiarly exceptional.

His mouth was moving but she couldn't hear the priest's words. She watched him flick oil at the polished timber and bow solemnly but she wasn't listening. Way over his head she watched the trees sway gently against the clear blue autumn sky, their leaves discolouring beautifully, just waiting to be carried to the ground to decay and complete their life cycle, just like the coffin that was without doubt a coffin fit for a king, now resting in the rectangular hole which was its final destination, primed to decay and rot. It was nature's way.

"Mum," Enya prompted from her left, waking her from her evanescent thoughts and nodding to the flower in her hand.

The lily: William's least favourite flower. Barbara cast it from her hands and waited for its quiet, comical thump as it hit the wooden box below. If she could have chortled aloud and got away with it she would have, but it just wasn't appropriate for the grieving widow to snigger at her husband's funeral.

Around her, one by one, her children reached down to cast still-moist handfuls of clay on to the coffin. The organic, wet smell of it made her stomach lurch and her skin prickle. She didn't need to look up to know how they appeared or how they would behave. In the silence of the past few days she had come to know them well: the distinguished leader, the careful diplomat, the amusing joker, the rebellious doer and the sensitive carer. The remaining line-up of her team.

Part One

Chapter 1

Three weeks earlier

Like a startled rabbit he jumped instinctively, alarmed by the feel of his brothers wife's hand passing purposefully across his groin. He took a short gasping breath and checked himself. Did that *really* just happen? Watching her back as she moved about the kitchen like nothing out of the ordinary was going on, he wasn't quite sure. Perhaps he'd imagined it. But when Kathryn looked over her shoulder to throw a wicked, sinful glance back at him he knew he hadn't and she had meant it. Every provocative nerve-tickling nanosecond of it. He looked around, as if someone else might have noticed her move but, apart from himself and herself, they were completely alone in the expensive, solid and shiny red kitchen.

Cormac, spooked by the innuendo, swallowed nervously and tried to discreetly reposition himself out of her way, but it was pointless. Moving within her dominion she found a way to make contact each time she passed, which was without doubt unnecessarily frequent. Whatever he had been expecting from her, it wasn't this.

"You alright?" she asked casually, busy chopping and mixing and stirring. "Be a pet," she said with a wink, "and help me set the table."

His heart was beating double time and, in the absence of any better ideas, he did as he was told. Having found what he thought was the right moment to talk to her again about his predicament, this wasn't the anticipated response. And now, distracted by her unexpected but not inexplicable behaviour, he couldn't think straight. And while he may have been temporarily stunned, he wasn't completely stupid: he had a pretty good idea what was happening – he just wished he were wrong. Perhaps he had misunderstood, maybe he was misreading her constant skimming. Maybe it would be different with everyone around? But he needed her alone.

Frustrated by a situation slipping out of his control, he stopped trying and allowed himself to become her stooge for the afternoon and prayed for a moment to organically arise where he could talk to her properly.

"Be a doll and check the spuds."

"Do me a favour and get the serviettes from the top drawer."

"Reach in there and grab the opener for me, would you?"

"You wouldn't mind shining up the glasses, would you?"

"Be a pet and fill up the salt cellar for me?"

Attending to her every beck and call, hoping to win her favour, he did as he was asked and scurried around her while one by one the family arrived to take their places at the now beautifully set lunchtime table.

On the plus side, he consoled himself as he navigated between tasks, his activity served to legitimately remove him from the mindless, bullshit conversations around the table. He never understood why they did this to themselves: these 'first of the month' Sunday lunches were a form of self-inflicted torture that he and his siblings forced upon themselves in the desperate hope of actually becoming the close-knit family everyone in their acquaintance had them down as. Why and to whom it was so important he couldn't remember anymore.

His father was, as always, being difficult, finding fault with his younger daughter on her unannounced return from abroad while his mother, as usual, remained silent but pissed. Rian was indulging in excruciating displays of affection with his newly announced fiancée Martha while Seb and Ciara verbally scratched at each other like children.

Lunch at last served, Cormac could no longer avoid taking his seat in the dining room, where he silently celebrated another average Bertram Sunday lunch: whoopee. His knee hopped under the table in anticipation of the meal's end. He had no idea what was on his plate or how much of it he eventually ate – all he knew was that when the end came he eagerly sought the opportunity to follow Kathryn into the kitchen.

"I'll clear," he announced, leaping from his seat to pile the plates one on top of the other.

"What's up, Bro?" Enya asked, catching the wineglass that he accidentally tipped with the edge of a plate. "You look a bit pasty – you feeling all right?"

Cormac, lost in his thoughts, was unresponsive.

"Cormac?" she repeated and, placing her hand on his arm, asked, "What's up?"

Disrupted from his trance, he looked at her, confused and distant. "What? Sorry … I'm grand, really. Just a bit off. Must have eaten too much." He gathered whatever else he could carry in his already overladen hands and hurried into the kitchen.

He had done his best so far not to react to Kathryn's unusually tactile behaviour, but now he was unable to control his body's instinct to jerk as if electrocuted when, holding him from behind, she pushed herself against him. Was she laughing at him? He pulled himself away and turned to face her.

"Oh for God's sake, Cormac, don't go all innocent on me," she mocked. "I've seen the way you watch me. I'm not shy, I'm open to it. We're both too long in the tooth to play games. How old are you – forty-one, isn't it? Don't deny you fancy me."

She was a very attractive woman, there was no denying it, but she was his brother's wife.

"Don't be ridiculous. What about Seb?"

"What about him?"

"What about him? Are you serious? He's your husband for Christ's sake and my brother!"

"Is that all that's stopping you?" she asked, moving towards him.

"Don't," he begged, unable to trust himself.

"Well," she told him, "now you know what I want."

"What?" he asked incredulously, amazed that she had managed to translate his predicament into a salacious come-on. "When I came to your office the other day I asked for your help, that's all."

"And I said I would think about it, didn't I?"

"So what's with all this – this stuff?" he asked with a quiet shriek, prodding the air with a pointed finger.

"Well," she replied with a sigh, "let's just say I'm testing the water." Then, smiling sweetly at him, she turned to fix the coffee cups on the tray.

"Kathryn, for God's sake!"

Picking up the tray she shimmied past, keeping her back to him, moving slowly, enjoying their close proximity and making sure her curves connected fully with his groin as she passed.

"Why did you come to me?" she asked when she'd reached the door.

He didn't bother to answer. He wasn't supposed to. It was a game. Her game. He had handed it to her.

"You think I don't know what you want, Cormac?" She smiled while pushing the door with her backside. "I think you like me, and I think I'm intrigued by your . . . *frisky* little antics," she whispered, punctuating her words with a slightly caustic smile. And, like a conquering diva, she swept herself from the room, leaving her lingering scent and a powerful emptiness behind.

Jesus Christ, the woman was stark raving mad. He had gone to her because he'd thought she'd understand – she was a psychologist after all. Ha! She'd understood the situation alright and now was taking advantage of him.

What the hell had he just done? His phone vibrated in his back pocket. He knew what it would be. This day was just getting better and better. Taking the slender, state-of-the-art device from his back pocket he swiped his thumb across its screen and waited for the message to appear.

Just like the last time the image made him blush: he recognised the bare freckled arms of Mark, the fine sweep of his leg and the beautiful curve of his behind. And despite his fear Cormac felt a perfunctory yearning stirring inside. Oh for God's sake, he chastised himself, glancing down with repugnance at the bulge that had grown in his trousers.

The delicately patterned walls of the kitchen danced

around him, closing in tight, their edges blurring dangerously as the enormity of his situation intensified.

He had just assumed Kathryn would help. She was the problem-solver, the rational one. He could have used any number of adjectives to describe his sister-in-law: organised, mature, solid, calm, serious, boring even. And now, it seemed, he could add horny to that list too.

"Bloody hell," he sighed desperately, closing down the image and the words that goaded him: **"Two more sleeps. Don't forget now!"**

Forget? How could he possibly forget? It was a hundred grand they were looking for, not fifty cent. How the hell was he supposed to forget about that? He placed his phone carefully on the counter, wanting nothing more than to smash it. Bash it into smithereens. Past panic and knee-deep in trouble, his stomach churned as Kathryn's fake cackle rattled through the door from the dining room.

"Cormac, pet, do me a favour and bring us through more cream from the fridge!" she called.

Bitch! He stood, feet apart, and putting his hands on the island he dipped his head deep between his outstretched arms. He was free-falling.

His gaze followed the hairline cracks on the expensive and expansive tiled floor, their chaotic pattern so much like himself: erratic, confused and going nowhere. A mess. He was a mess and his single best idea for a rescue was fast turning into his worst.

Well, she might still help him. But in return she intended to take advantage of him and his weakness. For a split second, he was almost flattered by her proposition: she wasn't a bad-looking woman, fit for her age. But his ego was immediately subsumed in his fear and loathing.

"Oh, and bring in the brandy too!" she shouted from the dining room.

Cormac looked first at the door then at the bottle of expensively beautiful and utterly inebriating liquor, and he wondered what else he might do with it. The colour blanched from his knuckles as he gripped the marble top tight. Accepting he could fall no further, he felt an inner calm descend over him, beginning at his head, percolating all the way down to his Converse-clad toes. There was very little he could do now. He was well and truly snookered. Might as well just get on with it and accept the consequences.

Raucous laughter from Kathryn once again ripped through the room. He knew it was staged. Knew she wanted him to hear her. His family never laughed like that at these compulsory monthly lunches.

"Yep, I'm done," he said to the still-echoing kitchen and, standing tall, took a fortifying breath before sweeping up the brandy bottle and walking out the back door into the early-afternoon sun.

He secured the bottle to the back carrier of his bicycle then stuffed his jean bottoms into the tops of his socks, swung his leg effortlessly over the crossbar and freewheeled along the side passage of the house, down the short gravel driveway and out onto the street.

Turning left, he pedalled his way down the tree-lined avenue, oblivious to the iridescent amber, yellow and rust autumnal colours that collided overhead to hide the sky beyond. This was such a beautiful street – as a child he always dreamed of living here, with his gorgeous but imaginary wife with big boobs and full hair. When Seb and Kathryn bought on this street, initially he was so pissed off: they had invaded his dream. This was his entitlement not theirs. Now he could never fulfil his ambition. The fact that he didn't and probably never would earn enough to afford one of these detached mansions was irrelevant.

He crossed over Main Street and cycled the fifteen-minute journey without noticing the rain that had started to spit at him. He felt his phone vibrate in his back pocket but ignored it. It could wait. But its presence was like a burning coal against his skin.

Had it been it worth it, he asked himself as the rain, heavier now, peppered his scalp. The drops streaming down his face could easily have been mistaken for tears. How had he let it come to this?

But they did have a lot of fun together, he and Orla – well, the sad part was that he actually thought she had enjoyed herself too.

"What a fool!" he whispered into the rain, letting the breeze take his words.

He should have known it was too good to be true. As his grandmother had told him so many times when he was young: "*If it looks too good then it is too good.*" How right was she? Thank God she was dead, though. She'd never forgive him for this. Small mercies, eh?

The lights turned red at Hillview Road and he slowed to a stop.

He stared blindly down the pretty tree-lined street that led to the beach and remembered the first time he had seen her. She was dancing, well, gyrating really, on a table top at the club. They were all at it, the guys as well as the girls, but she was the master: every part of her body moved in fully synchronised rhythm. She looked absolutely incredible and she knew it too, knew they were all watching her. It was only his second or third time in the exclusive members-only venue. That night he was with Gillian, a great girl with a face as sweet as sugar and a body made to touch. But, with Orla, there was no real comparison: she was out of this world. Out of his world anyway. Her long, sculpted, chocolate-brown hair reflected the dull glow of the lights in the darkness of the club which intentionally made it hard to see faces that didn't want to be seen. Easy to keep secrets. And, when she lifted her head, everything about her seemed to shine. She gleamed: her eyes, her hair, the soft sheen of her skin, the sweet swell of her lips, the long undulating journey of her body from her head to her stiletto-clad feet. She was breath-taking and in the company of Gillian he did his best to ignore her, but oh my God that body was impossible to deny.

Yes, he would always remember the first time he saw her. He would have done well to remember his first instinctive thought. She's so outta my league, he had told himself. And he was right: she was.

Months later, long after Gillian had ceased to entertain him he almost wept when Orla approached him. Her tall, elegant and seductive frame bee-lined towards him through the red-and-yellow haze of the lights. Like the cartoon cliché of the geek, he actually looked around, first left then right to make sure it wasn't someone behind him that she was targeting.

Me? he mouthed silently, pointing towards his chest with his thumb.

She nodded, amused by his reaction, and crossed the

last few feet between them with a slow smouldering smile designed to disarm and hypnotise.

Without offering her name, she hooked her thumbs through the loops of his jeans and leaned in to kiss his lips. Forward and delectable, she felt soft but demanding and he responded accordingly.

"Orla!" she shouted into his ear.

"Cormac," he replied with a feeble swallow, amazed by what was happening to him.

"I know," she said, grinning, and he nearly choked. "You like us brunettes."

It was more of a statement than a question, to which he raised his eyebrows in response, amazed that she had even noticed him, never mind who he was with.

Again, she leaned straight in to kiss him. "You taste of JD," she remarked, licking her lips.

His confidence boosted, he took a nonchalant swig of his drink, allowing his lips to soak up the smooth woody liquor before lowering his glass to swallow and letting her kiss him again, enjoying the warm fuzzy haze that followed.

"Come on, let's dance," she invited, leading him by the hand to the small dance floor. She moved expertly around him, sweeping her hands over his torso, grinding her hips into his, making him see and feel her excitement. Gyrating she dipped and swung herself low, using the loops of his waistband to drag herself slowly back up, pausing briefly at his groin. A titillating move heightened by his intoxication. She was gorgeous. He was lucky.

But when the lights came on she left alone. She was like a whirlwind: a tornado that had torn through his senses. He returned to the club the following night and the following weekend but it was two weeks before she walked through those doors again, this time in a very tight and very short leather skirt and strapless top that left almost nothing to his imagination – just enough to make his heart skip and his groin tingle.

He turned his back to the door and watched her in the mirror as she descended the few steps into the club then paused, scanned the room, saw him and smiled. He assumed she would play hard to get, maybe ignore him and delay their undoubted encounter, make him work for her attentions, but she came straight to him.

"Waiting long?" she asked.

"Only about three weeks."

"Sorry it took so long, babe, but I'm here now," she said with a sultry smile and, draping her arms about his neck, asked, "Now, where did we leave off?"

She pulled him in to her and held him tight. He felt her heart beat and her hips move against him. She smelt of tangerine and vanilla, an aroma he discovered ignited each and every sense in his body. He could just about contain himself. She was incredible. He returned her fevered embrace with urgency. Taking hold of her face he brought his lips to hers and kissed her. She responded with roaming hands that made their way from his shoulders, down his back and inside his shirt to massage and awaken the flesh on his chest . . . The memory hurt.

A short beep of a passing car tugged him back to the present.

One of the most disappointing things about the whole sordid debacle, Cormac thought as he set off again and pedalled his way down Strand Road, was that he actually thought they were good together. He thought together they ticked a lot of boxes. Fun: *tick*. Laughter: *tick*. Conversation: *tick*. Sex: *tick, tick tick*. Damn, they even looked good together, although he had to admit she tipped the balance on that one.

By the time he reached his apartment the rain had stopped and a few weak spears of light fought valiantly to break through the grey muteness of the afternoon. He chained his bike to the railings, took the bottle from the carrier and went inside. His apartment was elegant, bright and beautiful. The first floor of the Georgian building was all his. Heading straight for the living room, he pulled back the shutters and opened up the full-height sash windows then sank into his wingback chair to watch the world go by: just him and his brother's bottle of vintage brandy. This was the brightest part of the whole four-room, one-bedroom apartment. From here he had the best vantage point of the whole street and the park opposite. This was where he sat of a Sunday, armed with the full spread of newspapers and a long coffee that chilled as he waded through the pages and pages of newsprint but he drank it anyway.

But this afternoon it was just him and the bottle. Looking out at the quiet streets it seemed that even passers-by had absconded in sympathy, leaving him to sit and stare and ponder his predicament alone. But he was being ridiculous, just feeling sorry for himself. It was still early, not even seven, yet judging by the level of the remaining liquid in the elegant bottle he'd have been forgiven for thinking it was later. Despite himself, in an almost drunken haze he let his head fall back as he smiled, recalling the memory of the incredible excitement he had experienced getting into this unfortunate mess and pondering the trouble he was going to have getting out of it. In the wonderful Cognac-induced languor he could almost taste the JD on his lips just thinking about her.

Always the free spirit, at forty-one he was one they had begun to ask: '*Would you not find a nice girl and settle down*?' But the very idea of it made him nauseous. He never dreamt of walking down the aisle, quite the opposite, but explaining that to his inquisitors was pointless. They wouldn't understand, so instead of wasting his time he'd smile forlornly, lift his hand to his heart and declare that he hadn't yet crossed paths with his soul mate. The notion that he wasn't even looking was really none of their business.

His phone, cast aside earlier on the side table, rang out then vibrated for the umpteenth time but again he chose to ignore it. It had been going nonstop but Cormac was too busy thinking about her and now thinking about *him*. Thinking about Mark.

Chapter 2

The middle one of the three brothers, Rian was always both Ciara and Enya's favourite. In their youth, when politics seemed to consume their lives, they found solace in each other and fun, somehow, in the endless packing of election envelopes around the dining-room table, walking the legs off themselves doing door drops and smiling saccharine smiles for the cameras at one chilly hustings after another. And, as they got older, he was the source of many boyfriends and unfortunately ex-boyfriends. But it worked both ways: neither tall nor handsome, he possessed a devilish charm that was a magnet for most if not all of the girls' friends. It was, most agreed, his smile that reached the depths of his deep brown eyes and the unkempt tufts of chestnut hair that made up for his slightly smaller than average stature.

His sisters always wondered where he got his innate nurturing instinct from as, it seemed, neither of their parents had a caring bone in their bodies. Instinctively he stood up for his sister at the 'family' lunch, irked as always by the way his father provoked and bullied them.

"Leave her be, Dad," he told their father as he needled and goaded her.

"*I beg your pardon?*" William Bertram blasted, apparently surprised by his son's insubordination.

"You heard me," Rian replied. "She's only just in the door and you're already on her case."

"How dare you!" William turned to him with furrowed eyes and squared-off shoulders, preparing it seemed to ramp up to one of his usual high-volume lashings, but a glance at Rian's fiancée Martha seemed to change his mind. Lowering his voice to a patronising hum, he said, "I'll ask you to remember just who it is you are speaking to, boy."

"Come on, come on," Seb interceded, standing up to refill the wineglasses while throwing dagger eyes at his little brother. As the eldest in the family he commanded a level of respect from his siblings that was unspoken. "What do you think of the wine, Dad?"

Infuriated, Rian turned first to make sure Enya was alright, then returned his brother's glare, hoping it spoke the words that were passing through his mind loud and clear. It was a bit late, he fumed, for Seb to be playing the protective brother. Seb, he assumed, had something to gain by shutting him up. Over the years, particularly when they were much younger, Rian had learnt the hard way that Seb never went out of his way for anyone except himself.

Comforted by the calming squeeze of Martha's hand on his knee, he took a deep breath and allowed the moment to pass. And as happened every now and again, although less so recently, Rian found himself transported back to their boarding-school days where he and Seb, although brothers, were divorced from each other, both emotionally and empathetically.

Water flushed down his neck and filled his ears. It smelled of bleach, lemons and urine. He coughed and spluttered as it filled his nose and emptied into his mouth. He couldn't breathe. They lifted his head up by the hair at the back. A moment's respite, enough to spit it all out and gasp in some air. Then into the water again. In between, he could hear them laughing.

"One more time! One more time!" they squealed like sugar-crazed kids.

And so he was dunked again, closing his eyes to the white porcelain bowl just in time before the water rushed around his head.

"So, numb-nuts," Fitzer said, hauling him out of the bowl, "who did you say was the boss around here?"

"You are," Rian spluttered, spitting the remaining toilet water out as he spoke, splashing his assailant in the face.

"Oewwww!" he moaned, wiping his face with his sleeve, the look of disgust intensified. "I didn't hear you, Bertie!" he sang. "Say it again!"

"You are!"

"Still can't hear you! Louder so we can all hear you."

Rian opened his eyes to the cubicle and turned to his audience who giggled and jeered while he dripped and spat.

But before he could say it one last time someone whispered "Sketch!" urgently from the outskirts of the gathered crowd. "Sully on the loose!"

And like cockroaches in daylight they scattered in every direction. Fitzer, ever the ballsy lad, hung on to Rian's soaked collar a little bit longer.

"I'm not done with you yet," he whispered close into his ear then let him go. Rian flopped to the seat, not caring that the headmaster was on the prowl. It couldn't

really get much worse than Fitzer. Once he had you in his sights, well, that was it until he got bored or found someone else to torment. He sat in the cubicle and closed the door over, listening to the sound of the slow, heavy footsteps. The fluorescent lights flickered overhead, emitting a high-pitched buzz that you could barely hear and hardly notice, but when you did it was the loudest noise in the room. In the distance the comforting sound of his two hundred or so schoolmates chattering in the dorms from across the hall filtered through the lightweight partition walls. He looked up from his seat, following the priest's progress in his mind's eye.

This isn't my fault, he rationalised. I can't get into that much trouble really. He counted the splats of once-sodden toilet-paper balls that had been fired over the years at the yellowing ceiling. The footsteps stopped at the door into the toilets. This, he knew, was where Sully had to choose: right to the dorms, left to the toilets or straight down the stairs to the classrooms. Rian held on tight to his breath for fear Sully with his rumoured bionic hearing would hear him pant. Deathly still, he waited to see which way the priest would go. But he couldn't hear a thing. He stood up and stretched forwards towards the white melamine door, as if doing so would help him listen better. But it didn't help. Still nothing. He must have gone down the stairs, Rian thought, because if he'd opened the door to the dorms he would have heard the increased volume of noise from inside. Just as he was about to sneak a peek out of the cubicle door it crashed in on top of him.

"What's going on in here?" the priest bellowed, having used his foot to kick open the door.

Rian fell back onto the toilet seat as his heart leapt

from his ribcage to his mouth, his lunch threatening to follow. His knees turned to jelly and from his lips escaped the girliest of screeches in fright.

Father Sullivan took stock of the dripping, quivering mess of a boy in front of him.

"Take yourself to the showers, then come see me in my office," he said without as much as a hint of sympathy.

Rian's heart dropped. He knew what was coming and it wasn't going to be nice. Trudging out of the toilets, he crossed the hall and went into his dorm, his hair dripping and his jumper soaked, smelling like something close to a toilet freshener.

He stopped one cubicle short of his own. The curtain was open and his brother sat reading on the bed. He stood and looked in at him.

"Thanks," he said quietly.

"What for?" Seb asked, looking up from his book.

"You could have stopped them."

"You could have kept your big stupid mouth shut."

"Really? So I should have just stood by to watch that asshole Fitzer beat the crap out of Robbie?"

"That's the one."

"Robbie is our friend."

"Your friend."

"You're a shit, do you know that?" Rian told him, feeling the drops of toilet water seep down his back.

Seb gave him a last sour glance, accentuated by his middle finger, then focused his attention back on his book.

"Wine?" Seb asked, hauling him back to the present reality of the lunch table.

"Please," Rian replied politely, not because he had any

kind of thirst for it, but because he wanted to have Seb serve him.

He watched the burgundy liquid fill his glass before looking up into his brother's face. Seb avoided his stare, as if looking into his eyes might give something away, his slightly flushing cheeks confirmation that there was another agenda at play.

They had never talked about what happened that night, or what happened next like a scenario deleted from the final cut of the play, but they both knew it was a moment that had shaped Rian's life forever.

Rian walked on past, turned into his own tiny cubicle and pulled the curtain across. Despite its flimsy construction – it was nothing more than a two-by-three open-top, three-sided, plywood box with a sink in the corner and a built-in chest of drawers to the side – he usually felt perfectly safe, but not that evening. Sitting on the edge of the bed, feeling the hostile vibrations from his brother on the far side of the blue painted wall, he felt anything but comfort. Gathering his wash bag and towel along with a clean vest, shirt and jumper he returned across the hall, to the showers, ignoring Seb with his head held high as he passed his open cubicle.

"What's the matter, Bertie?" Fitzer was standing in the hall with his moronic sidekicks, Decco and Murph, on either side.

Rian lowered his head, keeping his focus on the ground, unwilling to risk meeting his aggressor eye to eye.

"Had a little accident, did we?" Fitzer sniggered, looking to his companions for endorsement while sidestepping into Rian's path. "Now I hope you don't

plan on whining your heart out to Sully. I don't want to hear that you have. Understood?"

"Understood," Rian replied, dead in his tracks, clenching his fists tight, his eyes to the ground. He wanted nothing more than to punch Fitzer but resisted the urge, knowing full well what would happen if he did.

"There's a good boy," Fitzer mocked with a gentle slap to the back of his head. "Because if you do, there'll be more of this," and with the threat he lifted his knee fast and hard till it come in contact with Rian's groin.

Immediately on impact his world imploded into whiteness, like a veil had fallen in front of his eyes. The pain shot like a burning rod, running the route straight to his brain and back again, a pain so bad it brought tears to his eyes and turned his legs to water – they wouldn't, couldn't and didn't hold him up any longer. Holding himself, he fell to his knees and bit down hard on his bottom lip, doing his best to contain both himself and his scream, making sure both it and his balls stayed inside. When he opened his eyes Fitzer was gone. The door to the dorm was open with Seb standing at its threshold, books and pens in hand, looking down on him. Seeing his brother lying buckled on the hall floor, he reversed back into the room and closed the door after him. Rian closed his eyes and waited for the pain to subside and his vision to return to normal, then slowly uncurled and heaved himself up off the cold linoleum floor. Unable to stand upright, he hobbled like an old man to the showers. Choosing the only lockable unit in the row of twenty open showers, he fell into it and slammed the plywood door behind him. Safe within its confines he stripped down, threw his clothes onto the stool and turned the dial to release the water at full blast. He stood under it, letting the spray drench him all over, not caring nor noticing that it was hot enough to burn. Somewhere deep inside he felt brave for standing up to them: Robbie was too small to fight for himself. But weightier was the feeling of humiliation at being knocked down. In the end he had let them take him down. It was that or fight and be battered. But, above all else, he felt abandoned by his big brother who as good as gave him up to the shellacking. Despite their antipathy for each other, Rian never thought that in a moment of danger Seb would forsake him like that. If their roles were exchanged he knew for sure he would never do that; he knew instinctively he would safeguard his brother at all costs. They were the same blood: he would take his side over anyone else. They should stand together and fight together, as brothers. As family.

Feeling let down, empty and alone, he slowly slipped to the floor and sobbed. At thirteen he wasn't yet the man his family expected him to be. Even at sixteen or seventeen or eighteen or ever, he would never be the man that could match the eminence of Seb. He was and always would be just Rian. And that would never be good enough.

He sat in the water spray until his skin turned soft and lumpy and his tears ran dry. Picking himself up, he took a deep breath and, shoving his feelings of self-pity to the back of his mind, accepted for the moment he was what he was. Slowly he washed himself, starting at his head and working his way down, checking his groin on the way for any visible damage, mentally preparing for what he knew was still to come with Father Sullivan.

"Are you okay?" Martha asked him quietly, squeezing his arm gently.

"What?" Rian asked, returning to the moment, his unseeing eyes still trained on his brother.

"You're shaking," she remarked, wiping his brow. "I hope you're not coming down with something."

"I'm fine, just thinking, that's all. Just thinking ..."

Chapter 3

Sebastian blushed under the intense scrutiny of his brother's glower. He needed to rein it in: his unusually affable behaviour was arousing suspicion. Until yesterday he'd forgotten that it was his and Kathryn's turn to host the monthly family gathering. He could have done without it but, given the circumstances, to cancel would have been the wrong thing to do. Anyway, he reflected, it did afford him some time to think tactically and figure out how best to handle this latest crisis; he hadn't, however, appreciated it would be as difficult a task as it was now turning out to be. Seb was well used to dealing with one catastrophe after another, but this one was that bit different because it involved his father. And the emotional aspect of this particular conundrum was having an unusual effect on his ability to think clearly and rationally.

Doing his best to ignore Rian's glare, Seb navigated the table to top up the wineglasses. This was his house, his home, his table and it galled him to see his father lord it over the group. Somehow he and his siblings had become used to it: regardless of whose home the lunch was hosted in, it was a given that William Bertram would somehow usurp the seat at the head of the table. But today, knowing now what his father had done, it stuck in his throat.

Be smart, Seb, he told himself, replacing the wine on the credenza and retaking his seat while Kathryn brought in the main course.

What the hell is she at, he thought, momentarily distracted by his wife's bizarre behaviour, prancing in and out of the kitchen with that look on her face that he tended only to see when she'd got what she wanted. Well, at least she's smiling, he told himself – one less thing to worry about.

He let his chin rest on his interlocked fingers to observe his father. Going into business with his dad was never a good idea, but his involvement had, he thought, been minimal.

"What harm can it do?" he'd asked his friend and business partner Dermot.

"Just keep it simple," Dermot had warned and that, or so he thought, was exactly what he had done – kept it simple. But lunch with an old friend told him otherwise.

Only a few days previously his phone had rung out from his pocket. He didn't recognise the number when it came up on screen and almost didn't answer, but curiosity got the better of him.

"Jesus, Tim. How the hell are you?" he said once his old school friend identified himself.

With the pleasantries aside, Tim suggested they meet "for a catch-up".

Seb was intrigued. Why all of a sudden was it so important that they should catch up?

"My shout," Tim offered.

Well, he's changed, Seb thought, remembering Timothy

Burton as the meanest guy in his year who got away with it only because he was so bloody entertaining. Must be looking out for a new job, he assumed.

They met in the city for lunch.

"Good to see you, mate," Tim greeted him with a hearty slap on the back and a knuckle-crushing handshake.

"It must be what, four, maybe five years?" Seb calculated.

"About that," Tim confirmed. "And we're still in one piece."

"Just about," Seb half-joked.

"Tell me about it – it's been a crazy couple of years."

They both nodded slowly as if paying silent homage to the memory of their recession-inflicted wounds.

"You still in the bank?" Seb asked after they had ordered.

"Yep. For my sins!"

"Someone's gotta do it," Seb teased.

"True. True," Tim conceded, matching Seb's wide grin.

And when their drinks arrived they touched glasses and toasted their re-acquaintance.

"So," Seb enquired through a mouthful of overpriced burger, "how is the bank?"

"Well, that's why I wanted to meet with you," Tim replied, putting down his cutlery and clearing his throat. "I'm heading up a new team. It's part of a high-value risk-assessment procedure that the Financial Regulator's brought in since the recession."

"Sounds pretty interesting."

"It is," Tim replied, dropping his eyes to the table. "Our job is to review all loan transactions over five million euro and basically make sure they are processed correctly and risk-free – for us, the bank, I mean."

Seb laughed. "Isn't that always the case?"

"Well, normally yes. But in the years before the recession it was all pretty lax to be honest. Before, money was handed out to people who would never, ever, have had the means to pay it back but now – now everything has to be checked and double-checked, triple-checked sometimes and – well – that's how come I asked to meet."

The sudden injection of trepidation in Tim's voice made Seb look at him properly.

Then out of Tim's mouth came words meant to soften a blow. "I respect you, Seb, really I do. I've followed you all these years and I admire the way you've managed not just to keep it together but have actually managed to grow your business at a time when everyone else failed. You have a really good reputation."

"Thanks, Tim," Seb replied, no longer interested in his food nor flattered by Tim's compliments which he sensed were nothing more than a sweet coating on a bitter pill about to be administered. Feeling a tiny flutter of fear in the pit of his stomach, he laid down his fork and wiped his mouth with his napkin. "I appreciate it," he finished, steeling himself for whatever was about to be revealed.

"I would hate to see everything you've built for yourself ruined by what could be just a small error." Tim paused, his face – from his cheeks to his chin – now coloured to a deep crimson.

"Tim, what's this all about?" Seb demanded.

"I'm not even sure I should be meeting you," Tim replied, "but then we're just two old friends having lunch, are we not?" He laughed nervously as if justifying their reunion to himself as much as anyone else who might see them and ask what they were doing together.

"Tim, I'm sorry," Seb interrupted with a degree of controlled impatience, "but you're freaking me out here. Spit it out, man – what's the problem?"

Tim looked over his shoulder apprehensively.

"Something's come across my desk with your father's name on it."

Seb felt his mouth go dry.

Watching his father now holding court at the top of the table, Seb hoped Tim was wrong. It was the kind of mess that was alien to Seb and he found it impossible not to be concerned. If the allegations turned out to be true, it had professional and personal implications that were both far-reaching and irreversible.

Seb took a deep breath. It was going to be a long, difficult afternoon. He could hardly wait for Monday morning to arrive when he'd have all the information he needed to see for himself.

Chapter 4

The phone rang out until his rehearsed voice invited her to leave a message.

"Hi, Cormac – it's only me – Enya. Just checking to see where you got to. You left me there to fend for myself," she quipped, a joke with a serious edge. "You were a bit weird earlier. Give me a shout when you get this. Bye!" She hung up. Throwing the phone on the duvet, she couldn't ignore the snoring heap that lay sprawled and fully clothed over on the bed.

Lunch at Seb and Kathryn's ran on until just after five thirty and it was almost six by the time they'd got back to Ciara's house. Enya would quite happily have left hours earlier but as her sister's houseguest she was at her mercy. Only when they turned into the tree-lined driveway did she feel her shoulders relax and the knot in her stomach unravel. Much as she loved her siblings, she'd had about as much of her family as she could take and needed a drink: not a polite glass of wine, but a dirty great big whiskey. Having wisely decided that morning not to introduce Joe into the 'family' mix at lunch, she now used him as her excuse to get to the pub.

"He's been here alone all afternoon – I think he'd probably like to get out – change of scenery, you know," she said, knowing it to be far from the truth. Joe was quite happy where he was: in the sitting room, his feet comfortably resting on the coffee table with a beer in hand, watching the footie.

"You don't mind if we don't go with you, do you?" Ciara asked. "It's just we have to be up early in the morning."

"God no," Enya gushed, feeling only a hint of guilt. "Anyway, I think Joe and I need to talk."

She and Joe walked hand in hand the short distance to the local pub, the gesture feeling awkward to her and out of place now she was home.

"So how'd it go?" he asked, oblivious to her ruminations.

"Grand. The usual. Nothing changes."

She didn't elaborate and he didn't look for her to tell him any more. She had shared very little about her family with him and, realising she couldn't be bothered to tell him about her lunchtime experience, she wondered what on earth she'd been doing bringing him back home with her in the first place.

She'd picked him up, literally, in a bar in Amsterdam: he'd tripped over her bag and ended up face-down at her feet. She'd helped him up and bought him a drink – it was the least she could do – and had been with him since. That was about six, maybe seven months ago, and in that time she'd never mentioned home. Not until she'd got the email from her solicitor.

And here they were now. She watched, troubled but focused, while he dribbled in his sleep onto the floral-patterned sheets. She couldn't bear to get into the bed beside him and instead moved in the darkness to sit at the window. Pulling back the curtains, she sat into the deep sill and drew them back around her, hiding her from sight. The moon was bright against the night sky, an iridescent magical orb shining down on her as she pondered her past and considered her future. Pushing up the sash window she took a cigarette from her pocket and lit it, waving the smoke like a defiant teenager out into the night air. Drawing her legs up to her chin, she wondered if there was any magic in that shining dot overhead. What would she wish for, she asked herself with a sigh and a deep pull on her cigarette. Ciara definitely wouldn't approve of her smoking at all, never mind in her house, but the whole day had been such a nightmare she deserved it. She shouldn't have gone to the lunch, she didn't want to, but Ciara was impossible to say no to and Cormac had promised to protect her from the anticipated intrusive questions that were bound to be fired at her. And they were. But Cormac had deserted her even before they'd finished their pavlova and Ciara, too focused on her spat with Seb, was useless, leaving her to bat the questions off alone.

The family monthly get-together was just as she'd remembered it: great if you weren't the centre of attention, torturous if you were. And, having just returned from an almost two-year absence, or adventure depending on which way you looked at it, she was very much in the spotlight.

Her father still knew how to push her buttons. Even after all this time, after all that he'd done, despite her abhorrence for him and all that he stood for, and in spite of the fact that she hated him, she still expected more from him. Alas, just as he had done the day she left, he'd made her blood boil this afternoon too. What a prize prick, she mused, flicking the ash out the window.

So, what would she wish for? To have her life back and her baby and be somewhere else, anywhere else far away from here? As wishes go, it seemed like a good combination. But something inside her, she wasn't quite sure what, told her it was time to grow up. Her life had changed. Fundamentally. There was nothing in her wish that was achievable.

Is it not time, she asked herself, to wish for something that is actually possible to achieve? She knew and accepted that the days of living outside of reality had to come to an end and now, she told herself, was as good a time as any. She had already tried to put thousands of miles' distance between herself and her home, but emotionally she wasn't able to disconnect. Accept it, she lectured silently. This is where you are, this is where she is and this is where you need to be.

A quick spray of deodorant and the room was as good as new, well, almost. Leaving the window open and the curtains drawn back she let the light of the moon brighten up the room and highlight the body in her bed. It was time for her to stay, and him to go. Bending down, she plucked the duty-free bag from under the bed. Taking it into the en suite she took the bottles from their plastic and poured their contents down the sink. He'd be cross, she thought, but she didn't care. It was time for change. Taking a pillow and a blanket she snuggled into the corner of the couch and snoozed, waiting for the morning to come. Maybe there was magic in that moon after all.

The smell of cooking breakfast woke her the following morning. Stiff from the awkward position through the night, she lifted herself from the couch to find the bed was empty. Nor was he in the bathroom. He must have made his own way downstairs, enticed by the smell of eggs and bacon no doubt. She hoped he'd at least dressed himself and smirked just thinking about the conversation he and Ciara might be having. Joe was a fantastic distraction but definitely not her sister's type.

She showered, changed and went down to rescue one or the other of them.

But, as she approached the kitchen, she was almost alarmed to hear a pleasant conversation in full swing.

"Enya!" Ciara called, seeing her sister enter the room. "Did you sleep well?"

Enya nodded in silence, looking at Joe who was digging into a full Irish.

"Sit down, I'll get your coffee," Ciara buzzed, getting up to busy herself with mugs and water and spoons – she knew that the first thing Enya needed was her caffeine fix. "Joe was telling me that you've sold some of your work."

"Huh?" Enya asked, disorientated by the unlikely companionship that seemed to have sparked between the two. "One or two. Nothing special."

"Seriously, Sis, I didn't know you were painting again."

"You didn't even know where I was, never mind whether or not I was working," she replied unkindly then immediately was sorry for her bad behaviour.

"Well, for what it's worth, I think it's great that you've found something that inspires you," Ciara, ever positive, responded, ignoring her sister's acid tone. "Did you take any photos?"

Enya shook her head and threw a chastising glare at

Joe who smiled back deviously, well aware of the friction he was stirring. She doubted if Ciara would appreciate the darkness of her art. Gratefully she accepted the hot mug of coffee and sat down beside Joe, cringing as he placed his hand affectionately on her knee.

"So," she asked, looking to distract herself from his unwelcome touch, "what's the story with Rian and Martha?"

"She's nice, isn't she?" Ciara replied, clearing away Joe's plate. "They've been going steady a good few months and now the engagement."

"How much older is she, do you reckon?" Enya asked.

"No idea, but isn't it great to see him smile?"

No longer interested in what was going on, Joe made his excuses and left the two women chatting.

"You did well yesterday," Ciara said once Joe had left the room.

"You think?" Enya replied with a shrug.

"No, really. Dad didn't make it easy but you stayed calm."

"It took everything in my power not to tell him to bugger off." Enya let the words hang before continuing, "But he's right. Much as I hate to admit it, I've got to stop hiding my head in the sand."

"Why did you come home?" Ciara asked nervously. "Not that I don't want you here or anything, but you've stayed so very far away from us for so long and then all of a sudden you turn up – I'm just curious, that's all."

Enya laughed. "I wondered when you'd ask. The divorce papers have come through."

"Oh," was all Ciara could offer in response. She let the silence settle before asking the next apparently obvious question. "And what about Joe?"

Joe was sitting up on the bed strumming his guitar.

"Hey, babe," he greeted when Enya returned to the room.

Closing the door behind her, she watched as he ran his coarse yellowing fingers over the strings. The sound, despite the roughness of his fingertips, was a sweet melody: a sad melody, like he knew what was coming, but, if he was perturbed by her stare, he didn't say so.

"I think it's time you went home, Joe," she said to him eventually.

"*Awwww* what? But we've only just got here!"

"No. I'm staying but you're going."

"Babe?" he asked, confused, putting down the instrument and kneeling on the bed. "Why?"

"I'm sorry, Joe, it's the best thing. Not just for me, for both of us," she replied quietly but with an unmistakable firmness, not looking to hurt him but making sure he understood that this was the end of their journey together. "It's just not the right time for you to be here." Her words sounded hollow and weak even to her own ears, but it was true. Joe was past. It was time to move on, get on with her life.

"But we're going to go back to France, the festival, a little R&R." He made a little pelvic movement, lest she should misunderstand what he meant.

His lewd performance sent a shiver of bad taste down her spine. Yes, it was time for him to go.

Chapter 5

Ciara stood by her sister, watching as Joe took off in his taxi. She was proud of her, always had been, but never more than right now. It was a tough call but it was a choice she knew Enya had to make and had confidence enough in her to know that it was the right one.

Long after the taxi turned the corner, Ciara steered her inside and without saying a word they walked arm in arm to the kitchen. Ciara sat and watched while Enya made the ever-soothing potion of a '*nice cuppa tea*'.

They had always been close. As kids, despite their age difference and the dissimilarity of their personalities, they somehow seemed to gravitate to each other. She never felt that inherent sense of separation that she felt with the others. She assumed it was because they were boys and that little bit older as well as being just plain different, but behind it all lay a constant notion of being somehow mismatched. And as they grew older that feeling intensified, born mostly from her insecurities rather than their actions. She was sure they didn't mean for her to feel like that; they weren't maliciously inclined. It wasn't, she often reasoned, that they didn't get on with her, more like they didn't connect with her. She always felt like she was hard work for them and interpreted every encounter as a measure of their tolerance of her. But not so with Enya.

Taking the mug of steaming hot tea that was offered, she smiled up fondly and was rewarded with an equally fond but desperately sad grin. They sat opposite each other in silence, sipping their tea, happy in the calm quiet of the kitchen. Somewhere outside a dog barked and a cat mewed. Despite the million and one questions that whirred around in her head, dying to be answered, Ciara remained mute, knowing that Enya would open the conversation when she was ready. It was good to have her home, she thought, observing her over the rim of the mug. With Enya she felt calm. And safe. That horrible feeling of being perched on the edge of a cliff with nothing to hold on to disappeared. The uncontrollable and overly dramatic compulsion to be the centre of attention lessened. Enya somehow had the power to dull the panic that always seemed to surround her. Enya and Robert: they were the two people in Ciara's world who were able to see beyond the high emotion and bizarre histrionics. Ciara smiled, thinking of Robert. How lucky was she to have found him? He was a godsend. A gift. They met while on a retreat in the wilds of County Galway. She was there under direction – Father Maguire thought it would be good for her – while Robert was there of his own free will: "to think," he'd said. It was one of the many interventions Ciara's parents had tried over the years to keep her 'disorder' at bay. Highly strung was how she was described, with no real diagnosis, prognosis or remedy aside from meditation, visualisation, relaxation and every other alternative treatment available.

She noticed him first at registration – it was impossible

not to. It was the sound of his laugh that grabbed her first. He had arrived on the bus that followed hers and was plucking his bag from its underbelly when for whatever reason he laughed out loud, a hearty sound coming hard from the base of his belly. Tall and handsome, well, to her anyway, with a few days of stubble around his jaw, he didn't seem the usual type for an event like this.

Maybe he's working here, she thought, watching him throw his bag over his shoulder.

But no, he was there that evening as a guest when they sat by the campfire talking about their lives' journeys, each having the opportunity to reveal their highs and lows thus far. He was funny and smart. She couldn't help but watch him over the flames, his face dancing with the flickering orange and black shadows. Their courtship was a fast one. He'd quickly passed most of her tests, from meeting both her brothers and Enya to dealing with her strange and oftentimes irrational behaviour. But Robert was generous with his love and soon became her stabiliser. The afternoon that Robert went to her father to ask the old-fashioned way for her hand in marriage, she was sure she saw relief in her father's eyes. She was never sure if it was relief that she was finally happy or that she was no longer his responsibility. Over the years she had tried her best to win his favour, to make him see her, like her even, but it never seemed to go according to plan. Invariably she ended up behaving more like a simpering idiot, which he seemed to take pleasure time and time again in telling her, while her mother, as always, appeared indifferent. "You'd get a better reaction if you'd told her you were marrying Barry from the off-licence," Enya and Rian had joked, so obvious was her disinterest.

And Robert's mother didn't like her very much either.

At one of their very first and few encounters she openly informed Ciara that Robert was a soft and gentle soul who always had some sick bird with broken wings to tend to, concluding with an acerbic smile that it appeared she was latest in a long list of ailing birds so not to get too comfortable. In a way she was right: Robert was a sympathetic sort always looking to fix things and people. And while there may previously have been a long line of sick birds with broken wings, Ciara was the last one he ever took home. In his heart he wanted to give flight back to those wings and mend her forever. And he almost had.

Enya put her mug down and traced her finger around the rim. "I'll miss Joe," she said as much to herself as to Ciara and, looking up, grinned weakly. "Thanks, Sis."

"No problem. It's nice to be able to be there for you for a change. You'd do the same for me. Correction – you *do* the same for me all the time."

"Not recently I haven't," Enya replied quietly.

"Well, you had your own stuff to deal with."

Enya huffed and let flashes of the two years past taunt her. "Well, I'm here now," she stated, pushing the memories aside firmly, sitting up in her chair and focusing on her sister. "Sorry it's taken so long."

"Good to have you back!" Ciara told her with a smile.

"Well, enough about me!" Enya replied with a lift in her voice. "How are you?"

"I'm good," Ciara responded but the light in her smile had gone out.

Seeing it go and knowing why, Enya probed gently, "And what about . . . ?"

Ciara responded with a slow shake of her head.

"Nothing?"

"It just didn't work."

"How many times did you try?"

"Three," Ciara replied with tears in her eyes.

"I'm so sorry," Enya sighed, taking hold of Ciara's hand across the table.

"Don't be, it's not your fault. You couldn't have helped even if you were here."

"But that's exactly what I *am* sorry for," Enya stressed. "I should have been there for you."

"Robert was brilliant," Ciara sniffed, tired of trying not to cry. "He's so amazing."

Enya dropped her head and suppressed a small hint of jealousy. She really was lucky. Robert was a great guy, and so good for her.

"Can't you go again?" she asked.

"We just don't have the money."

"And what about Dad – surely he can afford it?"

"We did ask, but he said no."

"*What!*" Enya shrieked. "He did what?"

"He said no," Ciara confirmed with a sorry grin.

"You're joking. What an asshole. Well, ask him again," she told her decisively.

"No," she said quietly. "Robert won't do it again."

"What about adoption?"

"Well, we're approved, but it could be years, maybe never, before we might get chosen as parents." Ciara lowered her shaking head. "We'd be great parents, Enya," she sobbed. "Rob would have made an amazing dad."

"He will," Enya stressed. "He will make a great dad. You can't give up hope. Not yet."

"Seriously? At this stage there really is very, very little hope."

"I'll help you. I have some money. We can borrow the rest."

"Stop," Ciara replied holding up her hand, uncharacteristically calm. "We can't. Robert has said no and I have to respect that. You can't help. Not unless you want to have it for us."

Enya's head dropped and her face coloured wildly.

"I was only kidding!" Ciara laughed, amazed at her sister's response. "You didn't think I was serious, did you? No, you being here is the best help you can be. Just don't run away again, okay?"

The sweet chime of the doorbell gave Enya the diversion she needed to change the subject, for the moment anyway.

"Expecting anyone?" she asked, looking at the clock on the wall.

"Nope, not that I can remember. Maybe it's Joe coming back for you?" she teased before getting up and heading out to the hall.

In the kitchen Enya, relieved to be extracted from the moment, took a deep breath and put her head in her hands, unsure why she felt so bad.

"Hey, Rian!" she heard Ciara cry out. "What are you doing here? Are you not working today?"

"I thought I'd drop by to see how Enya's doing after Dad's performance yesterday."

"Me?" Enya yelled out from the kitchen, hearing her brother's remark. "You took a bit of an emotional battering yourself. In fact, I'm surprised you even noticed Enya – you hardly took your eyes off your fiancée all night!"

Ciara hauled him into the kitchen, positioned him at

the table then stood back. It was like old times: the banter blossomed and took its own natural and unpredictable course. It was always the same: a little stilted at first but, slowly, as the effects of the copious amounts of tea and endless chatter began to bed in, the quick-fire joking was never long to follow. Yes, she was glad Enya was back if only for this moment. They were liquid gold: so rare, so beautiful, the laughter resonating so lyrically, the mood so buoyant, optimistic enough to combat even the heaviest of hearts. Unlike the forced Sunday gatherings, this felt real. It was real. They were here by choice, because they wanted to be, performance free, relaxed and enjoying themselves. This was the dream she had for her own children: that they might sit like this and laugh like they didn't have a care in the world, with each other to look out for and care for. But it seemed the harder they tried, the less likely her dream would ever become a reality.

Chapter 6

"Morning, Mr. Bertram," Lucy his receptionist welcomed Seb as he exited the lift on the 14th floor of his building.

"Lucy," he acknowledged without stopping.

From behind her elegantly illuminated glass desk she watched him go, expertly judging his mood by the speed of his legs and tone of his greeting. Today, she registered, wasn't going to be a good day.

Lacking the humour to entertain small talk, Seb lengthened his stride to take him quickly out of conversation's way. At a great pace he strode down the corridor past the mash-up of the old and new office interior. A refurbished grain store beside the canal, the building boasted beautiful red, gold and ochre brick walls slapped with flashes of ivory plaster where the new was forced to marry the old. Polished dark-timber floors, expansive glass partitions and low-level lighting created a warm but very masculine workplace. This was his realm, his space, and he was very proud of what he had achieved. On a normal day he liked to absorb the atmosphere while making the journey down the glazed corridors to his office. It was thrilling to witness the flurry of activity going on beyond the various glass walls: the meetings, the deals, the negotiations, all for the greater good of Bertram and Guilfoyle. Yes, he was a proud man, but today he was happy to charge past, unable to fathom the potential impact his current situation would have on the stability of this kingdom which he and Dermot Guilfoyle had built together.

The smell of furniture polish pleasantly assaulted his nostrils as he opened the door to his corner office. Fully glazed on two sides, it gave him a privileged view of the city. His city, he often titled it as he soaked up the light and the atmosphere of a country in the full swing of recovery. Closing the door with a cursory glance outside, he marched over to his desk, placed his briefcase on its top then pressed the intercom to Lucy.

"Yes, Mr. Bertram?"

"I'm expecting a package – can you bring it in as soon as it arrives, please."

"Yes, Mr. Bertram."

Tim had promised he'd get copies of the documents to him first thing and Seb really hoped he'd follow through. The last thing he needed was for this to drag on all day. From the shelf beside his desk, he pulled a thick black file with **Ronson Street** typed in bold along its spine and took it to the meeting table where he opened it out and, finding the section he was looking for, extracted six pages and placed them down, one by one, beside each other on the table. Even with the information Tim had given him the pages appeared innocuous, resting innocently on the table in front of him. How did the bank even pick up on it? He scanned the sheets. He would never have guessed there was anything wrong with any of them.

A gentle knock on the door interrupted his inspection.

"Yes?" he called out without moving from the table.

Lucy came in and handed him a large padded envelope. "This just arrived for you."

"Thanks, Lucy."

Good man, Tim, he thought, not the least bit concerned about what Tim had to do to get the documents to him.

"Would you mind getting me a coffee, Lucy?" he asked as she was closing the door. He would have liked something a bit stronger but, tempted though he was, he knew he needed to keep his wits about him and resisted the urge.

"Sure," she replied with a smile then left him alone.

Opening up the package, he pulled out the individual bundles, each clipped together neatly at the top right-hand corner and a yellow sticky note placed beside the signatures on their respective first pages. Written in blue ink on each note were the words in block capitals *NOT VERIFIED*. The pages were the same as those in his own file.

The Ronson Street deal was the first and would be the last time he would do business with his father. Bertram and Guilfoyle had earned considerable recognition through the recession by engaging in high-risk but lucrative property deals on behalf of their clients. Their interest wasn't in the properties themselves but in the high fees that the deals earned as the sites were bought and sold on. They were the middlemen who found the best deal and squeezed the margins so tight it made financial sense to have them on board.

When his father suggested that Bertram and Guilfoyle might be interested in getting involved in an apparently fantastic property deal, Seb entertained it more as a gesture to assist his father than as a serious business venture. William Bertram and three of his political cohorts had, they said, researched the market, come across a number of opportunities and now planned to invest in one of the last remaining derelict buildings on Ronson Street – an up-and-coming address in the city with a fast-developing almost celebrity status. Their intention was to buy the building, a relic of the recession, invest in its refurbishment and offer it to rent as a state-of-the-art office space and potential headquarter building. Once fully occupied, they would put it on the market as a high-profile signature building and make more money than their collective pensions would ever return on their retirement. It was, William Bertram described, a no-brainer. To Sebastian it was just another deal.

"A bank is unlikely to deal without the proper structures in place. You need to set up a limited company with the three of you as directors and equal shareholders – it'll protect you personally if anything should go wrong," he advised at one of their first meetings. The process was so simple it was foolproof, he thought. "The company will apply to the bank for the loan. They'll want each of you to raise a combined half of the property value and then they'll lend you the other half."

He cringed as he remembered how he had spoken to them as if they were novices, like they were completely ignorant of the process. But now, looking at the signed pages in front of him, he realised they weren't.

This was trouble. Since the economic collapse (what felt like aeons ago but in reality was only five torturous years) public and professional scrutiny was at an all-time high, nothing more so under the microscope than the behaviour of bankers and financiers. Even politicians didn't escape investigation if warranted, regardless of position or power. The media had become the public's unsympathetic watchdog, took no prisoners and like vigilantes loved nothing more than to delve into the belly of a story to expose its ugly truth. This was just the kind of thing they loved and as he was never media-shy they would love nothing more than to push him over then watch him fall. *Iron-willed. Hard-nosed. Tough. Bullish. Impervious. Aggressive.* They were the words often used to describe him, Sebastian Bertram. He was the one who dished out the whipping, not the other way around. He worked hard to protect his reputation, went the extra mile to make sure everything was above board and legitimate, so this injudiciousness, although not of his doing, would be like manna from heaven. He had managed hundreds of deals, some more challenging than others and some more contentious but, in all of his transactions, while getting what he wanted and being perhaps a little devious he was never, ever dishonest. His problem with this deal was all about being too trusting, a little naive and as a result more than completely stupid.

Lucy returned with his coffee and, seeing the sour look on her boss's face, left without saying a word.

Holding the mug in his hand, Seb took it to the window to look pensively over his rejuvenated city, sipping but not tasting, looking but not seeing the extraordinary view below. Theirs was one of the tallest buildings in the district and on this side he had perfect sight of the picturesque if busy canal landscape and the fastest point on the rail line that skirted the building way below. Here the trains whizzed past at speed, a symbolic measure of Bertram & Guilfoyle Enterprises. Nothing annoyed him more than having their success described as lucky. There was nothing lucky about it. Both he and Guilfoyle worked damn hard at being successful and he didn't plan on letting anything, never mind his father's apparent stupidity and notable greed, destroy it.

There was a knock at the door and Dermot Guilfoyle popped his head around its edge.

"So how did it go?" he asked.

"I haven't been yet," Seb replied. "I've only just got my hands on the files."

"Do you need me to do anything? Look over the papers for you?"

"No, you're all right. I'll do it. I'm embarrassed enough as it is," Seb joked, but his laugh was only surface deep.

"If you're sure. But you know where I am – second pair of eyes and all that."

"Thanks, Dermot," Seb replied, appreciating the offer as a gesture of his business partner's support – support which didn't need to be expressed. There was an implicit trust between them that was solid. As soon as Seb shook Tim's hand after their lunch, instinctively he called Dermot. This was the first event to truly test the strength of that trust and so far, thankfully, it was proving sound. "I'm planning to head over there this afternoon and see what he has to say."

"Grand," Dermot responded with a nod. "Well, let me know how you get on," and with another, more enthusiastic nod this time, he turned to go, only to change his mind and turn back into the room. "You know, Seb," he said, "you're much bigger and smarter than this. It'll come right. Believe me." And, with that he left the room, closing the door behind him.

One of the things that Seb liked about Dermot was that he didn't waste his words so, whatever the sentiment of those he did say, he meant it. On this occasion, Seb wasn't sure that Dermot's prediction was right. But yes, he was bigger than this. He just needed to keep a level head and be prepared for his father's reaction. Seb wondered if William would admit what he had done. Unlikely, Seb guessed, remembering how compliant William had been when first told about the bank's demands for guarantees from all three of the company directors.

He had met them in his father's private office in Government Buildings. They were all there, all four of them like overexcited pups eager to get the project moving. Seb had assumed their edginess was because they were afraid they'd lose the property; he had, after all, negotiated a really good price on it.

"Alright, so I've met with the bank and they're happy to approve the loan in principal but ..." he cautioned, handing to each a form, "they want individual personal guarantees from all of you."

In Seb's eyes, this changed the deal considerably. Now the risks were greater, now they weren't protected by their company. Should anything go wrong they would be personally responsible to the bank for this debt. Seb had anticipated a barrage of questions. It was a huge risk and he would have understood if at least one of them walked away completely. But there were no questions. Each of them looked up at him wide-eyed as he stood at the top of the meeting table.

"No questions? Are you clear you know what this means?" he asked. And when they mumbled and shook their heads he offered them his unsolicited but professional opinion. "Okay, well, as your advisor I have to ask that you consider the risk. Think about the consequences to each of you if it fails. Imagine it has failed. Do you think you could cope with this debt? Only sign these forms if you're happy you can."

There and then he should have smelled the rat. And if he didn't smell it then he was given another opportunity a week later when his father had barged into his office with steam in his turbine.

"You need to sign these," William had thundered, slamming the guarantee forms on the desk in front of his son who up until that point was in the final throes of preparing for a client meeting.

Irritated but not alarmed by his father's abrupt entry, Seb told him firmly, "You can't just come barging in here like that," then looked at the forms. "These can wait."

"Here, here, here and here," his father fired back, ignoring Seb's comments while pointing at the Xs marked on each page.

"I know that but I'm telling you they can wait, and anyway they're already signed." Seb looked up at his father's six-foot-four frame looming large over him.

"Mr. Bertram, they're ready and waiting in the board room," Lucy interrupted them from the door.

"Thanks, Lucy. I'm on my way."

"I know that," William replied impatiently. "I had them signed, you need to witness them. They're for the bank guarantee."

"I can't do that, Dad – you know that."

"Don't be ridiculous. You know who they are, you know who we are," he boomed, pointing at the forms signed by himself and his three Ronson Street partners. "I was there, I can stand over them – isn't that enough?"

"Look, Dad, I don't have time for this now. I'm about to go into a meeting – I'll call over on the way home – we can discuss it then."

"Discuss it? What's to discuss? You sign here, here, here and here and we're done. You can do that, can't you?" he said in his usual patronising tone.

"No, Dad, not really," Seb replied with controlled calm while pulling on his jacket and gathering up the small heap of files from his desk.

"Oh for Christ's sake, man, what are you saying? Do you not trust me?"

"I never said that, but the whole point of witnessing someone else's signature is that you actually *see* them do it. And I didn't."

"But *I* did."

"Well, you sign them then."

"Don't be facetious, Sebastian, it doesn't become you. Just sign the damn documents."

A heavy knock on the frame of the open door made them both turn.

"We're waiting for you," Dermot told Seb, looking pointedly at William Bertram.

"Jesus Christ, Sebastian, I'm not going back to them again. I signed them. They're real. What more do you need to know?"

"Seb?" Dermot prompted from the door.

"Oh, for God's Sake," Seb hissed, "give them to me!" and, leaning over, signed each of them in his characteristically swift but distinctive scrawl.

"That wasn't so difficult, now was it?" his father taunted as Seb quickly left the room, his fury silent but evident in his passing glance.

Thinking back on it now, it didn't seem implausible that his father had timed it well and on purpose, knowing that at that point he would have signed anything just to get him out of his hair.

"What a bloody disaster," he stated aloud, inspecting the documents again. He closed his eyes and shook his head. It was rare for him to feel emotional but this was an unusual circumstance: this was the ultimate betrayal of trust and entirely his own fault. Although on the one hand he hoped his father had a reasonable explanation, he knew on the other that it was unlikely. With a heavy heart and a rising sense of anger, he gathered up the documents, reassembled the file and began to consider his options. It would be a long afternoon.

The vibration of his phone made him jump. He looked, more from curiosity than the intention to answer it, until he saw who it was. A client as well as a sibling – he had to take it.

"Enya," he said as cheerfully as he could. "How are you?"

"Grand," she replied. "That was some show Dad put on yesterday, wasn't it?"

"Yep, it sure was," he sighed. He hadn't really got a chance to talk properly to her over lunch – with so much else going on around him he didn't have the mental capacity to deal with her too.

"He's going to have to stop with the jibes though," she told him, "especially now that I've decided to hang around."

Seb had been expecting her to stay, and was quietly pleased for her.

"I'm really glad to hear it," he replied. "Really, it's time to stop running."

"I know," she sighed, "and, well, with the divorce coming through it kind of makes sense, doesn't it?"

The pause in her breathing didn't go unnoticed by Seb and despite her obvious trepidation he launched at her anyway.

"And what about this fellow Joe?" he asked, unable to contain himself and without trying to conceal his tone of disapproval. "Is it serious?"

"Joe ..." she repeated his name with a tint of regret. "Joe has gone on without me."

"Good, it's for the best," he said, without even a hint of pity. "He wasn't your type really, was he?"

"How could you tell?" she retorted good-naturedly. "You only met him for a split second."

"Good God, Enya, seriously, I always thought you had taste, but he, well, he was a bit rough, wasn't he?" He was glad to hear her laugh at the other end of the phone – he didn't intend to upset her. "I mean," he ventured, trying out his dry wit on her, "even you can do better than that." Then switching back to a more serious topic, he warned, "Look, don't mind Dad, I'll deal with him. There's no point rocking that boat unless you absolutely have to. Let me have a word with him. Okay? I'm heading over to see him later."

"Sure," she replied. "Anyway, now that I've made one decision, I really need to think about what to with the house and everything. I could do with some advice ..." She let her sentence hang, ready for him to pick it up, which he did with remarkable and uncharacteristic enthusiasm.

"Advice? Of course. Yes, sure. Look, why don't I call you in the morning?"

"Thanks, Seb, I appreciate it."

"And, Sis," he finished, "don't worry about Dad, okay?"

"Okay ... talk to you tomorrow so," she replied slowly.

He ended the call with a deep sigh, bracing himself for what he had still to do.

Chapter 7

How bizarre, she reflected, placing the phone back in its cradle, baffled by her oldest brother's responses. What on earth's up with him?

She was so accustomed to her brother's poor manners that to experience his unusual empathy was disconcerting to say the least.

Despite his gruff and sometimes inexcusable attitude, she loved her eldest brother and trusted him implicitly. And even though they hadn't been terribly close – Seb didn't do 'close' – he had been there for her when she needed him and for that, if nothing else, he had earned her respect.

The house was perfectly peaceful without Ciara buzzing round. She and Robert had done an amazing job restoring it from the ruins of its former and neglected years. An old gate lodge set into the shadows of the imposing oak trees on the eastern peripheries of a fine old manor house, it had long been a forgotten and tarnished jewel in its original owner's crown. Although beautiful, refurbished as a home with all the comforts of a five-star retreat – and she would never admit this openly to Ciara – it wasn't really Enya's preference. She could never cope with its isolation so far away from the city. Today, however, in the aftermath of her relationship break-up and her decision to stay, she was enjoying its comforting seclusion. She poured herself the last of the coffee and sipped it, savouring the silence while exploring the gallery of family photographs that lined the walls and decorated the various table-tops around the bright, open-plan living space. There was no doubt that despite their differences the Bertrams were a handsome group, she noted proudly, meandering from one image to the next, smiling with each memory the trail of pictures evoked. But only one picture, set into a beautiful but plain silver frame, stopped her dead in a sunlit corner of the room.

She peeped out from the photograph. Her baby girl. The abrupt and unexpected recall of those perky pigtails as she posed innocently in her party dress made Enya's heart race. Instinctively she clutched at her chest, grasping the pain that tore through it. That dress: it had been her favourite with its blue frill around the collar that matched the sapphire blue of her eyes. Enya tried to complete the dynamic memory of that moment timelessly caught in that single photo. The smell of the three candles that danced on her princess cake, the shrieks of delight as she opened her presents and her feather weight as she eventually slept in Enya's arms, exhausted from the excitement of the day. Picking up the picture as if holding it in her hand would bring that moment back to life, she closed her eyes to again feel those beautiful pigtails and the soft caress of her baby's breath against her cheek as she snored through the rest of the afternoon safe in the arms of her mother.

There wasn't a day that passed when she didn't think of her beautiful daughter Lia. But it was so long since she had looked at a physical image of that perfect little face, seeing it now, so surprising, so beautiful, there was no stopping the tears that fell freely down her cheeks. She didn't even try.

After Lia died, in the height of the drama, she had spat furiously at her father, "This is all your fault!" and, while in her heart she knew there wasn't a grain of truth in it, still she had continued to shriek, urgently needing someone to blame, "I only went with him because you forbade me to! And now look. Now look where I'm at!"

That was true: her father had forbidden her to see Cathal O'Neill.

They first met at a fundraiser for one of her father's earlier political campaigns which Cathal had attended with the sole intention of inciting William. A member of the opposition and running in the same constituency, at the time Cathal was considered the front runner, a young whippersnapper, biting at the heels of the established set and branded as the one who might just usurp the esteemed, deep-rooted and old-style William Bertram from his seat. Working the room, Cathal spied a very bored-looking Enya and when she took a seat at one of the tables he deviously seized the opportunity to antagonise his already piqued rival by making a beeline for the vacant seat right beside her.

Just as the introductions were underway William approached the table.

"Apologies, ladies, gentlemen," he nodded to the group, making sure there was no eye contact with Cathal, "may I be so rude as to steal my daughter away for just one minute?"

Enya felt embarrassed by the fact that he had addressed this request to the guests rather than her, as if she had no say in the matter. Indeed, it was less a request than a demand which left her little option but to smile politely and go with him.

"What is it, Dad?" she asked, aware that they were being covertly watched by the table of intrigued guests.

Already antagonised, she met his command that she move tables with a rebellious "Absolutely not".

"You do realise, don't you," William informed her cruelly, "that he's only sitting beside you to get at me?"

Enya looked at her father then back at the offending guest who was gleefully aware of the reaction his move had prompted.

"Is that so?" she replied.

"Yes, so find somewhere else to sit," he commanded with the weight of his authority evident in his voice, moving her along, expecting her to acquiesce.

"Don't be ridiculous, Dad," she replied with a smirk. "He's harmless."

"Just do as you're told, for once."

"Sorry?"

"I asked you to move, so move seats, find somewhere else to sit. I don't want you beside him. Is that clear?"

There was no recognition of her being there for him, no offer to help her find an alternative place to sit, no suggestion she might join him at his table.

'*Move*' was all Enya heard. If he hadn't been so nasty in his request, she might have politely complied. But his conduct triggered the quirk peculiar to her that ran through her like a river, provoking an instinctive no, and without another word she returned to the table.

A chivalrous Cathal rose and pushed in her chair as she sat.

"Interesting," he remarked, nodding towards his retreating and fuming opponent. He sat down and reached for the wine to fill her glass.

"Really? In what way?" Enya replied, casually accepting the wine with a grateful bow of her head.

"Oh, it was easy to interpret that body language," he said with a smile. "Hmmm ... I didn't think I'd ever meet anyone who'd say no to William Bertram."

"Well, you hadn't met me, had you?" she said.

So began what was initially an unexpressed symbiotic relationship, each with their own ulterior motive: to irritate Minister Bertram. Each more childish than the other.

On their first date they made a pact not to talk about him, which in itself Enya saw as an indirect insult to him.

"It would kill him to know we're *not* talking about him," she laughed as they sealed their agreement with a toast and moved on to find out more about each other. It was remarkably easy not to mention him and the cynic in her was silenced by the amount of things she and Cathal actually had in common. By the end of the night Enya found herself looking at her relationship with her father's opponent in a different light: less as an act of rebellion, more a prospect she might actually enjoy.

Not surprised by her father's refusal to accept their relationship, Enya found herself exiled to the family peripheries. Even after William by the tiniest of margins won the political battle at the polls, he still refused to acknowledge her. She was still, of course, invited to family get-togethers but Cathal was never made feel wholly welcome and in the end he made his excuses and nobody lamented his absence. Insulted, he forced Enya to choose: stand with him or with her father. With no other option, uncomfortably and with silent misgivings, she made her choice and stopped going altogether. Ciara was devastated at the time while the others, including Seb, said it was for the best. Although they were disappointed by her absence, no one liked the atmosphere that Cathal and their father created – the mood became explosive when they were present in the same room at the same time. Many years later, after their relationship began to disintegrate, she wondered if their marriage lasted as long as it had out of sheer defiance of her father.

In hindsight, with the exception of having Lia, she regretted almost every single minute of her time with Cathal. Her charming man with his handsome good looks and irresistible grin turned out to be nothing more than an arrogant, self-obsessed schmuck. A classic Aston Martin shell with a rusty, knocked-off Skoda engine underneath. Enya hated the way he managed to tie her in emotional knots, making her feel inferior to his apparent greatness. Like a ferret he burrowed under her confidence, taking it down from its foundations up until she wasn't sure of anything anymore. It was only after he was gone that she realised just how much of herself he had emasculated and, more devastatingly, how much she had let him.

It took William, who neither forgot nor forgave, with his festering resentment and bruised pride, to exact his revenge and bring Enya's world tumbling down.

He called her on her mobile when she was overnighting at a conference in Galway.

"Nothing to worry about, but Lia's not well," he told

her. "She's with your mother back at the house."

"Where's Cathal?" Enya asked, concerned but not worried – his tone lacked the urgency to suggest it was an emergency.

"The crèche tried to call him but he's off air. I know he's been involved in this constituency think-tank thing out in the back of beyond so he won't have coverage. That's how come we've got her. She's with your mother at the house, so nothing to panic about."

The idea of Lia with Barbara on her own in the house was disconcerting. It wasn't that her mother would intentionally upset Lia but, without knowing her state of inebriation, it could go either way. Eyeing up the remainder of the conference agenda, Enya reckoned it wasn't worth the stress or the guilt if anything happened to Lia while in her grandmother's care. So, checking out early, she made her way home. It was a two-hour drive during which she tried to remember giving the crèche her parents' number but couldn't, but was glad she had, wondering what would have happened otherwise. Taking her father at his word, she didn't try to contact Cathal. There was no point. She'd see him soon enough and then, she decided, they needed some sort of contingency plan for next time she was away and he had to work.

But there was no '*think-tank thing*' at all. William watched from the opposite side of the road, his Mercedes tucked in behind a van. From there he saw Enya pull into the driveway and look curiously at Cathal's car parked in its usual spot and, less than ten minutes later, Cathal and his half-dressed and dishevelled secretary leaving the house in a flurry of arms and shirttails.

"Gotcha!" William declared and, beaming, he started the engine and pulled out into the road, delighted he'd discovered the malicious rumours were true after all.

His phone rang not long after he'd driven away.

"*Where is she?*" Enya shouted without introduction.

Expecting it, William replied simply, "She's at the crèche."

"How could you?" she spat.

"What? You'd prefer that he carried on behind your back, making a fool out of you, out of me?"

"Admit it, Dad, you don't give a damn about me, or Lia for that matter. All you're interested in is settling the score, isn't that right?"

"It's for your own good," he told her smugly without an ounce of remorse.

"Oh, fuck off, Dad," she spat and hung up the phone.

The memory of that day and those that followed still made her want to throw up.

Hearing a key in the door she dried her face and busied herself at the sink, pouring the now stone-cold coffee down the drain and rinsing her mug.

Ciara trudged into the kitchen, calling her name only to stop as she spied her at the sink.

"Oh, you're in here." She heaved two large shopping bags onto the island countertop. "It's murder out there," she puffed, slightly out of breath, oblivious to the state of her sister. "Bloody traffic on Mercer Street is mental, lights are out and everyone's going berserk!" She stopped to take a breath, looking at Enya's face for the first time. "You okay?" she asked, noting her red eyes and the scarlet hue on her cheeks.

"I'm grand," Enya replied, pointing to the wall of pictures by way of distracting her sister. "I was just taking a walk down memory lane. You've got quite a collection."

It worked a treat: like a magpie lured by shiny pretty things Ciara was off on a tangent, delighted Enya had noticed the effort she'd put into collating them. Out of all the family Ciara made most effort to keep everyone together.

"So," Enya asked, needing a definitive distraction, "have you heard from Cormac yet?"

"Actually," Ciara replied thoughtfully, "no. No, I haven't, the little fecker." Her curiosity was once again triggered by his as yet unexplained disappearance from Seb's house at the weekend. "Give him a bell there while I empty these bags and let's see what happened." It was only as she was leaving the room to hang up her coat that she noticed the silver frame out of place. The image of her beautiful goddaughter on her third birthday leapt up at her. She threw a look back at Enya busy dialling their brother's number and realised she had disturbed a long-awaited and much-needed moment between mother and daughter.

Chapter 8

Cormac couldn't ignore her. He'd already dodged her two earlier calls and knew her well enough to know she'd keep calling till he answered, so he might as well get it over with. Sitting upright, he picked up his phone and took a deep breath to armour himself. Swallowing hard to moisten his parched throat and disguise the tell-tale still-in-bed rasp in his voice, he answered her call, checking his watch to establish the time.

"Hey, Sis, how's it going?"

"Where have you been? Didn't you get my calls? Ciara and I, we were worried about you. What happened to you last night?"

Knowing this grilling was bound to happen and despite his inebriation the evening before, he'd had the foresight to prepare an elaborate and relatively credible tale. But panic and the smell of his own fear ripped the story right out of his head and he had no idea what to say.

"Something just came up," he blurted, saying the first thing that came into his mind, instantly cringing, knowing full well she was unlikely to swallow such a feeble excuse of an excuse. "You know me, always somewhere to be," he tried cheekily and when she didn't respond he felt silently pressured down a more likely route. "To be honest, Dad was driving me nuts. I don't know why you let him talk to you like that."

"But why did you have to leave?" she argued. "He was driving everyone mad, but we stayed."

"I know, I know, I just couldn't hack it. He's so bloody self-righteous."

"If I can put up with it, so can you. Seriously though, are you alright, really?"

"I'm grand," he assured her. "Really, I'm fine." And for a split second he thought about telling her. For a split second he imagined the relief that sharing with her might bring. For a split second he wondered what exactly she might be able to do to help. What would she say? What could she say? '*You absolute idiot!*' he imagined her shout. '*How could you have been so stupid?*' And she would be right. How could he have been so stupid? But he didn't have the answer and didn't even know where he should start to look for it. Neither did he have the courage nor the humility to say the words out loud: '*Enya, I'm in real trouble here. I need your help.*'

"Are you even listening?" Enya huffed sharply down the phone.

"Sorry, I was miles away."

"I said I'm already back a few days but we haven't had a chance yet to catch up. What's the matter? Are you avoiding me or something?" When he didn't answer she pushed him, irritated and more than a little cross. "Are you even still there?"

"Seriously, Enya, I'm grand."

"Grand? You keep saying that. So if you're so grand then tell me where you got to yesterday?"

"I had somewhere to be, that's all. Nothing to worry about, honestly," he told her. Then salvaging a small part of his intended story he continued, "I have a problem with one of my students. He's buggered up his thesis and I'm trying to help him fix it up. That's it. I swear."

Despite the silence her suspicion was palpable. "All right so," she said, more determined than before, "come over later – call it a late lunch."

"I can't later, I've got classes all afternoon," he lied.

"Tomorrow then? Ciara's cooking."

"I'm not sure I can."

"Of course you can and, anyway, I'm not going to take no for an answer."

"Fine. I'll see you tomorrow."

"Perfect! Call over about six. Dinner will be around seven thirty."

"Sure," he replied, already thinking of potential excuses to bow out.

Casting aside the phone, feeling like he was teetering on the edge of a cliff, he flopped back into the pillows, exhausted and hung-over. Last night's brandy bottle lay empty on its side on the duvet beside him, its wafting woody aroma a dull reminder as to why his mouth felt so woolly and his bladder so full. He needed to pee. Picking up the bottle he dragged himself from the bed and padded barefoot through the shimmering room to the toilet, placing the bottle on the dressing table as he passed. Without turning on the light in the bathroom he stood in the dark and let himself go, watching his shadow in the mirror before him. This was a reflection more used to being admired than castigated. With his back to the light he studied the structure of his darkened frame. Where his face should be was nothing more than an oval black mass wrapped in the outline of his tussled hair. No features. No shame. No words.

He imagined the stream carrying all the waste from his body. He wished it all out and away, wishing he was man enough to cry and be done with it.

One hundred thousand euro, he mused tragically. One hundred thousand euro. It wasn't much in the grand scheme of things but to him, personally, it was massive. He repeated the words aloud. And what for? For a collection of slightly out-of-focus photographs. Was that four or five zeros, he wondered as he shook off the last few drops and tried to visualise the vastness of the amount in his head.

And there was likely to be plenty more images to come, he presumed, thinking of the four that he had already received. He didn't need his phone to see them; they were indelibly imprinted in his mind. Their naked flesh and co-joined bodies, the white powdery line, dull but apparent in the seedy darkness around him, his face leaning over the glass table with the rolled-up twenty at his nose. Ugly.

Done, he returned to the safety of his bed and throwing himself face down cast his mind back to what had been one of the most salacious nights of his life. The mere thought of it gave him a hard-on, which he didn't have the energy to suppress, and he felt it press into the bed, its head rubbing rough against the fabric of his shorts. He moved, just a little bit: a slight hip shift to the left, then to the right, enough to feel his tantalisingly sensitive skin spark. Inhaling deeply, Cormac let the sensation tickle up his spine but kept his hands where they rested above his head, torturing himself, punishing his error of judgement by not letting those expert hands indulge his building lustful hunger. Out of bounds.

"What a fucking team," he huffed bitterly into the pillow. The pity of their combination of talents. What a waste. The warmth of their lips, the softness of Orla's hands, the strength of Mark's arms, the sinews of his thighs, the mass of his own body compounded by the deviant wild response to Orla's touch and the volcanic force of their combined climax. Cormac's skin hummed at the memory. It seemed real then, at the time, and even though he now knew otherwise it still felt real now.

What an asshole, he berated himself, balling his fists to drive them hard into the pillow, feeling his fingernails bite into the clenched palms of his hands.

He was duped all right. Well and truly beguiled by them. How thick was he not to see it? How arrogant? He searched his memory of what now felt like nothing more than a tawdry incident for something, anything that screamed *fake!* What had he missed? He couldn't find it. Nothing. Even with the pictures from his phone he still found it hard to believe that the whole thing had been a set-up and he never guessed. How the hell was he to know he was being watched *and* filmed? How could he have known it was a full-scale hustle? How could he have known that the bastards had probably been planning the whole thing for months? He'd been set up and he had, so eagerly, devoured the bait.

He had tried to call Orla the minute he received the pictures. They were coming from her phone. Was it some kind of perverted joke, he wanted to ask, feeling the pit of his stomach pulse and grow heavy as he waited for her to answer. It had to be a joke, it couldn't possibly be real.

Things like this didn't happen in real life – in the movies, yes – but not to him, not in his seemingly charmed life. But her phone rang out and the pictures kept coming one after the other and, when she'd sent through the last one and with it a polite financial demand, there was no denying he'd been deceived. He had so many questions but none more pressing than the simple 'Why?' Yes, he knew it was for the money, but why him? Why not someone else?

"Oh, for God's sake, Cormac," she said patronisingly when eventually they spoke. "Don't be an idiot. Why do you think?" Her tone as cold and hard as ice.

"But, but," he stammered like a broken-hearted horny schoolboy trying to make some sense of what was happening, "I don't understand – what went wrong? I thought we had fun."

"For Jesus' sake," she moaned, exasperated by him. "Get with the programme, would you? This was never about fun. It was all an act, a game we played, but you lost."

It was as straightforward as that: he lost.

And so he stood like a moron, in the middle of his living room, wearing nothing but his boxer shorts and socks, his feet unable to move as she fired her words at him down the phone.

"Yes, it was fun. Yes, we had a laugh. But you know what, Cormac, you were easy prey. People talk, you know, and you do have a bit of a reputation. It wasn't that hard. We had you weeks before you ever knew it." She chuckled as if he should share her apparent sense of accomplishment.

He felt small and helpless. She had the upper hand and knew it.

"You bitch!"

"Yeah, yeah, whatever," she responded, the laughter quickly disappearing from her voice, bored by him. "You've got a week."

"And what if I decide not to play your shitty little game?"

"Well, then, they go live. All of them."

"And what if I don't care?"

"But you do, don't you?"

The obvious sneer in her voice sent shivers up his spine.

"What guarantee do I have that you won't come back for more?"

"You don't."

"Well, I'll need more time than that – I don't have that kind of money, I don't even know where to start looking."

"You're a smart guy, you'll figure something," she scoffed. "But no more time. This day week. Ten a.m. sharp. Starbucks on the corner of Dame Street."

The alluring lilt of her voice mid-climax that he remembered had been replaced by her hard-bitch routine. And it worked. To be fair to her, he thought, she was expert at both.

That call was five days ago and with only two days remaining he still hadn't managed to pull the money together. No doubt he had blown his chances with Kathryn by running out on her after the family lunch. By not playing her game. Feeling physically ill, he hauled himself up and made his way to the kitchen, his feet making quiet suction noises on the polished wooden floor, leaving moist toe and heel prints in their wake.

Drenched in golden sunlight Cormac knew, ironically,

that it was going to be another beautiful day.

So what if he had a healthy appetite for flesh? So what if he liked to mix it up a little, take a risk or two? He wasn't harming anyone. They were all consenting adults; he was single with the capacity to entertain as well as pleasure. Why shouldn't he be allowed to behave the way he wanted to? Most men, he reckoned, would love to have the balls to take the risks he did. The impression of the photographs once again came to the fore and made him blush.

There was no question as to why he did it. He knew why, although he doubted many would understand if he had the will to explain. Some people smoked, others drank, some ran marathons and climbed mountains for kicks but he – he liked sex, loved sex. He loved the sight, the touch, the smell of it. It was his only real vice.

The drugs thing on the other hand, well, that was harder to put in plain words. Ordinarily he wasn't a user, it never really did it for him, but in this instance it was part of the act. Orla was so hot for him to try it. It became part of their play: she poured his share across her breasts and offered him the tube. At the time he remembered thinking: Sure, why not? It would be rude to say no.

What a dick.

"Take it," she offered, pulling him down to her. "Go on," she encouraged, toying seductively with her powdered nipple, "take it!"

And so, unashamedly, he obliged and snorted it deep into his nostrils before licking her clean. It had no taste but hit him hard, its fast-forward pace thumping like a piston through his brain. Everything seemed quicker, more intense. He wanted it to slow down but he couldn't and it wouldn't. His brain fought against his body but he had no idea how to connect the two. They were acting independently of each other and, as the full effect of his white stardust took hold, he couldn't have cared less.

His cheeks coloured as he remembered the scenario.

God, Cormac, you're such a fool, he told himself, his heart sinking at his naive and foolish error. Yep. He'd been had. Good and proper.

From the bedroom he heard his phone tweet. Taking two Paracetamol, a glass of water and his coffee back to bed, he picked up the phone tentatively, dreading the words he was about to see. But it wasn't Orla.

"Sorry for yesterday. Come see me my office tomorrow. Noon. Please. K"

Kathryn. His stomach lurched while his heart soared. A lifeline. She *was* going to help him? But at what cost?

Terrified but without hesitation he replied: **"OK. See you then."**

He checked his watch. He had time for a quick snooze, he decided, his spirits lifted and the throb in his head feeling more like an ache.

His phone tweeted at him again.

"Forget at your peril, Bro. Dinner at 6. Tomorrow. C&E"

He'd go see Kathryn and maybe he would pop in to Ciara's, but not for dinner – maybe tea? He'd see how he felt once he'd seen Kathryn. It was going to be a good day. A better day. He could feel it in his bones.

Chapter 9

Enya put the phone back in the dashboard compartment, pleased with the masterful way she was handling Cormac. They'd get to the bottom of whatever was going on with him: He couldn't keep a secret to save his life. Even as kids, one maybe two prods, not even hard ones, and he'd open like an envelope. She smiled to herself – he was putty in their hands!

"Sorry, Sis, what was that? I wasn't listening."

"I said I like her," Ciara repeated, keeping her eyes on the road. "I think she's nice."

"Who're we talking about again?"

"For God's sake, Enya, concentrate. Martha. I like her."

"Ah right. Martha. A little too intense, maybe?" Enya queried, back on track.

"How do you mean?"

"Well, do you not think she asks an awful lot of questions? She's always looking, you know? What about this? What about that? Why? Why? Why?"

"Not really," Ciara laughed. "Anyway, she makes Rian happy and that's all that counts, right?"

"Yeah, I suppose."

"Having said that, Kathryn says she thinks she's a little odd."

"Yeah, well, Kathryn would – she's nothing but a spoilt bloody princess," Enya replied sharply.

"Leave Kathryn alone, she's been very good to me." But, curious to know, she asked, "I take it you don't like her then?"

"It's not that I don't like her. I'm sure, deep down," Enya qualified with a smirk, "she's lovely. I'm mean she'd want to be something special to put up with Seb, right?"

"Definitely!" laughed Enya, enjoying the moment with her sister and happy for the distraction, given where they were going.

"But she's pretty superficial, happy to help, but only if it serves to make her feel good. Patronising, if that makes sense. You know, like she's pulling you up on the one hand and looking down her nose at you on the other."

"I never really looked at her like that."

"Well, you wouldn't," Ciara teased. "You always see the best in everyone."

To which, knowing Ciara was right, Enya replied with raised eyebrows and a nod of her head.

A protective but nervous quiet filled the car as they neared the house. The radio was on but neither of them was listening. It was mere noise.

So close now, Enya let herself wonder if it still looked the same? The house. Their house. She wondered if she would feel that warm glow as they turned the last corner to speed up the hill and make the final part of her journey home. Home. What a concept. It wasn't her home any longer. She didn't have a home, not anymore. Enya fought hard to dismiss the bitter, sad cynic in her which depressed and smothered any positive emotion before it had the time to blossom. But all this anger, it was hard work, and more and more she found herself becoming increasingly tired of the constant rage, the never-ending resentment and unwavering hostility that appeared to have taken up permanent residence in her heart. Knowing these feelings to be anomalous, she longed for normality. And, although she knew she could never get back the *normal* that she once knew, she was ready to at least try to start again, from scratch, to find her 'new' normal. Her impending divorce seemed like an appropriate moment for that fresh beginning; she just hoped she had the strength to see it through. There was so much to forget but plenty that was important to remember. Segmenting them properly was the challenge: admitting honestly what had to go and what needed to stay. She needed to, had to, get beyond the fury and incessant blaming of everyone else for what happened.

She had returned home that day over four years ago, completely unsuspecting. A sick daughter was what she expected to see but what she found was a foreign body, literally, in her bed with her husband. She wasn't sure which part of the ridiculous scenario was worse: the fact that Cathal laughed openly as she looked on aghast while his lover fled the room, or that he didn't even bother to pack his things when she roared at him to leave. But a strong contender for the '*Worst Part*' accolade was how her own father had been the catalyst for this great reveal. He'd heard the salacious gossip about Cathal O'Neill and his rumoured affair and, irrespective of the destruction he knew it would cause, he went ahead and devised his long-awaited revenge. He wanted the damage, craved it, but even he couldn't have predicted the ultimate tragic outcome. And that's exactly how Enya perceived it for a long time after: a heart-breaking and unforgivable consequence of her father's actions.

The last time she saw Cathal was at Lia's funeral. He sat bandaged and bruised in the wheelchair, dry-eyed and vacant, his face devoid of expression. Enya, heavily sedated and propped up on either side by Cormac and Ciara, remembered very little of the day. It passed in a blur of sorry faces and handshakes and apologies. All she could recall were the clouds that passed overhead and birds that sang a mournful tribute in the trees beside them. In the immediate weeks after she berated herself out of frustration because she remembered so little and then it just became easier not to bother and to forget. Sometimes she pretended her little girl was still alive, and that it was Cathal who was thrown from the car. She imagined that beautiful smile that lit up her entire round and rosy little face and the urgency of her soft, plump arms wrapped tightly around her neck every morning for her hug. And her soft lips, the colour of a perfect pink cherry blossom that puckered so adorably to press hard against her cheek. How she missed that child with her scrunched-up smile and eyes that sparkled no more.

He was supposed to have her back by seven. He'd promised, but then, what was new? Cathal couldn't keep a promise to save his life, or Lia's as it transpired. It had rained hard all day, like someone had turned a hose on in the clouds and forgot to turn it off, making them slate-grey and plump with rain, litres and litres of it. So much water fell from the sky that day that the roads were slicker than a greased ice rink, all shiny and spewing up spray to blind and soak whatever trailed in its path. She knew he'd been driving fast. Too fast. He always did. Even when they were together, even before the gleam had vanished from the silver lining of their once-frantic romance, he still liked to show off. Like it made him feel more manly or perhaps it simply felt good to see her squirm in the passenger seat, a demonstration of his prowess, making her plead desperately for him to slow down. Power. He liked to have power, or at least think he did. But it never came naturally to him – he hankered after it more than he possessed it: that was the problem. In managing his natural inferiority, he behaved with an air of synthetic superiority that he just didn't have the intelligence to cope with. Few people recognised it as such. What his friends experienced and admirers loved was a confidently arrogant, cheeky but charming socialite. But she knew him well enough to know that beneath the charm was nothing more than a selfish, ignorant and conceited manipulator.

She imagined him that evening, in the rain, whizzing along in his flash arrogant Beemer, full of his own self-importance, satisfying his pompous, deadly need for speed. When he hadn't turned up by eight, she'd called him to see where they were but he didn't bother to answer, sending her a text instead saying they'd be back when he was good and ready.

"She's got school in the morning, please try not to be too late," Enya pleaded in return, knowing that there was no point in arguing, especially not by text.

She never stood a chance. He swore he'd clipped her belt in. Vowed on his life that he had made her safe. She must have undone it herself, he argued pitifully but Enya didn't believe him. Not for even a short, sharp moment. Lia never knew how to do that. When the car in front slammed on its brakes for whatever reason, Lia was beltless and thrown from the car through the windscreen. A traumatised witness spoke tearfully about seeing her limp and bloodied body skating fast along the slick, shiny black surface of the road. She didn't have a chance. The doctors said she probably died instantly. *Probably*: a word that would haunt Enya for ever after. *Probably*. But what if she didn't? What if the trauma of the crash didn't steal her soul? What if there was life still in her, even a small, tiny breath? What if she had felt the pain of her shattered limbs and bruised flesh? The very idea of it hurt so badly that still to this day, every time she thought of her angel, Enya whimpered.

She had lashed out at Cathal in the hospital. He was lucky to be alive they told her, like she cared. But then *he* was wearing his safety belt.

"More's the pity," she swore at him with such venom it poisoned her heart.

And as always happened whenever she thought of that time in her life – the initial phone call, the urgent drive to the hospital, those horrible catastrophic hours and the night that followed – she cried.

Ciara put a hand on her quietly weeping sister's knee and squeezed. No words were necessary.

When they eventually did take that final corner Enya felt nothing but a burning need to turn back and run. Had she been the one driving, she probably would have. But Ciara geared down firmly with her foot on the gas, pushing the car hard as it made its way up the final hill. Symbolic, they both thought independently of each other, listening to the engine of her bright yellow heap of a Citroën struggle, as if it too was reluctant to go the distance.

Enya watched the landmarks pass outside the window, their familiarity somehow comforting. The trees seemed fuller and the grass greener. Was it possible that the street was a bit wider than before? Recognising gardens and house names, pillars and posts, she felt her stomach churn furiously as they approached and pulled in at the kerb. An expensive white Mercedes Jeep was parked in the stubby cobblelock driveway, beside it a child's purple bike with glittery tassels bursting from the handlebars was thrown casually on the lawn. It still looked beautiful, the house: so striking, a contemporary sculpture set in amongst the tradition of red brick on the street. But it didn't jar or look abnormal in its setting; like true opposites the surroundings and house complemented each other perfectly.

Ciara turned off the engine. Enya didn't move, but remained looking out her passenger window at the place she had once called home. She had put so much effort into this house, nurturing the warm, safe ambience to create a space where they could grow together as a family. It was designed that way, she thought sadly, looking at the bike strewn so unceremoniously in the grass, like it belonged right there. And it did. It just wasn't Lia's.

Curiosity lured her out of the car and, passing through the gates, she let her hand brush against the name painted in bronze on the column: *Tanglewood*.

Bracing herself mentally, she walked slowly towards the door. The house itself looked just as she had left it.

The day following Lia's funeral Enya had turned to Seb.

"I can't stay here. I have to go."

"You can't just up and leave," he had argued.

"I have to, I can't stay here!" she cried. "Everywhere I look she's there. I see her in every room in that house – I see her, I smell her, I can almost hear her."

Seb didn't argue. He didn't understand but he could see her distress and the urgency in her need to escape.

"Where will you go?" he asked, taking her into his awkward embrace.

"I really don't know," she sobbed into his shoulder.

"There's a friend of mine from school," he said. "He runs a vineyard in France. Amazing place. Why don't I give him a call and you can start there?"

"Thanks, Seb," she sniffed. "That would be great. I appreciate it, really I do." And, looking up to him, she asked, "Will you look after the house for me?"

"Absolutely," he replied. "I'll take care of it."

And he, it appeared, had been true to his word. She vaguely remembered an email from Seb telling her about the people to whom he had rented it, but there and then she couldn't retrieve the detail.

Gingerly she took a sneak peek through the window of the sitting room. They had moved none of the furniture but the photographs had changed; now the house played host to someone else's story. She stood for what seemed like for ever, remembering the copious amounts of colouring done at the table, books kept on the shelf, movies and CD's on the organiser and little feet that meandered happily from room to room.

With a heavy heart and poignant emotions, she turned to walk back to the car.

"Can I help you?" a woman called from the side passage,

her hands clad in soiled gardening gloves and her knees stained with mud.

Enya jumped, clutching her chest in fright.

"Oh. I'm sorry, do you live here?" she asked nervously, spying a young girl peeping out from behind the woman before legging it quickly to retrieve the discarded bicycle as if Enya might steal it.

"Yes, yes, we do," the woman replied assertively. "Are you looking for someone?"

Enya paused, looking towards Ciara in the car, unsure how to answer, not knowing what to say.

This is my house, she wanted to scream as loud as her voice would allow but instead she stepped back.

"No," she responded, "I'm sorry, I must have the wrong house."

The woman nodded, obviously thinking 'How odd' and, taking hold of her little girl's hand, watched Enya go, making sure she actually left the property.

Enya got back into the car at speed. She didn't know whether to feel anger, gratitude or grief.

"You okay?" Ciara asked.

"Yep," Enya replied in no more than a whisper, "but can we just get the hell out of here? Please?" The quiver in her hands was making hard work of the seatbelt buckle.

With neither a word nor a second glance, Ciara put the car in gear and pulled off, driving away much faster than when she had arrived.

"Alright?" Ciara asked quietly once they were far enough away and she was sure Enya had stopped shaking.

Enya replied with a nod, her heart heavy but her resolve clear: it was time for change.

"I think I have to sell it," she told her sister. "There's

no way I can go back there. Not without Lia."

Ciara replied with silence. It didn't need any verbal response.

"Do you think we could maybe go to the cemetery?" Enya asked, feeling the sting of her tears as they swelled once more.

Seeing her grave all tidied and perfect, with her name carved out of the grey granite with the delicate angels wrapped protectively at either end, was almost comforting. She knelt and placed her hand flat down on the grass and wondered if Cathal ever came to visit their daughter's grave. If he did there were no signs of it. She hadn't asked about him since her return and no one had made any mention as to where he was or what he was doing. She was sure they knew. She wondered if he thought about Lia or if he, like her, found it too hard to bring her to mind.

She wasn't sure if she was making it so or if it was her mind playing tricks, conjuring up feelings that weren't actually real, but she was certain she felt her, a presence and a spark that triggered a bizarre chemistry with nothing more than a memory and an ache in her soul. But she felt her there. It wasn't a time for tears and there were none.

She had spent so much time focusing on her past she had forgotten that she still had a future. Lia might be physically gone but she was in her heart and would stay there forever.

Chapter 10

Ciara watched as her little sister faced her fears. She could almost feel Enya's renaissance: kneeling for a last moment before slowly sweeping her hand across the cold stone then leaning in to kiss it. Standing. It was time to go. Ciara took her sister's arm and, with Enya's head on her shoulder, they walked towards the car.

It was impossible to ignore the ironic similarities in their emotions: Enya, grieving for her beautiful baby that lived for so few years, while she mourned every day for her tiny babies that never managed to take even a short breath on their own. The past weeks had been tricky. It seemed that everything was working against her, including Robert: "No more," he had told her only days before. And despite the distraction of Enya's arrival she was still trying to process the impact of this simple but extraordinary statement. Witnessing Enya take such a painfully brave step forward, so far out of her comfort zone, on the one hand made Ciara feel proud of her but on the other pierced her with a shard of jealousy somewhere deep in a bitter, twisted crevice of her sinking heart. Time to move on? Was it even possible for her to take example from her sister, she asked herself, hopeful but not convinced.

She needed time to think, time on her own. Dropping Enya back to the house she was glad to see relief in her sister's eyes when she suggested that she take a nap while she nipped into town to do a few things. They both needed head space: time to manage their thoughts.

Finally alone, lost in the whirlwind of her ruminations, Ciara drove aimlessly through streets and junctions. A blast of a horn dragged her from her cheerless introspection and back to the reality of her car. Taking stock of where she was, she parked and got out, not in the least bit surprised to find herself within walking distance of the entrance to the city zoo. This was *her* place. It was where she always seemed to end up when she needed time to herself and invariably it seemed to signify the end of one thing and the beginning of something else. This time however, by contrast, she wasn't quite sure what that 'something else' needed to be.

Having paid her fee, she walked through the gates and immediately felt exorcised, as if the stresses and worries of the last few weeks that had weighed so heavily on her conscience had flittered gently away. Swaddled by the inexplicably tranquil and hushed atmosphere of the almost wild gardens, as if accompanied by an old friend, she followed the familiar path into the estate.

On a weekday, at this time in the early afternoon, the inner network of winding lanes was almost empty: she was as good as alone. And on such a beautiful day, with the sun shining bright and a cold bite to the air, she felt charmed and had no intention of wasting either it or her solitude. Opening up her lungs as she walked she sucked in as much of the chilly air as she could manage then released it slowly back to the atmosphere in a translucent puff of warmed vapour. Pulling the black fur collar of her coat tight around her neck she wandered along the narrow tarmac tracks. Here there was no rush, here she could think, her thoughts like cogs in a finely tuned clock slipped effortlessly, one by one, into their paired slots, untangling even the most complicated dilemma. Here she made sense even to herself.

Stopping at the kiosk beside the high top-viewing platform, she bought a coffee and took a seat in what had become over the years her usual spot, overlooking the flamingos. Wrapping her hands around the warm Styrofoam cup, sucking from it whatever warmth she could, she watched, intrigued by their pink elegant one-legged stance as they occasionally dipped their heads into the water, happy to huddle, happy to preen, happy to do apparently nothing.

It wasn't an accident that she always ended up at the zoo. She had history here; this was now part of her story. It was in this exact spot that Robert proposed to her almost seven years ago. She shook her head as a gentle smile curved her lips – was it really that long ago? She remembered it as if it were yesterday: him on his knees dressed all in black, the blue velvet box that he offered up to her, presenting the ruby-and-diamond ring delicately placed inside, in return for her hand in marriage. She remembered his face and how it shone brighter than all the gemstones in the world when she finally, between gulps, said yes. He had completely surprised her – had she been asked about him before then she would never have described him as a romantic: passionate certainly, mysterious maybe, but romantic, not really. However, on that evening he had orchestrated the proposal so beautifully, right down to the timing of his proposition at sunset, that whatever his disposition she thanked her lucky stars that he had chosen her.

And there was no doubting that Robert was an incredible man, so kind, so patient. She knew he loved her, of that there was no question, and if she tried hard enough she could kind of see why he didn't want to try again. But this could be their time. This time it might just work. This might just be the last chance they needed. This time, the time *was* right, she felt it in her heart. And what if it was and they didn't try one more time? What if …? She would never know.

He had been adamant. "*No more.*"

Yes, there was the money and, yes, she didn't react well to the disappointment: grief just didn't suit her. But despite all the arguments and, yes, they all made perfect sense, there was a chance, a small chance but a chance all the same that this could actually be it: the one that worked, the one more they needed. How could they not take this one last chance? Then, if it didn't work, she'd let it go, but she needed to try one last time. She didn't dare dream of one day holding her own baby in her arms, that was too dangerous, but she knew what it felt like to have her baby growing inside her and it was that feeling that she returned to time and time again in her hope and dream of motherhood.

Feeling a chill, she shivered and got up to continue her visit, pausing as she passed each enclosure, recognising changes to the contrived habitats since last time. Interesting, she acknowledged, that she should find wandering almost alone in a forest of caged wild animals so comforting. She felt a peculiar empathy with these creatures, caught in a situation they too had no control over. They had no say. She had no say; she was what she was, just as they were. She stopped and stood in front of the tigers and watched while the male paced back and forth along the perimeter: relentless, slow and rhythmic. Bored with his lot, stuck behind a thick wall of glass and impeded by boundaries that were beyond his capabilities to overcome. While the other, his mate, watched from further up the enclosure, equally bored but lazy and not bothered enough to care. They were a magnificent presence behind the reinforced glass: So wild and strong, their movements, or lack of, filled with anticipation of what might come, if they had the chance. Outwardly calm, just waiting for their moment to pounce, their frustration palpable and captivity unnatural. That's how she felt: unnatural. Her respect for these creatures hadn't changed since the last time she stood before them, watching, feeling caged, echoing their frustration and disappointment, but fully aware of the possibilities and opportunities. If only she had the chance.

They had been so excited the first time they discovered she was pregnant. To this day she had found nothing remotely comparable to that feeling of something so delicate growing inside her. And for the first time ever she felt truly useful. Special: like she had finally found her purpose. And while some of her friends objected when their shape swelled and their breasts enlarged, she loved it, relished it even. She adored her fullness and would stand naked in front of the mirror to marvel at how, as each day went by, her body changed that little bit more. She was happy, inside and out.

But just like that, it was over. How cruel life could be.

In her twenty-fifth week she had gone to bed feeling perfectly fit and fine, their baby fluttering away inside her like a little busy butterfly in her belly. They fell asleep that night in each other's arms with Robert's hand resting protectively on her tummy. But in the morning the baby was still. At first she didn't worry. But as each minute passed and morning became afternoon she felt the panic rise rapidly inside her. She lay deathly still on their bed for near two hours waiting, feeling everything else move inside her except her baby.

She lay on the hospital gurney with Robert holding her hand while the doctor squeezed the thick gloopy liquid straight on to her belly. He smiled compassionately, catching her eye every now and then, his eyes brimming with silent sympathy before he'd even started the scan. He knew, as did she, but he couldn't say. He listened first. She didn't take her eyes off his face, desperately watching for a sign, a positive sign, any visible change in his features that might give away even a hint of the truth and, although he did his best to give nothing away, she saw the slight movement in his mouth and knew instantly it was not going to be good news.

"Let's take a look then," he told them, going through the motions, to be sure.

All the while she lay there and hoped, prayed for a miracle, silently begging for an explanation as to why those incredible little flutters in her belly weren't there any more: a reason other than the obvious. Slowly and methodically he moved the scanner over her rounded abdomen while she and Robert stared at the screen expectantly. It was torture. She couldn't stand it. She just wished he'd say it and be done. He's just being thorough, she told herself, he's just doing his job. She felt her fingers tighten over Robert's and his lips on her forehead. He knew it too.

When eventually those horrible words passed through her doctor's lips she wasn't able to cry.

"I'm so sorry," he said, putting down the equipment and wiping the gel gently from her tummy. And taking her hand he told her what she had been dreading: "I can't see a heartbeat."

It was like every muscle in her body tensed. Like every pore dried up. Small cat-like sounds, alien and obscure, came from her mouth but they weren't real, it wasn't her.

Robert held her tight and wiped her tears before his own.

There were only three people in the room to help bring her small helpless, lifeless baby into the world. Limp and inert. They gave her pictures, so she could grieve over him, they said. He was tiny, so physically minute. Her contractions were sharp but he was born quickly and without fanfare. And while there was little pain after, it hurt deep inside her. It hurt where medicines could never reach and where the healing takes forever, if ever.

Afterwards she slept and when she woke it was dusk. The curtains weren't yet drawn, giving the room an almost purple hue. Beyond the door the hospital hummed with activity and in the distance, but not that far away, babies cried. But not her baby.

She lay, looking through the window at the greying clouds against the deep blue, almost black sky, watching their shapes merge and extend to form obscure, sometimes familiar patterns.

A gentle knock on the door disrupted her melancholy

but sedate mood. She turned just as he stepped into the room, the small visible square of his detachable white collar contrasting brightly against the black of his suit.

"Is it okay to come in?" he asked, entering without waiting for an answer. "I'm Father Anthony."

Uninvited, he was already sitting in the chair at the bedside and had grasped her hand in his.

"I am so sorry for your loss, my dear," he told her with an ethereal glow.

She was momentarily dumbstruck – why was *he* sorry?

"Was it your first?" he continued, either ignoring or not noticing the bewildered look on her face.

It, she repeated in her head, taking a minute to think about what exactly he was offering. Sympathy? Solace? Silently she rejected them both. Withdrawing her hand from his grasp she turned in the bed, to look out the window again at the patterns in the clouds that made more sense than anything else around her.

The following morning they were directed to the morgue outside the main building on the hospital grounds from where they collected the smallest white coffin they ever expected or wanted to see. Clutching it tight, she held it in her arms as they drove the short distance to the church. This wasn't the way it was supposed to be. Her excited imaginings of that new baby smell, the touch of softer than soft skin, the quiet little murmurs, the strong grip of tiny fingers and the fast-beating heart had been shattered. Her fingers felt every raised fibre of that tiny timber casket. It felt so light, so delicate and small. Robert drove slowly and silently while she mindlessly watched the journey melt away through the window.

He had asked the priest who had married them to say

a few words with them before the baby was buried. The words were simple but unremarkable and utterly pointless to Ciara whose mind was miles away, immersed in the thought of their baby and how far, how close, they had come. So, so close.

They called him Patrick, a good, strong name. He deserved that. The hole was dug. She almost laughed when she saw it: it was huge. Unnecessarily huge. The size of an adult coffin. And he was so very, very small. Aside from the priest there was only herself and Robert there to witness his burial. Someone came and put a ladder into the gaping wound in the ground and Robert climbed down to put Patrick in it. He would lie in the same plot as Ciara's uncle who she knew would look after him in his next life, wherever that was supposed to be. And she really hoped he would have one.

After Robert emerged from the ground and took up his position beside Ciara, he put an arm around her shoulders and clutched her tight. She shook in its protective circle.

That day and night they lay in front of the fire, not bothering to go to bed, and comforted each other. She cried for her dead baby. She cried for herself who felt so empty. And she cried for her husband who she prayed would love her still.

The next time, less than four months later, she carried for only eight weeks, and the time after that it was thirteen and the most recent was twelve. Four lost souls in total but "No more".

It was pointless trying not to cry: it never worked, she knew as much, and just let them come. But they gave her no comfort. A quiet respectful few tears shed in the memory of her lost children: nothing wrong with that.

A family of three screeching children and their exasperated mother shattered the moment. They stopped right beside her with their buggy and bags and moans and bickers.

"*Pleeeeeease,* Mummy!" one of them pleaded.

"Look at the lovely tigers," their mother angled, doing her best to distract them from whatever it was they were after.

"*Mummyyyyyy,*" they persisted, "*pleeeeeease,*, just one more?"

"There are no more," Mummy tried to explain. "Oh look!" she exclaimed dramatically, pointing again at the tigers. "Here comes the daddy one!" But they weren't listening.

Ciara didn't move. The kids were about as interested in seeing the tigers as Ciara was in sharing her moment with them. But neither, it seemed, had a choice. She observed them curiously through their reflection in the enclosure glass.

"For God's sake, look at the tigers!" their mother quietly yelled with a quick self-conscious glance at Ciara.

"I don't want to," said the girl. "I want to go home."

"Tigers are gay," said the boy.

"Sam!" reprimanded their mortified mother with another quick glance towards Ciara who couldn't help but smile.

Had Robert been there he probably would have tried to cheer her up by pointing out that babies grow up to be terrible toddlers and eventually surly teenagers, just like this lot. And he was right, but there and then Ciara would have given anything to swop places. To be that happy and have a family, her own family, one that she had created:

something that came from her. She yearned for a baby and couldn't understand why such a gift escaped her. Without it she felt empty and helpless. It was an impossible feeling to describe. Yes, she had her siblings, her parents and of course Robert, but despite them she felt inexplicably alone.

Eventually the whining invaders moved on and Ciara listened to their drone as it disappeared along the neatly manicured route, headed towards the penguins until, thankfully, peaceful silence was restored and she was left alone again with her thoughts.

Daylight was fast fading, the hush of the zoo disturbed only by the screech of the baboons and drone of the camels, with an occasional roar of the lioness.

Reluctantly she made tracks towards the exit.

A warden appeared, collecting the various bits of discarded rubbish as he went.

"Sorry, love, time to go." Seeing her melancholy expression he asked, "Long day?"

"Something like that," she replied, holding back a sigh, choosing instead to reciprocate his friendly gesture.

"Well, chin up, love! It could be worse!"

It could be worse, she repeated, rolling the words over in her head. But Ciara had reached rock bottom. Just as the light was beginning to fade so too was her hope.

After the first miscarriage Kathryn had warned her that this might happen – that she'd dip emotionally. She actually used the word *dip* and, at the time, although Ciara had nodded appreciatively at her sister-in-law's advice she never imagined it would go this far. Never, not for a single second did she consider that her trying to have a baby would fail so epically. This wasn't a *dip*. A dip was far too gentle, a dip was something that only went halfway, that was easy to recover from, to get out of, to reverse. No, this wasn't a dip, this was more like a nosedive.

Chapter 11

Kathryn was bored senseless with her life. Aside from her naughty little frolics at Sunday lunch, this would be the most exciting thing to happen in her dull, monotonous life since – well, for as long as she could remember. Flicking her compact open, she expertly rolled up her pink Chanel lipstick and with one hand applied it, watching its glossing coverage in the small mirror. Pouting, she examined the result, catching sight of her eyes as she lifted her chin: ice-blue and cold with only a yellowing hint of the bruise remaining, they looked back at her, determined and unsmiling. She knew what she was about to do was rather unorthodox, cruel even, but something had to be done to cut through the cycle: he wouldn't hear her otherwise, and she wanted him to listen. Snapping the compact shut, she smoothed down her skirt, fixed her hair and tucked in her shirt. She was ready.

Sitting into the high-backed leather chair behind the vast bulk of her desk, which put as much distance as possible between her and her patients, she partially pulled out the drawer beside her, placing her beautifully manicured hand on top of the padded and full ochre envelope, and inhaled deeply.

They'll be here soon, she told herself, surprised by the butterflies that fluttered in her perfectly toned and flat stomach. A lot of time, effort and money was spent on that tummy, keeping it looking perfect in her size-eight tailored suits. She worked hard at making sure that she looked the part: attractive wife of a thriving entrepreneur and a successful medical consultant in her own right. Not that Seb seemed to notice these days and when he did it was only the bad things: the little imperfections that she simply couldn't hide. Yes, she worked hard at looking this good and to what end? Because *she* believed she really was worth it and worth so much more than *this*. It was, she conceded, unfortunate that Cormac was to be the vehicle through which she had decided to communicate the end of her marriage and for a split second she actually felt sorry for him, but he had unwittingly handed her the opportunity on a plate with his worried little wide eyes. And who was she to turn away from a gift like that? Life, she had decreed a long time since, was far too short for regrets and passengers. And while it was easy to feel a smidgen of remorse for what she was about to do to Cormac, it was just too hard to feel sorry for Seb. She let her head fall into her chest: feel sorry for him? It wasn't that long ago that she felt nothing but love for him. While it could hardly have been described as love at first sight, more a mutual and professional respect, it was without doubt intense and genuine. He was driven and ambitious, while she was intelligent and pushy. Both high achievers, high maintenance, demanding and unrelenting, they were a perfect fit, their passion burgeoning from each other's triumphs.

How ironic, she thought. It was the same hard edge

that attracted her to him in the first place that now made her feel so nauseous. They took no prisoners, she and Seb, and often marvelled pompously at the tales of their individual conquests, regardless of the inevitable collateral damage, human or otherwise. In hindsight, she conceded, like wild dogs it was only a matter of time before they turned on each other.

Life with Seb had become a chore, something she did because she was bound to rather than wanted to. She didn't like to be ignored and certainly wasn't going to put up with moods. Kathryn understood his commitment to his work; she accepted it, it was what made him who he was. She couldn't imagine his dedication to be anything other than one hundred and ten per cent. The recession almost broke them, but they managed their way through and survived. She should be proud of him, he should be proud of himself, but no – whatever was going on he had become unbearable. His pomp was replaced by petulance and distemper. She was being cast aside like some spent business deal.

Restless and impatient she stood to pace her office, pausing at the window that overlooked the hospital car park just in time to spot Cormac glide in on his bicycle. A wave of patronising pity washed over her: he looked so ridiculous in his tweed brown blazer and trouser-legs tucked into his socks. Despite their private school education, of the Bertram brothers Seb was really the only one with an ounce of decorum. While Rian was tolerable, his do-good mentality irked her immensely. And then there was Cormac.

"Look at him," she whispered to the empty room. "How pitiful! Cormac Bertram, pedalling furiously on his teenage racer."

For a split second she was stung by a pang of guilt: she was about to turn his world upside down when all he'd done was ask for her help. Certainly she was flattered that he came to her in the first place but his trust was misplaced and it was unfortunate that the day he called to her office to tell her his tale of woe was the same day as her argument with Seb. He had never hit her before so she was completely unprepared for the back of his hand when it met her cheekbone. How was she to know a throwaway remark about his underperformance would trigger such a violent reaction? Had she known, she wouldn't have said it aloud. That blow marked the end of their already struggling marriage.

"What happened?" Cormac had asked her that day, nervously taking his seat opposite her.

"Nothing too dramatic," she'd told him, gingerly touching the bruised and tender part of her face. "Just an overzealous morning in the gym, I'm afraid."

"Jesus, it looks pretty sore!"

"I'll survive," she replied with a reassuring smile. "Now! To what do I owe the pleasure?" Thankfully he was too distracted to interrogate her further.

Was that only a week ago, she asked herself, watching Cormac lock his bike, take his trousers from his socks and fix himself before making his way towards the hospital entrance.

He had been terribly edgy during his first visit. It was her job to read people and he was like an open junior-cycle book. So damn awkward and simple to read – his knees bounced, his fingers fidgeted and his eyes darted around the room like pinballs. When he did look at her it was uncomfortably, gauging her, second-guessing her reaction. His eventual humiliation and absolute mortification when finally he whispered, with his head hung low and his eyes almost closed, "Kathryn, I'm in trouble – I need your help," weren't lost on her. And in those first moments she actually felt sorry for him.

"What kind of trouble? Are you okay?" she asked with appropriate levels of concern and kindness, moving to sit opposite him.

"Not really," he replied with an uneasy chuckle.

"Go on," she encouraged him, "tell me."

An expert at masking her thoughts, she let him speak without showing either surprise or curiosity at this new and intriguing side of her not-so-innocent brother-in-law. She could feel his ignominy, could taste his helplessness – his body pulsed servility.

And when he was done, she simply nodded and let the silence, like a gentle snowfall, settle around him. Observing him while he sat, her mind tripped into action and a plot began to take shape in her shrewd head. She let him wallow in the stillness while she nurtured her scheme. He wanted her help, needed her help. Just how badly she was about to explore.

Sitting back into her chair she clasped her hands in her lap, dropping her eyes to inspect them dramatically, and for effect took a deep breath before looking back up.

"I have to say I'm a little surprised," she lied. "Can you leave this with me for a bit?"

"Sure. Sure," Cormac replied emphatically, squinting painfully while trying hard to catch her eye and gauge her thoughts.

But she refused to meet his stare. She knew what he

was thinking: '*At least she didn't say no, not immediately anyway*.' And when she didn't move, he knew it was his cue to leave.

"Okay. Well –" he said awkwardly, "I'll get going so," and gathering himself together he stood up.

She remembered the look on his face as he turned to open the door: confused and unfinished.

"You are coming to lunch on Sunday?" she asked his tweed-clad back.

He turned with a weak smile and nodded.

"I'll see you then," she said. "We can chat again there."

That day she gave him hope.

Kathryn used the next few days to think. It was both the first and the last thing she thought of every day until Sunday finally arrived. Filled with anticipation before even getting out of bed she paced through her plan, working through the potential variations of what might happen. Regardless of the path each scenario took they all ended up in the same deviant place. She hoped he wouldn't let her down but she doubted he would. She knew his personality type: he simply wouldn't be able to resist. It wasn't in his nature to say no. They both knew she was his only option; he'd said so himself. And heading to the shower, for the first time in as long as she could remember, the prospect of the monthly Bertram luncheon was quite enjoyable, for all the wrong reasons.

Cormac was the first to arrive, so eager was he to hear her answer. But she played him like a tightly strung fiddle, using the excuse of preparing the meal to appear flustered and distracted, and managed to gleefully and credibly withhold the attention he coveted.

She could feel his eyes on her, tracking her like a cat about to pounce, watching her every move. Laughing brazenly to herself, she thrilled at how edgy he was and how wicked she was about to be. So far, so good – her plan was coming together nicely.

Arriving into the kitchen after they'd finished the main course she geared up her game and, stepping in behind him, placed a hand on each forearm and slowly pushed herself against him. She felt him stand firm and hold his breath as if its rhythm would betray him. She knew he was aroused but working hard to hide his reactions. He was the startled gazelle leaping for the safety of the long grass.

"Oh for God's sake, Cormac, don't go all innocent on me," she mocked, just about able to contain a laugh that threatened to burst from her. "I've seen the way you watch me. I'm not shy, I'm open to it. Don't deny you fancy me. We're too long in the tooth to play games."

He was so easy to read she could imagine the thoughts that were rushing through his brain.

Go on, she silently prompted, say it . . . And he didn't disappoint.

"Don't be ridiculous. What about Seb?"

"What about him?"

"What about him? Are you serious? He's your husband for Christ's sake and my brother."

"Is that all that's stopping you?" she asked, moving towards him till she could smell the frustration on his heavy breath.

"Don't."

"Well," she told him, taking a step back, "now you know what I want."

It was done. The seed was sown. She was playing a cruel game, she knew that, but it was fun. Now she just needed to get him alone again. There was only the tiniest of doubts in her mind that maybe he wouldn't turn up but the temptation of a solution to his problem would win out.

Kathryn wasn't surprised when after dessert she returned to the kitchen to find he was gone.

And here he was. The phone on her desk rang out, bringing her straight back to the here and the now and Cormac who, Janice her PA announced, was waiting to see her.

"Send him straight in," Kathryn told her, standing only to sit again and run a hand over her perfect hair.

Well, this is it, she said to herself, picking up a pen and making herself look busy.

"Come in," she replied to the quiet but firm knock at the door.

She heard him enter.

"Punctual. I like that in a man," she said without looking up. "Sit. I'll be with you in a minute."

Obediently he sat into the visitor's chair opposite and waited for her attention. She glanced quickly at him. His eyes were pasted to the floor as if even to look at her was betraying his brother.

"So, thanks for coming," she said, finally putting down her elegant fountain pen to sit back in her chair. "You left yesterday without giving us a chance to agree the detail."

"The detail of what?" he asked politely.

"You know," she teased. "Our deal to save your ass."

She got up from her chair, shimmying seductively around to perch herself on the edge of her desk in front of him, making it impossible for him not to at least notice her provocatively placed stocking-clad legs.

Swallowing hard, he did his best to keep his eyes anywhere but on her.

"Kathryn," he whispered, "you are my brother's wife. Please don't do this."

She considered him for a minute, checked her watch and wondered how much more he could take. Deciding for immediacy – she only had so much time – she stood and walked around to the desk drawer. Opening it she removed the envelope, placed it on the table and pushed it towards him.

"It's all there. A hundred thousand euro."

Cormac looked at the package resting innocuously on her desktop: his future concealed inside an insipid yellow wrapper. This time when he swallowed his throat was dry and the air caught in his throat, making him cough.

"And in return," she told him, "I want you. Just once. Here. Now."

She knew she'd presented him with an offer that was just too irresistible to refuse. Here she was: willing, gorgeous and oh so tempting. She could almost hear him rationalise the offer inside his tiny little mind. They were alone. No one would see. She watched him blink, watched his eyes widen, knew what he was thinking. Knew what the voices in his head were saying, how the '*No way!*' that started out so vociferously was being smothered into almost silent insignificance by the voice that said '*Just once*'. It was incredible to watch: textbook stuff really. She was all too familiar with the type, having dealt with quite a few in her professional career. He was nearly there. Working through to the next phase of her beautifully conceived plan, she picked up the phone to remove the final obstacle.

"Janice, why don't you take an early lunch? "

Now they were really alone. No one to disturb them. No one to know.

"Just once," she repeated softly as if to answer the last remaining question and convince his conscience.

She stood before him, her legs slightly apart, and with both hands slowly lifted the hem of her navy pinstripe skirt up to just below her hips, revealing the lace tops of her silk stockings and the tanned toned stretch of soft sweet-smelling skin. She waited for him to lift his eyes to hers as she knew he would once he had passed the point of refusal and, when he did, she paused for a moment to hold them before stepping closer to him.

"Just once," she whispered, "and I promise I'll make it worth your while." Her words rang empty even to her own ears. For a split second she almost lost her bottle. Almost didn't, couldn't go through with it. Almost.

But now that she nearly had him, his control all but gone, his last remaining efforts to restrain himself and refuse her were weak and unconvincing.

"God, Kathryn, please," he begged aloud and half-heartedly, shaking his head in an attempted protest, "he's my brother for God's sake!" but the hands that moved to investigate beyond the hem of her skirt betrayed his now feeble protests.

"Oh, Seb won't mind," she replied bitterly. "He's far too busy with his little kingdom to take any notice of me, let alone you. Do you think he actually cares about either of us?" Leaning over, she gave him full view of her ample cleavage: her best feature, she often thought.

It was almost time.

Taking him by the collar of his awful tweedy blazer she pulled him up, slipping it over his shoulders and out of his arms to cast it carelessly onto the opposite chair. He didn't stop her but she could tell he was pushing himself to the limits of his restraint.

Only a little farther, she sang inside her head.

Standing up, taking a few steps back, dragging him with her, she felt the edge of the desk against her backside and stopped. Reaching up to take hold of his face, she angled it down towards her own so her eyes met his.

"Just once," was all she said, taking hold of his hand and placing its clammy palm inside her shirt, against her skin.

"Just once," he repeated, unable to hold back any more.

It was too much. He simply wasn't designed to say no.

It was almost time. With Janice gone he would come straight through, unannounced. Probably wouldn't even knock. Sensing Cormac's response to the feel of her skin, she encouraged his touch and lifted her leg to wrap around his waist, bringing his head down to her chest. Any minute now. He reciprocated accordingly, releasing her breast from the lace confines of her bra and taking it full into his mouth.

"Not so fast," she told him, willing him to ease his pace, holding him back by the hair at the nape of his neck, the edge of the table biting hard into the cheeks of her bottom.

She only wanted him and needed him to go so far. Then it was done.

Cormac didn't see or hear the door when it opened. He didn't see his brother stand in the frame, looking on while he suckled his wife. He didn't see the look of confusion morph first to shock, then disgust.

Their eyes locked, Seb and Kathryn. She thought he'd at least say something, anything, shout maybe, object, but instead he backed up a step or two and without taking his eyes off her closed the door, cutting her off from sight.

A guttural groan mixed with a pleasured laugh followed her husband's exit, loud enough for him to hear and confusing enough to convince the idiot Cormac that he had administered pleasure sufficient to extract such a feral response.

He should have been relieved when she pushed him away, and moved to take herself out of his reach. He should have thanked her for saving him betraying his brother further. But instead he looked wildly at her, bewildered and unfinished.

"What the ...?" he objected.

"I'm sorry, I can't do this," she told him calmly. "This is a mistake. You need to go."

"What?"

"You heard me. Go."

Kathryn moved out of reach, buttoning up her shirt, pulling down her skirt and fixing her hair.

"I don't understand," he exclaimed, dumbfounded by her sudden and unexplained change of mind. "I thought that was what you wanted?"

"It was, but I've changed my mind," she replied, throwing in, "We can't do this to Seb," both for good measure and as a vehicle to bring him and his feet back down to earth.

"Changed your mind?" he almost shrieked. "Are you bloody serious?" Then, reality dawning, he looked at the envelope that still rested on the desk. "About everything?" he asked, looking at her, his eyes pleading and his tone disbelieving.

"Oh for God's sake, just go!" she spat sharply and, stepping forwards, opened the door.

He pointed to the envelope, to his future, but she shook and bowed her head.

Confused, like it was a big joke, like she'd stop him, like she might explain what the hell just happened, he shrugged on his jacket, unfulfilled and reluctant to leave empty-handed.

She closed the door behind him and leaned heavily against it, her heart pounding in her chest. She heard him pause outside, mumble a few indecipherable but imaginable words, then leave, slamming the outside door behind him.

She hadn't intended to keep it. She had actually withdrawn it for him but, as her plan unfolded and thinking about what lay ahead for her now, she knew she'd need it more than him.

Chapter 12

Sebastian Bertram, forty-six years of age, confounded and humiliated, walked out of his wife's office and closed the door behind him. It was shut not in anger or disgust but with resigned defeat. Slow but walking tall, he made his way down the horrendously garish corridors out into the bright daylight and fresh air beyond the hospital doors. He stood for a moment to take a breath and measure for a minute what he had just walked away from, unsure as to how he should process it, his rational brain conflicting with the apparently preposterous nature of what he had just witnessed. It wasn't an accident. She meant him to see it. She had invited him there and knew he'd be on time: he always was. She expected him and planned for him to walk in on them. Poor, stupid Cormac. He almost laughed at the thought of his ridiculous brother wrapped around his wife. Not just anyone, but his *wife*. How was he supposed to deal with that? That idiot was just a pawn in her freakish little game show. A chump. Her first ploy in a move to the end which he never saw coming and which Cormac was unlikely to realise he was a part of. She had launched a surprise offensive in a war Seb stupidly wasn't even aware was being waged.

Patients and visitors flanked the doorway, dressed in a collection of parka jackets and dressing gowns, puffing away to save their lives in the filthy butt-covered health-facility entrance. The comforting tar-laden fumes snaked their way into his nostrils and deep into his lungs. He hadn't had one since breakfast and longed for one right then but couldn't quite see himself hanging with the patients, no matter how desperate he felt. Leaving them to their own destruction, he went along the covered walkway to the car park, paid for his ticket then made his way to the intimate comfort of his Jaguar.

Sitting into its ample interior and closing the door with a quiet *thunk*, he sat back into the leather seat, placed his hands on the wheel and lowered his head over them, rocking his forehead rhythmically against his knuckles.

He knew she wasn't happy – hell, he wasn't happy. With deep shame he also knew the point at which he had lost her completely. He'd overstepped the mark and recognised it as a detrimental move the moment he raised his hand. But he had been unable to stop it. Although only a week before, it felt like months ago. He'd been under enormous pressure and just snapped, tired of her caustic tongue. He shouldn't have touched her like that, he knew it the second it was done and told her as much as soon as the haze cleared and he could think straight again. Obviously from what he had witnessed as her revenge, his apology wasn't enough. But she had pushed him to it with her patronising, supercilious sneers and her barking remarks – that constant, endless, mindless pushing. Why did she have to go that extra mile to humiliate him? Why couldn't she have just let him be? Why did she have to be so bloody tedious? Regardless of the multitude of excuses he could concoct, he knew he just shouldn't have done it. At least now he knew the price he was expected to pay. A bit rich perhaps? How could they possibly move on from this? Did he even want to move on? Did she? What next?

He pressed his forehead hard against his knuckles. How was he supposed to deal with this on top of everything else? In an instant once again he felt the now familiar fog close in, felt the panic grip his heart and squeeze him tight. He felt the sweat build on his back, and his underarms heat up. Leaning back with his eyes closed, instinctively he reached to loosen his tie. His throat closed over so much he couldn't breathe.

A knock at the window brought him rushing back to the reality of the darkening car park.

"Are you alright, son?" an elderly man asked, peering in at him through the closed and slightly tinted window, his look a combination of concern and curiosity.

Startled, Seb lifted his hand in acknowledgement.

"I'm good," he said, lowering the window. "Just taking a moment." He gave him a grateful reassuring smile, ignoring the temptation to tell him to bugger off and mind his own business.

The man returned his smile, nodding in recognition. "We all need one of them some time or other. As long as you're okay." Satisfied that Seb was in no danger, he walked towards his own car, started the engine and drove away.

Seb felt sick, his stomach reacting to the adrenaline that pumped through his system.

He shook his head in a desperate attempt to rid himself of the image of his wife's leg wrapped seductively around his brother's waist.

"What am I supposed to do with that?" he asked himself aloud, still reeling. Did she really have to go that far, with his *brother*, of all people? And for the first time since he was a teenager he actually felt vulnerable and afraid. The temptation to lie down and roll over, his will to fight depleted, was beyond tempting. They'd love to see him like this, his detractors. This was what she wanted. To hurt him. To demean him, see him suffer.

"Well done, you!" he saluted his absent wife, sorry she wasn't there to hear his words. "It worked, you should feel quite proud of yourself, if that's how you want to play it."

As was his nature, it didn't take long for the anger to build, his defence mechanism to recharge and his will to fight return, fully loaded.

"I'll deal with you later but first I have to deal with a different bastard!"

And, putting the key in the ignition, he revved the engine and sped from the car park.

If anything the encounter with his brother and wife gave him the impetus he needed to tackle his father and put the adrenaline to good use. In his mind's eye they were one and the same: his father, his brother, his wife, all serving together to do him harm. In the car as he drove he made two calls: the first to the bank, the second to his solicitor.

Fired up, the thirty-minute drive through the city passed in a mélange of grey, morphing into a shapeless, fast-moving blur passing outside the window, but inside everything was still. Just as it should be. Moving at the same speed as himself: in tune and synchronised. The familiar rattle and hum of the car as it drove over the uneven surface of the bridge was the signal of a ten-minute arrival time at his parents' house. Pushing against the steering wheel, he braced his arms and took a deep breath, steeling himself for what was to come.

Slowing right down he turned into the tree-lined street and seconds later to the entrance of the elegant five-bedroom Victorian villa. Overshadowed by the tall oak and ash trees that provided the all-important privacy to the Bertram family, natural light didn't stand a chance in amongst the dense foliage and thick weave of branches. Getting out of the car he pressed a short sequence of numbers into the key-pad mounted on the perimeter wall and returned to his car as the tall wooden gates glided open. The slow sound of tyres on the short stone driveway was like teeth biting into burnt toast: a crunching, brittle sound that had been the same, never changing, ever since his childhood. He pulled up between his father's white Mercedes and his mother's hardly driven Volkswagen Golf. Instinctively locking the car, even though he probably didn't need to within the safety of his parents' little enclave, he walked up the majestic granite steps to the front door and banged the brass knocker, as old as the house itself, against the solid door. He had keys somewhere and there was always the secret key out here but he hadn't used either since the day he moved out over twenty years ago. He had no need. The knocker was good enough for him: it defined him as a visitor, which he was more than happy with. Poised and ready, he waited for the faint sound of footsteps and the glossy black door to open.

It was impossible to deny that the house was beautiful, despite the colouring of his grim childhood memories. As children, they seemed to exist in a constant state of belligerence. Someone always fighting with someone else. His own fights with his father, the endless battle of wits, the constant scrapping with his sisters, their mindless bickering and his seemingly endless gripe with Rian who annoyingly rarely fought back. Weak, insipid Rian. Even the girls put up a better fight than him. He was easy and very, very irritating prey. And as for Cormac, the bastard, he was the mover within the group without, it appeared, upsetting anyone. The constant playmaker, he had the vision to lead and the charisma to bring people along with him, the ultimate politician – how he hadn't followed their father into either the law or the party he didn't quite know. The hand-shaker and peace-negotiator, the defender and the operator, always in some way serving his own end but never in a malicious way – someone else always came out of it thanking him. Once again the image of Cormac buried in his wife reappeared to torment him and despite himself a smile crossed his lips. Kathryn was the manipulator in this case, of that he was sure. She had obviously seen an opportunity and leveraged it to her own ends. If it were anyone else's plan, he'd probably admire it.

Seb's heart pumped in anticipation of what he still had to do and, with no sign of anyone coming to the door he knocked again, louder this time, and leaned around to see if he could see any movement through the sash windows. Even when it was bright outside, inside the house was always cold and dark. There was always a light on and today was no different but with the curtains half drawn it was difficult to see beyond them. It used to irritate him as he grew up that no one ever pulled the curtains back fully

– always seeming to struggle with daylight, like vampires afraid of what terrors it might reveal. Either that or someone was more worried about what others would see from the outside in. In total there were twenty-four rooms across the three floors of the house, only ten of which as children they were allowed to enter: their individual bedrooms, the kitchen, the playroom, the bathroom, the utility room and, most importantly, the pantry. All others were strictly out of bounds unless in the company of either parent or their nanny. Out of fear of physical retribution from their father they never disobeyed the order. He was never afraid to use the back of his hand. To this day Seb couldn't confidently map the rooms within the various layers and along the different corridors. Now, no more than then, he neither cared nor bothered about what lived behind the discoloured and ancient six-panel doors.

A third, louder knock resulted in the sound of clunky hurrying footsteps and eventually an out-of-breath Gladys opened the door.

"Sorry, sir – I was in the kitchen and didn't hear you – my hearing's not what it used to be."

Gladys had been their housekeeper for as long as he could remember and just like the house she hadn't changed much over the years: a little smaller perhaps, definitely greyer, but despite her faded sheen she was still the same old Gladys.

"Gladys," he greeted her patiently. "And please," he said as he entered, inflicting a forced smile on her, "as I've said countless times before, 'Seb' will do just fine, thanks." He hated being called *sir* – well, in this house anyhow. 'Sir' was his father's title and within these walls it had different connotations to elsewhere socially.

"Is my father here?" he asked.

"Just in," she replied formally. "He's in the study." Standing back, she waited for him to pass into the hall. "Can I get you some tea?" she offered, doing her best to buffer the tension that oozed from him.

"No, thank you, Gladys, I'm fine."

Taking off his coat to hang on the ornate hall stand, he checked his reflection in its mirror before turning away.

Taking a breath, he ignored the nerves that tingled in the pit of his stomach and took confidence from the defensive fury that smouldered dangerously inside him. Pausing for a moment, he reminded himself that he was a man in control and he had a job to do. He needed to think strategically. His father was a complex individual who would fire everything he could at him so he needed to be prepared and try to think one step ahead.

As the eldest child, Seb's relationship with his father was tense. Very much in the public eye as the longest-standing government minister, one of the few to keep his seat since he first earned it, William Bertram demanded a lot of his children. It was only as Seb matured and experienced the compassion demonstrated by other parents that he considered perhaps William was never cut out to be a father. Certainly he was wise and engaging with his voters, his smile appearing to be all-encompassing – definitely a commanding leader who was often described as charismatic by his peers. But to his family, whom he wheeled in and out of his public life as was needed, he was always dispassionate and disturbingly aloof. He didn't seem to care or connect unless there was something in it for him. His family didn't appear to be of any use to him and, William himself admitted, if it were up to him they wouldn't meet as a group. "A frivolous exercise" was how he was overheard describing their regular family gatherings. It was Ciara's irritating but secretly admired influence on the group that kept them bound together. He didn't know where she got it from as none of the others, including himself, seemed to care. He was his father's hereditary hope: William believed that, in the same way as he was a clone of *his* father, Seb should be just like him. A mini-me. A replica. A strong-willed, bloody-minded, commanding leader. From an early age he was taught to shake his father's hand rather than share an intimate hug. He was advised to call him *sir* rather than *Daddy.* He was trained to listen and observe all around him.

"Fear is merely an expression of respect. If they do not fear you, they do not respect you," his father preached and Seb prided himself on being somewhat distant, almost superior to those around him. But he, much to his father's disappointment, not having inherited the political bug, was destined never to covet his father's ministerial seat of power or show even the slightest interest in joining the firm of solicitors set up by his grandfather many, many years before. Seb was his own strong-willed, bloody-minded and commanding leader with his own unique dreams, and his own seat of power that he was now primed to defend and protect.

"And Mum?" Seb asked Gladys, moving across the hall towards the closed study door.

"She's upstairs, sir, in her room," Gladys replied, lowering her eyes, hoping he wouldn't ask her if she was either awake or sober.

"Thank you, Gladys," he replied, ignoring her

persistence with '*sir*'. Striding towards the door he pulled back his shoulders and tensed his core, banged three confident knocks on the door and entered without waiting for his father to respond.

If his father was taken aback by his son's impertinent entrance he didn't show it. He stood with his back to the door behind the vast antique and claw-footed desk with its red china desk lamp and leather blotting pad.

Heavy brocade curtains draped low to almost cover the windows without actually being closed. Side-tables and standard lamps littered a room already cluttered by stacks, piles and shelves of papers and books accompanied by an array of vintage ornaments and furniture gathered over the years. The warm lamplight struggled to fully light up the room, barely reaching the heights of the high ceiling while only the crackling of the fire and the tick of the clock on its mantel disturbed the heavy hush.

"Father," Seb announced, taking four long steps into the room, clutching the file firmly in his hand.

"Sebastian," his father returned without lifting his head from what he was reading, as if expecting him to have been there sooner. "Sit," he ordered with a careless wave of his hand, as if commanding a dog.

Ignoring the instruction Seb remained standing and patiently watched as his father continued to read. This was the game. A familiar, age-old tactic and one he himself played well having learnt from the master: make them wait and sweat. Recognising it for what it was, he smiled inwardly and played to his father's opening gambit. The silence stretched out but, refusing to rise to it, he continued to let the time pass, watching his father's back gently inflate and deflate as he breathed. Once again Seb wondered what had possessed him to do business with him in the first place. He must have been mad. Even Dermot had been reluctant. With the benefit of hindsight he knew he should have listened to his instinct, which he trusted in every other aspect of his business. But never could he have imagined an outcome such as this.

With his father's company established, Bertram and Guilfoyle administered the purchase of the derelict and half-finished office block on Ronson Street. He was actually quite proud of the price he'd negotiated on their behalf. They really were getting a great deal with fantastic potential for growth. With the money in the company bank account from the four directors and the paperwork in place, including the guarantees, they closed the sale and work started on site. Surprisingly, it appeared to be a seamless operation. All that remained was the final approval on the company loan from the bank to come through.

At the time Seb was pleased to help this group of almost celebrity politicians prop up their apparently meagre state salaries. Standing now with the file in his hand, in his father's lair, with allegations of fraud biting at his heels he told himself once again that he'd been a fool.

"So," his father finally responded and, turning to look at Seb, he placed the apparently captivating document on his desk, "what's so important that you have to burst in here like this?"

"I'm here to discuss some issues with Ronson Street." Seb, still standing and ignoring the intended sting, replied, his voice strong and his diction clear.

"Really? What problems?"

Forewarned by Tim, Seb knew that his father was already aware of the situation. Apparently William had called to see what the delay was with the final loan approval, which was supposed to have been in the bag.

Standing tall, holding his ground Seb continued. "It seems there are some concerns over the signatures in the guarantee documents."

"What kind of concerns?" William asked innocently, looking calmly at Seb over the rim of his glasses. There was no shock, no faltering speech, no fidgeting, no rising red in his cheeks. His serenity was almost unnerving. Again, a calculated strategic tool: play dumb.

Maintaining an even tone, Seb continued. "The bank has raised a question over the validity of the personal guarantees on the loan application."

"Have they now?"

"Yes. Yes, they have." Opening up his file, Seb took from it the printed sheets with the five signatures and their comparisons on it: his own, his father's and the three partners'. "You remember these, don't you, Dad?" he asked and paused to see his reaction. "The signatures, it seems, might not be ..." again he paused, searching for the appropriate term, "... exact."

"Really? How extraordinary," William replied.

"Yes, and funnily enough the only one that seems to be genuine is my own. You remember, Dad – you brought these to my office and created such a fuss when I didn't want to sign them. Don't you?"

Seb extended his hand, offering the wad of pages for William to see.

"I don't exactly recall," William replied vaguely, ignoring them.

"Well," Seb continued, "I do. As a lawyer you should know that the bank have procedures. They actually check these things. Here," he offered again. "See for yourself." And extending his arm further, pushed the pages at his father.

Taking them this time, William flicked casually through them before handing them back.

"Well, I can't tell for sure," he said flippantly as if it meant nothing to him, like he'd nothing to worry about.

"Can't tell for sure?" Seb mocked. "But you told me yourself that evening. You said you'd actually *seen* your partners sign them, so really you should be sure. You told me to trust you and I did. Can't tell for sure? Bullshit. You know damn well."

His father looked him straight in the eye but said nothing.

"You've been caught, haven't you?" Seb dared and when William remained silent he shook his head in disbelief. "What's interesting here is that you didn't take the process seriously! You didn't bet on them verifying the signatures at all, did you? Not yet anyway."

"I have nothing to worry about," William finally said.

"Really? Are you serious? Nothing to worry about?" Seb asked incredulously. "But you do and I'll tell you why." He took a step closer to his father, close enough to see the defiance in his eyes. "At the very best they'll want to know why we submitted fake forms and, assuming they're satisfied with our answer, they'll make us resubmit them, properly this time. Then you really will have to carry the debt. There's a chance they might rescind the loan offer completely and in that case you're screwed too because you're already on site and spending money faster than you're bringing it in. But at worst they'll take this further with the fraud team and probably the police and, with you and your buddies involved, it's guaranteed to hit the media. That's when you really need to worry."

"Me?" William asked with feigned innocence.

"Who else?" Seb challenged.

"Well, you said it yourself. They're not our signatures and yours is the only one that's genuine ..." He let the sentence hang for Seb to digest.

"Jesus, Dad, we both know it was you who did this, not me."

"But I've done nothing," William protested.

Seb shook his head in disdain. "Dad, this is between you and me. You told me, remember, to my face. We both know what's going on here and you can spin whatever fairy tale you want, but you and I, we'll know the truth. Don't forget that."

William turned his back on his son in what Seb assumed was an attempt to hide his weakness. It was a rare occasion to have the upper hand over his father. Seb could feel his discomfort and watched him squirm. William couldn't argue, nor could he deny it, but would he admit what he had done?

"Here's what I think," Seb offered. "I think you deliberately forged those signatures. I think you did it so that *if* there was a problem you could hold your hands up and say, '*Oh no, that wasn't me, I didn't sign them!*' The bank then, you assume, wouldn't be able to hold the guarantee over you and all four of you get to walk away scot-free, while *I* bear the brunt of the blame as the person who prepared and submitted the application. But, and this is where it gets interesting, is it possible that you didn't bank on the fact that these days they do have processes in place to catch people like you and your band of merry men. They do actually check signatures. And they do catch people out. But you must have known that. Your problem is that they discovered your fake signatures too bloody soon, didn't they?" Seb paced as he spoke, no longer looking at his father, with the parts of his hypothesis that he didn't quite get just falling into place. It made sense and in the absence of any defence from his father he knew he was on the right track. "In your plan they would only inspect the guarantee if they needed to use it. I'm right, aren't I? And I'll put money on it that you're all in on it. Not just you but all four of you." Seb waited for his father's response and when none was forthcoming he let the silence linger before asking, "So I'm supposed to take the blame for this?"

He stopped again and waited for a reply from William who still had his back to him.

"Come on, Dad, at the very least have the balls to admit I'm right."

Finally William turned. He had a gleam in his eyes and a provocative smirk on his lips.

"Well, if it's the truth you're after then yes, that was the plan." He stood firm, waiting for Seb to react.

And, even though Seb had pieced the scheme together for himself, hearing the admission aloud from his father was a breath-taking blow.

"You really are a bastard, aren't you?" he said with a deep sigh, his pulse picking up speed.

"You asked for honesty. And really, it's as much your fault as it is mine – you should really have checked them."

"You forced my hand."

"I can't be held responsible if you haven't the gumption to say no."

"I took you at your word. I didn't think I needed to say no," Seb replied, feeling the acid taste of panic rise in his throat.

William, apparently guilt free, shrugged.

"Okay," Seb swallowed, taking a different tactic. "Let's say, that afternoon you came to my office, if I asked you then whether they were genuine, would you have told me the truth? Would you have let me in on your ruse?"

"Probably not."

"I never stood a chance with this, did I?"

"Not really, no."

Seb didn't know whether to be reassured by his father's honesty or astonished. It was as if William had disconnected completely from the reality of what he had done, emotionally and professionally.

But Seb recognised the shift in power. Incredibly, William had regained the upper hand.

"So now that you've been caught, what's your plan?" he asked.

"No change," he replied, sitting into his desk chair. "There's no need."

"They'll probably withdraw the loan offer, you know that, don't you?"

"Well, we'll just have to re-apply then, won't we?" William's tone was condescending, as if speaking to a child.

"Well, count me out," Seb scoffed. "And if the bank decide to report this – what then?"

"We'll cross that bridge when we come to it." William shrugged, like it was plain that this was the best solution.

"And again," Seb asked, feeling his anger rise with the nonchalance of the answer, "you expect me to take the blame for you."

"I do."

"You are completely nuts, do you know that? Do you think I'll risk everything I've worked so hard to build so you can get away with attempted fraud? And even if I wanted to, do you think Dermot would let me? My reputation is everything." Seb stopped and dropped his head, suddenly feeling tired.

"You might not have an option," his father replied, his composure unnerving. What did he have that gave him this much confidence, Seb wondered nervously.

"It'll be your word against mine," said William. "And not just that, there are any one of about fifty tests we can take to prove that I didn't sign those forms. Do you understand? This will come down to you. Without fail."

Seb watched his father's reactions, or lack of, stunned by the absence of remorse or concern for the consequences of his actions.

"What I don't understand is why you'd do such a thing?"

"Don't be an idiot, Sebastian – because the bank wouldn't release the funds without the guarantees."

"I wasn't talking about the bank, I was talking about me. Why would you do it to me? Your son. But, now that you say it, why not just give them what they wanted? Why not do it properly? This is a risky game. I explained it to you all from the start. It has huge potential but it's a gamble, and if you can't afford to lose you shouldn't play the game. You can't afford to play the game, Dad. Not if you're doing this."

"Don't patronise me, son."

"Well, stop acting like an idiot!" Seb spat, waving a dismissive arm at him. "*You* and your kind are the reason they check!" His voice was rising, his composure shot. "And you charlatans are running this country. Unbelievable. God help us all."

William watched his son's display dispassionately, his arms folded across his chest.

"I could be prosecuted or disbarred! Dad, you could be prosecuted, we all could."

"Oh for God's sake, Sebastian, get a hold of yourself. Obviously the bank was never supposed to find out. You've already said that this is a fantastic project. Nobody ever set out to deliberately defraud anyone. We were just trying to protect ourselves, that's all. Is that a crime?"

"Jesus Christ, Dad, yes, it bloody well is!" Seb shouted, running a hand over the top of his head. Feeling caged, he turned on the spot. "My future is in the hands of a bunch of politicians, as genuine as a virgin prostitute."

A knock on the door put a stop to his diatribe and an embarrassed Gladys cautiously slipped her head around the door.

"Ehhhh ... sorry to disturb you, Mr. Bertram ..." She looked quickly towards Seb who immediately turned away. "I'm done for the day – do you need anything else before I go?"

William ran a hand over his balding head and looked straight at her as if the argument with his son was business as usual.

"No, Gladys, that's fine. Thank you and have a nice evening."

She stalled at the door as if about to say something else, looking from father to son, as if concerned that they might do each other some harm should she leave them alone.

"Anything else?" William asked her.

"No, sir. Goodnight," she said timidly and withdrew.

"*Sir*," Seb mocked quietly, retreating to the fire.

Grasping the mantelpiece with both hands, he shook his head. What was it about this room? Nothing went right in this room. Being in it meant trouble, it always had, even when they were young this was where things went down – never good, always bad. His memories of being humiliated and lambasted rushed back to haunt him, feelings not so different to what he was experiencing right now. Furious, frustrated and vulnerable, he couldn't help but think of Rian.

Chapter 13

Unlike Seb, hardly a day passed by when Rian didn't relive, even briefly, the undesired recollections of that house, standing with his thirteen-year-old hands clasped tightly behind his back, sticky and tight. Like a moth to a flame he couldn't help but be drawn into the memory of the subdued study and how he had faced his father who was sitting bolt upright and livid behind the antique rosewood desk, his face lit up by the desk lamp like a horror-show ghoul. The image remained as vivid as the day he had first experienced it. He could still feel the tension in the air, smell the smoke from the spitting coals in the fire, hear his heart beating loudly in each ear and sense Seb's presence on the far side of the door, listening, waiting to be called in, waiting to let him down. It was a moment he would never, ever forget.

The last three weeks of term had been nerve-racking: looking over his shoulder every minute, acutely aware of every whisper, every footfall, and every creak of the old school floorboards. Keeping an eye out for Sully was agonising, and at the same time making sure he steered clear of Fitzer and the strife that inevitably followed him was exhausting. But the idea that once he got home he would be okay was all he needed to keep going. For some ludicrous reason, inside his thirteen-year-old head Rian had thought that confiding in his father was the right thing to do. He assumed he would help, would stop the predictable from happening. It never once crossed his mind that his father wouldn't believe him.

"How is your father?" Sully had asked that evening in his study, sparking a tremor that ran from Rian's head to his toes, his voice a silver icy sliver that burrowed its way deep into his heart.

"He's good, sir," Rian had replied with a desiccated and shaky swallow.

"And your mother? She looked so well the last time they came to visit."

Rian looked down at his hands, feeling tears sting the backs of his eyes and all the while Father Sullivan's hand rested menacingly on his thigh, just above his knee, burning through the coarse material of his grey school trousers to scorch his skin. Where was Seb, he asked himself – he could stop this. Rian didn't want to be alone with Sully. Why wasn't he here?

He could help me. Maybe if I scream …

"So, what have you got to say for yourself?"

"Nothing, sir," he offered, feeling his headmaster's hand slide further up this thigh, wanting more than anything for the ordeal to be over. Was Father Sullivan looking for him to snitch on Fitzer? He searched his brain for what might, even remotely, be the correct answer. Is that what this was all about, he asked himself hopefully. If that was true then he would gladly tell all and maybe that would stop the hands moving.

"He wouldn't believe you, your father," Father Sullivan remarked quietly. "If you told him, that is, would he?" The words were delivered almost as a whisper, seductively.

"About what, sir?" Rian asked, genuinely confused by what he meant: Fitzer or this, the hand that wouldn't let him go?

"That's the good lad," Sully replied, misinterpreting his response as an affirmation.

Bewildered and lightheaded, madly trying to make sense of what was happening to him, Rian thought he might be ill as he tried to decipher how he should respond and tried to weigh up his options.

I'm not tied down, why can't I move?

"He won't believe you," the priest went on, confusing the boy further, "when you say you're not protecting anyone." But sincerity was missing from the words, the sly leer undeniable.

"No, sir," Rian replied, trying to push himself further into the back of the chair, hopelessly, desperately struggling to achieve even just a few inches more of separation between them.

I can stay here and let him touch me.

"You're obviously good at keeping things to yourself," Sully remarked as if talking to himself, as Rian wasn't even there.

Or I can get up and leave. I could explain, tell Seb what happened.

"You don't like to tell tales, do you?" the priest continued.

I can go straight to Dad . . .

"It could be our secret," he continued absently, the

palm of his shovel-shaped hand now covering Rian's groin and closing gently around his penis.

Get up! Rian's inner voice screamed. Get up and leave. Get the hell out of here!

"Let me just check here to see if there is any damage."

Get off me. Stand up. Stand up! Inside his head the sound of his own voice was deafening.

"He did kick you here, boy, didn't he?" Sully asked with a small squeeze. "It might be bruised."

Maybe if I scream, someone will hear me. Maybe he'll just stop.

"Let me just look and see ..." The priest took hold of Rian's trouser zip and started to tug it down with such calm, like it was the most normal thing he could do. Like he did this kind of thing every day: examined his students' penises to see if they were bruised.

Rian was rooted to the chair, unable to move, unable to scream audibly, unable to say anything. But inside he was bellowing wildly. At that moment he felt exposed and like a baby abandoned to the wild. He felt utterly helpless and, despite himself, started to cry.

Maybe if I let him do it, say nothing, he'll let go.

The tears that had prickled the back of his eyes now flowed freely down his cheeks.

Maybe if I ask him, he'll stop.

The tears tasted salty in his mouth, the sharp tang of humiliation.

Maybe I just won't tell. No one has to know.

He let the priest put his hand inside his trousers to touch him. He clutched tight on the arms of the corduroy-upholstered arms of his chair. He let the old hands rotate his balls between his fingers and rub its palm roughly on the small bulk of his shaft. It didn't feel right. It wasn't right. His flesh was unresponsive and for a horrible fear-splitting moment he worried that it might not stay that way. What if, despite his terror, he might go hard and make Sully think he liked it. His breath stuttered and his chest shuddered. He had no control. He didn't know where to look: down at the hand that fondled him or straight ahead into the leering eyes of his violator. Or straight up to the sky and heaven where God was watching and taking notes.

"That's a good boy," Sully whispered. His eyes closed over and his previously free hand moved to massage his own groin.

Please, please, God, help me! Rian implored and with nowhere safe to look closed his own eyes and stopped listening, his booming heart drowning out the sound of his headmaster's malevolent, moaning, saccharine voice.

A frantic knock on the door made the priest pull away, withdraw his hand instantly from Rian's trousers and stand up quickly like he'd been electrocuted.

"Fix yourself, boy," he said sternly.

Rian thanked God for the intervention, his head light with the white noise that blasted in his ears and an ethereal aura blurring his vision. Standing up, his legs like jelly, he pulled up his zip.

Sullivan sat back into the chair behind his desk and ran a hand through his hair.

"Come!" he roared to the unexpected visitor.

An apparently hysterical Robbie burst into the room.

"Sir, sir," he panted, "I think there's something burning downstairs. I can smell burning!"

"Calm down, boy," Sully boomed. "Tell me where

exactly you think you smell burning."

"In the back stairs, sir, down to the ref!" he screeched excitedly, referring to the dining hall.

"And what were you doing on the back stairs?"

"I left my assignment in the ref at supper. I went to get it."

Sully looked discreetly down into his lap, checking himself before standing up to make his way out of the room

"On your way, Bertram," he said to Rian without looking back at the boy who stood pale-faced and quaking by the chair. "I'll see you for confession tomorrow evening."

Confession? It's not till Saturday – that's three days away. Why tomorrow? What have I done wrong? Rian asked himself, watching the holy robes sweep and disappear through the door.

Before he left Robbie looked back at his friend, his eyes telling Rian that he knew exactly what had been happening to him before being interrupted by what they both knew would turn out to be a false alarm.

"This way, sir," Robbie said, running to get ahead of the headmaster.

"Don't be an idiot, boy! I know where the refectory is."

Rian made his way slowly back to his dorm. Lights were out but the yellow beams from the multitude of illegal torches bounced from the ceiling to light his route. He stopped outside Seb's closed cubicle curtain, contemplating whether or not he should call in to him. Through the thickness of the patterned fabric he saw the flicker of the torch as it was put out. Deciding against it he walked past and went straight to his own, pulling the curtain across behind him.

"Is that you, Bertram?" Johnny Jackson asked from beyond the baby-blue partition wall.

"Yeah."

"You okay?"

"Yeah."

"So did Sully slip the tongue then?" Johnny asked with a childish twitter.

"Very funny, asshole," Rian replied, careful not to sound too serious lest Johnny should guess from the defensive tone of his voice.

"Just askin'," Johnny finished with a snigger.

"And anyway, if he did I wouldn't bleedin' tell you."

He stripped out of his uniform, got into his pyjamas and lay on the flatbed cot face down with his head buried deep into his pillow. While his relief at being safe was palpable, he knew he had just had a very lucky escape. He also knew that what happened wasn't his fault. He hadn't done anything wrong. But what confused him was, if he didn't do anything wrong why did he feel so bad? His guilt and unease consumed him to the extent that he couldn't remember what it felt like to be without it, even though it had started only minutes before. His head was a whirlwind rushing round and round, his reason raging madly, round and round, thoughts chasing thoughts, answers never quite stopping to be read or understood. And then there was Robbie: the catalyst. If he hadn't stood up for him in the first place, if he hadn't challenged Fitzer, if he hadn't told him to back off then none of this would have happened. Lying on his bed, breathing in the dust and the mites from his feather pillow, there was a moment when he asked himself why he had bothered. He should have just left him be. Turning in the bed he examined the ceiling, the dirty grey ceiling with its nasty hanging lights with their dust-covered bulbs and even dirtier, nastier, glass shades that had seen much sparklier days. No, *despite his perplexity he knew for sure that he couldn't have stood by and watched his friend have the crap beaten out of him. That would have made him feel worse. If there was one thing he was really sure of, it was that he had done the right thing by standing up for his friend in a moment when no one else bothered.*

And catching Robbie's poignant, troubled blue eyes standing in the doorway of the office, Rian had understood that he had returned the favour. Now, between them they had something more than just the wrath of Fitzer in common.

It took hours for him to get to sleep that night. Every time he closed his eyes he saw Sully's big white head looming over him. He thought about Seb and what he might do if he confided in him. But, knowing the answer to be absolutely nothing, decided that there was no point. He had turned away when he saw Fitzer tear him down. He had walked away when Rian was lying on the floor. He had watched him walk from the dorm like a lamb to the slaughter. And he did nothing. He did nothing to help him. He offered him neither a silent word nor nod of either support or sympathy. He threw him knowingly to the holy wolf then turned a blind eye. Rian didn't know what was worse: the image of Sullivan's ugly head or the idea that his own brother couldn't care less. Unable to face the pictures that formed so vividly in his head, he tried to see if he could keep his eyes open all night. It worked for a while but eventually, despite himself, he simply fell asleep.

When he woke the following morning he dressed then listened and waited for the sounds of his brother leaving the dorm. He followed him down the stairs to the refectory where he sat opposite him. Seb threw him an irritated look but said nothing, focusing on the disappearing contents of his cereal bowl. Without offering his little brother as much as a smile he scooped himself a second bowl of half-stale cornflakes. Rian followed suit, their fingers meeting at the milk-jug handle. Seb looked sternly at his younger brother who immediately withdrew his hand in obedience. Seb was often irritated by his little brother but this morning he was particularly prickly: if his looks were terminal Rian would have expired at the first soft spoonful.

In his own awkward way Rian wanted to know, needed to know, if Seb was on his side in the matter of what had happened in the priest's office. What did he think of what had happened? Because, even though Rian had said nothing, Seb knew damn well. Everyone had heard the rumours. But his brother didn't raise his eyes from the milky bowl. Spoon after spoon, scoop after scoop, they ate their cornflakes in silence. This was the test, Rian thought. If he says anything now, I know he's with me. If he doesn't, then he's not. Simple as. Throughout breakfast, as each disappointingly silent minute passed, he felt and acknowledged the various pats on his back from his student comrades. They suspected but didn't know for sure what had happened in Sully's office and they never would know. He'd not tell, that was certain. His fellow classmates, it appeared, cared more than his own brother.

"What the hell do you want?" a vexed and grumpy Seb finally barked impatiently, throwing his spoon into the bowl with a heavy clang, sending a wave of milk crashing over the side and all over the table.

But Rian didn't bother to reply. So the test was complete. He had hoped for more and felt like his brother had thumped him. Unmanly tears threatened so rather than expose himself further in front of everyone he dropped his gaze and shook his head.

"Well, then, bugger off, would you?" Seb told him callously. "You're giving me a pain in my face."

Done. Gathering up his bowl, spoon and glass, Rian took them to the dishes trolley and left to get his books to go to class, stopping off in the toilet on the way to sort out those unwanted but inevitable tears.

He did think of sharing his experience with his mother, but in the end decided against it. She held no weight with his father and wouldn't really be able to support his desire to leave. So, when term finally ended and he had plucked up the courage to approach his father, he had expected a tricky but eventual end to his ordeal.

"What in the name of the good God are you up to?" his father accused him, his flaring nostrils accentuated by the light from the desk lamp. "Father Sullivan is your headmaster, he's a teacher for God's sake, a man of the bloody cloth, of integrity." The more he spoke the more incensed he became, his arms gesticulating rigidly in anger, as if cataloguing the reasons why he shouldn't believe his son. Pushing his chair back violently, he stood and walked around the desk to approach Rian.

Knowing better than to avoid his father, Rian stood firm and waited for what was to come. Having thought long and hard about whether or not to confide in him, he had worked through every detail about how he should say it every night since and all the way home on the school train. 'Just spit it out' was his decided approach and now, standing with his knees like jelly and his father bellowing at him, he wasn't so sure he'd reached the right conclusion. His father was angry but for all the wrong reasons.

Arriving at the feet of his son, William raised his arm and swung to slap him hard across his soft, flushed face. Rian's body swivelled from his hips with the force of his father's hand but he didn't fall over.

"How dare you?" William spat. "Of all people. You don't honestly expect me to believe that he, a fine, intelligent, educated man is about to squander his reputation, his faith for God's sake, on a little squirt like you, now do you?"

Rian's face hurt, but not as much as his feelings. He didn't expect his dad to believe him immediately but he at least expected to be given a chance to explain, to present his case. Raising his hand to touch the cheek, gently feeling the stinging welts that were blooming beneath his fingers, he managed to stifle the small cry that would only irritate his father more.

But I've done nothing, he said to himself and to his father he insisted, "I am telling the truth. He did ... he ..."

"He nothing." His father spoke firmly, lifting his hand to take a second swipe, but changing his mind mid-swing. "Why, I ask you, why would you do such a thing?" Then, without waiting for an answer, he roared at his quivering

son, standing so valiantly in the face of his father's and his own shame: "Get out! I am utterly disgusted with you. Go to your room and don't come down till I tell you to!"

Rian stood for a long minute staring at his father who stood now in front of the fire, hands buried deep in his pockets. He couldn't believe that that was it. No questions, no inquiry.

"Go on," his father instructed. "Get out and send your brother in."

Turning on his heel he walked slowly to the door without the energy to stop or even wipe the tears and the snot that ran in little rivers down his face. Bewildered, tired, hurt, defeated and weak: that was how he felt. Now he knew how Sullivan had managed to get away with it all these years, how his reputation had managed to become almost mythical amongst his peers. It was incredible to believe; too incredible it seemed for his father and probably many fathers before him. He pulled open the door, leaving the warmth of the study to exit into the chill of the dark and wide-open hall where Seb waited for his turn.

Rian stepped aside and watched his brother pass. Their eyes met briefly but all he saw was contempt.

"Please!" he whispered desperately to his brother as he walked through the door.

Seb paused for a split second but, without acknowledging his brother, entered their father's lair without even a fleeting glance back.

Rian didn't have the will to move, praying that his brother would do the right thing, but knowing miserably that he wouldn't. He listened with his ear to the door and waited for his father to speak.

"What do you know of this?" he heard William ask Seb.

"Nothing," Seb replied confidently. "I didn't see anything."

Rian listened no longer. He didn't care to.

Seb could have helped. He should have told the truth. Sure he didn't see what happened, but he knew. Just like the rest of the school knew.

Sitting at the end of the stairs he waited for Seb to come out.

"Why did you do that?" he screamed in a whisper. "Why couldn't you just tell him the truth? Tell him what really happened? Why couldn't you say it? Why didn't you say?" The slow-running river turned into an ocean of salty tears that sizzled as they passed over the heat of his throbbing cheek.

"You're a bloody looper, do you know that?" Seb spat, bunching his fist and driving it into this little brother's soft stomach. "You can't just keep your mouth shut, can you? And now look where you are and you want to bring me down with you. You are a weakling and a pain in the ass and, do you know what, no one really likes you very much, you know? You think you can go round fixing people and making people like you. Well, you can't. This is what happens when you try too hard. Stop trying, Rian." He stepped around him to make his way upstairs.

"I hate you, Seb. Really. Really hate you," Rian whimpered helplessly.

Seb didn't hear and even if he had he wouldn't have cared.

It was a day that Rian would never forget and one that forged the foundations of his future. Dogged by low self-

esteem and the even lower expectations of others, Rian threw himself into showing them how wrong they were. He wasn't stupid or weak and, while he couldn't avoid Father Sullivan and his vile persuasions, he didn't stop trying. During the course of his remaining five years at Ashton College he had to suffer Sully's repeat performance only five more times, one for each of his seemingly penitential years. Each time was easier to endure than the last. He learned to think about where he was going and what he was sure he would become. He would come back and show them all that he was someone to respect, not someone to abuse. He promised himself that he would find a way to show them and, when he did, they would all be sorry. When he qualified from college, he would be better than Seb, with better grades, better friends and a better life. He would be a different kind of success to his big brother. He would actually give a shit.

The morning after he graduated and left Ashton College he woke up to the new day feeling different: lighter, brighter, taller, wiser. Now he could breathe properly for the first time. He opened up his lungs and stretched long and tall to let the air rush and sweep away the thoughts of his past morning horrors. The tension was gone; he didn't have to think three steps ahead of himself anymore. He was no longer a pawn in someone else's twisted game. His only regret was that a substitute would be sought to take up the position that he and a few others from his year had left vacant. But that was not his battle, for the moment.

Most nights now he turned in his bed to face his newly crowned fiancée and couldn't help but feel like the luckiest man alive. For the first time ever, genuinely, he had happiness in his heart. Ten years his senior, she wasn't the prettiest, or the smartest or the fittest, but inside Martha was by far the most beautiful woman he had ever met. He could never resist the need to place a gentle, delicate kiss on her nose. Now he could leave the cold chill of his childhood behind as he had such a warm, loving future to look forward to.

She was good to him. Attentive, sensitive, she understood him and the things that were important. And while she didn't need to get on with his family, she made an effort, particularly with the girls. And despite what she knew of Seb, she tried with him too.

"He's not a bad person really," Martha explained. "He just knows no better."

She made sense. She was real. He liked that. It made him feel secure.

Chapter 14

In his father's study, still gripping the mantelpiece firmly, Seb's head was a blazing inferno, all notions of reason and calm abandoned. The game had changed and he was being hung out to dry.

Sitting down, taking his head in his hands, he immediately switched to crisis mode and, as he did with any challenge he faced in his day-to-day professional capacity, he sought to logically scrutinise the situation, understand the problem, assimilate an appropriate response and from there formulate a plan of action.

"Grow up, Sebastian! Are you telling me you've never told the tiniest of white lies to get the upper hand? Are you telling me you're squeaky clean?"

"Actually, yes, I am!" he shot back with force. "In my business I am squeaky clean, I'm as clean as whistle, as straight as a die. We're all of those things, we have to be. We don't mess around, we can't mess around. Our reputation depends on it." As he spoke his mind was processing the implications of the situation. "We deal in millions, Dad, tens, hundreds of millions, and one small cock-up, one small dodgy deal, one small *white lie* could ruin everything. *This* could ruin everything. Do you understand? Do you *really* understand what you've done?" He could feel his pulse amplify and his temper rise. "Anyway," he concluded frantically, "they won't believe you. Why would I do it? Why would I conjure up fake signatures for a deal that I don't benefit from? I waived my fee for you, remember? I get nothing out of this."

"Well, that's not technically true," his father replied.

The words rang dangerously loud in Seb's ears. He watched his father move to the opposite corner of the room and from the safe remove a brown manila folder.

Handing it to Seb calmly, he told him, "You see, this ties you to the deal."

Seb opened it and stared at its contents, feeling his eyes blur and his head buzz. How did he think it couldn't get any worse? *Tanglewood*. The name jumped from the page.

"How did you get these?" he asked quietly, holding the deeds tight in his hand. "Where are the originals?" he asked, his tone more urgent.

"I can be very persuasive when I need to be," William replied, remembering how all it took was a smile and a convincing story to get Lucy, his secretary, to retrieve and hand the file over. He was Seb's father after all. She could trust him.

When his father had told him months back that the bank had agreed in principle to lend him his portion of the money, Seb was more than a little surprised and wondered at the time how on earth his father had convinced them to finance his share of the project. Now he knew: he had used Tanglewood as collateral. His own signature, *Sebastian Bertram*, danced beautifully on the page in front of him. The implications beyond the legal were profound. Seb felt his temperature rise. He hadn't felt this much contempt for his father in years.

"How dare you?" he whispered and, raising his voice, repeated the words with fervour. "*How bloody dare you!*"

"*Don't speak to me like that!*" William responded with equal intensity.

"You son of a bitch!" Sebastian stood to face his father. "This was your deal. You asked me to do this. You were the one who came to me." His voice was quiet but strong, realising with incredulity that this was always part of his father's plan. "And all the while you used me," he continued, taking a step towards him. "You and your bastard friends used me. And if that's not bad enough, like you haven't done enough damage already, you have taken advantage of your grieving daughter. What kind of a mean-minded, sadistic prick does that?"

William stood fast, firm and silent, pulling back his broad shoulders and lifting his chin in defiance.

Seb took another step forward. "Tell me," he said quietly, only to release a second short, sharp roar seconds later that made the big man in front of him jump. "*Tell me!*"

Was he imagining it or did he see a flicker of consternation in those cold, old grey eyes?

The pressure and stress that had been gathering pace all week and had risen even further this morning was finding its release. Anger at his wife and fury at his brother combined with rage at the nefarious intent of his father to form a cataclysmic explosion of livid emotion, all directed at William. His towering, traitorous father.

And with the floodgates opened and the adrenaline pumping, even if he wanted to there was no way for him to stop the words from coming out. Along with his voice Seb's index finger lifted and pointed, driving home his words. Without realising it, he was shouting and for the first time ever standing up to his father.

"You gathered your players. You organised their money. You wrote the damn investment brief for Christ's sake and then you played me for an idiot, that's what you did. And what, Father dear," he raved, his voice laced with derision, "are you going to tell Enya? Now that she's back and plans on selling the house, you'll need to tell her something. Without the deeds of the house she can't sell it, can she? How are you going to tell her she can't? How are you going to explain that?" He was bellowing, taking single steps, like punctuation marks, closer to William. "You can't, can you? There's no real way for you to explain how or why you forged my signature and stole from your daughter for your own greedy satisfaction, now is there? Nothing you can say now could possibly make what you have done right."

Spent, he took a breath and turned away, counting in his head, trying his best to regain his composure.

"So," he resumed carefully once he'd recovered a level of control, "this is how this is going to pan out. If they ask, you're going to own up to what you have done and make it crystal clear that I had nothing to do with it. Right?" He waited for his father to respond but when he didn't he turned back to face him and prepared to repeat his words. "I said –"

"I heard what you said," William replied firmly, the calm crust of his exterior firmly intact. "But I will not."

"Why the hell not?" Seb growled. "If you don't tell them, I will."

"Don't be an idiot," William snapped. "It'll be your word against ours."

"Ours?"

"Yes, ours," William retorted.

"What? You and your political playmates? Dad, you don't scare me!"

"Look at the facts, boy! You witnessed signatures that were already there. You should have checked. That's your job. But that has always been your trouble. You never attend to the detail. Even as a child you were sloppy." William chose his words well, each designed to unnerve and distract sufficiently to manipulate the blame from himself to his son who, he was right, should have checked.

"Don't call me 'boy'!" Seb spat, furious because he knew his father had him on one single point. The fact that he trusted his own flesh and blood would be neither a sufficient nor reliable defence. If anything it worked against him and he knew it. "They'll take away our licence, you do know that, don't you?"

"Oh, don't be so bloody melodramatic. We'll make sure it won't come to that. I'll see to it personally."

"They'll rescind their loan offer, they won't give you a penny."

"Poppycock. You've as good as said yourself it might not even come to that."

"You think you've got it all worked out, don't you?" Seb laughed. "You've actually thought this through, haven't you?"

"Look," William told him, changing his tone to one of reasonable assurance, "there's no reason for them to call in the guarantees, so they're unlikely to do anything too severe. The project is going well – yes, it's a risky one, but we've already got an enquiry book full of interested tenants. It'll earn a reasonable profit, it really will. So this is nothing more than a technicality, a blip. We'll say it was an oversight. No harm done." He spoke like it was already all wrapped up neatly. "You've seen what the regulator has done to the banks for much worse. Nothing, that's what." He laughed. "You've nothing to worry about. You'll be reprimanded, a proverbial slap on the wrist, nothing more."

Utterly flabbergasted, Seb almost choked on the breath catching in the back of his throat which felt like it was closing fast. He wasn't sure what to be most amazed at: his father's total lack of shame or his willingness to throw both himself and Enya under the bus.

"Do you seriously think that I'll let you do this?" he said. "Aren't you at least expecting me to defend myself? Or do you think I'll just roll over and let you, of all people, destroy everything I've built? What do you take me for? How weak do you think I am? And what about Dermot? He'll never let this one fly. Not a hope in hell." Unable to control the crack in his voice he found himself shaking. "Am I that useless?" he blared. "And Enya? What about her? Does she not matter? Are we both that worthless to you?"

William in response simply shrugged carelessly and in that single, simple action, without uttering one word, he managed to ignite every trigger in his eldest son's body. Seb's fists closed, his knuckles white and his neatly trimmed nails cutting into his palms. He was primed and ready to launch at his father.

He rarely lost his cool completely but when he did it tended to be cataclysmic, as Kathryn would vouch. The shameful memory of his hand hitting hard against her skin told him he should calm down.

Needing to put space between him and his father he turned and walked back to the fire, sat into one of the armchairs and rested his head in his hands. The temperature off the smouldering coals felt hot on his already burning skin which was fuelled by the adrenaline that pumped harder and faster than if he'd run a marathon. He could feel the pulse throb in his neck.

"Tell me," he said once his fury subsided to a manageable level, "did you imagine your reputation would carry you above the law? Was that it? Was that what you were depending on?" He looked up to see if his father showed any signs of offering any insights but William remained silent, with eyes full of irritation at his naive son. "And, to be honest, it doesn't matter whether or not the regulator does anything or not. Our clients will know. Our business relies on trust. *Trust.* Do you even know what that means?"

But William remained mute. Uncaring. Fed up of his son's performance.

"It won't matter a damn if they take our licence or not. Our reputation will be shot!" Seb threw his arms open. "Everything I've worked for all these years gone because you are nothing but a corrupt, self-serving bastard! I trusted you. Like an absolute idiot, I assumed you were an honest man. How wrong I was! You're all the same, you politicians. Shame on you all."

He got up, and walked to the door. He had more than he could stomach and needed to figure out what had to be done to manage the threat.

"You should have checked," William twittered to his back, rubbing it in, his trump card that would protect him above all else.

In his mind's eye Seb could see him shake his head like he used to when they were kids. It galled him then just as it galled him now. Turning, he paced back into the room.

"I should have checked? And what good would that have done? It was in your plan that I wouldn't. You planned to abuse my trust of you. If I'd checked you'd have found some other way to cheat. Wouldn't you? '*You should have checked*'!" he mimicked with a theatrical shake of his head.

William smirked at his son, assuming the higher ground by remaining silent.

"Is that it?" Seb roared. "Are you *seriously* laughing at me?" His face contorted reflecting the ferocity of his anger.

Instinctively William took a step backward.

"You connive to ruin my reputation and then you have the audacity to mock me." The relief he felt through his verbal tirade was immense. "And you're a disgrace to your office, to your profession –" he inched closer to his father, his index finger raised, to finish finally with "to this family."

"Control yourself, Sebastian," William shouted, "and for God's sake put down that finger!"

"You've got to be joking? Control myself? For as long as I can remember you've controlled me, us, all of us. Well, not anymore. Today is the beginning of the end for you and me. You are dead to me." His pointed finger pushed hard against the embroidered crest on his father's jumper.

Backed up against the desk William had nowhere to go. His face furrowed at the brow, his mouth opened and the colour began to drain from his cheeks. Taking pleasure from the visible signs, finally, of fear, Seb pushed his finger in harder.

"Yes, I should have checked and no, I should not have trusted you. But I will not let you ruin me. I will fight back with every ounce of my being and promise you here and now you will not beat me. Not now, not ever again." His words felt good, liberating. "What have you got to say to that?"

William's hand covered his chest in what Seb initially assumed was a defensive gesture, but it was impossible not to notice the cool grey pallor that was washing over his face. Retreating, Seb almost felt sorry for his father who appeared to shrink in front of his very eyes and, shaking his head, he accepted he was done and turned to leave.

"*Seb . . .*" he heard his father whisper.

Shame? Remorse? What was the tone he registered in that voice? But it was too late. The damage was done and, turning with the intention of telling his father so, he was surprised to see fear in his father's face. It felt beautiful. William's shoulders had slumped with one hand clutching the edge of the desk and the other now gripping his chest.

"Seb, my pills," he murmured, almost inaudible but just loud enough to hear, his knuckles white for the effort it took to keep himself upright.

Seb took a moment to take stock.

"Where are they?" he asked.

"My jacket." William pointed to the other side of the desk. "On the chair."

Slowly Seb moved back into the room then stopped, his father looking up at him, his eyes pleading. Oh, how the tables had turned!

"Hurry," William rasped, his body faltering before he fell to his knees.

Considering him for a moment, not so fearsome now, Seb debated silently without taking his eyes off his father's shrinking presence. Then, he walked calmly out of the room, careful not to slam the door as he left, and into the hall where he stood to catch his galloping breath.

"Mother!" he called half-heartedly into the darkness. "Father needs you!" Then, without waiting to see if she answered he walked out of the house, down the beautiful granite steps, got into his car and left.

Chapter 15

Barbara was unusually sober, just about, for that time of day. Only because an extra tiny blue pill had made her afternoon nap that little bit longer. The sound of raised voices earlier had aroused both her body and her curiosity. Was it real or had she dreamed it? The sound of the front door banging encouraged the wide opening of her heavy eyes. Perhaps Will had gone out, leaving the downstairs free for her to roam. These days she tended to spend her time alone in her room in a drunken haze, bored by her own company but equally disinterested in the company of others.

She stepped out onto the landing in her nightgown and listened. The sound of silence was delicious. In her bare feet with glass in hand she wandered down the stairs. A loud crash from the study made her jump.

"William?" she called into the silence.

Slowly she made her way across the hall to the closed study door. Cautiously, like it might burn, she placed her hand on the brass doorknob, turned it and pushed open the door. The apparent emptiness of the room both greeted and unnerved her. It looked but didn't feel empty. She took a step further into the room and called out again.

"William?"

A harsh rasping sound, like a cat's defensive hiss came from the other side of the room. Quietly she put her glass down on the table by the door and picked up a heavy plaster statuette. It was heavy to hold but she hardly noticed, focusing on the possibility of an animal lurking somewhere in the room. Raising the weapon as she walked, trying her best not to bump into the various pieces of furniture that cluttered her way, she ventured across the room.

She saw his feet first, protruding out into her line of sight. Putting down the statuette, she rushed to him. He lay on the floor, his eyes furrowed and closed, his hand clutched desperately to his chest. Beside him was the source of the crash – a smashed table lamp – she wasn't sure if he'd knocked it over when he fell or pulled it down on top of himself as he tried to get back up. She didn't even know if he was alive or dead. She couldn't see his chest move and when she bent over him not a breath, or so she thought, passed his lips. Helpless, she stood up. She didn't know how to resuscitate and even if she did know how she didn't have the wits to do it. With no idea what else to do she picked up the phone from the desk and dialled 911.

She knelt by his side. The minutes that passed felt like hours.

"Come on . . . come on . . ." she pleaded.

William didn't open his eyes. He lay limp and lifeless on the floor but his hands remained warm.

In reality they were there within minutes and the room flashed blue to the rhythm of the ambulance lights.

Barbara let go of his hand and opened the door.

Gladly she stood back to let the experts take over. He was alive, they assured her, but in a grave condition. They stretchered him out of the house with an oxygen mask covering his face and nose. His eyes, relaxed now, remained closed. There was nothing like near-death to sober you up, she thought, and considered her chances of sneaking in a quick shot before she piled into the back of the ambulance with him. No sooner had the thought crossed her mind than she was ushered up the steps of the ambulance, still in her nightgown and a coat she had thrown over it. The doors were slammed shut and seconds later the wheels spun on the gravel outside, spitting up pebbles and grit behind them like fuel-filled boy racers. She sat beside him, rocking and swaying with the fast motion of the ambulance. One of the paramedics attended him all the way, his face serious, fully focused on the task at hand. Seán was his name. He spoke gently to her throughout the short journey, but she had no idea what they talked about. She couldn't take her eyes off her husband. He looked so pale, so vulnerable, lying there defenceless and sleeping, his face covered by a mask with his mouth almost open. Her hand swept a loose hair from his forehead and strayed to explore the lines and creases that catalogued his life. He was a bastard, she mused, wiping a speck of dust from his cheek. She hated him. Really hated him. But in calling the ambulance she had saved his life. How ironic. She had wished him dead more times in the recent years of their fifty-five together than she should really admit, and now when the time came to actually see her deep-rooted fantasy come to fruition she forgot herself and let it pass. Why? How?

It wasn't always like that: she wasn't always this bitter,

like an old lemon. She had loved him. Once. And it lasted for many years. Really loved him. And, she assumed, somewhere in the residues of that love lived the apparently impulsive need to keep him alive.

From the moment she'd first met him he had captivated her. She had just turned eighteen when they were first introduced: she, the pretty debutante, he the slightly older son of a wealthy solicitor and successful politician. As close to a celebrity as she was ever likely to meet. He was, everyone agreed, a highly eligible bachelor and would be a wonderful catch. Educated, smart, entertaining, witty and with prospects to boot, all he needed was the looks and he'd have been perfect. Perfect husband material. He wasn't particularly good-looking, in fact he was decidedly ordinary, but there was something extraordinarily charismatic about him. He had presence and the most alluring male pheromones, enough to make any young girl lose herself in his company. And what he lacked in looks he made up for in confidence. She and the rest of the young ladies discreetly competed for his attention. But in the end, he picked her – why, she could never really understand. In so many ways they were opposites: he was gregarious and outgoing, the life and soul of the party while she was happy to sit alone in his company. He was the acidic joker and entertainer and the audience, both male and female, that invariably gathered were without fail seduced by his charm. And while he stole the show, she would observe and bask quietly in awe of him. He was tall while she was the perfect petite package: there was nothing she liked more than to be wrapped in his arms, to be held deep into his chest, his musky aroma intoxicating and his heartbeat mesmerising. She felt so safe, so lucky that he chose her. They were the perfect couple that in the early days were the must-have guests at every party. He was always so dashing with his lean physique apparent in the sharp slim-fitted tailored suits often topped with inimitably matching Stetsons. She wore only the finest dresses, perfectly pinched to show off her delicate waist and sculptured torso, and quickly became the most envied woman in the town. But in private circles, beyond theirs, they were branded Beauty and the Beast.

In the early years Barbara never doubted his love for her. He appeared impervious to the many female advances and was always attentive and caring. It was only after Sebastian was born that things went awry.

The news that she was pregnant was met with great joy and celebration. And when the first-born boy, his successor, came into the world, she and William thanked the Lord for their beautiful gift. He lavished her with chocolates, flowers and a stunning diamond-encrusted eternity ring. The menfolk celebrated for days while the womenfolk fussed. There was champagne and cigars and many late nights of chest-beating celebrations. But it had been a difficult labour and Barbara lost a life-threatening amount of blood. She suffered hard with depression and found it almost impossible to bond with her whimpering little bundle and even harder to admit her failing. To try and help her, William immediately arranged for a nanny to come and help and she was a godsend. Barbara was weak and William understood, encouraging her to take her time to recover, which she did. And when that recovery, almost a year later, was deemed to be complete and she could no longer use her depression as an excuse for ignoring her little boy, she begrudgingly re-established her position as lady of the house.

And as William's career flourished and he quickly rose up the ranks of power, Barbara drank cocktails, smoked though her long tortoiseshell filter and played bridge from one end of the week to the other. She was too self-obsessed to notice that William was fast becoming less and less attentive and came to her bed less often. They had always had separate bedrooms. William wanted it that way – he liked the idea of having his own private space and she didn't mind it either. He was often out late with his politics and she hated to be disturbed. With the children it made it easier and, as she too discovered, she liked her own space just as much as he did. Rian arrived not much more than a year after Sebastian and Cormac three and a half years after that. She lost a baby, a little girl, Emily, when Cormac had just turned two years old. The fact that she had become pregnant at all was nothing short of a miracle. The enjoyable intimacy of their sex life had all but disappeared and his rare visits to her bed were out of carnal necessity rather than true longing. But she never turned him away even when he so obviously abused his privilege. On occasion he would come to her and, without removing his clothes or engaging in any sort of foreplay, enter her roughly, take her hard and quick then pull out, wipe himself on her nightclothes and leave without uttering a single word. It was on those evenings when she lay still and shaking on the bed that she wished herself somewhere, anywhere else. She didn't have to bother pretending to enjoy it because he didn't care, being not in the least bit concerned about her pleasure.

After Seb, the joy of being pregnant never really came to

life again in Barbara. She spent the nine months in a constant state of regret and sadness. On the day Emily Bertram was born, the same day she died, a little bit more of Barbara died with her. The once attentive husband had become bored and disinterested while she responded with relief to his waning attentions. But what never crossed her mind was that an insatiable libido didn't just disappear. She never stopped to think about where and how he was now being satisfied.

Enya was a different story. Enya was her choice. She was never sure why her body wanted a last baby so badly: her biological clock, perhaps. Or maybe it was a much-needed distraction, a balancing of rights, after the arrival of Ciara. Perhaps.

In the ambulance, William opened his eyes briefly, like he was checking to see if he was alive, or dead and en route to heaven or hell. He didn't open them again until he was admitted and safe in the private hospital bed with the nurses and doctors flurrying around him, dashing and shouting all sorts of complex statements and instructions. And Barbara watched from the corner as they worked. Eventually, with William stable, noticing her they enquired as to her wellbeing. She looked frail and slightly confused: distantly traumatised. But all she wanted was for them to leave her be.

"Can I call anyone for you?" a young nurse asked while handing her a cup of tea. "One of your children perhaps?"

"I don't know any of their numbers."

"Don't you have your mobile with you?"

"No," she replied with a small shake of her head. "I don't have one."

Nurse Cathy, as she introduced herself, threw her a sympathetic but slightly patronising smile then sat down in the leatherette chair beside her with a squeak and gave her knee an uninvited squeeze.

"Will he live?" Barbara asked vacantly.

"Yes," Cathy replied earnestly with a reassuring pat on Barbara's hand, misinterpreting her quiet tone as one of concern rather than doubt. "Yes, he'll be just fine. He mightn't be on his feet for a bit though. How about their names?"

"Eh?" Barbara responded, feeling slightly bothered by this nurse's insistence on talking to her.

"Your children," she prompted. "Their names. We can always try the old-fashioned way through directory enquiries."

"Right." Barbara thought for a minute before remembering the obvious. "My daughter-in-law Kathryn Bertram, she works here. You could contact her husband through her – my son Sebastian – he's the eldest."

"Perfect. Well, let's see what we can do." And with a smile and another small comforting pat on Barbara's hand, she got up and left.

Barbara sat, lost in thought, wondering, amongst other irrelevant things, about the bang of the front door and who it might have been who had left the house.

She got up and stood over William, inspecting his grey features and wondering if he was in fact a little greyer than before. His eyes flickered open. She caught them with her own and, although she wanted to, she didn't look away. He tried but couldn't hold her stare, trying to keep her in focus with each slow blink of his lids. He was obviously heavily sedated and she was surprised he could actually see her at all.

"You got help then," he slurred almost inaudibly, his voice tacky.

"I couldn't help myself," was the best she could respond with. But it was the truth.

His eyebrows attempted a weak lift.

"Are you surprised?" she asked but he didn't reply. Either he fell back into his drug-induced stupor or he just didn't want to admit aloud what he had been thinking as he lay motionless on the floor.

So he did realise what he had been doing to her all these years. She smiled to herself sadly. He was afraid – not of dying, but of her. The power had shifted and he knew it.

Chapter 16

Almost every day Seb drove past the bar and every time wondered what it was like inside. It was exactly as he imagined, except perhaps for the smell – like cinnamon and dark chocolate, not what he was expecting. Dark and dingy with Thin Lizzy streaming from an old-style juke box in the corner, it was just what he needed. No one would recognise him here. This wasn't his kind of place and these weren't his kind of people.

He took a seat at the corner of the well-worn bar where many an elbow had rested as punters drank to their woes, just as he intended to do now.

"What can I get you?" asked the barmaid, wiping the counter in front of him with a sodden cloth.

"Double Jack Daniels on ice."

"That kind of day, huh?"

"Yep."

"Well, this isn't goin' to make it much better, trust me," she advised, nodding towards his fellow drinkers with a knowing glance, pouring him his drink.

Seb smiled up at her. "That's not going to do business much good, turning the customers off their booze, now is it?"

"I know, don't tell the boss." She smiled at him, a cheeky grin with eyes to match. "You just don't seem the sort, and I haven't seen you in here before."

"What's your name?" He asked her.

"Nico."

"Very exotic."

"Not really, just suits me better, that's all."

"Short for Nicola, I assume?"

"Don't tell me – genius, right?" she asked with a smartass tilt of her head.

He raised his glass to her with an apologetic nod. "What's wrong with Nick or Nicky then?"

"Do I look like a Nick or a Nicky to you?" she asked, standing with one hand on her stuck-out hip.

He didn't dare answer.

"Thought so," she huffed, continuing about her business.

But she wasn't serious and he knew it. He liked her. She was sassy as hell and curvaceous to boot with a look in her eyes that said more about what she would do than wouldn't. He watched her move behind the bar and thought about Cormac, about Kathryn and Cormac. And then Cormac again. The bastard. What would he do if he were here now, watching that fine backside strut behind the bar? Would he fancy her? Seb didn't even know if she was his type – but then he reckoned Cormac probably didn't have any particular type: they all went down the same way. The family all knew what he was like, even if they never discussed it openly. But Kathryn, of all people. He took a swig of his drink, wincing as it seared the back of his throat.

"Same again!" he called and watched as she poured his seconds.

"So what do you do when you're not here?" he asked, surprising himself.

Nico smiled. "Not a lot really. I study when I can."

"Ah, educating yourself. Interesting."

"I don't plan on being here for the rest of my life. I've got plans."

"Care to share?" Seb invited, sipping his Bourbon, enjoying what he thought was frivolous banter.

Was this what Cormac did? Was this his kind of opening line? Seb felt dangerously alive, putting himself in Cormac's shoes. Call it research, he told himself. Anyway, did it really matter? His marriage was over, so why the hell not?

"Not really. I tend not to share with strange men who walk into my bar."

"More's the pity." He shrugged. "We could have had a little fun."

Nico laughed out loud at both him and his appalling chat-up line.

"You're obviously new to this." She pointed at his ring finger, eliciting an immediate blush.

Mortified, he instinctively yanked his hand away from his glass.

"Oh, don't worry," she placated him. "I get all sorts in here – first timers, old timers, even the odd virgin, believe it or not. I'm no prude and I don't judge."

Seb's eyes dropped.

"If it's fun you want, have a chat with Sadie over there – she'll look after you."

Seb threw a surreptitious glance over at Sadie. She didn't look so bad. But was that what he was after, coming here, because he couldn't go home?

A bearded man joined Nico behind the bar.

"All quiet?" he asked.

"All quiet," she replied, taking off her once-white apron and disappearing out the back.

Feeling safe, with anonymity once again, he took a closer look at Sadie. She could have been anywhere between twenty-five and forty-five, her hair bleached beyond recognition of its original colour. She had a pretty but tired face that looked down onto the screen of her phone. As she was half obscured by the table, he had no idea what she was like from waist down but on top she was well endowed, very well endowed indeed.

Nico reappeared, this time on the right side of the bar, a bag slung over her shoulder with a hoodie in her hand. She went over and flopped down in the snug next to Sadie. Seb immediately dropped his eyes to the remains of his drink, not daring to lift them, but only minutes later Nico was by his side.

"Now she *is* a bit of a Nicky, so be careful." And with a wink and a smirk she was gone.

"Will I top you up?" the bearded barman asked, hating to watch a man hug an empty glass.

"Please do. And one for my friend." He nodded towards Sadie who was making her way over from the other side of the bar.

For a while he was Cormac, promiscuous, wild and dirty, and Sadie became Kathryn. *Slut. Whore. Bitch.* He slammed into her hard, her head thumping off the inside of the passenger door, but he didn't care. She didn't seem to care either. Every thrust was a knife plunged deep into Kathryn's heart. Punishment. His eyes clenched tight, the image of her smiling at him with Cormac stooped over, buried in her. *Bitch*, he slammed. *Bitch*.

And then he was done.

They drove back into the city; the hills it had seemed was the place to go. She had offered that they should go to hers, but he didn't have the stomach for it. One step at a time.

"Jeez, man, you need some help," Sadie complained, fixing herself while massaging her aching head. "I've had all sorts in my time, but that's hard, man."

"I'm paying you, aren't I?"

"You fuckin' bet you are."

He pulled up outside the bar, two hundred euro lighter, to let her out.

Sadie went to slam the door only to bend into the car again. "Whoever the fuck she is, I hope you got her outta your system. No bird's worth that much pain. Trust me, I know, I'm one o' them. But hey," she scoffed, waving her fifty-euro notes, "don't be a stranger!"

He stopped at the garage to make sure the back of the car was clean before finally making his way home. His anger was gone, replaced by profound resignation.

He put his key in the door and wondered if she would know. Would she be able to tell? Would she be able to smell Sadie on him?

Four Louis Vuitton bags lined the wall of their ample hall, stuffed it seemed to the brim. She was in the kitchen, waiting, sitting at the table, a bottle of Bordeaux open and half gone. She looked up at him as he entered, her eyes wide open and filled with defiance. Taking a glass from the drainer, he pulled out a chair and sat opposite her. He filled the glass.

Neither spoke. Neither wanted or needed to.

She was still beautiful, Kathryn, his wife. In the silence of the kitchen, observing and contemplating each other from their opposite sides, he couldn't help but notice she still had the spark that had first lit up his heart. Seb found himself filled with regret. Not because of what he had just done but more for what he hadn't done for the hundreds of days and nights before. He would miss her, his wife Kathryn, but they both knew she was long gone.

Chapter 17

William remained still and silent for the hours that followed. The first few were fine. Wide awake, Barbara used them to reflect on their lives, her feelings and her future. But then she got bored. She really could do with a drink.

Nurse Cathy had eventually returned to report that she had located Kathryn and Sebastian's numbers but had so far failed to get in contact with them. She had left messages on their phones, including their landline. Armed with the names of the other Bertram children, she left promising to attempt to contact them through directory enquiries.

Then, in the early morning hours, like a tornado Ciara rushed through the door.

"Oh my God! Dad!" she gushed when she saw him lying so still, so grey.

Barbara prickled at the sight of her.

"I came as soon as I could." She threw her coat and bag on the empty chair in the corner, firing questions at her dazed mother. "Why didn't you call me? What happened?" She took her father's hand in hers.

"He's had a heart attack," Barbara answered, clearing

the dryness of her throat with a cough, doing her best to sound neither patronising nor sarcastic, wondering who'd told Ciara.

"Oh God! Will he be alright?"

"They seem to think so." Barbara looked around, wishing herself to be anywhere but here. She had spent her time, years of her time, avoiding situations like this. "Are you going to stay long?" She pulled herself up from the chair. "I should really go home to change and get your father some things."

"Sure, I'll stay," Ciara told her, only then noticing Barbara's nightdress underneath her coat.

Relieved, Barbara said, "I'll get back as soon as I can. I'll give your brothers and sister a call from the house."

But Ciara wasn't listening. She had taken hold of William's hand and was fixing his grey fringe over his eyes.

Barbara glanced briefly back into the room as she left and caught the look of absolute devotion. The poor girl. She worked so hard and was rewarded with so little. But, despite it, she never stopped trying.

It was dark and cold inside the house. She had no idea what time she had called the ambulance and had even less of an idea as to what time it was when she got home. She looked at her watch: it was almost five in the morning. She kicked off her shoes and made her way to the lounge where she headed straight for the drinks tray and poured herself a very generous whiskey. She deserved it, after the day or night she'd had. Just the one, then she'd get herself together, gather his things and make her way back to the hospital. She welcomed the soft comfort of the couch and savoured the burning assault at the back of her throat as the neat spirit made its way down. She didn't even bother with the ice. She needed to feel its anaesthetic power, needed it to turn down that bloody voice that had spent the night questioning her every single feeling and every tiny action. She, it seemed, had put herself on trial and had become her very own judge and jury, her conscience. But the voice she heard wasn't her own – it sounded just like her long since dead mother – a tormenting commentary from the grave, criticising and harsh.

The first whiskey didn't help. Maybe a second would kick its ass, she hoped as she poured a double measure of the amber liquid into her glass. Four rounds later and her eyes were heavy and the inner voice, although not entirely quiet, was reduced to a simpering whisper. Enough to let her sleep.

She was woken what felt like minutes later to urgent shakes and persistent whimpers that in her dream were the wailing cries of a dying cat at her window and no matter how may curtains she pulled in front of it, curtain after curtain, it just wouldn't go away.

"*Mother! Mother! For God's sake, wake up, Mother!*" the voice eventually broke through.

She opened her eyes to see what or who was causing her such violent disruption. The looming and undeniable shape of Ciara stood over her with her face all tied up in an ugly grimace, looking like her father.

"Mother, what are you doing?" she shouted, her tone laced with acid fury, which for Ciara, usually the quiet, subdued one was significantly bizarre.

"Ciara?" Barbara asked through her groggy 'almost

but not quite aware' stupor. "I fell asleep." She tried to pull herself up – steady as a newborn fawn, her mouth as dry as a sawmill.

"Came home and got plastered more like."

"Well, if you knew the answer why did you bother asking?"

"You were supposed to bring Dad's things to the hospital!"

She didn't bother to reply – instead she got up and left the room.

"What the hell are you playing at?" Ciara called, following her to the kitchen.

"Good Lord, girl, will you stop mithering," Barbara pleaded, holding on to her head as if keeping it all together in case it should explode.

"Dad is lying in hospital, he could be dead by now for all you know and you're home here getting drunk."

"Did you not hear me?"

Barbara called, exasperated and headsore. "I asked you to shut up. *So. Please. Will you shut up?*"

"Don't tell me to shut up!" Ciara stood back, aghast at her mother's outburst.

Barbara had surprised herself, never mind Ciara. She had never spoken to her, or any of her children like that before. Maybe it was shock. Maybe it was exhaustion, but something had switched inside telling her enough was enough.

"Too late," she cracked. "I already did and if you don't like it you know where to go. You waltz into this house – my house – and order me around like you own the place."

"He's not dead yet, you know. You do realise that, don't you?"

"I beg your pardon?" Barbara demanded, surprised by the comment. "Why would I think he was dead?"

"Well, isn't that what you've been waiting for?"

"Don't be so bloody childish!"

"You heard me. We all know you and Dad are in trouble."

"*Really*? In trouble?" she repeated with feigned curiosity, encouraging her to continue.

"Yes. And don't even bother denying it."

Barbara picked up an empty wine bottle from the counter and shook it desperately before throwing it down again. She bent down and picked a fresh one from the wine rack in the central island.

"Really, Mother, it's eight thirty in the morning!"

"Oh, would you ever just go back to the hospital and leave me alone!" she spat. "Go look after your *father.*"

She pulled the cork from the twenty-year-old Bordeaux and raised a glass to Ciara's exit from the room. She listened to her pound up the stairs, apparently transferring her anger to her feet which marched heavily across the floorboards overhead – to William's room, Barbara guessed.

Barbara's relationship with her children was almost non-existent: they didn't figure much in her world and therefore neither did she in theirs. It had always been an enigma, why she never held her children dear like other mothers whose families grew alongside her own. It wasn't that she didn't notice her indifference – she had recognised it as being unusual very early on but was more intrigued than worried about the difference between her and the other mums.

"Give Mummy a kiss," the other children were invited

by their attentive parent. Barbara would watch curiously as the tiny pursed lips covered in saliva, snot and God knows what else were pressed untidily against perfectly glossed lips. *Ewww*, she would internally cringe. The last thing she wanted was mucky handprints on her blouse and demanding whinges from children pulling at her petticoat tails. No, she was content to keep them at a safe distance. There were more pressing issues to attend to, like who'd won the last bridge rubber.

Listening to Ciara's progress upstairs and for her eventual departure from the house, Barbara wondered if any of them had sussed that William didn't like them much either. They were without exception an intelligent brood: they must know – he wasn't that good at concealing it. It was the public's perception of him as a fine upstanding family man worthy of their votes that stopped him from ignoring them altogether. And in return they tested him to the nth degree. All except Ciara who, God bless her, like a little puppy just wanted to be loved. Barbara was almost impressed by Ciara's outburst and imagined her heading into the hospital telling her tale of finding her mother drunk again, and passed out, to her sick father who quite frankly didn't give a damn.

Chapter 18

William lay, eyes closed but awake. He heard her come in and felt her gently touch his hand and fix his fringe. But he didn't open his eyes. She was close: he could feel her breath and smell her slightly citrus perfume. It reminded him of their holidays spent in Spain and the aroma of the tangy cologne that seemed to hang in the air wherever they went. Of all of their children Ciara loved Spain. He hated it: so common.

The door opened again.

"He's sleeping," he heard Ciara say.

Was it Barbara, he wondered. Was she there? His eyes were too heavy to open and see for himself.

"Good," one of the many efficient but slightly nervous nurses charged with his care replied in a whisper. "He needs the rest."

He heard the sound of the chart being pulled from the pocket at the end of the bed and felt her presence at his side, checking his pulse, fluids and monitors.

"There are a lot of photographers outside," the nurse remarked, "and Mr. McDaid, the government press secretary, has arrived. He wanted to come straight though, but he's been told to wait for you in the visitors' lounge.

You might explain to him it's family only at the moment."

"I will. He'll be looking for us to make a statement, I suppose," said Ciara.

William could hear the confidence disappear from her voice.

"My brother, Seb, isn't answering his phone," she said fretfully. "He's the one who should deal with this – Mum's useless at this kind of stuff."

William heard her sigh. Even from his sick bed he wanted to tell her to stop her snivelling and just get on with it. And yes, where *was* Seb?

The door opened again and one of them left – the nurse, he assumed. Listening to Ciara shuffling and moving around the room, he still couldn't bring himself to sneak even a quick look. He didn't want to see her pity. Vulnerable wasn't ever a trait he quoted as his own. He was strong. Masterful. Proud. In control. She idolised him, he knew that, and he couldn't bear to see the pity that was bound to be in her eyes. Him, the commanding would-be leader, lying here helpless and old. The last time she looked at him it was with admiration and awe. Not pity. She was incredible – no matter how many times he put her down, disparaged her with some patronising, condescending or demeaning remark, she always took it, would retreat for a while but invariably came back for more. Sometimes he did feel a slight pang of remorse, but it was for her own good. Now it was he who felt vulnerable and exposed, an ironic twist of fortune. He almost felt angry with her for it and wished she'd just go so he could relax and rest in peace.

He heard the digit beeps of her phone then the soft sound of her breathing, quietly waiting for a reply.

"Seb, it's me again – Ciara. I'm at the hospital now. Dad's very ill but he's stable. They say he's had a heart attack – sorry –" she then laughed, "I already told you that in my other messages. Look, can you give me a shout as soon as you get a chance? Simon McDaid is here and wants us to make a statement. I don't know what to say. Please come ... I think you're better at this than me, than any of us. Anyway, you're the oldest – sorry, I'm babbling. Just give me a shout. Bye."

William didn't need to open his eyes to see how she looked. He could picture her well enough with her cheeks flushed, feeling stupid. Seb got so irritated when she prattled on like that. William was sorry when she ended the call, obviously doing her best not say anything else that would annoy Seb – more's the pity – he deserved it after what he'd done.

William didn't think Seb would be returning the call and wanted badly to tell her not to bother and to try Rian or even Cormac instead. Even Barbara would be better. She, apparently, was not in the room – he wondered where she was and suspected she wouldn't be back in a hurry. *Do I blame her?* Maybe not: he knew she'd had enough, but then she had amazed him already. If he had been a betting man he would never have put a single cent on her saving his life. That said, neither would he have put Seb down as a cold-hearted bastard. Which, in his father's eyes, was exactly what he was.

'How dare he do this to me?' William silently thundered, feeling his pulse race in tandem with his simmering anger and the colour flush into his cheeks.

To which his conscience replied, *'Well, he is your son.'*

'But, really, what son does that to his father?'

'You're as bad as each other. You made him that way,' his conscience advised before asking rhetorically, '*Would you not have done that to your own father?'*

But William answered anyway. *"If it were a means to a goal, then, yes, I would. No one stands in my way."*

He thought of Ronson Street and the deal that they were so convinced couldn't go wrong. But just in case, like every good politician and strategist, they wisely made sure there was a cover: a Plan B. How easy and logical their apparently foolproof, simple scheme sounded. If he were being honest with himself, he'd say that Seb was right to be furious. Yes, they knew what they were doing when they devised their plan. They were well aware of the implications, both legal and moral. And they had consciously set Seb up to take the fall. Yet somewhere, well camouflaged within the conniving and scheming, was a minute, almost indecipherable, faint beacon of regret that it was Seb's trust in his father that would ultimately be his ruin. But they hadn't been completely dismissive of him and as a group had debated furiously about his fate at one of their many late-night planning sessions and eventually, in the early hours, came to the convincing conclusion that realistically it would only really be a 'short' fall and worth it if the worst came to the worst. And even then, William could, he was sure, use his circle of influence to 'bury it', Haughey-style. He'd get a rap on the knuckles, a warning of sorts, but nothing more.

At the end of the day, William rationalised quietly in his own mind, it was what it was and Seb just needed to man-up. He'd get over it, in due course. Yet the persistent memory of Seb's face and the look that poisoned it right before he walked out the door suggested it might take longer than he'd thought: it was a hard, well-considered look, a concoction of pain, disgust and hatred, targeted precisely at him. William felt his fists clench under the light-blue hospital cover.

I am lucky to be alive, William admitted, curious to know how Seb reacted when he was told that death was not his fortune that day – *Hoo-Ha!*

One by one they had arrived to visit. They whispered about him in the third person like he had passed away already, and debated the doctor's prognosis which was the prospect of a by-pass. Silently he laughed, entertained by the idea that they should decide his fate. Operation or no operation, it was his decision to make, not theirs. He'd bide his time and tell his doctor so.

'*But let them at it,*' his conscience told him. '*They'll get bored in a bit and go away, but for now leave them to it.*'

So he listened to his better judgment and let them worry while he slept.

He woke some time later. The room around him was deathly quiet and, risking a quick peek, he thanked the Lord that finally he was alone – still tired, still disenchanted but, most importantly, still alive. He didn't know whether to be grateful or disappointed. This was his life, his lot. In his adult years he had achieved a lot, but not everything that he wanted. There was more to do, so much more, he surmised, thinking of the unexplored and exciting opportunities open to him to attain further greatness and financial betterment, if he wanted it. Was there sufficient life left in him to do that? Did he really want it? Did he have the energy for it? And what about happiness? Was there a chance for that too? He thought of his life so far, his wife and his children. They were all damaged in one way or another. Did he want that or them? Was there a future for them in his life?

He had tried so hard to give them direction and guide them in the ways of the world – the real world – to impart to them the ambition to succeed, to instil in them a hunger to do better, to be better. But, with the exception of Seb, none of them quite 'got it'. None of them, he deduced, either understood it or needed it or wanted it badly enough to take it by the horns for themselves. Instead they did it their own way regardless and, in his opinion, failed miserably.

Barbara's genes, he mused, thinking of his subservient wife who had, in his enlightened opinion, neither backbone nor gumption. Yes. He was disappointed.

He drifted in and out of sleep, disturbed at moments by voices and nurses and needles and noise and a pressure in his heart that still hurt like hell. Time became an enigma, teasing him with hints of light and night, but they passed so quickly it couldn't possibly have been real.

He thought he heard a male voice plead, "But why won't he wake up?"

In a fleeting moment of lucidity he silently answered from the safety of the hospital bed: *Because I don't want to look at you, any of you.*

"Your father is a very sick man," he heard the doctor reply. "His body has gone through a serious trauma but his vitals are strong. He'll wake up when his body is good and ready."

When I am good and ready, he affirmed silently, wondering who was asking so urgently.

"He's not unconscious," the doctor said, "just sleeping."

Stupid boy, William thought ungraciously in response to his son's concern.

"He can't die, not yet." A woman's voice this time.

Martha, he assumed, not unpleasantly surprised by the level of emotion in her voice.

"He won't die," the doctor told her kindly. "For now he needs to rest – we're looking after him."

William wished they would leave him to wallow in his own illness.

When he did finally decide to open his eyes and face the world the nurse called for a doctor.

"You've had a lucky escape, sir," the young medic told him, delighted they'd managed to save his life, while William smiled up at him weakly.

"Lucky?" he rasped.

"Yes, sir. If your wife hadn't caught you when she did, you'd be a goner."

"I don't believe in luck."

"Well, call it what you like – just be grateful you're still here and you can thank your wife for it." With that he smiled, issued a round of orders to the nurse then dropped the chart back into its cradle and left her to it.

"Has she been here ... my wife?" William asked.

"You've had lots of visitors with you over the last few days," she told him. "Isn't it just typical that, the moment you wake up, they've all gone?"

"And Barbara?"

"I've only just come on shift myself so I can't tell for sure, but I can ask." She stopped what she was doing to look at him. "Do you want me to call her for you?"

"No. No. It's fine," he replied, closing his eyes again.

Things had changed. He could feel it. There was no way for him to come back from where he and Barbara had arrived. He had, he admitted, lost an element of control, which he considered he might never have had in the first place. Seb was a strong man. He should be proud of his son's confidence and tenacity in standing up for himself, even if it was to the detriment of his scheme and probably his reputation. It was the flaw in his plan, William admitted: he never considered that Seb wouldn't stand for it. Never thought he'd react as he did. He had overlooked Sebastian Bertram's strength and force of character. As it was, he knew he'd have to defend his position in government against the vultures that were bound to circle: even the slightest whiff of weakness and they'd swoop. He'd done it himself so he both knew and recognised the form. And he *was* weak, between the heart attack and what might be the fallout with Seb. He needed to think, circle the wagons, and defend his territory. He needed to get the hell out of here, regroup his troops and prepare. It would have been good to have Barbara there as his moral support, good for the papers. He'd have to work on her, get her back, so to speak.

Chapter 19

For three days Barbara allowed herself to wallow in an alcoholic stupor. She had no idea who came and went during that time. Gladys obviously was around every day but she knew to steer clear of Barbara when she was like this.

When on the third day she decided to surface without the aid of her whiskey crutch, her head throbbed and her stomach heaved.

Sitting up slowly, she massaged her brow.

"Jesus!" she gasped, the throb in her head pulsing against the inside of her skull and the stench of her breath lifting her stomach.

She sat still on the edge of the bed to let everything settle and align before standing up. The air in the room was heavy and stale and, as if on a tightrope, she took small, considered steps, placing one foot gingerly in front of the other to get to the window, pull open the curtains and drag up the glass. The light burned the back of her eyes but her face welcomed the cold breeze that wafted into the room to drive out the dead, alcohol-infused air. From her bedroom window everything was as it should be: the cars were parked below in the regular positions and the wind danced with the trees to the quiet hum of traffic on the main road. Inside was silent, as always.

Turning, she took stock of the evidence of her recent activities strewn on and beside her bed. She winced: it wasn't a pretty sight. Empty bottles, dirty plates, spills and soiled, crumpled-up tissues littered the bed, floor and bedside locker. Taking a deep breath she walked past it, opened her bedroom door and unsteadily made her way across the corridor. Warily and out of habit she knocked first before entering the room.

The smell of William's musky aftershave filled her head, evoking instantly a mental image of him. His tall frame and still full head of hair came to mind. Even in his absence his presence in this, his space, was strong. And it was immaculate. The bed was made, his pillows plumped and not an item out of place: books, bottles, brushes and all his bits, pristine except for a jacket thrown casually across the back of the chair in the corner, like it had been cast there only moments before and he would return any minute to retrieve it. She sat on his bed, partly because her legs wouldn't hold her anymore and partly because she just wanted to sit a while and think. She struggled to clear the fog in her head. She wished it would dissipate quickly because the desperate need to understand from where she had come and where she was going wasn't helping her already throbbing head. But inside her head was chaos. She had tried and tried to untangle it, bit by bit, breaking down each phase of her life to a bite-size piece, small enough to digest, but she could only achieve so much before getting the pieces caught up in the pandemonium and having to start all over again. Her frustration was blinding.

In here, though, there was a feeling of calm. Looking around, taking in the atmosphere, the arrangement and the smell of the room, she let the impression coalesce. A small stack of books sat on the bedside table, topped off with Richard Branson's *In His Own Words*, beside it an ancient picture of the whole family from one of his political landslides. She picked the photo up to take a closer look. They all looked so young, not particularly happy nor fashionable but content. There were no big grins or funny gestures. It was just them, the Bertrams, facing the camera, standing straight and tall. Barbara placed it back on the table and lightly touched the pile of books, eyeing each of the titles. Among them, Mandela's *Long Walk to Freedom* and Hawkins' *My Short History* – all thoroughly intellectual reads with not even a sniff of fiction inside any them. Typical William, she thought. Never a fan of creative writing no matter how literary or noble, he preferred the facts, the science, and the actuality of the world. Is this what he's reading now, she wondered, admiring the handsome Branson on the front cover, with a bookmark halfway through the book. Would he want it in the hospital? She always liked Richard Branson: a tenacious and attractive, not to mention exciting, entrepreneur. William had met him many years previously at a seminar at which he was the guest speaker. So normal, so down to earth, William just couldn't fathom it. How could a man who had achieved so much and had everything be so normal?

"We strive each day," he had remarked after the encounter, "to be different, to make a difference, so I'm baffled as to how one who continually achieves such an ambition can be so humble."

The memory of her husband's remarks aroused her curiosity and lifting her legs up onto the bed she curled up and started to read, eventually drifting into a deep sleep.

When she awoke it was pitch black outside. She must have slept through the rest of the day – and perhaps the night. She flicked on the reading lamp and winced as the light hit her eyes. It was midnight according to William's alarm clock. She noticed the book back on the bedside table and a blanket over her. Her head felt a little woolly but clear. The marshmallow-like softness of the pillow and the heat of the duvet under her made it difficult to do anything else but snuggle deeper.

Reluctantly she got up and made her way to William's en suite where she stripped and got into the shower. She let the hot jets pelt down on her for a minute before turning the dial and the heat down, extracting as much energy from the freezing-cold spray as she could. It felt good. Refreshing. Now she was awake. And cautiously ready to face the day – or, rather, the night – ahead.

Wrapping herself in his bathrobe she went to her own room and dressed, then returned to his room to pick up the book. His overnight case and wash bag weren't where they should be – she wasn't expecting them to be, assuming Ciara had already taken them to him.

She gathered her things and left the house.

She could only imagine what he'd be like cooped up in that hospital room. He hated being indoors too long. It wasn't always the case, but a health check about three years previously had given him a warning: shape up or face the medical consequences. Heeding the consultant's counsel, he accepted the prescribed medication and defiantly took up running, swam every day at the local health club and once a week in the freezing Irish Sea. He was, it seemed, a fit and healthy man and if he survived this would soon, she reckoned, be driving the doctors to distraction looking for answers, and cures, for his health failure. It was a sobering thought: he had almost died.

Unsettled by the fondness in her thoughts, she drove on autopilot and unseeing to the hospital. These were affections she had wished to feel for years now, so why then did she feel disquiet when it appeared that her wish to a degree might be coming true? She thought about their children. In normal circumstances like this, she supposed, families regrouped and comforted each other, but not hers. She, it appeared, had been left to her own devices. They didn't come near her.

Now, Barbara, she chastised herself, how would you know who came or went? Sure you were too pissed to notice. And why in the name of God would they even bother? And anyway, it's a two-way street: I wasn't there for them either.

It was self-criticism, which she accepted gracefully.

At the hospital she had to ask at reception where he was because she couldn't remember. Once directed she walked the long insipid corridors and rode the lift to the fourth floor, the smell of disinfectant stifling and the presence of all those sick people nauseating. Tentatively she pushed open the door, afraid and wondering what to expect. But she needn't have worried – he was sleeping and alone.

Quietly she slipped into the room, took off her coat, lifted the chair closer to the bed and sat in silence to watch him sleep in the soft light of the overhead lamp. He was whistling rather than snoring – he never snored – he was far too dignified for that, she always mocked. He was looking older and greyer than he ever had before and she noticed the wrinkles that seemed more pronounced along with the dryness and flakiness of his skin. Leaning in a little closer, comfortable in the safety of his slumber, she took a good look and tried to remember his good bits, the bits of him that had made her laugh, the part of their life together that they had actually enjoyed, that she had enjoyed. She tied to re-imagine those moments, those smiles, their best bits. But the memory was terribly fuzzy; it was after all a very, very long time ago. Was there anything left? There were more unhappy times than happy. Instinctively she placed her hand on his chest to feel its gentle rise and fall, his every breath, feeling its rhythm – closing her eyes, she imagined its journey through his body, keeping him alive, making her drowsy.

"You're here," he muttered and as if burnt she withdrew her hand instantly and he smiled.

"I am," she replied, self-conscious at having being caught red-handed.

Neither said anything more, each lost in their own thoughts, thinking along the same lines: how had it come to this? Both equally surprised by the idea that she had acted to save him. Both intrigued at the obvious sentiments she was experiencing. Why should that be a revelation? Probably because their marriage was a wreck and had been for some time and they both knew it. It wasn't just over between them: they actually hated each other, couldn't stand to be in each other's company. Or so they had thought. But there in his hospital room, after their brush with death, the hours slowly ticked by and something triggered between them. A mutual and tired concession of regret perhaps, that sparked a fragile pulse in their once unyielding bond to keep it alive along with the delicate rhythm of his heart.

The night came and went. Barbara stayed and dozed in the fake leather chair. She didn't dare leave, afraid that if she did she might not come back.

William fell in and out of sleep, disturbed by the regular interruption of the nurses on their rounds. Each time he woke he knew if she was there still when he opened his eyes then she would be with him forever, however long that would be. Between them there was a lot at stake in that single night.

A quiet polite knock preceded Ciara's entry into the room and immediately the atmosphere tensed. Barbara felt her nerve-endings prickle all the way down her spine, the halted step at the door demonstrating that Ciara reciprocated those same uncomfortable feelings.

Casting a glance towards her father and then back to her mother, Ciara entered the room and closed the door behind her.

"Mother," she greeted curtly in a whisper, afraid to disturb him. "How is he?"

"He's doing well, the doctors said," Barbara replied politely, sitting up in her chair.

"Have you been here all night?" Ciara asked, noticing her slightly dishevelled state, surprised by her attendance in the first place.

"I have," Barbara responded.

"Why?"

"I beg your pardon?"

"Why? I mean, you're no Florence Nightingale. Did something happen?"

"Don't speak to your mother like that," William quietly ordered from the bed without opening his eyes or lifting his head.

Both women turned in quiet alarm towards him.

"Dad?" Ciara went to stand beside him. "You're awake. How are you feeling?" She took his hand and leant over to kiss him on his forehead.

Barbara couldn't look at the display and instead stood and picked up her bag.

"I'm going to get a coffee."

"I'm here now so you don't need to come back," Ciara told her.

"Excuse me?"

"I said I'm here so you don't have to come back," Ciara repeated, looking back at her mother over her shoulder. "If you don't want to, that is."

"I heard you," Barbara fumed. "I just can't believe you said it."

"Why not? We all know you'd rather be somewhere else," Ciara told her with feigned innocence.

"Is that so?"

"It is," Ciara continued childishly. "So you can head off and do what you do best, if you like."

"If you two are going to start bickering you can both leave," William told them, feeling stronger than he had in days, but not strong enough emotionally or physically to deal with the women.

"Right," Barbara said, smarting, knowing that Ciara had every right to feel the way she did and, in the absence of the courage needed to take her on, she decided it was time to go. "Don't worry," she told them both, "I have things to do anyway." And, picking up her coat, moved to the bed and placed a hand over William's. Without seeing it she could feel Ciara's glaring scowl in response to the rarely shared gesture.

"I'll pop back later, okay?" she told him and from the corner of her eye saw Ciara throw her eyes and chin upwards.

Barbara looked up at her, wanting nothing more than to slap her face, hard. But there were bigger things at play – both she and William knew that. She wasn't the 'cold turkey' kind and each had a pretty good idea where she was going and what "things to do" actually meant. For William there was a silent acceptance that, while he had his choices to make, she had decisions of her own to deal with.

Despite her little squabble with Ciara, Barbara's composure was still intact as she pushed her way through the hospital doors and went back to her car. Making her way home she made a quick stop en route. Getting out, she ran straight into the off-license where she bought herself a litre bottle of the best whiskey they had on the shelf, got back into the car and continued her journey home.

The house was silent and empty. She had no idea where Gladys might be and didn't really give her a second thought. Throwing her coat and bag over the back of a chair in the kitchen, she placed the long bottle on the counter, grabbed a glass from the cupboard, threw a few cubes of ice in and topped it off with a double measure of the whiskey. But she didn't pick it up: instead she listened to the ice crack and watched the cubes sink into the rich caramel-coloured liquid.

There were two voices in her head. The first, the voice of reason, which spoke firmly to her. It said: '*Don't touch it, Barbara. You can't control it but it controls you.*'

The other was the voice of seduction: '*Drink it, Barbara,*' it said bewitchingly. '*It'll make things feel so much better, just for a while. That's just what you need. Isn't it? You can always call it quits tomorrow. Not today. Tomorrow.*'

Picking the glass up she held it in her hand, swirled the liquid round, watching it cling to the sides of the glass as it spun. The smell was so tempting, so smooth. The fumes tickled her taste buds. It would be so easy, just one sip. Why stop now? Just one tiny drop.

'*We can start tomorrow*,' the voice of seduction repeated. It was so sweet, so alluring and so much louder and convincing than reason.

The front door slammed, shaking the foundations of the house, their vibrations breaking through the reverie of her moral dilemma. She put the glass down. She could guess who it would be but didn't try to hide either the bottle or her thoughts. This was just Barbara and her conscience. She recognised the familiar click-clacking on the expensive parquet floor and, letting out a deep sigh, waited for her to appear.

"Well, isn't that just lovely?" Ciara launched her attack, her arms folded across her chest and her hip cocked to one side. "How did I know you'd be here with ..." she nodded towards the glass, "with this."

Barbara looked across at her from the far side of the counter. How smug, she thought, observing the bitter and contorted face, the face of a woman she found so difficult to look at and so impossible to love.

"Well, I'm glad not to disappoint," she mumbled, raising the glass to catch the sunlight that poured in through the kitchen window. But she didn't let it touch her lips, she just watched the ice cubes swirl and dance in the delicious liquid.

"I thought you were going to stay with your father?"

"They took him for tests. So," Ciara continued, irritated and unnerved by the eerie calm being displayed by her mother, "what did you do to him?"

"What do you mean by that?" Barbara threw back, allowing herself be distracted from her ruminations.

"You heard me – what did you do to him?"

Barbara shook her head in disbelief. "Now you're being ridiculous," she snapped. "Of course I didn't do anything to him."

"Well, you must have done something. Normally he can't stand to be around you, then all of a sudden you're the loving couple holding hands by his sick bed?"

"You listen to me, madam." Barbara turned to look straight at her. "Don't come into my house –"

"*Your house?*" Ciara shrieked dramatically. "It's Dad's house too, you know – don't forget that."

"Like you'd ever let me forget it," Barbara muttered under her breath, recognising the venom for what it was and the fact there was no point in rising to her hysterical challenge.

"Look at you," Ciara sneered. "You're a disgrace, hardly fit to be a mother, never mind a wife."

Barbara carefully placed the glass of very tempting and now slightly diluted whiskey on the counter, breathing steadily through her nose.

"Who do you think you are," she asked with quiet

calm, "to come into *my* house and speak to me like this?"

"Actually," Ciara continued, unhearing, her tone laced with sarcasm. "I don't even know why you bothered to have us at all!"

"Oh for God's sake," Barbara interrupted, exasperated and irked, "don't be so childish!" She sensed control slipping from a situation that was fast developing into something dangerous.

Ciara yanked out a stool from under the counter and sat her bottom on its edge.

"You know," she said bluntly, "all of us, we spent our entire childhood wishing you'd be a mum: a real mum, not some lush half pissed most of the time." She shook and bowed her head. "You were – no – you *are* a shit mother." Then she looked up with a sad, forlorn smile. "I spent years hankering after you but you were always somewhere else." It was a simple but honest statement, filled with heart.

"How dare you!" Barbara replied nervously, knowing what Ciara had said was true, but pride combined with a substantial dose of shame refused to let her admit it. Why now? she thought. Why does she have to do this now?

"You ignored me for as long as I can remember, you made me feel like I was nothing, like I was a piece of dirt on the sole of your shoe." Ciara stopped to take a shaky but measured breath. "I never felt the same as the others, you made sure of that. You really were an absolutely rubbish mum and ..." She paused, as if realising something for the first time or at least admitting it openly for the first time. "And I despise you, really I do. I actually loathe you."

Barbara sat down into one of the chairs at the table

and listened stony-faced to the rant, shocked and more than a little bit fearful of the toxic tone in Ciara's voice. It didn't sound like Ciara; she had her characteristic penchant for drama of course but in all her years she had never exhibited this much vitriol towards her, towards anything in fact. There was no sign of the affectionate child, or the young girl turned immature woman who still craved love and emotion to the point of irritation. Could this be her response to the upset of her father almost dying or did something more specific happen to spark this tirade? And with a sizable measure of dread, Barbara wondered where the conversation was going.

Ciara was always too emotionally demanding for the detached Barbara who tended to steer away from her: never looking her in the eye, never holding her hand, never mothering her, never trying to demonstrate even the smallest bout of affection for fear that the girl would see right through her. And Ciara was right. She did treat her differently and, yes, she was an appalling mother. It was impossible to hide and absolutely true. She was never any good at concealing her true feelings and Ciara, despite her oftentimes histrionic behaviour, was an intelligent individual who would, Barbara was sure, eventually discover her for what and who she really was. It wasn't that she didn't like Ciara, or love her even – of course she did, in a way. No, Barbara's indifference towards the girl was much more selfish and far less pleasant than she cared to admit, even to herself. She had done her best with her, really she had. She had tried very hard but obviously not hard enough.

Perched, legs apart, on the edge of the chair she let her elbows rest on her thighs, listening to Ciara who wasn't yet done, letting the years of bitter disappointment spill over, impossible to hide the snarl in her sorrow.

"You sit there," she ranted as if living out the days of her past, "pissed most of the time – even after Patrick died you couldn't manage to step up and be a mother!" And as each statement escaped her lips the release worked to lift her shoulders. "You never held me then, you never even tried to tell me it would all be all right."

Ciara had never spoken like this to anyone, having bottled it all up inside her for years. And now that the dam had been breached there was no stopping the deluge of suppressed truths that poured forth.

"Robert was right about you. You really are nothing but a selfish drunk."

As Barbara listened she wondered at what point was it acceptable to stand up and fight back. It was the alcohol that tended to keep things quiet. Never an aggressive, troublesome drunk like one typically imagines, she didn't get loud and bolshie nor did she morph into some obnoxious bitch. No, she was a quiet drunk: the precarious kind. The alcohol helped silence the voices in her head that oozed guilt, shame and abject disappointment, keeping the simmering honesty from bubbling over. But, having not had a drink in over twenty-four hours, she was sober and there was very little holding her back. She was in perilous and unknown territory. The more Ciara upbraided her, the easier she felt it would be to take a dose of whatever Ciara was on and simply let go. It was ironic that Ciara should feel so uptight, like she was the only one to feel anything. How selfish, like all these years were easy for her. Barbara had stopped listening to her, concentrating more on keeping her own mouth shut.

It was unsurprising that the tears had started to fall from Ciara's eyes and she watched the translucent snot begin to escape unchecked from her nose. It was a cute little nose, so unlike her own and definitely not like William's. In her mind's eye she pictured herself standing up, slowly, with her chin held defiantly up and candidly blurting it out. She envisaged Ciara's reaction, visualised the response, which she knew, of course, would be disbelief and contempt.

"I have no idea why Dad hasn't thrown you out on the street," Ciara's confidence was fuelled by the emancipation of the harsh truth and feelings for her mother, "so you can live in the gutter, because that's all you deserve. You don't love him. You don't love any of us. You just use us. You always have."

She sounded so childish, Barbara thought, fighting through the daze, biting her tongue. How easy … consequences be damned …

"I don't understand how you can live with yourself. How can you? Tell me, I'm intrigued?" Ciara spat, pointing and prodding the finger of accusation at her, standing now, goading her with the tightening of her jaw and stretch of her lips. "How can you live with yourself?" She gesticulated wildly.

Always impetuous, almost always hysterical, Barbara silently remarked, knowing for sure she didn't get it from her.

Only then did she notice that Ciara was silent and standing, waiting.

Oh my God! Barbara thought. She actually expects an answer. What was the question? Oh right. How can I live with myself? Well, let me see … She processed the question silently, taking only a few minutes, the words no longer willing to remain silent and lining themselves up to come out. Straight.

"How can I live with myself?" she repeated aloud. "Well, I'll tell you how … Because you're not my daughter, that's how, and I've had to put up with you for years."

There. It was out. She had been dumb for far too long.

The instant the words were out she felt a sense of relief, immediately followed by an urgent inclination to take them back. And just as quickly a realisation that, no, it was time Ciara knew the truth. The regret she felt was not for what she had said but more the fact she had to say the words at all. It was the truth. Ciara wasn't her daughter. It wasn't Ciara's fault. She and William could claim that blame all as their own. They had committed their secret to silence so many years before and had managed to maintain that obligation, almost never mentioning it or discussing it, ever. But now that their proverbial dirty linen was laid bare it was likely to trigger a series of events that were unstoppable. Barbara meant no harm to Ciara, but even she had her limits. This situation was forced on her.

She thought of William and what this would mean to him. His fury was inevitable.

This is not my fault, she thought, justifying her actions. She should have been told sooner.

Between them they had assumed all those years ago that eventually events would naturally evolve to the exposure of the truth. But it didn't happen that way and remarkably the question never arose. Barbara felt her cheeks burn with a rising sense of indignation. It *was* time the truth was told. *It was, really*. She watched Ciara's reaction, or lack of it, as she waited for the words to sink in.

The moment after her response passed in slow motion. She saw Ciara's jaw drop, her eyebrows lift and her eyes widen as she processed the words. Barbara watched the colour drain, drop by drop, from her cheeks. They had reached the point of no return and there could be no going back. And when Ciara's mouth opened but no sound emerged, Barbara's blood chilled, like she had been cloaked in a damp dense fog.

Silent shockwaves reverberated from Ciara's body with ripples coming tight and fast, noiselessly emanating her disbelief, her horror and her loss. Turning on the spot, raking her hands though her hair, not knowing what exactly she was expected to do, she quietly melted into a drama that this time wasn't imagined or misinterpreted. This drama, this time, was real.

For the first time in years, ever even, Barbara felt the need to protect Ciara: she didn't deserve this. It shouldn't be her burden. She really was the innocent victim. The secret that had destroyed Barbara, that she had allowed to fester and eat away at her, was no longer hers. She had passed it on, like a poisoned chalice, to continue its virulent journey. And she had given it to Ciara. A wave of regret and shame washed over her. And, unlike her fantasy, the release was nothing like she had imagined. She had so often dreamt of this moment: the relief, the weightlessness, the liberty of a burden removed. Barbara always assumed her liberation would be monumental, like it would make her better somehow, but right then she only felt worse. She watched as an almost hysterical medley of emotions passed over Ciara's face in alarmingly recognisable succession: shock, confusion, realisation, acceptance and hurt.

Instinctively Barbara went to her. "Ciara!" she sighed. "I'm sorry. I didn't mean ..."

"Oh yes, you did. You meant every word." Ciara took a step away, shaking her head. "So, if I'm not yours, whose am I?" she asked with mascara-tinted tears streaming down her flushed and burning cheeks, the uncharacteristic calm of her words unsettling.

It was a question that despite years of visualisation, years of imagining how it would sound and feel, she had no idea how to answer. It had always been about the truth but never the consequence. She knew the question would be asked but never, stupidly, considered what the response should be. Faced with it now, she didn't have the courage to answer.

Chapter 20

By the time Barbara realised that William was bored at home and seeking solace and satisfaction elsewhere, it had gone too far. Unbeknownst to Barbara, amidst the joy of their first-born was Irene Philips with her voluptuous breasts, skinny waist and alluring blonde curls. She was the first and certainly not the last of many misadventures of the adulterous kind. After Irene came a pointy-nosed, cavern-faced brunette, Judith Hayes, to entertain his wandering eye and after that again there was Maureen Judge: Barbara's bridge partner and supposed friend. And so the list grew steadily and, as the years passed, it became almost endless. He managed his women like he managed his politics: with dexterity and charm. Although rumours were hard to suppress, there was no one willing to put their own head on the line to expose him. He made sure to choose his women well – they each had as much to lose as he would: the house, the car, the kids, the holidays, the generous allowance ... And inside the house, when Barbara wasn't willing to satisfy his casual carnal needs, Lillian seemed willing to step in. In between Rian and Enya, just after they lost Emily, at a time when Barbara was at her lowest, Lillian arrived to replace a former nanny. Tall and slim with beautiful clear skin, bright-blue eyes and long straw-coloured hair she had an innocence that was almost irresistible. At eighteen, with already three years' experience, her job was to help Barbara with the kids, not satisfy the man of the house.

Educated by the nuns in County Galway, she was a bright young thing with a promising future that at fifteen was extinguished the day her father ran away with a bottle of gin and their meagre savings, leaving Lillian with her mother and younger siblings, a boy and a girl, to fend for themselves. Lillian's mother Maeve did what she could but, in the end, as the bills stacked up unpaid and intimidating, Lillian was left with no choice but to leave school and the rural safety of Roundstone to get a job. Her first family, the Mahoneys, weren't that far away – only fifty miles separated them from her home – but even so she missed her family terribly and they missed her more. She did her best to get home to see them as often as she could but, with the constant tiring demands of her young charges, making the short trip home wasn't as easy as it sounded and, soon, seeing them only once a month became the norm and something she could look forward to. A new job and a new country for Mr. Mahoney meant that Lillian needed to find a new position for herself too. Mrs. Mahoney and her three young girls begged her to go with them but America was so big and so far away a shy young Lillian said no.

Maeve was so proud of her when she'd called to tell her that she'd be working for a rich family in Dublin. It would mean she'd be home much less, but it was a good job and the salary meant her mum could give up her night shift at the hotel.

So Lillian moved into the house with the Bertrams, looking after the children alongside the listless Barbara who seemed to care less and less as each day passed. Lillian was amazed at how she could be like that, with everything she had: beautiful clothes, incredible children, amazing house, enough money to buy whatever she needed and a husband who, she thought, tended to her every need. How could she be so despondent? She didn't understand her at all but knew what she'd do if she had all this: enjoy life, that's what. And so she said to her mam during one of her visits.

"You just keep your head down and your remarks to yourself, young lady," said her mam.

"Yes, Mam," she replied, dropping her head.

"The last thing we need is for you to lose that job."

And so, when William laid his hand over hers in the first of many intimate encounters, saying no didn't even enter her head. She couldn't let her mother down.

Ciara was born three and a half years after Cormac and almost two before Enya. For Barbara the shame of the pregnancy was worse than the humiliation of his indiscretion that apparently everyone knew about except her.

It was a day she would never forget: a wet Wednesday when she found Lillian crying and vomiting simultaneously. She didn't need a doctor to tell her what was wrong with the girl but Barbara took her anyway just to confirm what she suspected.

"I'm so sorry, Mrs. Bertram," Lillian cried from the edge of her chair, wringing her hands and the hem of her dress into a knot.

"Well," Barbara asked calmly "who is the father?" and

when Lillian didn't answer she stood over the quivering young nanny to demand, "Who is it, you stupid girl?"

But Lillian couldn't bring herself to answer.

"Well," Barbara informed her unsympathetically, "you can't stay here – you'll just have to go home."

"Please, please no! Please!" Lillian cried. "I can't go home . . . my mam ..." The sentence didn't need to be finished.

Barbara got it completely and, seizing the opportunity, looked down, almost smiling at the weeping girl. "Tell me who is the father and I'll think about it."

Lillian looked up at her, weighing up the options presented and spoke in a spontaneous instant without thinking about what she was doing.

"Mr. B-b-bertram," she whispered.

"Mr. Bertram what?" Barbara asked, not understanding what the gibbering girl was trying to say.

"He ... he ... he is the ..." but she couldn't finish her sentence for her intense sobbing.

"Is the father?" Barbara finished, paling. "Are you trying to tell me Mr. Bertram is the father of your child?"

"Yes," she sniffed, her face drenched by her tears.

But Barbara didn't need to hear her; she got it the first time but just didn't believe it.

"You lying bitch! How dare you!" she spat instinctively, slapping the girl hard across her already burning face.

Lillian recoiled, raising her hand to her face and looked up at Barbara, her eyes filled with shock and terror.

She was no more than a child herself. She looked so innocent, so angelic, so credible. Doubting her was pointless. This wasn't the face of a liar.

At least now she's stopped blubbering, Barbara thought, while between her ears her blood raged like a torrent inside her head. She felt its rapid course through every vein and artery until it pounded in her head, ready to explode. She might have screamed, or maybe just cried aloud, but one way or another she couldn't speak, her pain was that intense.

William steered clear of her with nothing to say and no apology on offer while she couldn't bring herself to look him in the eyes. She didn't challenge him or ask him how he could have done this to Lillian, to her, to the children. She knew exactly how it happened. She even knew why it happened. But knowing it and saying it were two different things. For a week Barbara was left to her thoughts and could think of nothing else but Lillian and William.

"What a fool you are," she told herself as she worked through what could and should happen next.

Her room became her jail. She was too ashamed to be seen by anyone – not her friends, not even Gladys who must have seen what was going on. Even the children, she thought, looked at her with pitying eyes. How could they? They're so young. Oh, they know all right, she tormented herself, they can smell it. Shame has a powerful stench.

When William eventually came to her it was with embarrassment rather than humility.

"May I come in?" he asked politely from the doorway.

"You already have," she answered bitterly as he entered without waiting for an answer.

"This ... eh . . ." he paused, seeking out a word that might be least offensive to her ". . . eh . . . this situation . . ."

She replied with a slow shake of her head.

"Well, I think the best thing is for Lillian to leave."

"Leave?" Barbara asked in disbelief. "And go where?"

"Well, it has been suggested –"

"By whom?" she shot at him. "Who else knows about this … about this '*situation*?" Her words slurred slightly at the end, the effects of her first few drinks of the evening kicking in.

William bit his tongue in recognition of his error in talking about their situation to anyone outside of their own circle.

"There is a community in the North that welcomes girls …" He left the sentence open-ended, inviting her to pick up the meaning.

"Oh really?" she asked politely. "And what then?"

He looked back at her, confused.

"What then, mastermind? What does she do with it?"

"With what?"

"Oh, for God's sake, William! Are you being purposely obtuse? The baby. *The bloody baby!* What do you do with it?"

"The child will have a home," he stated with dispassion.

Barbara was too incensed to ask where.

"And what if she won't go? What if she won't give it up? What if she wants to keep it? Have you thought of that?" she asked instead with shaky calm.

"I think she knows she can't stay here and she doesn't want to go home with the baby, so …"

"You think? You've spoken to her about this?" Barbara asked with an acid laugh. "How cosy! Post-coital chit-chat. Just bloody lovely."

Affording her, in the circumstances, the right to be childish, he ignored her jibe and told her, "She leaves on Monday."

"She leaves tonight," Barbara corrected. "I don't want her a night more under this roof. And you can go with her."

William moved around the bed to sit into the chair in the window. There was more.

"Not me," he said. "You."

It took a minute for his words to sink in.

"Me?" she asked with a confused laugh. "I'm not going anywhere!"

"I've thought about this and there is only one way to keep this quiet."

"You are insane, do you know that?" Barbara interrupted, knowing but not believing the direction of his instruction.

William continued as if he didn't hear her interjection. "The baby will come here after it's born."

"And Lillian? What about her?"

"Lillian will keep quiet. She doesn't want the child."

"She's told you that, has she? So what does she want? Money? Is that it?"

"Don't be ridiculous!"

"I don't think it's an unreasonable question. If she doesn't want the baby and she's not after money what exactly is she after? But never mind that – where is she going to go?"

"Well," he shrugged, "then she goes home."

"Home where? Here?"

"*Think, woman!*" he almost shouted, his patience wearing thin. "Back home to her mother in Galway of course."

"And if she won't go?"

"She will. We'll give her a healthy allowance and a glowing reference. She won't be able to refuse."

"And what about me? Do I not have an opinion?"

"Barbara, you *know* this is the only way. You don't want this getting out any more than I do, do you?"

He was right. She didn't. But to take the child as her own? He must be mad. She thought of Emily. She still felt her loss every single day: her little girl. Maybe this child would be a girl …

"Well?" he asked, looking for her response, like she had a say.

"You have it all worked out, don't you?" she asked him quietly. "What if I don't agree?"

"You will," he told her confidently. "You'll do what's best, for us all."

"How could you do this to me?" she demanded, between sobs.

"I have needs," he told her. "I didn't set out to hurt you, it just happened."

"William, things like this don't *just happen*. And what about the others?"

"What others?" he asked, taken aback by her suddenly forthright questions.

"Don't take me for a fool!" she sighed. "I may be a drunk but I'm not stupid."

"Well, maybe if you stopped drinking and took some notice of what was going on around you this might not have happened."

And there it was. The blame. And it was hers to accept and keep. Ever the politician, William managed to deflect both attention and blame away from himself. It was his parting gift as he left the room, delegating the responsibility for their dysfunctional marriage to her.

On the Monday morning the car came to collect them and

almost immediately an agency nanny moved in. The children, not that they really understood, were told that "Mammy has to go away for a while. She's not feeling well because she's going to have a new baby but needs some special care. Lillian is going to go with her so she can take care of Mammy".

Barbara often wondered what would have happened had she not got into that car. How differently things might have turned out. But it was the 1970s, she was the wife of a promising young politician, a future Taoiseach perhaps. She didn't have a choice.

On paper, it was a simply explained exercise but in reality it became an arduous journey of self-inflicted punishment and flagellation for Barbara. She accompanied Lillian to the wilds of Donegal and remained with her for the remainder of the pregnancy. Proving that everything had a monetary value, she and William were guaranteed discretion by the nuns and Barbara was treated like religious royalty, if there was any such thing. It might have been cheaper to stay at the Ritz, she quipped to herself as Mother Superior took her to her room. She was given one of the larger cells to sleep in which had privacy in its favour and a view from a small window that looked over the fields and out to sea. Lillian on the other hand slept in one of the dormitories with the other girls of which there were at least fifty, all young, all scared and all very, very lonely. No one, it seemed, ever came to visit, there were no letters and no phone calls to or from the makeshift booth in the main hall. It was like they had been lost or just simply forgotten.

Such a cold place, always dull like the sun never shone and if it did the rays were devoured by the grey boundary walls before they even had a chance to shine through the windows. Barbara kept to herself, steering clear of the loud clatter of the girls as they marched through the corridors at lunchtime or in the evenings when their work was done. They were kept busy, working twelve-hour days. Waking up at six in the morning and finishing at six at night they spent their days washing and scrubbing for the community. It was their penance, Mother Superior told her when she first arrived. These were girls, troubled girls, in need of reform and guidance, she said with a smile that had no heart.

Even though they were all pregnant or recent mothers there was neither sight nor sound of their babies. She never saw them together, the mothers and their children. Never a cry or a whimper, although sometimes, even through the yard-thick masonry walls of the convent she heard the girls cry while the nuns screamed – *guiding* them, Barbara thought, pushing the morality of what she was witness to out of her mind completely.

It was only years after she left the convent that she thought about what went on in that house and wondered what had become of those girls, so many of them abandoned by their families, all in the name of repentance and the need to hide their shame. How misguided. How hypocritical. How evil. It was easy to blame the Sisters, brainwashed in the unnatural environment of their own captivity, but all of those girls had parents who had knowingly sent and left their daughters there to suffer. They were the culpable ones. They were the heartless bigots. People just like herself and William.

For Barbara, it was her longest period sober since Sebastian was born and for seven months she walked the harsh and unforgiving weather-beaten coastline. Although Mother Superior often offered her time to share her thoughts and worries, Barbara never quite trusted her and chose instead to keep the story of how and why she ended up in the far north of the country to herself. The magic and beauty of a landscape that was different every day became her best friend and her captor, keeping her lucid and in control. Despite herself, she did miss her boys in her own peculiar way but even so she was happy to be alone. She felt she could quite happily have remained there had she been allowed but as the seven months ran out so did her patience with her own company.

The baby arrived early on a Monday morning. It was fast and sore with no medicine to ease the pain. The novice attending the delivery, Sister Jude, without consultation named her Ciara and Barbara didn't care to object. She was taken from Lillian and delivered straight into the arms of Barbara who held her for only a minute before handing her back, repulsed, to Sister Jude.

She did ask after Lillian, out of curiosity rather than concern, to be told that she had cried and hadn't stopped yet but would get over it eventually.

On the eve of her planned return home to Galway some weeks later, Lillian left the house bright and early only to return lifeless and limp in the arms of a stranger. He had pulled her from the sea which was just too wild for such a slip of a thing. And, despite seeing the fragile girl in the early minutes after life, Barbara secretly counted it fortunate that sweet Lillian had passed.

And as if to add a final insult to Lillian's family's hurt and inconsolable pain, they buried her where she died rather than sending her home.

"How will she ever be able to rest in peace there?" her mother wailed. "Why did you leave her there? You should have brought her home to me."

William, having taken it upon himself to 'manage' the situation, having delivered the news that not only had her daughter passed away but was already buried, took her hand and with well-practised remorse captured it in his own and leaning forward told her in his most sympathetic guise, "She loved the country. It's what she would have wanted."

Lillian's mother cried while her little sister listened from the stairs outside.

Chapter 21

For as long as she remembered Ciara always knew she was different. Not physically, but inside. And now she knew why. Without a second thought she left her mother to contemplate her drink, got into her car and drove straight to the hospital, distracted to the extent that she didn't even think to call Robert. Her head was chaotic, her thoughts a blur. It was impossible to index the words that tripped so easily off her mother's lips so processing them into any kind of bite-sized intelligible pieces was hopeless. By the time she reached the hospital she had worked herself up to an almost hysterical frenzy.

"*Is it true?*" she shouted, storming into her father's room without greeting but not without seeing Rian, Martha and Enya sitting around William's bedside like good attentive children.

How hypocritical, she thought, cringing inside, not knowing how she should feel about her siblings now she was only halfways related. Each of them turned in surprise at her abrupt entrance. Glancing briefly at each with accusing eyes, like this was as much their fault as his, she ignored their stunned stares and instead focused her attention fully on her father.

"*Is it true?*" she repeated with a force sufficient to make her sister jump. Betrayal bubbled inside her as she waited for him to answer, her eyes searching his pale and insipid complexion. She wanted to feel nothing but anger towards him, but his frail demeanour refused to let her fury completely consume her. Doing her best to push her compassion aside, she shifted uncomfortably from one foot to the other.

"Is *what* true?" Enya asked, glancing first at Ciara then at her father.

"Not you," Ciara rebuffed her angrily. "*Him.*" A hint of desperation had crept into her voice as she pointed at William.

"Ciara!" a shocked Enya cried in return, her tone a mixture of impatience and concern. "What on earth's got into you?"

Ciara didn't think it possible but she was sure she noticed her father's already ashen face turn a shade lighter.

So, he thought, the day has come. Just as she said it would.

But, unlike his wife, it wasn't a day that he either anticipated or thought about to any great degree, but now it was here he wished he had, because maybe then he'd know what he was supposed to do. He might have at least rehearsed it mentally in preparation. His mouth dropped a jot, as did his eyes, with an audible intake of breath.

Ciara thought he was about to say something. But he didn't and couldn't or wouldn't meet her stare.

He knew exactly what she was asking, of that she was sure: his face said it all. Without him uttering a single word he answered her question. It was true. But she already knew it was – why would her mother lie about such a thing? She just needed to hear it or see it in her father.

"Ciara, what's going on?" Rian demanded quietly, standing up to take charge.

She could tell he was thinking, 'Oh, here we go again! Drama! Drama! Drama!' And he was probably right; she was a drama queen and a damn good one at that. But this time, at the root of the fuss, she was entitled to a little commotion. Turning, Ciara smiled. He knew no different, she knew that – he was behaving as he always did, trying to maintain a level of calm and, because of his ignorance of the situation, he had every right to look at her in that way. But she knew that when he found out the truth behind her actions he would look to protect her, at least she hoped he would. For a split second, a moment of fear, she wondered if her newly defined title within the family would change how he treated her. Rian always maintained the voice of reason, especially around her, so she wasn't surprised when he stood beside her and, wrapping a reassuring arm around her, looked to steer her away from danger. But even Rian's embrace wasn't sufficient to extinguish her fire.

With damp and mascara-smudged eyes, she pleaded silently for him to leave her be. She felt the pressure of his fingers on her shoulders, a reassuring and genuine pressure, the kind to make her heart sigh with the shame of disappointing him. But she had no alternative, she knew he'd see that, eventually.

"What's wrong with you?" he asked, more gently this time, searching her face for an answer.

"I'm sorry," she whispered to him and, releasing herself from his embrace, stepped towards the bed. "I asked you," she said with restrained calm, due mainly to Rian's composed influence, "is it true?"

Rian let her go and looked expectantly towards the bed, curious to know what had triggered her hysterical agitation.

Only the sound from the corridors outside that buzzed with activity and the heave of Ciara's breath filled the room as they waited for him to respond.

"From your behaviour I can only assume," William eventually replied, lifting his eyes to look petulantly at her, his words a bored effort, "that you've been fighting with your mother again."

Spiked with such condescension, they were all Ciara needed.

"*But*," she stressed with almost rabid glee, leaning closer to the bed, "she's *not* my mother, is she?" A deep thrill swept through her, triggered by the sharp intake of breath from her audience, their reclassified relationship weighing heavy on her heart but almost instantly giving her the distance required to see just how peculiar the dynamics of their dysfunctional family really were. Rian with his love-struck fiancée and Enya sitting at the bedside of their almost tyrannical father who enjoyed nothing more than terrorising and demeaning each of them at every opportunity. The absence of Sebastian and Cormac was interesting. And then there was their mother: not *hers*, but theirs. Drunk probably, unconscious possibly and damaged definitely.

Both Enya and Martha stood as if repulsed by the revelation. Enya stepped forward to place her hands on Ciara's arm. Martha dropped her head and Ciara saw her eyes shut slowly, likely mortified by the family she was about to marry into. The thought flashed through her head: how much damage would this revelation cause to Rian's relationship with Martha?

"Take a breath," Enya told her quietly.

Ciara smiled, wondering if she was sorry she ever came back. What a joke.

Then turning back to her father, Enya, standing firm beside Ciara, asked, "What is she talking about, Dad?"

Funny how she asked him and not me, Ciara thought, but said nothing, willing to wait and see if William would answer her, curious to see what he'd say.

"Do we have to do this now?" William asked, dropping his head back onto the firm white pillow.

"Yes. Yes, we do," Ciara replied, incensed further by his frigid and almost blasé return. It just didn't matter to him. Bunching her hands into fists, she squeezed them tight, quelling the urge to grab and shake him wildly,

"I'm not sure this is the time," he told her, true to his patronising form.

"Why not?" she asked him. "Is it because *they're* here?" She nodded towards Rian, Martha and Enya. "Or because you need time to concoct some kind of pathetic excuse for what happened?" She stopped to catch her breath which was beginning to run away from her. "You know, when she told me for a split second I didn't believe her." She shook her head as again William diverted his gaze. "But she was telling the truth, wasn't she?"

William didn't answer. In his mind, he was asking: why now, why here? What had he done to deserve the last week of angry insolent outbursts from his family? Could this possibly get any worse? Maybe if he were lucky, he told himself, he'd just close his eyes and fade away.

"*Wasn't she?*" Ciara repeated, raising her voice to an angry snarl, breaking through his self-obsessed reverie.

"Dad, please, answer her!" Enya pleaded.

Sensing a situation ready to implode, Rian stepped up again.

"Ciara," he said, taking a gentle hold of her arm, "seriously. Now isn't the time." He steered her away from the bed. "Whatever it is, it can wait. Dad's having his operation in the morning – he needs to rest."

"Everything all right in here?" The previously friendly nurse popped her head around the door, her voice cheerful but with a 'don't mess with me' edge. Expertly assessing the situation, she entered the room, giving each of them a brief but stern glance, changing it as she approached William to a warm smile. He was her charge, in her care, and she took the task seriously. Fixing his pillows she quietly asked if everything was okay.

"It's fine, a minor family spat," William told her, oozing charm despite his fragile disposition.

"I'm right outside if you need me," she told him before patting his bruised and punctured hand.

At the door she turned.

"I'm going to have to ask you to keep it down, or leave," she said to the others. "Your father is a very sick man and this is not helping." With a superficial smile she then left the room.

The silence that remained was excruciating, the tension thick.

Ciara waited and let the silent tension build.

When he did eventually lift his eyes to hers they were empty: no sorrow, no shame, just blank.

"You bastard," she whispered, "I have tried so hard

for you to like me! So bloody hard. No wonder it's never worked." Turning on her heel she left the room, wishing she could slam the door behind her.

"Let me –" she heard Martha say and heard her trot down the hall after her.

"Ciara!" she called. "Wait up!"

Despite herself Ciara slowed down and, without turning, waited for Martha to catch up. Although different in so many ways, they got on well together. While the others seemed worried about the age difference, Ciara just got on with getting to know her. And it wasn't just because she was Rian's girlfriend and so merited a special effort: she actually liked her.

Overtaking her, Martha stopped in front of Ciara, her breathing fast. Sensing immediately her abject despair, she opened her arms, inviting Ciara to walk into her embrace.

As soon as Martha's arms wrapped around her the tears came.

"*Shhhh!*" Martha soothed, rubbing her back and stroking her hair.

Ciara's body quaked as the tears came fast and furious, both of them ignoring the looks that came as they stood in the middle of the corridor, Ciara weeping oblivious to her surroundings while Martha silently cursed William Bertram and everything he stood for.

Chapter 22

Martha returned to William's room and all heads turned as she entered, their collective sigh of relief when they realised she was alone undisguised.

"Is she alright?" Rian asked.

"Not really, but she will be," Martha replied, unable to meet William's gaze.

William watched her from the bed, acutely aware of her purposely averted eyes. Although she did an excellent job at concealing it, her revulsion was palpable.

Shame, he thought to himself, I liked her. And almost immediately his trust in her was lost. Who the hell did she think she was anyway? Waltzing in with her presumptions and misconceptions. Catching himself, he wondered if the sneer he felt inside him was visible on his face. She doesn't know what she's dealing with. There are two sides to this story, he silently warned her, and made a mental note to make sure she saw it that way.

If he was hoping that her return would distract his children from their interrogation he was to be sadly disappointed. They weren't about to let the matter lie.

"I'm sorry, Dad," Enya pleaded, "but Ciara just said that Mum is not her mother. You can't expect us to let that go without explanation!"

William sighed. The only way to stop them plaguing him was to tell them the whole truth.

"Yes. Your mother is not Ciara's mother."

"Mum is not Ciara's mother?" Enya repeated slowly, trying to get her head around what he meant. "*How could that be?*" she almost shrieked, standing up in surprise.

"She's adopted?" Rian interpreted and, feeling Martha's hand find its way into his, he squeezed it tight.

"No," William replied, finally demonstrating an element of discomfort as the need to spell it out became apparent. "Ciara is my daughter, but not your mother's."

"Holy shit!" The words fell from Enya's mouth, followed by a burst of nervous laughter that quickly morphed into a solemn groan of melancholy. "Ciara," she whispered, falling back into the chair. "Oh Jesus!" she finished with her head in her hands.

"And us?" Rian asked.

With a sigh William shook his head. "Your mother is ..." He paused, realising how ridiculous he sounded, but with nowhere else to go with it finished his sentence, "well, your mother is your mother."

A snort masquerading as a laugh again escaped Enya, much to the annoyance of her father.

"So who is her mother?" Rian followed impassively, like conversations like this happened every day. He watched as their father took the question and processed it, probably wondering how he should answer: be direct and tell the truth or distract and point to another source for the truth, inevitably their mother. Rian could almost hear the cogs in motion behind those cold blue eyes and didn't expect him to answer. Turning from him to stop the queasiness, he walked to the window.

Now, he thought to himself, now it all makes sense: Ciara, his mother ...

"Can we not do this now? Please?" William asked, feeling genuinely weary.

"No, seriously, answer the question," Enya said, in a gentle but unrelenting tome. "Who is her mother? We deserve to know."

There was no point in holding on to it any longer; they were going to find out soon enough and it might as well be from him.

"Lillian," he answered. "Lillian was Ciara's mother."

Who the hell is Lillian? Enya was puzzled – the way he said her name it was like she should know her.

But Rian knew exactly who he was talking about.

"Lillian?" He spun to look back at William. "Lillian our nanny? Are you serious?"

But William was lying back, looking up to the ceiling.

"Jesus, Dad, she was so ... so bloody young ... she was there to care for us for God's sake!" He was too young to really remember her but what he could recall was that she was more like a big sister than a nanny. "How could you? I mean really, how? She was so young, like ..." He couldn't find the words and looked at Martha, embarrassed by the filthy secret being revealed in front of her. What must she think? But he couldn't tell; she held her head low, eyes to the floor.

"Good news, William," the nurse announced, entering the room, heading straight to the chart at the end of the bed. "Your tests have come back clear so we're good to operate tomorrow." Sensing the tension, she eyed William directly and judging the situation for what she understood it to be responded accordingly. "Okay. I'm afraid you all need to leave now. Your father needs his rest. We'll be operating first thing so he needs his strength."

She stood watch over them and waited while they gathered their belongings in silence and prepared to go. Rian led Martha out first without so much as a sideways glance back but Enya took her time, pausing at the door to look back at her father. He didn't see. His eyes were closed. But he felt her chilling stare wash over him.

William wasn't surprised when later that evening Ciara returned, just as he knew she would. He braced himself for what was likely to come. Notably calm and controlled, she pulled up the chair to his bedside and sat down, taking a moment to gather herself together before speaking.

"So, Dad," she enquired politely, "can you tell me who I am?"

The level tone of her voice wasn't what he had anticipated.

And Ciara wanted him to notice how calm she was, how controlled and neutral her tone was. She wanted it to register with him that she was trying to be mature and wasn't taking her usual often-hysterical approach even though, for once, she had every right to do exactly that. She wanted him to recognise that this time, this was different. She was different. And he needed to be different but honest in his response.

Come on, you can do it, she silently encouraged herself while preparing for the encounter. Surprise yourself, do something extraordinary, be different, it'll freak the hell out of him if nothing else.

Although outwardly calm and in control, inside she

was quivering like a plucked string on a fiddle. She knew what she needed to achieve and consciously made an effort to do something remarkable, for herself if no one else. Determined and focused, she trained her eyes on him and it was without venom.

William considered her for a minute then leaned forward in the bed. "Here," he said, "help me sit up," struggling a little to stay up and pushing himself forward as she moved in to fix his pillows. It was an intimate gesture purposely planned. He wanted her to feel like she had the upper hand and so presented her with the impression that he was the vulnerable one, in need of her care. It would help, he reasoned, to gain her sympathy and break down her anger – a tactical move he'd learnt in his early days in politics. Use your weakness to your benefit. And it worked.

"Is that okay?" she asked with a weak smile and a lingering hand on his arm.

He was ready. "Yes. Thank you." Then, lowering his eyes, he took a seemingly unsteady breath and began. "Your mother ..." he paused to immediately correct himself, glancing at her quickly, "Barbara . . . was telling the truth. She isn't your mother."

"So who was? She wouldn't tell me."

"Lillian – Lillian was your mother."

Ciara felt every drop of blood pump through her veins, her heart pulsing at full throttle while her breath caught in her chest as if she were sprinting a three-minute mile. All she knew of Lillian was that she had looked after the boys when they were little.

"She died shortly after you were born," he continued, his voice quiet, and pausing he waited for her response.

When it didn't come he kept going. "She drowned, in a swimming accident."

He had, William assumed, given her sufficient information to trigger a barrage of questions, but she remained composed and neutral in her chair. The only signs of distress were the white pressure-lines around her tightly pursed lips. Nodding slowly, accepting his words, she silently indicated for him to continue.

"Your mother ... Barbara," he again swiftly revised, "and I thought it was best that we took you on."

He knew as soon as they were out that, although true, it was an unfortunate choice of words and registered their effect through the instant fall of her eyes and tight balling of her fists. But still she remained silent.

"Best for you," he qualified and as if to justify their decision to her. Putting her control further to the test, he challenged her. "I'm not sure you quite grasp what that meant for us, what we did for you."

Ciara brought her clasped hands to her face and closed her eyes. Counting each breath, slowly, creating a hypnotic rhythm. *One ... two ... three* ... slowly she counted, unwilling to let herself down.

Please, she begged herself, just this one time, keep it together. And only when she was ready, certain she could remain composed, did she open her eyes again.

William, becoming more unnerved by her uncharacteristic quiescence, scanned her body language from head to toe, searching for the usual tell-tale signs of discomposure: redness around her neck, puffing of her cheeks, and jittery movement of her legs. It was always easy to detect when she was out of control. But they weren't there. It was as if she were hypnotised, like she'd taken something, but when he caught her stare there was no denying her eyes were clear and focused.

"But I am yours?" she asked him directly without letting go of his gaze.

"Yes," he replied.

"You are my father," she solicited steadily.

"Yes, I said. Yes," he told her, losing degrees of his cool, unnerved by her behaviour. "Barbara wanted to do it, to take you. I was against it from the start. I thought you should be with your birth mother. After Lillian died, I thought it best for everyone that you should go to her family, her mother. I knew this day would come. But Barbara insisted."

"So you didn't want me?" she challenged, placing him firmly into the emotional quicksand.

"That's not what I said. Well, not what I meant." The more he tried to weasel his way out the deeper he sank. "I wanted what was best for you, as a child. I simply thought you should be with your birth mother – or, failing that, with her family."

"So, what, it's Mum's fault, all this, is that it? You had nothing to do with it?"

William didn't know what to say. She was on form, dancing round him, making him say things he didn't mean or want to say.

"Does it even matter now?" he protested awkwardly, uncomfortable under her intense scrutiny. "What's done is done. We can't go back and change anything."

"It matters to me. This is my identity we're talking about, not some stranger. It's me."

Reasoning that as Ciara already had issues with Barbara he could see no harm in placing responsibility firmly on her doorstep, he offered her a version of the truth that would be a means to his own end.

"Well, if we're being honest here, then yes, it was her fault really. You know your mother when she gets an idea into her head."

"So if she didn't want me, you were happy to let me go?"

He didn't answer, he couldn't. She had backed him into a corner and right then and not for the first time he wished she was never born.

"You just can't help yourself, can you?" she laughed. "This had nothing to do with Mum at all, did it? This is about you not being able to keep it to yourself. This is about your mistake that Mum, God love her, tried to make right. This is about Mum making up for you being a prize shit. That's what this is." Her voice was measured and her tone dismissive.

Neither heard the knock at the door, nor did they notice the nurse and an orderly stall at the threshold as they registered Ciara's words.

"I'll never forgive you for this." She was matter of fact, like a schoolmistress addressing an unruly teenager. "Do you know that? All these years you made me feel like a piece of shit. All these years trying to be something I already am. I am a person, and a good one at that. All these years trying to impress you, trying to make you notice me. I loved you so much all I wanted was you two to be my mum and dad, to behave like proper parents and at least pretend to love me back. I watched you pick any one of the others over me. You isolated me, made me feel so inferior."

"Please, lower your voice," the nurse said sternly, placing a hand on Ciara's arm.

Ciara ignored the attempted intervention without as much as a glance back at the nurse. "This isn't Mum's fault at all. No wonder she's a bitter twisted bitch, married to you all these years. You don't love her. You don't love any of us. The only person you give a shit about is yourself."

"Right. That's enough!" the nurse interjected emphatically, trying to take control of a scene that was degenerating in front of her.

Ignoring her completely, Ciara continued on her charge. "You think I don't know about all the others. We all know. You're about as discreet as a nun in a whorehouse. But you are the whore. You don't deserve me, you don't deserve any of us."

"I *said* that's enough!" the nurse said. "And if you don't leave by yourself I will ask security to help you."

Ciara didn't resist any further. She got to her feet and allowed herself to be almost pushed from the room, her breathing erratic. Once outside she leaned against the wall to steady herself.

On instruction, one of the nurses stayed with her and, cognisant of her delicate state, asked, "Are you okay?" Her tone was gentle and brimming with concern. They were used to seeing families at loggerheads and knew there was always two sides to every story.

Ciara nodded, afraid that if she opened her mouth she might cry.

"Look, I know it's none of my business, but your dad is really quite an ill man. Do you really want him to leave him now like this? You don't need me to tell you that these could be the last words you speak to him. Are they really the ones you want to remember him with?"

Ciara looked at her, too ashamed to admit that yes, they were just that.

Sitting in the sickly yellow corridor with its brash and flickering fluorescent strip lighting and that stomach-churning smell, she held her head firmly in her hands and asked herself again: *Is this really what I want? To leave him with those horrible words, to have the last thing I ever utter to him be so vile? Am I prepared to live with the guilt if he dies, if I never get to see him again?* This was the man she had spent all these years idolising and shadowing like the lost puppy she was. Had she changed that much? Was she willing to take that risk? With her thoughts in chaos, feeling so alone, she cried tears for her mother and for herself.

Despite the distance down the corridor she could still feel his presence and it made her skin crawl. She needed to get as far away from here, from him, as possible.

She rose to her feet and hurried down the corridor, oblivious to the attempts of the nurse to detain her.

She ran from the hospital and out into the fresh air. Ignoring her car, she turned and walked. Driving was too normal and she couldn't imagine doing anything normal, not now, not today. Today her normal had changed.

The faster she walked the quicker they came, the questions, relentless, one after the other, like little grenades going off inside her head. She knew almost nothing about Lillian. Nobody talked about her – why would they? To everyone else she was just one of their nannies from years ago. Wanting a baby so badly she couldn't understand how anyone could willingly give their child away. Why? By the way her father spoke about it Ciara guessed Lillian wasn't given much of a choice and, knowing him and his gruff manner, as a theory it didn't sound that incredible. Maybe she did want to keep her after all but they forced her to walk away from her baby? There was only one person who could answer her questions and that was Lillian herself. But Lillian was dead.

Chapter 23

There were few people who managed to unnerve William Bertram but Kathryn Bertram was one of them. She knocked on the door early on the morning of his discharge and entered without waiting for a reply. As always she looked incredible in her slim-fitting grey-and-black knee-high dress, her legs long and luscious in sheer tights and black patent high heels.

"William," she said as she entered, "how are you feeling? I hear surgery went well."

"Kathryn," William responded, sitting up a little higher in the bed, surprised by her arrival. Of all his well-wishers he least expected her, his eldest son's wife whom he entertained as a necessary irritant only because he couldn't get past the formidable and seemingly impervious aura she cast around herself.

"A frigid bitch" was how he described her within his close circle but, to her face as was required, he was his charming self.

At this point in his convalescence he was almost beyond vulnerable embarrassment but, for some reason in front of Kathryn, lying there in bed still dressed in his pyjamas he felt exposed. And she knew it.

"You're looking much better," she remarked.

Much better than when, he wondered.

"You've obviously got a lot of fans," she said, acknowledging the impressive abundance of flowers. Taking an uninvited moment she explored the colourful array of cards on the window ledge, the height of her eyebrows a good indication of recognition for the senders. "Popular guy," she mumbled.

William watched her progress from his bed. He could see why Seb had married her, but for the life of him he could never understand why she had married him.

"I'm here to say goodbye," she informed him casually as she moved from one card to the next. "In case you're wondering."

"I'm delighted for you, but I'm not quite dead yet," he half joked to which, in response, she threw her eyes to heaven.

"William, have you ever considered that not everything is about you? Me. I'm going. Leaving. Not you."

"Really?" This time it was his turn to raise his eyebrows. "Anywhere nice?" he asked politely, intrigued by the innuendo.

"The States. New York actually. I've been appointed as research fellow in the University Hospital there."

"Congratulations," he replied, now honestly interested. "And Seb?" he asked nonchalantly.

She laughed wildly. "Really? I take it then you haven't spoken to him."

"No," he replied, "I can't say that I have, nor, it seems, have you spoken to your husband about me."

"Christ, what have you done now?" she asked sardonically but, not really interested in his response, quickly brought the conversation back on topic. "To answer your question, no. Seb isn't coming with me. I'm going alone."

Interesting, William thought, not in the least bit worried that he felt more pleasure than pain at his son's apparently impending separation.

"So you'll travel back and forth then?" he probed.

"Don't be an idiot, William," she scoffed. "No, I won't be *travelling back and forth,*" she mimicked while William tried to look surprised. "I'm leaving him. I'm not coming back, not immediately anyhow."

"Does he know?"

Again she laughed. "He most certainly does," she replied, thinking about their farewell drink and the bank statement that he had probably found by now, wondering which he would miss more, her or his money.

"And so you thought of me?" William enquired, curious to know why she was here. Now.

"Call it tying up loose ends."

"Of which I'm one?" he replied, fascinated by their exchange and its ultimate purpose.

"I've been a part of this family now for what ...?" She paused to theatrically add up the years. "Must be over fifteen years now." She sat into the visitor's chair and crossed her shapely legs, aware of the effect they had, especially on someone like him. Like father like son, she supposed deviously and, smiling inwardly at his impulsive and slightly repulsive honeyed glance, she continued, "And in all those years I've seen how you operate."

William raised his eyes in response, getting a good sense that she wasn't here to sing either his or his son's praises.

"I've watched how you run your children, torment your wife and quite honestly lord over your constituents and so often I've wanted to tell you what I think but out of respect I've said nothing."

"Until now," he interjected with a bittersweet grin, bracing himself, his adrenaline rising, priming for the game to begin.

She smiled and nodded, "Until now. Call it my swan song."

"I can hardly wait."

"Typical William," she mocked. "Always manipulating, always working. Can't wait, my backside! Admit it, William, beyond that charming, smiling exterior you're frantically trying to second-guess me. Well, in this instance I'm sorry to disappoint. There's no great mystery. All I'm doing here is pointing out the obvious."

"And that is?" he asked.

"And that is that you are a selfish, controlling swine."

"Is that it? Actually, I take that as a compliment."

"I assumed you would," Kathryn replied, "and that's what makes it so abundantly devastating that you would think that terrorising and marginalising your own family and the people who bizarrely care about you is a good thing."

"Well, thank you so much for your thoughts," William told her, doing his best to assert his self-appointed potency from his hospital bed. "If you're done, feel free to leave, close the door behind you and have a safe flight."

In the absence of retaliation she knew she'd found some kind of kink in his armour. "Don't try to dismiss me, William. I'm not one of your submissive children. I'm not going to roll over and bark. I actually bite. And don't you forget it."

"Are you threatening me?" he asked her with venom in his eyes.

"Good God, no! I'm not threatening you – just warning you. That's all."

William threw his head back against his pillow and laughed as if it were the most entertaining thing he'd heard in years.

"You're a piece of work, sitting there with your long legs, dressed up like some kind of high-class hooker. You don't scare me. You might take on that prim stuck-up-bitch attitude with your husband but it won't work on me. So why don't you take yourself and your friendly advice off to somewhere and someone else that actually gives a shit."

"William," she said in an apologetic tone, delighted to have ruffled his feathers and not in the least bit affected by his snide remarks, "I'm only expressing what everyone else is just dying to say but they're all simply too damn scared to open their fearful little lips." She stood up to go, smoothed down her skirt and stood tall. "For some reason you hold people to emotional ransom and now that I've taught two of your sons a very expensive lesson and have absolutely nothing to lose, I'm happy to confirm to your face that you are an unbelievable asshole and one day soon the karma of your manipulative and frankly evil endeavours will come back to bite you. Hard, I hope."

She walked to the door but before leaving stopped and turned.

"I suspect," she warned with a grin, "you're in for a little bit of a shock and when you get it I want you to think of me." Blowing him a kiss she made to leave, almost crashing into Barbara who was on her way in.

“Barbara,” she greeted her and kissed her on each cheek. ”I’m just saying goodbye. William will no doubt explain.”

Confused, Barbara stood back to let her leave, looking on in surprise as Kathryn threw a final wink back at a beautifully dumbstruck William.

Part Two

Chapter 24

Martha was an only child. It hadn't always been like that but, after her brother and not long after her older sister died, it was just herself and her mum. Although she tried every day to maintain the mental image of her sister, after so many years Martha could just about remember her. Her most vivid memory was of her in her purple coat with a pink scarf wrapped around her long hair pulled back in a tidy bun, stepping onto the bus the day she left to start her big job in the city. She remembered her mother's tears and gushing pride. For weeks she could talk of nothing else to her friends and neighbours: her brave and grown-up daughter who seemed to mature almost overnight. Although they both missed her they knew she had no option but to go.

Two years had passed since their father left for England in search of work. Every day for years her mother went to the small cottage post office at the end of their lane to ask them to check, and check again, for a letter from him until one day she just didn't bother. Two years without a word.

With no idea if he were alive or dead, they struggled to make ends meet so it made perfect sense for her sister, just like so many of her friends, to forgo her education in favour of a wage.

She had only just left when her brother was knocked down and killed. He was only thirteen and on his way home from school. 'Big school'. They said he ran across the road without looking but Martha didn't believe it for a minute. No, he was likely just another tragic victim of a careless driver on the road, a child from the flats that was dispensable, an accident that no one bothered to look into. Someone saw him, they said, running without taking heed of the traffic. But he always looked and made her look too, every time. Her sister couldn't come home for the funeral, she couldn't take the time from work, but when she did come, two weeks later, they all clung together and cried for their brother and son.

Martha's memories of her sister were scant. Without a picture to remember her by, she had to rely on her young and immature memory to recall her face. In her mind's eye her sister had been as tall as her mam and just as slim with narrow shoulders and a long straight-down kind of body, as straight as her hair. But in Martha's mind, her sister's pretty face had matured with augmenting soft focus, blurring more and more around the edges until eventually there was little definition left, just an indistinct pale smudge resting on straight shoulders.

She and her mother weren't told of her death until after she was buried. A tragic accident, they were told, and despite Martha pleading with her distraught mother to visit the grave, she refused, unable to accept that her daughter was gone.

Martha never understood why her mother insisted on blaming herself.

"I shouldn't have let her go," she cried desperately. "I should have let her stay right here. We could have found a way. We could have survived."

Inconsolable and taken over by her grief, she found solace neither inside nor outside the house. Martha tried hard to make her smile again. She tried to make up for her profound loss, but her mother was unresponsive to her desperate, often agonising attempts to connect and day-by-day slipped deep into a world where only she and her dead children existed. Alone.

Martha, helpless and useless, wanted nothing more than for her mother to come back to her: the child that still lived. But no matter what she did she couldn't disperse the gloom that like a shroud seemed to settle over her comatose mother and their little terraced house. The day her brother and sister died a piece of both Martha and her mother died too but, while Martha was young with her whole life ahead of her, it was different for her mother. The part of her that died was her will to live.

For months that persistent shroud sheltered them sufficiently to block out any sunshine that might have existed around them until eventually, for her mother, it smothered her completely.

Almost seven months later her mother passed away, from what their family doctor described as a broken heart. Martha had woken up one morning to find her lying cold and stiff in her bed.

A bitter poison seemed to take hold of Martha that day: at ten years of age she had been abandoned, left to fend for herself by everyone. Was she invisible? Was she that worthless? Did she not matter? Did anyone even care? Apparently the answer to each of her questions was *yes* with a single *no*.

Initially she had refused to leave the house. It was where she belonged. Just because they had discarded her, first her father, then her brother followed by her sister and now her dear mother, that didn't mean she should be punished by taking the only constant in her young life: her home. But, as she packed up what few belongings she had and was taken into care, it seemed that she should.

Martha moved from foster family to care home but she could never settle, deeply unhappy and confounded as to why and how she had ended up so alone.

"You're just not a very lucky lady, that's all," she was told with genuine sympathy by one of her many minders who polished, swept and cleaned around her. "Some of us," she told her with matter-of-fact precision, "are destined never to be blessed with happiness."

It was assumed that since she had been told to accept it, she should. And when she couldn't let their memory go, rather than help her they ignored her. In *the system*, it seemed, the only way to be noticed was to kick off: the bold ones got all the attention. But she was one of the quiet ones, never caused any trouble, never spoke out of turn, did what she was told and so faded into the background like whitewash in the snow.

Chapter 25

1982

The day she turned sixteen she once again packed up her things and left the care of the state to venture out into the world. All by herself. Again.

"Well, Martha," Helen, the Head of House, said to her least troublesome charge with a reassuring smile, "I've arranged a place for you with the Sisters of Mercy Nursing College. It's live-in so you won't need to worry about a place to stay. Here," she said, handing her a piece of paper with the address written down, "ask for Sister Josephine, she's expecting you."

With no other choice, Martha took it.

"Thanks, Helen," she replied, looking down at the handwritten note, not knowing what she should do next.

"Come on," Helen encouraged her, getting up from behind the desk.

Leading her from her make-do home-office with an arm around her shoulder, she walked her down the hall and out to the front door.

"Now. You have money in the envelope I gave you earlier. Don't lose it. and, if you need me, you can always come and see me, or give me a call."

Sensing Martha's nervous reluctance, she turned to

stand in front of the vulnerable young lady about to embark on the next chapter of her life. Placing a firm hand on each shoulder she gave her a squeeze, smiling affectionately as she lowered her head to chase and catch her gaze.

"You need to go now and make something of yourself. Show them they're wrong. You can be great, you *will* be great. You know that, don't you?"

Martha nodded with tears in her eyes.

"Well, go on! Be brilliant."

Helen watched her walk down the street towards the bus stop with her small check suitcase and silently wished her well.

It was peculiar to no longer be answerable to anyone. Martha didn't think she'd like it but nursing surprised her. She relished the idea that she was needed and was able to make a real difference, do something positive. And she was good at it.

"You've a lovely manner about you," the Matron remarked on her first day on the wards. "They'll like you." She nodded towards the old dears who dribbled uncontrollably in their beds.

The training-college boarding house was old-fashioned and rundown. It was managed by Elizabeth, an old spinster battle-axe the girls affectionately named Bad Betty. It smelled of cats and damp fabric but the new friendships she made with the rest of the girls in the house made up for the stench and the bad-tempered old bat. She shared a room with the maddest of them all: Joan. Like Martha, she had been in care since she was young, having run away from home, refusing to return to her abusive father and drunken mother. She too couldn't believe her newfound independence. Bonding immediately, they quickly became inseparable.

February 1983

When Martha asked Joan to make the trip to visit her sister's grave she was flattered and didn't hesitate for even an instant.

They left early on a misty Friday morning, making their way by bus into the city centre where they picked up the train that traversed the country, stopping in almost every town along the route, to the county of Donegal. It took forever. With the name of the town, Ballybeak, indelibly etched into her brain from the many times she heard her mother repeat it, over and over, Martha knew exactly where she was going and had worked their journey out, step by step, on the map.

On their way, sitting at the back of another rickety old green bus whose suspension had seen better times, going where they were going, it was impossible not to recall the day they were told of her sister's passing. At the time, she remembered, her mother wouldn't accept it was Lillian at all.

"Sure what was she doing there?" she asked, confused. "Isn't she working in Dublin, in that big fancy house? What would she be doing in the depths of Donegal?" But there was no one else to ask, no one to tell her why. A simple woman, it just wasn't in her mother's nature to question the authorities further, so with no other option apparent to her, she had to take them at their word and accept it.

It took what felt like days for them to get there along the narrow, potholed roads that tossed them about like rag dolls in the back of that little green bus. Nauseous and tired, the girls were both glad and lucky to arrive in one piece. The bus passed the cemetery on its way into the town.

"That must be it," Joan whispered over her shoulder, immediately setting off the butterflies in Martha's tummy.

"Must be," she answered, looking back at its stone wall which was just about visible in the failing light as the bus chugged past. She had waited all this time; another final night wouldn't make that much of a difference.

At a glance Ballybeak consisted of a single road that ran through its centre with a church at one end and a pub masquerading as a shop at the other. It didn't take long to find their Bed and Breakfast, sandwiched between two fast-food restaurants, halfway down the street. The day had turned into a dark, cold and eerily quiet evening, leaving the girls feeling much less brave than when they'd set out that morning.

In their room that night, Joan worked hard to keep the mood upbeat with her wild stories of the various foster homes she'd passed through. Some of the stories Martha had never heard before, others she'd listened to several times over but they were so outrageous and entertaining she was happy to hear them again. And Joan was a natural raconteur, transforming some truly toe-curling horrific episodes into hilarious comedic adventures. It was her defence mechanism, Martha knew that.

"You should write a book, do you know that?" she said to her friend when the giggles died down.

"Nah," Joan replied, lying on the bed with her hands

behind her head, "I couldn't be arsed," the comment triggering another round of uncontrollable laughter and a loud batter on the wall from the guest in the next room.

"Keep it down in there! Some of us are trying to sleep!"

The girls only laughed harder and louder.

When finally Joan could chatter no more, Martha closed her eyes to the darkness and tried to remember the face of her sister, but it refused to come. She tried to piece it together bit by bit: blue eyes, yellow hair with natural gold highlights that glistened in the sun, eyebrows that moved with the rise and fall of her voice and a smile that lit up her face like sunshine. But the image refused to coalesce.

Falling asleep as the birds were beginning their dawn chorus, it felt like seconds before she was dragged out of the bed and down to breakfast by a well-rested Joan.

"Jesus, I slept like a log. You?" Joan asked as she wolfed down the deliciously greasy Irish breakfast with all the trimmings: beans, mushrooms, tomatoes.

"We won't need to eat for a week, eh?" she remarked between mouthfuls without taking her hungry eyes from the plate.

"You'd swear you hadn't eaten in weeks," Martha joked, watching her stuff her face.

"You're not hungry?" Joan enquired and, without waiting for her answer, pulled Martha's plate closer to pick from it what she fancied.

They washed after breakfast then walked down the street towards the church which was set into the hill and surrounded by a low wall. They pushed open the heavy metal gates that whined in objection. Laughing nervously at the Amityville cliché, the girls walked along the pebble path to the back of the grey granite building. It was a sufficiently small town cemetery and didn't take them long to find the stone they had come to see. Plain and unadorned, flat and grey, a stone edifice emerging as if growing from the soil with her name etched simply in plain black letters. In front of it, lying delicately on its side, lay a small posy of daisies tied up with string.

Slowly Martha slipped to her knees and ran her fingers across the words cut deep in the cold slab. She'd thought she would cry, had expected tears to flood down her face but they never came. Instead she felt an incredible weight lift and her heart fill with a bizarre feeling of joyful release. Finally she was here and able to say hello and goodbye to the sister she barely remembered and hardly knew.

"Are ye relatives?" a gruff voice asked from behind them.

Both girls jumped and turned. Behind them stood a woman who looked like she had seen better times, her hair a tangled mess and her face grubby with grime from God only knew what. She held tight on to a variety of different shopping bags, each full to bursting with stuff. She looked down at Martha with suspicion.

"Yes, I'm her sister," Martha replied cautiously, wondering who she was.

"She didn't tell me she had a sister."

"You knew her?" Martha was immediately on her feet.

"For a while, a short while," the raggedy lady chortled, nodding her head with a rueful smile. "I knew her all right. I knew all them girls. Terrible waste."

"What happened to her?" Martha asked.

"Not very close then?" the woman retorted sceptically, taking a step back, her guard raised once again along with the return of the suspicious look.

"I was only nine," Martha told her. "Too little to know. And we didn't find out until after they buried her here."

Martha sadly looked down at the lush green grass, letting the soft sound of the wind whisper to her as it chased through the headstones into the trees.

"Where was the accident?" she asked eventually. "Where did she drown?"

"Over yonder," the lady relayed, using her head to demonstrate the direction of yonder. "Along the Golden Strand. But you'll have to ask them bitches in the big house what happened. 'Snot up ta me." She sniffed while shifting the bags between hands then turned to get on her way. "But I'll tell ya this much, lassie – 'twas no accident."

"No accident?" Joan repeated after her. "What does that mean?"

But the woman ignored her and began to walk away.

Martha hurried after her and reached out to stop her, placing her hand on the old woman's arm.

"Please, tell me what you mean?"

"Get your dirty mitts off me!" the woman shouted, lifting her make-shift walking stick defensively at Martha who jumped back to avoid being walloped.

They let her go and watched as, mumbling to herself, she waddled between the graves to the other side of the cemetery and out to the field beyond.

"Well, that was weird!" Joan remarked. "She was a bundle of laughs. What the hell did she mean by that?" She looked at Martha who was still watching the woman disappear from sight. "And where is this big house?"

Martha shivered. "We can always ask someone," she suggested, looking round at the empty graveyard before kneeling back down in front of the simple headstone.

"Well, we'll not get an answer in here," said Joan. "Let's ask at the pub – don't they always know everyone's business?"

"Can we stay just a little bit longer?" Martha asked, reluctant to leave.

"Sure. We can stay as long as you want," Joan said, plonking herself down beside her friend.

Together they let the serene calm of the country graveyard settle around them.

Martha and Joan marched off together, across the road and down the hill.

I'll be back later for a proper chat, Martha silently promised the spirit of her sister, who she hoped was somewhere watching and listening.

The walk to Donegan's Pub didn't take long and even at that early hour of the morning it was open and with good custom. Each of the patrons turned as the door opened and the two young girls walked the short distance to the bar that ran the full width of the thatched building.

Once her eyes adjusted to the dreary darkness, Martha took stock of the room, which smelled of stale beer and cigarettes.

A short, round man polishing a glass looked curiously at them from behind the counter.

"Can I help you there, ladies?" he called with humour in his voice, and a *watch-this* glance at his customers, like they had wandered in unwittingly and would be mortified by their mistake.

Confidently Martha approached the bar, unaware of the entertainment their presence was generating.

"I wonder if you could help us? We're looking for the 'big house'?"

He looked at them like they were speaking a foreign language. "Are ye serious?"

Martha looked nervously at Joan who shrugged her shoulders, equally confused.

"Yes," she answered cautiously, afraid she'd done something wrong.

"Well," he said, putting down the glass and leaning onto the bar with his elbow, "that'd be the big house at the end of the road there. Go out the door, look right and sure there it is, like the name says, the big house, right at the top o' the hill in front of ye." He waved his arms with a flourish, his voice laced with sarcasm.

Sniggers rippled through the dark and smoky room. Both girls blushed.

"What do ye want up there?" he asked, intrigued and feeling a little sorry for them and his mockery.

"My sister was there. I think she might have stayed there."

"Have ye lost her an' come to find her?" he asked kindly now.

"No," Martha replied bluntly and without thinking. "She's dead."

A deep pull of breath sucked the air from the room.

"I'm so sorry for your loss," he told her, standing upright and bowing his head at her, in a gesture of sympathy.

"Please, don't be. It was a very long time ago. I ... we're only here to see where she's buried." The room now fully attentive. "Me and my mam, we never got to say goodbye."

She spoke with such innocence that each patron in the bar felt like they had slapped those girls one by one with their ridicule.

In the resulting uncomfortable silence a man got off his stool and stepped towards them.

"Let me take you up," he offered.

"Good man, Jimmy lad," the barman commended. "Come back when you're done up there, ladies, and I'll make ye a nice hot Irish whiskey!"

"Thank you," both girls said in unison as Jimmy held the door open for them.

"So," he asked as he walked them up the road, "you say your sister stayed here?"

"Well, I think so – I only remember the name from when I was young," Martha replied cheerfully as Joan struggled with her tired legs and full stomach.

Sensing their complete ignorance, he asked tentatively, "Do you know about this house?"

"What do you mean?" Martha asked, her feet pounding the path.

"Well, has anyone told you about what things happened here, maybe when your sister was here?"

"No," said Martha uncertainly.

"Do you know how long she stayed?"

"No, but then I never asked. I think she was here on a holiday. She died in a swimming accident. So what kinds of things are you talking about that happened here?"

"What was yer sister's name?" Jimmy asked as casually as he could. Girls from the big house came and went. They hardly ever saw any of them in the flesh. They were just silhouettes in the windows. But girls who died in swimming accidents were rare and to his knowledge there was only ever one.

"Lillian Byrne," she replied, taking no heed of the brief stumbling pause in his pace.

They walked the rest of the way in silence, through the gates and up the weed-infested gravel drive, clearly in need of attention. As was the house: it stood gigantic, rambling and grey. A daunting cheerless place that made Martha shiver and wonder just what Lillian had been doing there.

A chill wind passed over them, prompting Joan to take hold of Martha's arm.

"Jesus," she whispered, like talking was forbidden, "this makes Butlin's feel like the feckin' Ritz."

"Can't say I'm liking this place much either," Martha replied as they reached the front door.

Jimmy leaned forward to press the doorbell which echoed loudly on the far side of the door. They didn't have to wait long before they heard the rush of feet and the pull of a bolt.

A grey-haired woman wearing an apron and a scowl pulled the door open.

"What is it?" she growled.

"I think these ladies are here to see Gráinne."

She looked at them quizzically then back at Jimmy. "What for?" she snapped. He didn't bother to answer. Turning to the girls, he shook Joan's hand first then gripped Martha's tightly, placing his other hand over it.

"Good luck now," he said, his voice soft and his smile meek. "Please, come back down for that whiskey when you're done." Then he turned and left.

They watched him go.

"I think he likes you," Joan joked with a giggle before they turned their attention back to the aproned lady grimacing at them in the doorway.

"Well?" she said with a snap that made them jump. "I haven't got all day."

Without knowing what else to say, Martha took Jimmy's lead. "We're here to see Gráinne."

"And who," she asked smartly, "might *we* be?"

"I'm Martha Byrne, and this is my friend Joan McCarthy."

"Wait here," the woman instructed, shutting the door in their faces.

"Bloody hell," Joan huffed. "She's a real cow. A million times worse than Bad Betty. And that's sayin' something."

They waited in silence at the door for what seemed an age, soberly taking in the miserable surroundings, before footsteps and muffled voices were heard again. The door opened for a second time and this time a woman who introduced herself as Gráinne greeted them.

"Come in," she invited with a smile. "You shouldn't have left them out here, Ita!" She threw the grumpy woman a chastising glare then stood aside to let the girls into the bare and hollow hallway. Sunlight struggled to get through the cracked and wired skylight overhead, making it dank and intimidating.

"Let's go where we can have a chat," Gráinne directed pleasantly and marched them at a smart pace down a corridor that led deep into the bowels of the house.

Joan and Martha struggled to keep up while Ita, thankfully, appeared to lose herself somewhere along the route. Trotting behind Gráinne, the sound of their footsteps bounced off the floor to the walls and back again. They almost ran into the back of her ample bottom when suddenly she stopped and turned into one of the many doors lining the route. Unlocking it, she led them into a cosy sitting room, with a small sash window that overlooked the avenue.

"Come in, take a seat," Gráinne invited as she went from lamp to lamp, turning them on to bring a warm glow to the room which smelled delightfully of vanilla. A clock ticked loudly, sitting on one of the book-lined shelves.

Both girls sank into the old-fashioned sofa whose springs it seemed had given up long before, while Gráinne took the wing-back chair opposite.

"So," she enquired looking from one to the other, "you're here to talk to me?"

"Yes," Joan offered, glancing at Martha. "We'd like to ask you about Lillian Byrne. She was Martha's sister. We came to see her grave. She'd never seen it before." Joan nodded towards her silent friend.

Gráinne looked to Martha with a sympathetic expression. "What can I tell you?" she asked kindly.

"Why was she here?" Martha asked nervously. "Lillian, I mean. Why did she stay here?"

Leaning forward, Gráinne took her hand and with a sympathetic tone said, "I didn't know your sister. She must have been here before my time, but she was likely here for the same reason as most of our girls. She had a baby."

"A baby!" Joan gasped.

Martha shook her head. She suspected as soon as they

started their trek from the front door that this wasn't a place anyone would come on holidays and that there was another, less pleasant reason for Lillian being here. But this? A baby? Gráinne must be confusing her sister with someone else.

"No, we're here to ask about Lillian Byrne. She was here but she died." Martha hoped her loose explanation might put Gráinne straight and get the right girl in mind. "I can tell you when," and, closing her eyes, she recited the date. "It was the 15th of September 1975."

Her eyes opened and she waited expectantly for Gráinne to stand corrected.

"Well, I'm not one-hundred-per-cent sure and it was certainly before my time – I can check for you if you have the right date – but," Gráinne paused, assessing the innocent young girls, Martha in particular, to make sure they were fit to understand what they had come to find out, "to the best of my knowledge there were very few girls who came here for any other reason but to have their baby."

"But why here?" Martha questioned. "Why not a hospital?"

"Well, there were lots of reasons why," Gráinne told them, "but mostly it was because many of the girls weren't married and had no one to look after them."

"Well, that couldn't have been Lillian," Martha told her categorically, "because we could have looked after her. Me and my mam. And anyway I don't think she had a boyfriend."

Her endearing naivety touched Gráinne. "You need to remember," she explained gently, "that girls don't like to be unmarried and pregnant – some feel huge shame and embarrassment. Maybe your sister didn't want you to know she was pregnant at all."

"Not Lillian," Martha insisted, sitting bolt upright and shaking her head. "My sister wouldn't have hidden away here. We would have helped her, she would have known that."

Sensing that maybe a little time to think was in order, Gráinne got up.

"I'll go and check," she said. "Tell me again when she was here."

"It was 1975," Martha said. "That was the year she died too. Like I said, the 15th of September."

"I'm sorry, dear. Let me see what I can find. Can I get you girls some tea, or maybe a mineral while you wait?"

"No, thanks," they replied in unison and watched her leave the room.

"What the hell is she suggesting?" Joan whispered indignantly. "Do you think Lillian was having a baby?"

But Martha didn't reply, too preoccupied and worried about what Gráinne was going to come back with. Inside her head the questions came and went.

Why was Lillian buried here? Who decided that? Why wasn't her mother asked where she would like her to be laid to rest? And if she was having a baby, where was it? Where was the baby? Did he or she die too? Oh, good Jesus! Maybe she could ask.

She only realised she was thinking aloud when she noticed Joan looking on, her mouth agape.

"But I can't. I'm too scared," she finished with tears gathering in her eyes and, leaning into her best friend, laid her head on her shoulder and cried.

Hours seemed to pass before Gráinne returned, cradling

a large box in her hands. She placed it on the coffee table.

"Well, I think I found your sister," she told them, averting her eyes, looking instead at the dusty old box on the table, pushing it toward them. "Look – it's got her name on the top."

LILLIAN BYRNE was written in blue block letters on the top and on one side. "These are a few of her things that somehow never made their way to you."

"We never got anything," Martha replied timidly, staring at it like it might move if she stared long enough.

Her sister's name vibrated against the discoloured cardboard. Her things. This was all she had left yet it was more than she had ever had of her. Touching it, Martha was sure she could feel her sister's breath on her skin and the touch of her hand on her cheek. Closing her eyes, she could sense her; she was so close right now, here in this sitting room, with her. Martha squeezed her eyes tighter and for the first time in as long as she could remember could see her sister's face as clear as if she were standing there in front of her. Relief and joy filled her. She didn't want to open her eyes in case the image never returned. She concentrated on the shape of her face, absorbing the colour of her skin, the pitch of her cheekbones, the curve of her lips and the sweep of her long yellow hair. Only when she was sure that she had etched her features indelibly into her memory did she open her eyes only to close them again quickly just to see and, yes, there she was again, set against the blackness of her eyes and she was smiling.

Martha opened her eyes again and pulled the box to her.

"Do you want to do this here?" Joan asked, to which Martha nodded.

Lifting the lid, a musty smell hit her nostrils. Inside, it appeared, were items from the top of a dressing table. She pulled first from the box a small tatty old photo frame with a picture of herself, Tommy and Lillian, taken not long before she left, their happy faces grinning out at her. If only they knew what fortunes were to follow that picture! A brown wooden hairbrush and mirror set. A little box that looked like it had at some time held something precious but was empty now. A bottle of perfume that still had some liquid in it and a container of sweet scented powder with a little pink puff and a perfectly tied bow on top. And at the very bottom of the box was a bundle of letters tied together with a blue ribbon. From the handwriting on the first envelope she could see that they were letters from her mother. She ran a gentle hand across the ink. Her mother and her sister present in the one spot. She missed them so much. She could almost smell her mother's perfume and hear the sound of her voice telling her to "*buck up, whist and stop those tears*". She tried but she couldn't stop them falling.

Joan's hand rubbed her back in a gentle circular motion while she cooed, reassuring her quietly.

"Can I have these?" Martha asked Gráinne when she had cried herself dry, wiping her nose with the back of her hand.

"Absolutely," Gráinne replied. "They're yours now. I'm only sorry it took until now for you to get them."

Removing the picture from its old frame she placed it into the sleeve inside her purse. Now she would never forget what she looked like. Replacing everything else into the box, she secured the lid and placed it back on the table.

Gráinne stood, suggesting their visit was over. Looking up at her neither girl moved, both with the same question on their minds.

"But what about her baby?" Joan asked.

"I'm sorry?" Gráinne asked.

"The baby. My sister's baby," Martha urged. "What did she have? Was it a boy or a girl?"

"Well ... I don't really know," Gráinne said, her hands clasped tight in front of her.

"What happened to it?" Martha asked, cringing as she said 'it' like it meant nothing. But it did. "After my sister died what happened to her baby? Why did no one tell Mam?"

"Again, I can't tell you ... I don't know."

"But you must know." Martha's voice shook but she persisted. "You have to know. If it was here, you must know where it went, who took it!"

Shifting on her feet Gráinne cast her eyes to the floor and cleared her throat. When she looked up again she appeared composed, her poise recovered.

"Everything that is here about your sister I have given to you," she said. "There is no file. The nuns who were here didn't really operate that way."

"Someone here must know – there must be records," Joan challenged.

Gráinne shook her head solemnly.

"Well, who can we ask?" Joan demanded, standing up so she could look at her properly in the eye. "Who will know?"

"It was usual for the women who came here to have

their babies adopted." Her eyes refused to meet Joan's. "It's best you contact the adoption board. We wouldn't keep records like that here."

"Where would we find that?" Martha asked, feeling bewildered by what she had found out and what still needed to be uncovered.

"Wait – let me get you the address and telephone number," Gráinne eagerly offered and hurried from the room.

"Do you think it's true there are no records here?" Martha whispered.

"I don't know, but then why would she lie?"

When Gráinne returned to give Martha the handwritten note it was as if she were sharing with her the address of a popular restaurant.

"Here you go," she offered with a smile. "Best if you call before you go there – you might need to make an appointment. I don't think they'd like you just turning up at their door."

Martha took the paper and stood up. Clutching the box under her arm, she took Gráinne's lead and left the room, Joan following after her. Their meeting was over, her initial delight at having received a treasure chest of memories dampened by the fact that she had more questions now than when she arrived.

They said their curt goodbyes at the door and Gráinne watched them walk away with Martha clutching the box tight to her chest with both hands. She stood watching till they were out of sight.

Closing the door she leaned against it and took a deep breath. She wasn't paid enough to do this. She wasn't there to lie for anyone and promised herself as she waited for her heartbeat to return to normal that she would never do that again. Enough was enough. While there were no girls left in the house, their memories were perpetually etched into the fabric of the walls and she was the only one left and charged to care for them. She knew only the last few to leave the house and held their stories in trust, watched over each and every last one of them, waiting for friends and relatives, just like Martha and Joan but more recently journalists and reporters, to come and ask. She walked back to her office and sat behind her desk. It was impossible to concentrate after a visit from someone looking for answers. Each time it happened a tiny piece of her once strapping faith chipped away. But she was never asked to lie, until now. She had witnessed so much hypocrisy, had a filing cabinet full of harrowing stories of young girls abandoned and shamed all in the name of their Christian faith. Good Catholic families who abandoned their daughters, hiding them away, in some cases never to return for them, ever. Yet still these morally staunch citizens had the audacity to look down on and disparage others who were apparently less perfect than they, families with religion in their blood and members of the cloth within their fold. How artful. How deceitful. How sanctimonious. This was the end, Gráinne thought. She couldn't, wouldn't do this anymore. Lillian Byrne's story was the lowest of them all. And for what? She lifted a yellowed page from the dusty old file. A child, a birth certificate and a guarantee of no questions asked. At a price. Closing the file over, she placed it on the pile beside the shredder. With the nuns preparing the house for sale there was no need to keep files like this one any longer.

There was no place for files where they were going, the few that were left.

True to his word, the landlord set about making both girls their Irish whiskey: their first, he assumed, in their young years. Jimmy still sat in his spot at the bar, smoking a cigarette while considering a seemingly never-ending crossword. Every now and then his eyes flicked keenly towards them. There was a peculiar tension in the air, like they were being watched and observed with bated breath.

Assuming it was because they were the only females in the dingy little pub, the girls were mildly entertained rather than bothered by the attention and took a seat by the fire. As soon as she was seated comfortably Martha opened the box again and took from it the bundle of her mother's letters and laid them carefully on the table in front of her.

The barman brought them over their whiskeys.

"Easy now," he warned in a fatherly tone. "I've watered them down a bit for yez, but they're still fairly strong now for the unfamiliar."

The whiskey burned as it went down, their comically squawky faces a giveaway that indeed this was their first.

"You alright?" Joan asked with a wrench in her voice.

Martha nodded her assent, lifting the glass to take another large gulp with her still shaking hand.

"What are you going to do with these letters?" Joan asked her.

"Read them, I suppose," she said with a weak grin.

"Is it not a bit creepy?" Joan asked. "Ya know, a bit like eavesdropping on the dead?"

"I suppose," Martha replied, picking them up to massage them in her hands. "Maybe I'll just keep them, you know – I don't have to read them." She didn't want to read them yet anyway – she dreaded to hear the sound of her mother's voice in her head without having her actually there. She'd wait till she was alone.

"Yeah," Joan agreed. "Fancy another?"

"How about we just have coffee?" Martha replied wisely. "It's only just lunchtime."

"You're probably right," Joan replied, returning to the bar.

Martha flicked through the little bundle, looking at each one: the date, the stamp, the feel of the paper to the curl of her mother's letters as they spelt her sister's name. By the time she got to the last one she was expecting more of the same, but this one was different: different because it wasn't the same colour, it had no stamp and most of all it was different because it had her name on it. Just her name. Her first name. *Martha*.

Her heart skipped a beat as she pulled it from the rest of the bundle. She held it up. *Her name*. She turned the envelope over in her hands to lift the flap at the back, and took out the faintly lined pages, each scripted beautifully with her sister's elegant joined writing.

Dearest Martha,

By the time you read this I'll be gone. I'm really sorry I didn't get to say goodbye to you, but I really couldn't face you. I can't let you look at me, knowing what I have done. I feel so ashamed, I wish I could pretend it didn't happen but it has. And soon you will know it. She is theirs now, so small and pretty. She looks just like you, Martha. She has your blue eyes and soft yellow curls. They'll be taking her away from me and I know they're right. What kind of a life could I possibly give her? And anyway, she doesn't deserve to know how she came to be. No one really needs to know. I don't suppose I could face her every day, but neither can I not have her near. I am lost. But I really don't have a choice. They expect me to go home in a few weeks when I'm back to normal and behave like nothing has happened. How can I do that knowing that my baby is miles away from me? And even though Mr. Bertram says he will find a way for me to see her every now and then, how will I be able to hold her or play with her knowing it's only for a short while and then she will leave me all over again? I can't bear to say goodbye to that beautiful face once more. And though I'd like to believe he means it, that in time he will be able to take me to her, even in secret, I don't think I'll ever see her again.

Please don't think badly of me. Please don't think I didn't care. Because I do. I miss Tommy, you and Mam every day. I wish I could just go home. I've made such a mess of things I can't see any other way out.

He's not a bad man, you know, Mr. Bertram. I didn't mean for this to happen, it just kind of did. I'm not sure I can explain properly, but he was always so very nice to me and I was so lonely. I have no friends in Dublin, no one except him. But now, after this he says we can't be together again and Mrs. Bertram, she hates me and I don't blame her. She says I have ruined her life. I think she's right. I know you look up to me, your big sister working in the big city, but now you know I'm not what you think I am. You need to have a better role model than me, Martha. You are such a wonderful, beautiful sister, the best anyone could ever ask for. You have your whole life ahead of you. Don't make the same mistakes I have and always remember I love you and will watch over you. Look after Mam.

I love you.

Always.

Lillian xxx

It might have been the animal whine that escaped her or perhaps it was Joan's repetitious calling of her name "Martha? Martha?" that alerted Jimmy and the rest of the bar to her plight.

"Is everything okay there?" Jimmy asked, turning in his seat.

"I-I don't know," Joan stuttered, taking the letter from Martha who sat stunned as if slapped.

"Oh my God, Joan," Martha whispered, bringing her hands to her face while Joan read.

Jimmy got down off his stool and moved towards them.

"It was a lie," Martha murmured before Joan could get to the end of Lillian's note. "It wasn't an accident." The realisation first that Lillian had died at her own hand followed by the reference to her relationship with her employer was shattering.

At first, they didn't notice him standing so near, so close he was almost breathing over them, his presence unheeded until he spoke.

"I found her."

Both Martha and Joan looked up at him from their stools, confused by both his presence and his words.

"I'm sorry?" they asked in unison.

"I found your sister. I was the one who brought her in."

Part Three

Chapter 26

Sober for over two weeks, Barbara was terrified by the lucidity of her thoughts. Bizarrely, the last time she was teetotal for this long was almost twenty years before during her stay with Lillian in Donegal. And just as there was back then, today there was plenty to occupy those similarly dark thoughts. So much had happened in such a short, concentrated period of time it was daunting being so clear-headed with nowhere to hide psychologically. And that had been her first conscious *dry* decision: to break down her mental cache and admit to what had driven her there in the first place and then to face what was to come. Having held on to the secret for so long it had managed to completely colour her vision of herself and her world. But once exposed it almost immediately became less intimidating. So now they knew. Now there was nothing more to protect, nothing more to hide, nothing more to hide from. Finally, she could relax. And whatever were the consequences, they had to be easier to deal with than the poisonous weight of the shame and disappointment that had cloaked both herself and her marriage for so long.

It was truly regrettable then that her selfish relief

should be contradicted by her palpable sense of guilt. And the maxim that every action suffers an opposite and equal reaction reigned true in Barbara's mind. Her liberation seemed to be balanced by her shame. But as there was no taking it back it was easier to accommodate the unusual equilibrium in her conscience than the disparity of the truth untold.

Her ultimate decision to stay with William was arrived at after infinite agonising hours of introspection in the silence of that room with only the blip of the monitors and William's deep breathing to keep her sane There was no real complex emotional rationale: she simply had nowhere else to go. No one else she wanted to be with. There was no one else who wanted to be with her. And it was no one's fault but her own. Over the years she had consciously isolated herself from her children, friends and family leaving her with no alternative beyond her own miserable company. And that idea, the very notion of being totally alone was more daunting than settling, finally, right where she was. And, despite his apparent disenchantment with her as a companion and a wife, coupled with his years of philandering, William too was still there with no apparent sign of going anywhere, except to hell maybe. Perhaps his motivation was the same selfish one as her own, Barbara couldn't be sure. But what she did know was that if he intended to leave he would have done so by now. No, she decided. It was better to stay and try to piece together some semblance of an existence from the residue of their marriage.

So they sat in the relative silence of their own company, each pre-occupied with their own thoughts, both conscious of the implications of her presence and what it meant to both their futures.

Even Simon McDaid, who visited daily to brief William on the events within government, thought her presence unusual. Not long in the job, he didn't know William well enough to ask how come all of a sudden she was there. He put it down to the shock of his near-death experience. Barbara didn't seem interested in making conversation with him so he nodded politely towards her when he entered and left the room, and wondered what was going on behind those sad blue eyes to warrant such a solemn presence.

On the day of William's discharge Barbara arrived at the hospital in time to cross paths with Kathryn who departed leaving an agitated William and the whiff of Chanel in her wake. But not before kissing Barbara on each cheek.

As Kathryn was normally so aloof in their company Barbara was slightly perplexed by her unusual and animated display of affection and watched as the door closed after her. Turning to look at William she mistook his flushed face and shocked expression as a response to the bizarre conduct she had just witnessed.

"What was that all about?" Barbara asked William.

"Something about her going to the States," he replied.

"How odd," Barbara remarked, taking the suit bag that was draped over her arm to hang it from the back of the door. "I brought your things. What time do you think they'll let you leave?"

"Mr. Murray is on his way now apparently to give me the all clear," he told her, pulling himself up and out of the bed. "I'll go perform my ablutions."

"Right. That's great."

She was feeling the familiar anxious sensations beginning to niggle. She had passed the small number of TV crews and journalists outside, waiting patiently for him to be discharged. She dreaded their intrusion and no doubt the performance that was required to entertain them.

She listened to the shower run in the hospital en suite and imagined him going through his rituals – his methodical, step-by-step, same every day routine since the day they met. Standing at the window she looked out without seeing, intrigued and distracted by the heat from the radiator that lifted the light particles of dust into the air, visible only because of the sun that beamed in through the windows.

Are you sure, she asked herself, watching their weightless rise and fall. *Is this what you want?*

But she didn't get a chance to answer as McDaid knocked and entered the room.

"He's in the shower," Barbara informed him as he looked quizzically from the empty bed to her like she'd done something with William.

He smiled with an awkward nod. "Great. The car will be here in about an hour to pick him up. We'll head straight to the house. If that's okay with you, Mrs. Bertram?" He never had to consult with her before now, so it didn't come naturally.

Recognising his discomfort and not wanting to upset his tenuous confidence, Barbara did as good a job as she could manage at a reassuring smile.

"Of course, that's fine."

"Great, great," he faltered. "I'll come back in a while so." Turning on the spot he left with speed.

Was it her or just him? Barbara wondered, slightly amused by the effect she had on him.

Dressed in beige slacks and plum-coloured V-neck jumper with an open-neck pink shirt beneath, William emerged from the bathroom standing tall and proud, already getting into character for the performance that was to follow.

"How do I look?" he asked.

"Very dapper. A picture of health," she declared kindly. "How do you feel?"

"Like a cooped-up hen. I can't wait to get the hell out of this place."

As he refused emphatically to leave the hospital in a wheelchair, they compromised by allowing him to walk the last few metres to the door with Barbara by his side. The orderly wished him well as he got out of the chair to make the last leg of the journey unaided – evidently irrelevant to William as he didn't turn to either thank or acknowledge him.

"Dickhead," Barbara heard the young man mutter under his breath before turning back without waiting to see him exit safely into the waiting huddle of journalists.

She cringed as they walked through the automatic doors, feeling like a fake, standing there with her arm hooked in his, the good wife, smiling as they fired questions at him, bulbs flashing and garish microphone heads pointing at them.

"Feeling better, Minister?"

"Are you relieved to be alive?"

"Is it true they're negotiating for your retirement, Minister?"

The questions were fired fast and furious.

Instinctively Barbara felt her fingers clutch at his forearm that was significantly less muscular than the last time she held him in that way. She almost leapt from her skin when in a seemingly instinctive gesture he placed a protective hand over hers. All part of his act or a genuine display of affection?

"Mrs. Bertram, Mrs. Bertram!" one of them called. "Are you glad to have your husband out and well? What are your plans for the day?"

But she didn't answer. She couldn't, she wouldn't know what to say and anyway, they didn't really care, did they? All the while she held the smile firm on her face and when finally William spoke it was slow but well-practised.

"Thank you all so much for your good wishes," he boomed. "Your thoughts and prayers were a reassuring presence during my operation and recovery." He gave them a smile to melt the hearts of the nation, oozing a captivating magnetism while his voice commanded silence over the sound of the clicking cameras. "I'm delighted to tell you I'm very well and I hope, after a couple of quality days with my family ..." he looked down at Barbara as he spoke, "I'll be ready to resume normal duties at Government Buildings."

Barbara thought she might choke. She could see the female journalists flutter their eyes at him – she had to admit he did still cut a very dapper figure – while the men in the group watched and listened with admiration and envy.

"I'd like to say a special word of thanks to the doctors and staff here at our excellent St. Mary's National Hospital – their care has been second to none. So, thank you, thank you all."

He paused for a moment to let the random applause finish.

"Now, if you'll excuse me, Barbara and I are going home," he finished with a dramatic flourish.

Even the way he referred to her by her first name in such a casual manner made her think that there was no doubting Ciara was his daughter: he was the ultimate diva.

Leading the way through the small crowd McDaid guided them to the waiting black Mercedes. Opening the door William stood back to let Barbara in and with a final royal wave stepped into the car before the door snapped shut and they drove away at speed.

Tempted but not brave enough to ask '*What the hell was all that?*' she sat the journey out in silence while the men talked politics, strategy and defending his position in the Dáil.

His illness, McDaid warned from the front seat, had the vultures circling and he needed quickly to re-establish his authority.

They needed something substantial to use as leverage, William mused, something that would attract the media to generate sufficient publicity to get him back in the mind's eye of the voting public and quash any insurgents brave enough to take him on.

"So what are the options?" he asked while McDaid consulted his iPhone.

"We've got the gay marriage debate – you could take a position on that?"

William shook his head.

"There's always the water charges, but I wouldn't recommend that – it could go either way and there's too much negative noise." McDaid flicked down through his list. "How about Syria or the Middle East?"

"Not really. I need something a little more edgy, something with teeth," William growled, clenching his fist. "No one understands what the hell is going on over there anyway."

"I'll have to come back to you on it. Let me see what I can come up with."

"Well, don't wait too long – we need to turn this around PDQ."

"Yes, sir," McDaid responded and turned to sit back properly in his seat and bury his head in his phone.

The house was deathly silent and overbearingly warm.

"Oh, sir, I'm so glad to see you back and looking so well!" Gladys gushed from the hall as they entered. "I have everything all ready for you in here." Proudly she opened up the sitting-room door.

"Thank you, Gladys," he replied. "Have you lit the fire in the study?"

"Yes, sir," she replied earnestly.

"William, do as the doctor said," Barbara suggested. "Take it easy for the next few days – you need to rest."

Back in command, he told her, "I'll join you in a minute," and nodded to McDaid to follow him to the study.

Once inside with the door closed McDaid handed William a thin file from the brown leather satchel that hung loosely across his body. "This is what you asked for," he said as William took it. "Nothing really in it."

"You read it?"

"Well, yes," he faltered.

"Why?" William quizzed.

"I don't know." McDaid shrugged. "I didn't think it was a secret."

"Of course it's a bloody secret! Why else would I ask you not to mention it to anyone?"

"But, you asked me to find out, so I thought –"

But William cut him short. "Well done and for God's sake, man, don't argue."

McDaid watched eagerly as William opened the file, extracted the single sheet and read though it once, then twice.

"I told you," McDaid offered, resulting in a death-stare from his employer.

"When I want your opinion I'll ask."

"Sorry, sir, I was just –"

"Well, don't," William warned without lifting his eyes.

"Pretty boring really," McDaid mumbled because he just couldn't help himself.

"Don't you have something better to do?" William growled.

McDaid, suitably warned, sat down and buried himself in his iPad.

William wasn't really sure what it was he was looking for. He had hoped to find something, anything that he could use to get rid of her: He wasn't happy to have people who judged him watching his every move. It made him uncomfortable. But McDaid was right. She was pretty unremarkable. Single, never married, trained nurse turned social worker and volunteer. Born and bred in wilds of the West of Ireland, she seemed harmless enough. But something just didn't rest right with William. There was more, there had to be, but he was feeling tired and just couldn't make his mind work any harder.

Taking the bunch of keys from his belt he opened the safe concealed in the corner alcove cupboard and laid the file safely inside.

Despite the health warning from William's consultant for him not to consider doing anything resembling work for at least two weeks, Barbara, after her token protest, happily let him disappear into his study with his side-kick, grateful for even a few short moments to herself.

She'd made her way into the sitting room and immediately pushed up the window. The heat was stifling: she could hardly breathe. From the window she saw the car pull up. Her stomach turned as she watched with bated breath to see who would get out. She had successfully avoided her children so far since the great reveal and dreaded the prospect of answering the questions which she knew they would have. She had run from them not out of badness or any malignant purpose, but because she had no idea what to say to them, or more specifically Ciara. She didn't know if she should hug her or apologise to her, knowing that neither would feel quite right. But she needn't have worried because Ciara kept herself clear of the hospital and, Barbara prayed, she was unlikely to turn up to the house, not unless it was to cause trouble – and, in spite of everything that had passed, Ciara wasn't the sort to do that.

Instinctively she let out a sigh of relief when she saw Enya and Cormac emerge. They were alone.

Minutes later they joined her in the sitting room.

"How about I get you all some tea?" Gladys asked cheerfully, delighted by the busyness of the house, but also fully aware of the tension the guests brought with them and doing her best to dissipate it.

"Thanks, Gladys, that would be great," Enya replied with a reassuring smile then went to her mother to place a stilted kiss on her cheek.

The sentiment of the gesture, while strange, wasn't lost on Barbara who smiled gently at her daughter as she took a seat beside her on the couch.

"So I take it he's in his study then?" Enya asked.

Barbara replied with an exaggerated roll of her eyes.

"How are you, Mum?" Enya asked noting her sober and seemingly sound demeanour.

"I'm doing fine," Barbara replied shyly, finding the attention unsettling.

"You do know we're here for you, all of us?" Enya said.

The sentiment disturbed her. Never before had any of her children asked over her welfare – well, perhaps they did but she neither noted nor remembered it.

"I'm fine, really. But thank you, I appreciate it. Truly." She lowered her eyes, embarrassed by the intimacy of the moment.

"I know now probably isn't the right time, but I'd, we'd ..." Enya looked up at Cormac for reassurance, "we'd all like to know what happened and, well, what it means, I suppose."

"I know," Barbara sighed. "Your father and I will of course sit with you all to talk about it but not just now, not yet, if that's okay?"

"Absolutely. We understand. When you're ready," Enya told her with a sideways glance back at Cormac.

"How is she, your sister?" Barbara asked, the words

seeming hollow but she was genuinely interested to know.

"She's okay-ish," Cormac replied, kneeling down to stoke the burning embers of the fire. "She's at home with Robert. I think they're planning a bit of a trip – you know, get away from it all."

Barbara responded with a nod. Yes, she could identify with that. She knew just how Ciara was feeling: that instinctive and almost uncontrollable urge to escape. Unconsciously her eyes found the drinks tray on the dresser beside the door. She had chosen to get away from it all years ago and had only just now, it appeared, come back to land. Her mouth was parched. She swallowed the emptiness in her throat and bit down on her lips, relieved by the sharpness of her teeth sinking into the soft flesh.

A gentle knock at the door preceded Gladys's entry.

"Can I get you anything before I go?" she asked.

"That would be lovely, Gladys," Barbara replied with as much normality as she could manage. "Can I ask you to get me some iced water?"

"Of course," Gladys replied and scurried away, delighted to be of use.

The sound of the front door ringing brought with it the arrival of Rian and Martha. The living room hadn't seen this much activity in months, the family all gathered – well, almost.

Gladys clattered back into the room with Barbara's water, not a minute too soon, and then went and brought more cups for the latest arrivals who chatted politely amongst themselves.

Barbara was just about to send one of the boys to fetch him when William entered the room, prompting the boys and Enya to stand to attention and greet him one by one.

"Sit down, Dad," Rian said. "You're supposed to be resting."

"No need to fuss." William was delighted, playing to his audience.

"You look much better," Rian told him as he took up position in his usual spot at the fireside end of the couch opposite Barbara.

"Yes, you do – much better," Martha affirmed, leaning over to kiss him on each cheek, a gesture which William accepted reluctantly.

Watching her sit back in the chair offered by Rian, William waited till their eyes met and held onto her gaze for a short but intense moment. Both Barbara and Rian noticed it and Barbara sensed in her husband a hint of aggravated stress that had been pleasantly absent recently.

There was no denying the tension that filled the room with William's arrival: no one spoke, like the words were too frightened to come out. Concentrating on drinking their tea, between them the children passed an apprehensive eye-raising glance from one to the other, unsure how to behave or what to say.

"So," Cormac started, breaking the tense silence with a smart-alecky comment to his brother, "I hear you two are off again to save the world?" Then he smirked, just to take the edge off his jibe. But he needn't have worried as both Rian and Martha grinned in response.

"That's right," Martha told him, speaking to the room as if they might all be interested. "We're heading to Darfur this time."

No one noticed their father's flaring nostrils nor the increasingly fast rise and fall of his chest.

A polite knock at the door preceded McDaid's head

popping around its edge.

"I'm off now," he announced. "I left some options for you on your desk, sir."

William made to get up,

"No, please," McDaid insisted, "stay as you are, I can make my own way out. I'll see you in the morning."

"Thanks, Simon!" Enya said and once they heard the front door bang shut, remarked, "He's a nice guy, isn't he?" She looked to her family for affirmation.

William responded with an irritated guffaw.

"Seriously, Dad?" she challenged him.

Cormac put a calming hand on her leg, telling her silently with his eyes not to rise to it.

In his pocket his phone pinged and vibrated. Ignoring it, he got up to close the window, the draft giving him a chill down the back of his neck.

It pinged again. And again.

Simon McDaid had stopped in his tracks, turned and was racing back towards the door, almost tripping on the first step, his eyes being glued to the screen of his phone. Briefly he lifted his head, alerted probably by the noise of the window dragging in its frame. Their eyes met briefly. Cormac recognised the look: it was the look of fear and he saw it full and furious in the young man's eyes. Cormac's heart stopped and his mouth filled with bile, knowing without seeing what was about to happen. The doorbell rang three times in fast succession.

"Jesus Christ, who's that?" William grumbled.

Rather than going to answer it Cormac sat down, calmly gave the event about to unfold a twenty-second time frame and silently counted.

One ... two ... three ... McDaid entered the room.

Four ... five ... six ... He glanced quickly at everyone except Cormac ... *Seven ... eight ... nine ...*

"Was that you?" William complained, turning in his seat to look at him, irritated by the apparent lack of manners, barging in like that. "What on earth's got into you?"

Ten ... eleven ... twelve ...

"Eh," McDaid faltered. "Eh ... I ..." He stuttered like a fool, completely lost for words while proffering his phone. Finally he looked at Cormac who lifted his head from his hands and nodded back.

Thirteen ... fourteen ... fifteen ...

"I think you need to see this," McDaid told William without coming any further into the room.

"Well, show me!"

"Not here," he replied nervously.

"Show him," Cormac told him quietly, feeling his phone vibrate again in his pocket. Refusing to check as he didn't need to, knowing that the shit in less than five seconds was about to hit the fan.

Sixteen ... seventeen ... eighteen ...

McDaid walked over and volunteered his phone.

"What do I do?" William asked.

"Just watch."

Nineteen ... twenty...

Boom.

Chapter 27

"You filthy dog!" William shouted, getting up from his chair and lunging at his youngest son.

Cormac fell to the floor, and almost comically adopted the foetal position, curling up his legs and wrapping his arms round to protect his head.

McDaid leapt forward to hold William back while Barbara shouted warnings.

Rian picked up McDaid's discarded phone to see for himself what had triggered such a ferocious response from his father.

"Holy shit!" he gasped, then laughed. "Go, Cormac!" Unbelievable. This was trouble. Just as his father had discussed with McDaid earlier, Rian too was aware of the media commentary about his father's health and had also wondered how his father could prove his fitness to remain in office. This video would do him no good in that regard, that was for sure.

McDaid, holding back his boss, shocked but also slightly amused, silently quipped: *Careful what you wish for, Minister, you did ask for teeth …*

"Stop it!" Enya yelled, stepping in to cover Cormac from her father's flailing arms and feet. "Dad! What on earth are you doing? For God's sake, stop! You'll give yourself another heart attack!"

"And if I do, this time it'll be *his* fault!" William shouted, pointing at the slowly unfurling Cormac. "It'll be your doing, you filthy pig. *Yours!*"

"Dad!" Rian called out. "Calm down. Please."

"Calm down?" William hollered, spinning to twist his incensed attentions on him. "How dare you tell me to calm down? Have you seen it? Look at it. You, standing there, Mister Self-righteous looking down your perfect little do-gooder nose at me. How dare you!"

"Alright, alright," Rian conceded, holding up his hands in assumed defeat. "That's enough."

"How could you?" William asked, turning back to Cormac who stood up, defeated.

"It's okay," Cormac said to an incensed Enya. "I deserve it. For what it's worth I didn't do this on purpose. I didn't know I was being filmed. I tried to stop them putting this out there but …" he shrugged with Kathryn foremost in his mind, "my plan kind of backfired." For a split second he considered the potential for his own confessional moment to his family here, but decided, and rightly so, that now wasn't the time.

"I don't give a shit about you," his father spat.

"I'd never have guessed," Cormac mumbled, making his way to the door, disappointed but not surprised that his father didn't seem remotely interested in asking how or why. "I'm going anyway."

"Good riddance and don't bother to come back! Don't dare darken my door again!" William roared.

"*William!*" Barbara shouted. "*That's enough!*"

"*William!*" he mimicked. "What? All of a sudden you

care about these . . . these . . ." he fumbled for words, "these *shits*. Sober for five minutes and what, you're the world's best mother? Look, woman, look at what they've done. To you. To us, all of them. Worthless. Have you been that drunk that long that you've totally forgotten? We've given them every opportunity and look how they repay us!"

"Enough, Dad," Rian stepped up. "Mum's done nothing. She doesn't deserve this."

Cormac stood rooted to the spot, stunned by their father's vicious verbal assault. "*Leave her be!*" he shouted. "I'm the one to be angry at, not her."

Turning back to Cormac, William's eyes filled with revulsion and he barked with such force it made Enya jump. "*Don't you even dare!* Go on! For once just do as you are told and get out!"

Not willing to have a second heart attack on his conscience, Cormac decided he needed to leave. "I'll wait for you in the car," he said to Enya. He knew his father would never give him the opportunity to explain. He could talk to the others separately.

"No, wait, I'll come with you," Enya said, leaning over to grab her bag.

"You are a real asshole, do you know that?" she threw at her father. "I can't believe I ever thought that you ever cared even a small bit about us. You're nothing but a selfish bastard."

"Oh, look at you. Like butter wouldn't melt. Like some kind of prodigal daughter. You bugger off, bury your head in the sand and come back expecting us to welcome you here with open arms?"

"Actually yes, yes, I do," she replied, shocked by the vitriol in her father's voice. "Because that's what families do. Normal families not like this ridiculous excuse of one."

"Normal? Well, that's almost entertaining coming from you. I saw the way you looked at *him*!" he shouted, pointing towards McDaid who instantly coloured

"Me?" He squirmed, wishing he were anywhere else but here witnessing this monumental and intimate implosion, waiting for the moment when he could secret himself away unnoticed.

"Where are your loyalties? Oh, I'm sorry," William stated with mock-apologetic ignorance. "I forgot, you don't have any. You never did."

"Don't be ridiculous, Dad – now you're being childish," Enya objected. "What the hell has got into you?"

But William was on a roll.

"Don't give me that. Look at you with your short tops and tight jeans. You're a harlot. That's all you are."

"Right!" Enya declared with a resigned breath. "I've had enough of this." Turning to her mother who sat looking horrified in her chair, she said, "I'm sorry, Mum, to leave you like this." She made her way to the door.

William shouted after her. "And take that pathetic excuse of a man with you! And you can give a message to that other idiot brother of yours. Tell him I'm alive and I'm going to make him regret the day he ever walked out on me. *Go on! Get out!*" he roared.

The scene was frightening. He raved like he was going mad and looked like he might collapse all over again.

If he didn't, Martha thought, it would be a miracle. She made her way towards a stricken Barbara.

"And as for you, Little Miss Innocence!" William spat

out, like some kind of sniper spotting her move, his mouth going full throttle with the word's tripping out of him like automatic machine-gun fire.

Seeing Martha about to fall victim to his next verbal onslaught, Rian stepped in front of her as if to shield her.

"Don't even go there, Dad. I know you're upset but you've gone too far, way too far."

"Have I really?"

"Yes, you have." Rian was using all his diplomatic powers to try to diffuse the situation. "And you know you have, so let's sit down and see if we can take things down a notch or two."

"Don't you patronise me. I'm not one of your poor little famine children. I am your father and I will do as I wish."

"Well, why don't you start by behaving like my father?" Rian countered politely without raising his voice.

The words were like a slap to his face and a stopper to his mouth. With a cavernous breath William turned to the fireplace and leaned into it, bracing himself with both hands.

"How in God's good name did I end up like this?" he asked the flames. "How did I end up with such a ridiculous, disrespectful collection of offspring? Not one of them worth any more than the next. Useless, all of them!"

Rian looked at Martha who instinctively placed a hand on Barbara's shoulder and indicated they should go.

From the corner of his eye William spotted her manoeuvre.

"*You!*" he barked.

Martha stopped, unsure if he was yelling at her or Barbara.

"You stay right where you are. This is as much your issue as it is mine. Did you not see your son's disgusting antics? Here I am trying to recover, trying to make sure we have a future: they're out there, you know," he raved, "waiting for me to fall, wishing for me to trip up. All I expect of my family is some support – is that too much to ask, to stand by me and help?"

He let out a deep sigh as if resigned to being let down and turned to Martha.

"You understand that, don't you?" he asked her with a devilish glint in his eye. "You know how important family is. You know how powerful the need for a family can be, don't you?"

Martha swallowed while Rian looked quizzical.

"You're just a Good Samaritan, that's all, aren't you, Martha? Just a good girl." His tone had a nasty bite making her skin prickle, her senses on high alert.

William hadn't intended on using the information he had gleaned, not yet anyhow, but he was so caught up in the momentum of his emotional steamroller he just couldn't help himself.

Earlier, looking at the dossier McDaid had given him, he knew something was off. It hummed trouble. William had always considered himself to be an excellent judge of character, it was his job. As an incisive politician he had to make snap decisions based on perceptive assumptions and he trusted his instinct implicitly. And his instinct told him that something wasn't quite right with this Martha woman. It was only after he'd locked the file away that the name began to vibrate somewhere deep in the archives of his mind.

"You know," he said to her, sitting back down into the

couch and crossing his legs, like he was holding court and about to recount an incredibly fascinating story, "at first I didn't think that was your name. Martha. I knew there was more to you the first moment I saw you." His composure miraculously regained, he appeared perfectly comfortable looking up at her.

Does he know? Martha asked herself, not for one minute duped by his capricious demeanour.

"You don't really look like a Martha. I couldn't quite put my finger on what it was about you. But at the time I didn't think it really mattered – I thought you were just some kind of predatory, unscrupulous cougar. Rian's always been a poor judge of character, but then you got yourselves engaged and that really changed everything. And then, in the hospital, I saw you in a different light. Something about you made me uncomfortable and I asked a few questions." He saw her blanch. "Yes, that's right, I know who you are."

"What are you talking about, Dad? You leave her be, you understand?" Rian took a protective step forward.

"Or what? What'll you do? Cry? *Oh boo hoo!*" he sneered. "But you need to hear this, boy ..."

Rian turned to Martha and put his arm around her, feeling her quake as he held her close.

She always knew that at some point she would ultimately have to admit to Rian who she was but she certainly didn't envisage it coming out like this. She always assumed it would be on her terms, in her own way. She only ever imagined a scenario where she was the one in control of not only the information but also the moment.

"He's right," she whispered, looking up and straight

into his eyes, knowing that this had the potential to rock everything, needing to make him trust her, if that were even possible now.

"What?" he asked. "What is it?"

"I was going to tell you, I just didn't know how and certainly didn't want to tell you like this."

"Well, then," he replied in defiance of his gloating onlooking father, "whatever it is it can wait till we're alone."

"Tell him!" William's voice rang out from the couch. "Tell him. *Now.* Or I will."

Refusing to look at William, wishing only ill on him, she took a deep breath, feeling as if she were standing on the edge of the deepest, steepest cavern with no strings attached.

"My name," she said, placing both hands on his chest, begging him with her eyes to understand, "is Martha Byrne. I am Lillian Byrne's sister."

"So?" Rian asked, irritated and confused. "Who the hell is Lillian Byrne?"

She didn't answer immediately, hoping he'd put two and two together, hoping the name that had caused such a stir in recent days would connect with him. But he didn't get it, forcing her into the final humiliation of spelling it out for him.

"Ciara's mother. Lillian was Ciara's birth mother," she said softly.

"Lillian … oh Jesus, oh Martha …" The words were filled with disappointment and anguish, his face a mass of contorted expressions.

"I knew!" William clapped. "Hard to believe, it took me a while. It wasn't even the last name that twigged it for me – it was Roundstone. How many girls from there are you ever likely to meet in a lifetime? And then I recognised the features, her face. You really are quite alike, do you know that?" He saw the tears well in her eyes but went on regardless. "Now I don't believe in coincidence and I'm assuming that this is not one, is it?"

She shook her head. "No," she whispered, wishing William would curl up and die right there on the couch, hating every single hair on his head and inch of skin on his body.

"So I assume it's money or some kind of childish naive retribution you're after," William probed like it was some immature game they were playing.

But she didn't hear him; all she saw were the eyes of her fiancé filled with sadness and anguish.

"Martha." Rian said her name like the very word hurt.

"Please, Rian. It's not what you think. Please, you have to believe me. Trust me. Please."

"Trust you?" William commentated from the couch, delighted with himself. "You deceived him, you deceived us all."

"That's enough, Dad," Rian interjected without taking his eyes from Martha. "This is our business."

"Your business?" he guffawed. "Then you'd better deal with it!"

He watched gleefully as Rian and Martha left the room. The front door slammed behind them.

Barbara had watched in horror from the couch as the whole malicious episode, like some kind of climactic TV soap opera, unfolded in front of her eyes.

This was her life. This was what she had bought into. *Again.* Here was the man she had decided she wanted to stay with but he, it transpired, was the Devil. Her heart, like lead, felt no happiness – only absolute repugnance. Had she really made her choice? *This* choice. Was he it? Was this the kind of person she wanted to be? Because by staying with him this is exactly what she would become. She would be as bad as him, tarnished by association. Remaining with him would be seen as an endorsement of his actions. And even if she were only tolerant of his actions, it would always be just her and him. Alone. But together, growing old, wallowing in each other's malice. Was that what she wanted?

Her lack of sobriety over the years had managed to mask the evil streak in him; she had been too pissed and locked up in her own troubles to notice what kind of a man he truly was.

She was so hot, her body convulsing inside.

"Are you happy with yourself?" she asked William, hoping the disgust she felt was apparent in her tone.

"I don't want them in this house again, do you understand?" he told her, his mirth spent. "Either of them. Any of them!" he hissed.

She shook her head in disbelief.

"Don't you dare shake your head at me!" he spat.

"How did you know?" she asked.

"About what?"

"About Martha."

"I knew as soon as we met her that something wasn't right."

"So rather than say anything to Rian you went behind his back and tried to sabotage his relationship."

"That boy couldn't hold down a relationship if he tried."

"Not with you working away in the background, no, he didn't stand a chance. And what about Seb? What happened there? Why was Kathryn with you this morning?"

He looked at her with contempt but didn't answer.

"What did you mean when you said Seb walked out on you?" she asked, pulling together pieces of conversations she'd heard and had. "It was Seb in the house, wasn't it, before, when you had your attack?" The realisation dawned on her. "He left you but I found you."

Immediately and despite herself she found herself thrown back to that event and imagined a totally different scenario. What if she hadn't found him?

"And what about me?" she finished. "Are you going to throw me out when I say or do something you don't like?"

But William had stopped listening to her, deciding he didn't like this sober Barbara. She asked too many questions, she was logical once more. He'd forgotten what she was like, the old Barbara: so unpredictable, so hard to manage. She was, he concluded, easier to cope with drunk and, turning on her, funnelling the hard edge of his remaining bitterness towards her, he lined her up in his sights.

"This is all your doing, all of it, a spiral of disasters one after the other. For years this has followed us like a bad penny with nothing but dire luck looming. I should never have let you talk me into it." He spoke like she wasn't capable of understanding, like she wasn't there. He got up to roam the room. "We should have left her there, just like I suggested. Why didn't I listen to Sister What's-her-name? It would never have come back to us: an unmarried mother, a bastard child? They're ten a penny. She told us so. No birth cert, nothing to trace her back. But no. You had to have her. You and your conscience. Living this – this charade, this lie. "

Out of breath, he flopped into the upholstered antique carver in front of the matching writing bureau that stood before the window overlooking the garden. With his elbows on the bureau he rubbed his aching temples.

"Now as usual I have to fix things. Pick up the pieces."

Barbara watched him from behind, his memory of events contradictory to the actual events. She had wanted none of this. It was his scheme. How dare he blame her? And as if by some cruel, twisted coincidence that same sick feeling that she felt in the pit of her stomach the day he told her she must go to Donegal with Lillian washed over her. Clutching her belly and swallowing hard, she fought the impulse to vomit. But still William ranted, his words as disgusting as the idea of her vomit. She stopped listening, internally turning down the volume of his voice. She was surprised at how effectively this blocked him out. Why hadn't she thought of doing this years ago, she asked herself. Because, she answered, she didn't need to: copious amounts of whiskey did the job for her. Relishing the memory of the lovely hot spirit, she licked her lips.

Bizarrely intrigued by the shape and form of his body, she watched his back in the chair and the hypnotic rise and fall of his breath. Unconsciously letting her own breath synchronise with his, her thoughts merged into each other to become incoherent and indecipherable.

Part Four

Chapter 28

Detective Inspector Alan Milford got the call just as he sat down to dinner. It was their anniversary and Jill, his wife, had prepared his favourite meal: beef-and-onion pie with creamy mash and overcooked mushy broccoli.

He sighed and looked apologetically at her as he reached behind him to the sideboard for the vibrating phone.

"You said you'd switch it off, really off, not just the ringer," she objected, although she knew he wasn't listening and in truth she really didn't mind – his work was his passion and that wasn't something she ever planned on getting in the way of.

Silently he listened as they gave the situation analysis. Then, pulling the napkin from his neck, he pushed back his chair.

"I'm on my way," he said with a heavy sigh and, looking sheepishly at his her, whispered, "Sorry, love."

Rounding the table to kiss his wife of eight years, he tried his best to appear upset but already could feel the excitement of a new case build.

"It'll keep," she told him, with a wave of her hand at the food. "But I'm not sure this will." She smiled, claiming the twenty-euro bottle of Bordeaux as her consolation prize and carrying it and her glass from the table to the couch.

"This'll be a long one, I think, so don't wait up," he told her with a quick peck to the top of her head as she settled in for her night alone.

She didn't intend to.

He took the briefing over the phone as he drove, with his sergeant giving him more details.

The blue lights of the ambulance and police cars parked randomly in the driveway lit up the night. With no space for him, how inconsiderate, he pulled up on the curb outside, locked the car and turned slowly towards the house, absorbing the leafy neighbourhood, the well-heeled neighbours standing whispering in small huddles and the arriving paparazzi vying for the best spot for a story that was without doubt 'breaking news'. Nodding curtly, he quickly passed them, picking up the pace when the ones who recognised him ran his way, hungry for whatever information they could scrounge only to be stopped by the Garda standing sentry at the gate.

Aside from the service vehicles, there were only two other cars in the driveway. A black Mercedes. *Nice*, he remarked to himself, taking his time to casually stroll around it, admiring the luxurious curves and the 151-registered white Golf beside it. The blue beams from the patrol cars bounced back at him from the glass. High-spec cars, beautiful house, political icon. Milford was curious to find out what was going on inside but before he entered the house he stood for a moment, hands on hips, and looked around him, soaking up the entire picture.

Taking his time he walked up the granite steps and through the open door into the impressive high-ceilinged hallway.

A young officer, Garda Rachel Evans, was waiting in the hall for him

"They're in there, sir," she informed him, nodding towards the open door opposite.

"Thanks, Evans," he replied courteously and made his way across the hall and into the study where two tearful and stunned women sat side by side, holding hands on the burgundy chesterfield sofa.

Lamps dotted around, along with the flames from the fire that roared in the fireplace, lit up the room. It was a sober space, and despite the disarray of its recently upturned contents its temperate atmosphere was apparent.

Books, lamps, ornaments and fallen furniture littered the floor.

Now that's a mess, he noted with increasing intrigue as he skirted around the interview that was taking place on the sofa between the ladies and one of his team. Wanting to observe the scene for himself for a while longer he chose to leave them uninterrupted and walked instead around the desk that had been wiped clear of its things which now lay in a heap on the carpet. The lamp had been smashed, papers were strewn around and in the middle of it all three drawers lay overturned and empty, one of them forced with its lock shattered and timber splintered all around. He watched his every step, careful not to tread on anything and followed the trail of destruction to the opposite corner where the cupboard built into the alcove had its doors thrown open. It too was now haphazardly devoid of most of its contents. And at the back of it, buried deep into its recess, the vintage cast-iron safe that it hid was sitting wide open with a ring of keys still in the lock. Files, loose documents and passports were reefed and cast aside, obviously worthless to whoever had perpetrated this havoc.

The place was a mess. Whoever did this, he assessed, had plenty of time and wasn't afraid of being heard.

As Milford went to leave the room to explore further someone handed him a clear plastic pouch containing a handwritten piece of paper. He took it and read.

"Interesting," he remarked and with a nod to his officer held on to it, putting it carefully inside his breast pocket.

The kitchen was clear, the housekeeper having left hours earlier he was told, but in the utility room a window had been forced and broken, the glass in smithereens covering the top of the counter and spilling on to the floor below. He ventured outside through the back door to inspect the side passage and the window frame. It was clear. No footprints, no marks, just bits of dirt and glass on the ground. The gate to the side passage wasn't locked but secured by a latch that could be lifted from either side. Having seen enough for the time being, he made his way back inside and retraced his steps from the utility room through the kitchen and back into the hall.

"Well, let's have a look then," he said aloud to no one in particular and made his way to the scene of the crime.

In what Milford assumed to be the lounge, William still sat in the Queen Anne carver, slouched forward with his head, cheek side up, resting cold and stiff in a pool of his now hardened and crusting blood on the top of the polished mahogany bureau. Careful not to touch anything Milford moved expertly and with great agility around the body, bending and stretching, interrogating every visual aspect of the scene, taking in the detail and cataloguing it in his head for referencing later. Photographs, he found, rarely captured the finer intricacies of a scene better than his own eyes. These were the details that in his mind could ultimately seal the case.

Taken by surprise? he wondered, curious about the bruise to his forehead and more importantly the gash to the back of his skull, obviously the injury that did the fatal damage.

And how come in here? he asked himself, looking around the room for inspiration. "Any sign of a weapon?" he asked the official sweeping the room for evidence.

"Not yet, sir," came the polite reply.

"Surely if it was a break-in he'd have heard the glass shatter? He'd get up to investigate, don't you think?" he asked without expecting an answer. "But from here it looks like he was taken by surprise." The house was big, but not so big as to muffle the sound of a breaking window. "Unless he's deaf?" he presented himself with a not unlikely alternate explanation and checked for signs of a hearing aid. "He didn't turn around so either he didn't have time or he didn't realise what was coming."

With the exception of the victim nothing in the room was obviously disturbed. Embers burned faintly in the fireplace, the aroma of the long-since dried-out logs still marvellously fresh in the room.

Nothing like an open fire, he reckoned. Next to the

fireplace, at the end of the couch that ran perpendicular to it, a book tower was piled high on the side table and beside that was a half-finished glass of water and a silver plate of bonbons.

How very chic, he thought, tempted but not daring to pop one of the sugary delights into his mouth. Instead he sat down and settled himself comfortably into the sofa's cushions to survey for a moment the lay of what appeared to be an ordinary room with little evidence of the crime apart from the corpse in the antique chair.

Satisfied eventually that he'd seen enough, he continued his exploration of the house, careful to keep his hands to himself as he went.

The dining room next door, with very little to upset, seemed almost untouched. The main ingredient of the sparsely furnished room was a long, perfectly polished chestnut-coloured table with two large candelabras standing majestically in its middle. An impressive feature as well as a functional piece of furniture, Milford could only imagine how sumptuously lavish it was when dressed for the many political gatherings this room had undoubtedly entertained. Elegant and sophisticated, fit for royalty. Far too big for his own house. And apart from the matching chairs and a serving bureau there was no other furniture in the room.

Nice, he thought as he made his way back to the hall to beckon the Garda standing watch at the door.

"Evans, get Fitzgerald to cover the door. I want you to check all the windows – oh and check the phone too – we'll need last dialled numbers and calls in."

"Yes, sir," she replied, scurrying off.

"Be careful not to touch anything else," Milford

warned as she disappeared in search of Garda Fitzgerald.

The house and its contents flaunted the wealth of the family, with an impressive array of silverware, elegant crystal, valuable antiques, state-of-the-art electronics, not to mention the impressive paintings on the walls. There were prime pickings in almost every room. If he needed evidence to prove that this wasn't a regular burglary, botched or otherwise, the fact that nothing obvious had been taken from the house appeared to be it.

He headed up the stairs, taking the steps two at a time, to see what else he could discover. He noted with interest William and Barbara's separate rooms in which, again, there didn't appear to be any sign of disturbance. He spent most time in Barbara's room. Feeling like an intruder himself, he placed his hand between the sheets of her bed. Feeling significant heat there he knew she wasn't long out of it. On the bedside table a half-empty bottle of scotch whiskey beside the small brown pharmacy-issue canister provided an explanation, perhaps, as to how and why Barbara apparently heard nothing from downstairs. Beside her bed, tucked in neatly between the bedside table and the bed itself was her handbag. Pulling it out he took a quick peek, careful not to disturb the contents, wondering what it was that made him think all was not well in the day-to-day goings-on in this fine house.

Satisfied that he had seen all that was necessary, Milford made his way back downstairs and into the study. The women still sat side by side on the couch by the fire. He nodded to his colleague who took the cue to let him take over and stood to discreetly whisper in his ear: "She hasn't said a word."

Milford smiled sympathetically in acknowledgement

and sat down in his place. Although he'd never met her, he recognised Barbara Bertram from the pictures he'd seen of her over the years. As he recalled she always looked very dour and always stood behind her husband, as if she were hiding. This evening she sat stony-white, looking straight ahead unblinking, and, he reckoned based on what he'd seen upstairs, very hung over. The other woman – the daughter, he assumed – held her arm tight around her mother's shoulders, gently stroking while she rocked, needlessly hushing her like a baby. Settling himself down, feeling the warmth of the fire beside him he leaned forward to introduce himself.

"Mrs. Bertram," he said quietly, "I am Detective Inspector Milford. Alan Milford." He paused for a response but she didn't move or bat an eye.

Looking towards the daughter who acknowledged her mother's silence with a helpless lift of her eyebrows, he tried again.

"Barbara, I know you're in some shock right now, but if you could tell me what happened ..." He let the sentence hang, hoping to see even a glimmer of a response in her unblinking eyes. Nothing. She was obviously and understandably in a state of shock. He turned instead to the daughter. "And you are?"

"Sorry," she replied, a little flustered, and paused before answering, as if waking from a trance. "I'm her daughter, Enya, the youngest," she said nervously.

"Enya. Beautiful name," Milford said with a smile, hoping to put her at ease. "So, can you tell me what happened?"

"I don't know." She shook her head, glancing again at her mother who remained statue-still with her hands clasped tight in her lap. "I came back – we were here earlier, you see, and I rang the bell, but there was no answer so I used the key."

"What key?" he asked.

"There's a key rock outside."

Milford listened attentively without taking notes, giving her all of his attention.

"And I came in and . . ." Her voice shook and body shivered despite the heat in the room.

"Go on," he encouraged gently.

"I found him, in there . . ."

"And your mum?" Milford pressed.

"She was upstairs." Ciara paused to look again at her mother and, lowering her lids as if to hide her embarrassment, added, "Asleep."

"Has she said anything about what happened? Did she hear anything?"

"No. She won't speak to me."

"Did she give you any indication when she woke about what might have happened?" he asked.

"No. She hasn't said a word."

"Can you remember what time that was?"

"I got here about eight fifteen."

"Okay," he said, nodding pensively. "And after you found your father, what did you do then?"

"Well," she replied slowly, "I called out for Mum and when she didn't reply I ran up the stairs to see if she was alright."

"You went straight upstairs? You didn't go to the kitchen?"

"Well, no. I knew where she'd be, see." She threw a quick glance at her mother, as if feeling the awkwardness of speaking about her like she wasn't there.

Milford didn't take his eyes off her, watching her closely, taking in how she moved and held herself, her gestures and expressions, where she looked and the words she used and didn't interrupt her.

"But she wouldn't wake up, so I shook her a little." She flicked her eyes up to see how Milford responded to that, but he didn't react.

"When she did wake up I called Seb and then I called you."

"And that was at ...?"

"Probably about eight twenty – maybe eight twenty-five."

"And which phone did you use?" he asked, searching his mental catalogue of images for the location of the handsets and mobile phones throughout the house.

"I used the landline."

"Seb is your brother?" he asked and she nodded in reply. "Why did you call Seb first?"

"I don't know – instinct, I suppose. He's the eldest and knows what to do in most situations."

"And what did he say?"

"He told me to call the ambulance and they called you. He should be on his way here now."

"Wise man," Milford said with a friendly smile, turning his attention back to Barbara.

"Mrs. Bertram?" he asked gently. "Barbara ..."

But Barbara remained perfectly still.

"Barbara, can you tell us what happened?" He gave her a minute to reply and when no response came he continued, "We need to see what happened here. Did you hear anything? Any shouts, conversations?" But he knew his questions were pointless, falling on deaf ears. Accepting her silence as an indication of her fragile state rather than a lack of cooperation, he turned his attention back to her daughter. "We'll get her seen by the doctor – he may want to give her something for the shock." In his mind he made a note to point out what she'd already consumed. "Enya, I need to ask you something. It looks like whoever did this came looking for something specific. Do you have any idea what that might be?"

"I've no idea. I don't really know much about Dad's affairs."

"And where are the rest of the family? Do you need to call them?"

"No, it's okay. They're on their way. I've called them already."

"We will need to speak to your mum at some point, but now isn't the time," he acknowledged with a sideways glance at her mother. "Are *you* okay?" he asked then, concerned for this woman, realising at that moment just who she was, remembering her story which was widely covered in the media at the time.

Enya replied with a fast nod of her head, afraid that tears might follow.

"Let's leave it at that for the minute," Milford concluded, seeing her struggle. "We can try again to talk to your mum tomorrow and see if we can figure this out. Is that alright?"

Again Enya nodded in response.

"Are you okay to stay here for a while? I just want to see what's going on out there." He indicated towards the door with his thumb and with her consent he got up and left the room.

Heading straight for Garda Fitzgerald he instructed quietly, “Let me know as soon as the rest of the family arrive. And don’t let them anywhere near him.” He pointed towards the lounge.

Taking the cigarette packet from his pocket, he went outside to think, and leaning against the wall lit up with a deep drag into his lungs. The first pull was always the nicest. He was supposed to have given up months ago, but his heart wasn’t in the effort: he still enjoyed it too much, not that he’d say that to his wife. Taking another deep pull, he relished the fresh evening that had a hint of moisture in the air. The sky was clear and the light of the moon was just about visible above the glare of the blue lights.

He thought about the situation inside the house, mentally summing up what he could gather so far. Whoever did this was in no hurry. At a glance it was safe to assume they knew exactly what they were doing and where they were going. He wondered if they knew Mrs. Bertram was upstairs all along. Wandering as he puffed, he made his way to the side passage and unlatched the door. Easy enough, he thought to himself. No one to see, he assessed, looking around. Tapping the cigarette into his pocket ashtray he walked down the passage and stood in front of the broken window. The frame was cleared sufficiently to open the latch and climb in without hurting anyone. There were no footprints and apparently no fingerprints either.

What were they looking for, he wondered, observing the detail of the glass, the way it had cracked and how it fell. Was it possible, he contemplated, that whoever it was thought William was still in the hospital, out of harm’s way? Already his mind had begun to dissect the jumbled-up pieces of evidence, ready to make a start on putting them back together again, right way up. This was the part of the game that he enjoyed most: the initial thrill of the puzzle, the intrigue of the individual elements coming together, and finally the supremacy of working it all out. Priding himself on his superlative instinct, he didn't ignore the gnawing feeling that something wasn't quite right. It just *felt* peculiar. He couldn't quite decide what was wrong, not yet anyhow, but he knew eventually he would. He always did.

The sound of a car horn blaring drew his attention and, stubbing out his cigarette, he made his way back out front. Coming out of the passage he saw a champagne Jaguar coming up the short drive. Popping a chewing-gum in his mouth, he quickly he made his way back inside, past Garda Fitzgerald who was standing guard at the door, and halfway up the stairs to sit and observe the behaviour of the family members as they arrived.

The first walked into the house confidently, cock of the walk, like he knew exactly where he was going. Of course he did, this was his parents' house. He was the loud one. The leader, who didn't want to waste any time in establishing who was boss.

"Who's in charge here?" he boomed at Garda Fitzgerald who was still standing guard at the door.

"Detective Inspector Milford is the lead investigator on this case, sir," he replied politely. Then, with as much authority as his inexperience could command asked, "And who might you be?" They were used to people throwing their weight around and getting impatient: it was all part of their training.

"Tell him Sebastian Bertram would like a word."

Milford put a finger to his lips as Fitzgerald glanced in his direction as an indication not to give him and his discreet position away, then watched as Sebastian made his arrogant way into the house.

Ciara arrived next, cautiously treading her way into the hall, like she was expecting someone to pounce: she was both nervous and afraid. Afraid of what, he wondered. Her dead father or something, maybe someone else?

She almost ran into the study when she was told where they were all waiting.

A younger man came last. Cormac, he assumed, as he too arrived with confidence into the hall. Taking a sweeping glance around, he was the only one who seemed in anyway curious about what state the house was in and immediately noticed the man sitting curiously on the stairs. He slowed and nodded and instead of following his brother and sister into the study he doubled back to the front door to ask Garda Fitgerald, much to his amusement, who was the strange man sitting on the stairs.

Interesting, Milford said again to himself. Very interesting.

Chapter 29

Milford looked at his hand-drawn sketch of a family crumbling right before his eyes. It was true, he thought, looking at the convoluted diagram. There is no such thing as the perfect family. We all have our secrets and lies. Some secrets are destined to remain just that – secrets – whilst others just cry out to be discovered. And for the Bertrams it seemed that theirs, of which there were plenty, were tripping over themselves in some kind of revelation stampede just dying to be uncovered. Over the course of the last few days he'd spoken informally to each of the siblings, piecing together the main thread of events on the day that William died. He liked to take time to observe his suspects from a distance and used the passing of William's funeral as the marker after which he would begin to question them formally.

Dotted lines crossed solid lines, which intersected double lines in seven different colours, one for each member of the family as well as Martha Byrne and Simon McDaid. To anyone else it might have looked like a jumbled-up mess but to him it made perfect connected sense. Standing back with his arms crossed, he went through the story again and again in his head, his eyes moving rapidly along the tracks of lines, trying to understand and if possible figure out the variables and possible explanations of just what happened. And there were quite a few.

According to the family William Bertram was alive and well when they, Rian, Martha, Enya, Cormac and the very nervous Simon McDaid, left the house at approximately four thirty. This concurred with a variety of sketchy witness statements, which confirmed that the three cars with their owners and passengers left the house at about that time. Traffic cameras on the busy intersection also corroborated their story: all three cars could be seen turning out of the quiet street within about ten minutes of each other. They all appeared to drive steadily with none seeming rushed or erratic. In the house then remained Barbara and the victim, apparently still alive. Forensics from the scene were inconclusive. His watch was still ticking when they arrived at eight twenty-six and on preliminary investigation it seemed that William died from blunt force trauma to the head, but there was no sign of a weapon at the scene, although traces of bark around the wound suggested a log from the fire might have been used. Evidence gathered from the scene suggested he didn't die immediately. Had he been caught in sufficient time he might just have lived, but William Bertram died a slow, miserable death. Indications from forensics suggested the approximate time of death was anywhere between five and seven thirty that evening. It was likely that he was knocked unconscious by the blow to the back of his head and may have regained consciousness at least once or twice before he died. Whatever hit him was delivered with such force that it caused part of his skull to cave in.

"Evans!" Milford called through the glass partition.

The young sergeant was at the door in seconds.

"I need a sounding board," he told her, deciding that a fresh pair of eyes might see things differently and help him break down what they knew as fact and what was mere supposition.

Happy to oblige, she took the seat Milford vacated and sat back to listen.

"So," he started, propping up the wall in the corner of the cluttered and stuffy office, regarding the board. With one arm crossed over his chest and the other clutching his chin, he stood: the personification of *perplexed*. "Some of the family, but interestingly not all, get together at the house, to welcome Bertram home having just been discharged from hospital."

Milford pushed himself from the wall to pick up a ruler and over the next ten minutes point at the different names and events to build for an attentive Evans a concise picture of what happened in the last few hours before William's death.

"Young McDaid, God love him, breaks the news of Cormac's pictures, stays to hear the start of the argument but scurries from the house first. The others, having argued with their father, exit the house, in ones and twos, pissed off and furious. Martha and Rian are the last to go, leaving only Barbara there and an apparently very much alive William." He paused to consider the detail so far.

"What about the housekeeper?" Evans asked from her chair.

"She left at about four ten, just before things kicked off," he told her quickly, eliminating her from the scene.

"Barbara Bertram isn't saying much but from what we can gather she and William then have their own domestic and, upset by his behaviour towards the children, she storms off and takes herself to her room accompanied by the Bushmills from the tray in the lounge and her little bottle of Valium."

Milford moved to the other side of the board to point his ruler at a slightly pixelated and not very flattering picture of Enya.

"At approximately seven fifty-five Enya arrives, apparently looking to talk to her parents about what's been going on with Ciara only to find the house in chaos, her father dead and Barbara passed out cold in the bed upstairs."

Here he paused to take a breath then turned to Evans with a curious sidebar to the events unfolding.

"We don't," he commented, "see any car arrive on the street – apparently she came by bus. By her own admission she called Seb first at eight sixteen from her mobile and then, after a full ten minutes, she called us from the landline."

"Why did she wait so long?" Evans asked.

"Apparently she was trying to waken her mother. Didn't want the police to see her passed out like that, or so she says."

"She might have been better off to leave her as she was," Evans offered. "You know, to corroborate her story."

"Hmmm," Milford pondered before continuing. "We arrive next. Bertram is dead in the living room, Barbara and Enya are in the study that's been completely turned-over. Both women appear shocked and a bit terrified and

Barbara can't say a word." He slapped the picture of Barbara's face with the ruler. "The bed upstairs, Barbara's bed, is still warm, with the bottle of whiskey now about half empty and the bottle of Valium down a few tabs on the bedside table."

Taking a few steps back he rested, feet apart and arms folded, to observe the story so far.

"So where did they go after they left the house? The children?" Evans asked. "Where were they in the timeframe of their father being bludgeoned to death?"

"Good question. Let's start from the bottom up." Moving back to the board he pointed to Enya. "Enya Bertram leaves the house in a huff with Cormac at about four thirty. They go back to Ciara's house to park the car then take a taxi to town where they go into a bar and stay there till just after six. They leave. She goes home alone as does Cormac, but she decides to go back to the house later on her own to take on the parents and so becomes the first at the scene to discover the body."

"Do we know for sure they stayed in the bar till six?"

"Yes and no. The cameras in the bar aren't working but the barman says he remembers them mainly because she, Enya, raised her voice a good few times, but he couldn't say for sure what time they arrived or when they left."

"What about credit cards? They must have bought drinks?"

"No cards," he smiled. "Only cash."

Evans raised her eyebrows in a 'how convenient' slant. "I assume then that we only have their word for it that they went home, separately."

"Exactly," Milford confirmed, moving the ruler up the

board towards Ciara. "Ciara claims to have been walking the beach at Strandhill. She too has no real alibi although the shopkeeper at the local store thinks she may have been in the shop and bought a coffee at about seven, but she doesn't appear on the CCTV."

"So she's not really clear then either? Strandhill Beach is only about twenty-five minutes away. On a good day she could have made it there and back easily."

"I know," Milford remarked, glad that the intricate weave was decipherable.

"Then there's Rian." He continued climbing up the family tree. "He and Martha, also pretty upset it seems, apparently went back to their apartment and didn't leave again till they were called by Enya. But again we only have their word for it. The CCTV from their apartment does show the car parked all evening in the basement car park and then shows them leaving, but we only have their alibi for each other."

"And what about Sebastian?"

"Ahh, the delightful Sebastian?," Milford mused. "What a charmer. Sebastian was on the move most of the afternoon, travelling between his bank and his office. His secretary confirms he returned just after five and was in his office when she left at about five forty. The security camera shows the car drive from the car park at eight forty-five, obviously heading to his parents' having got the call from Enya. Again, though, there doesn't seem to be any one to witness for sure that he was in his office building all that time."

"Right." Evans shrugged. "Sure that doesn't categorically rule out any of them – except Barbara who was off her head."

"Ah yes, but we only have her word for it that Bertram was alive before she made off with her pungent little cocktail."

"True," Evans pondered, "but do you really think she has it in her? I mean, look at her – she's a real mess and physically she doesn't look like she could have done it. She's pretty small."

"Hmmm," he brooded, mentally plotting a course of action.

"And you still don't think there's any chance it could have been an outsider, someone completely random?"

"No, it wasn't random," Milford replied firmly. "Whoever did this knew what they were looking for. They knew where to find the keys to the safe and then knew where the safe was. No. I'm convinced they were looking for something specific, so that rules out random. But as for it being someone outside the family, it's certainly a possibility, but in my experience logically and statistically it's unlikely. There's too much going on in this family right now for this to be a coincidence. I mean, look at them for God's sake!" He pointed back to the family portrait on the board. "An honest-to-God, good Catholic Irish family that makes *EastEnders* look like a playschool cartoon. No. One of them did this, I'm sure. I just need to figure out which one."

Chapter 30

They sat around the large kitchen table with their steaming mugs of tea and a visibly nervous Gladys.

"There's nothing to worry about here, Gladys," Milford assured her. "We only just want to have a chat about what's been going on these last few weeks – you know, the comings and goings, any disagreements, arguments ..." The open sentence was primed for her to pick up his lead and hopefully tell him what he needed to know.

"Arguments?" She shrugged. "There's always plenty of those!" She laughed shakily. "Mr. Bertram doesn't suffer fools gladly." Then she corrected herself sadly. "He didn't, anyway."

"With his wife?"

"Not really. Mrs. Bertram tends to keep very much to herself; they don't really spend much time together. In the early days, perhaps, they'd be snapping at each other every now and then, but not so much anymore."

"And what about the children?"

"He was always very hard on them boys," she told him with a slow disapproving shake of her head. "The girls too but in a different way."

"You've been with the family for many years, haven't

you? Did you know about Ciara?"

"I did," she said, lowering her eyes. "I didn't agree with it, I thought it was wrong and Mrs. Bertram was mad to do it. But it wasn't my place to say."

"You see a lot here," Milford remarked in a sympathetic tone.

"That I do, sir," she affirmed proudly, her chest inflating slightly. "I hear many things in this house long before they ever come up in the papers, but I know my place. I don't blab. And Mr. Bertram knows that. He knows he can trust me," she told him firmly.

Gladys, it seemed, blended into the background. She was a cornerstone of the inner workings of the house that no one seemed to notice anymore. She heard most things, personal and professional, and it transpired had quite a strong and entertaining political opinion more left wing than she would ever have admitted to William Bertram. She was never asked her opinion and she never offered it. In her eyes this was a professional working relationship and personalities didn't come into it.

"Tell me what's been going on here these last days," he probed, feeling that now she had relaxed a little.

The argument between William and Seb captured his interest and he fully expected Seb not to mention it.

But he was wrong. Seb was very open about the argument and the reasons for it.

"My father," he told them from the comfort of the couch in his office, sipping his Nespresso from a miniature glass cup, "was about to ruin me."

"How so?" Milford asked the remarkably relaxed Seb lounging with his legs crossed and one arm draped across the back of the sofa.

"Well, although I'm sure you already know this, my father was involved in a property deal that is being investigated."

"And how were you involved?"

"Basically I helped him and his business partners to set up the deal for the purchase of the land, but my father it appears was foolish enough to forge some key signatures on certain documents relating to the bank loan as well as ownership of other properties that he used to guarantee his own personal loan. And I 'witnessed' the signatures – on my father's say-so without actually seeing the documents being signed."

"I see," Milford responded. It was a good summation – he already knew about that. "And tell me what the implications were for you?"

"Worst case scenario, in simple terms, I'd be barred from working in the industry again, my reputation would be shot and essentially I'd be ruined." He laughed sardonically. "Best case scenario, I'd get a fine but the negative effects on my reputation, which in this industry is critical, would make it difficult to recover."

"So what happens now that your father is dead?" Milford enquired, prompting a heavy huff from Seb.

"I see where you're going with this," he said, "so let me get straight to the point. You're asking if I'm better off?" Shrugging his shoulders, he thought for a minute then replied, "Yes and no." Putting the cup down on the table he rested his elbows on his knees, leaned in closer and looked intently at Milford. "Professionally, am I better off now that my father is dead? No. I am not. The problem still exists. Whether I like it or not or meant it or not, I did actually falsely witness signatures that weren't performed in my presence." Again he shrugged his shoulders. "Simple as that." He put his head down, still fuming at his naive error in trusting his father. "That said, I do have evidence, emails between my father and his partners that show I didn't purposely set out to mislead the bank. It shows they set me up."

"So, it's not as bad as it could be?" Milford suggested.

"No, thankfully it's not."

"And personally?" Milford prompted.

"Well, personally am I better off without him? Then, truthfully I have to answer yes, yes, I am. But did I kill him?"

"Well, did you?" Milford asked, equally straight and to the point.

"No. No, I didn't," Seb said with a patronising smirk, "and even if I did I'm not likely to admit it to you now, am I?"

His tone ground on Milford's nerves.

"These emails you mentioned, did you get those off your father, as evidence, before he died?"

"No, actually, I have my own team working on this. It's all my own handiwork."

"And what about your father's reputation?"

"Who cares?" Seb threw out coldly with a wide sweep of his arm. "He's no longer with us."

Milford's skin prickled. He didn't like Seb much and he was sure, without being bothered, that the feelings were likely to be mutual.

"So, you're glad he's dead?"

Seb considered both Milford and the question for a minute before answering.

"I wouldn't say necessarily that I'm *glad*, but I won't miss him. My father was a bully who put himself above everyone and everything else. He deserved what he got."

Milford looked at him with wide eyes, not in the slightest bit thrown but slightly astonished by Seb's cavalier and overly candid attitude.

"Can I ask what you did after Enya called you from the house?"

"You can," he responded smartly. "I was here in the office and –"

"Do you often work late?" Evans interrupted from her standing position behind the couch.

Seb looked at her with disdain. "Yes, I do. Often. If you must know I'm working on trying to unravel the mess my soon-to-be-ex-wife left behind her. I was in my office, the call came through on my mobile, I took it, told Enya to stay put, not to touch anything. I told her I'd be there as quick as I could and I left."

"What time was that?"

"About five or ten past eight, I think."

"Was there anyone else here with you?"

"I don't think so, not from about seven onwards. Unlike me, my colleagues all tend to have lives outside of here."

"How long does it take to get from here to your parents' house?" Milford asked.

"Fifteen, maybe twenty minutes?"

"And that night?" he probed.

"Fifteen, maybe twenty minutes," Seb repeated with bored, half-closed eyes, irritated by the question.

"So, just to be clear, Enya called you at five or ten past eight but you didn't leave the office till close to eight thirty, because if memory serves me rightly you arrived at the house at about eight forty-five, correct?"

"That's right."

"Why the delay?"

"Obviously I had to close up the office – that takes time." His words were off-hand and dismissive, his face poker-straight, giving nothing away except contempt for their presence.

"I understand," Milford said, "that you had access to the safe?"

"No". Technically that's not correct. Without the key no one had access and Father kept the key with him at all times. It was up to him who he chose to give it to."

"Interesting. But you, I have been told, were the only he allowed use the key, in his presence as you say."

"True," Seb answered, but offered no further explanation.

"So as the only other person to gain recent access to the safe, you should be able to tell me if you've had any thoughts on what might have been in there that was so desperately sought after by the apparent thief."

Sensing a trap, Seb looked directly at him. "I wouldn't say recent access – it has been some time since I opened the safe. The last time was almost a year ago now and, no, I have no idea what might have been in there or what might have been taken."

"We've come up with a pretty straightforward theory –"

"Well, good for you," Sebastian said, eyeing the silent Evans. "You must be very proud of yourselves."

"The idea is that whoever came into your parents' house came with the specific intention of retrieving something that perhaps your father was holding from them, or even against them."

"Well, now," Seb replied, "aren't you and your officers a hive of intelligent ideas! For the record, yes, I would agree with you. It makes perfect sense."

"Was your father holding anything back on you?" Milford asked directly.

"I don't know. You tell me. You're the detective." He looked at his watch. "Now. If you don't mind, I have an appointment and I'm late, so ..." he stood up, the meeting, in his eyes, over, "unless you've got anything useful to tell me about the death of my father, I suggest you leave and if you have any further need of me, let me know, and I will gladly come to the station. With my solicitor."

Striding to his desk he picked up the telephone.

"Lucy," he instructed firmly, "the officers are ready to leave. Please show them out."

With a pleasant if superficial smile Lucy promptly entered the room, eyed Seb briefly and held the door open.

"If you'll follow me."

Pulling up outside Cormac's apartment Milford admired the neighbourhood and instinctively priced the location. Cormac didn't drive so there was no car but chained to the railings was a high-spec hybrid bike missing its saddle. Milford rang the bell then turned to appreciate the view of the private park and hushed tone of the square. At ten o'clock on a bright Saturday morning there weren't many people about.

Evans stood behind him, upright and official with a neutral expression, waiting patiently for the door to be answered, delighted she had become such an integral part of the investigation.

If he was surprised to see them both at his door on a beautiful Saturday morning Cormac didn't show it. He brought them through to the living room and offered them a cup of the coffee whose aroma was tantalisingly apparent from the moment they entered the apartment. Gathering up the array of open newspapers and magazines, apologising unnecessarily for the non-existent mess, he invited them to take a seat.

"Lovely spot," Milford complimented pleasantly, breaking the tension that hung in the air.

"I think so," Cormac replied. "Again, sorry about the mess. I wasn't expecting guests this morning."

"Just a quick call, Cormac," Milford assured him with a smile. "I just need to get some things straight in my head."

"Sure. Well, make yourselves comfortable and I'll get you that coffee."

He left and returned minutes later with a tray and invited them to help themselves to milk and sugar.

"So," Milford started when they had all settled down with their coffees, "tell me about the argument with your father."

Cormac shook his head with a knowing smile. "I'm assuming you're referring to his upset at my recent '*misdemeanour*'," he said, making finger quote-marks in the air while raising his eyebrows. "Am I right?"

"Yes, we did hear about it alright. Interesting videos," Milford remarked with a slow, sympathetic and non-judgmental nod.

"Well. Let's just say it wasn't one of my finest moments, and I didn't have the money to stop them."

"You were being bribed but never reported it?"

Milford asked curiously, already knowing the answer.

"Yes and no respectively."

"You do realise that blackmail is an offence?"

"I do and so is taking cocaine," Cormac said smartly. "I've learnt my lesson. A big one at that and I'm lucky not to have been fired outright, so really I just want to forget it."

"Do you know who it was?"

Cormac nodded. "I certainly do."

"Well, at least you didn't pay them." Milford paused, looking at Cormac whose smile was tinged with regret.

"No," he replied, "I didn't pay them." A wave of nausea rose in his throat at the memory of what he had done in trying to gather the funds to do just that.

"Well, to be honest, and I know you probably don't think so now, but if it's any consolation it's the best outcome. In my experience if you'd paid them they'd only have come back for more. You'd never see the end of it. At least this way it's over."

Cormac nodded, actually believing him. It was the best outcome really. He could learn to live with the nasty taste in his mouth every time he thought of it and the irritating sniggers in the uni corridors would eventually fizzle out once they found something more tantalising to talk about.

"So, this argument with your dad then?" Milford encouraged him.

"Well, as I'm sure you can imagine, Dad wasn't happy. He was furious to say the least and only just out of hospital – they probably timed its release to coincide, maximum effect and all that."

"So he kicked you out?"

"Yep, he did that alright," Cormac replied,

remembering his harsh reaction and vitriolic words. "He went a bit nuclear. It wasn't very pleasant. I had ruined his reputation, apparently, like I did it on purpose."

"I'd say that didn't go down well, him shouting at you like that at –" Milford paused to feign a mental calculation, "all of forty-one years old and in front of a practical stranger? McDaid?"

Cormac gave a little laugh. "No, it didn't. But would I have killed him for it? I don't think so. My father was a nasty man. He was always horrible to us all. He tormented us for years but we were used to it. He'd be dead a long time ago if that was the approach we took and, in that case, any one of us would have done it."

"Did you try to borrow money from him?" Milford probed.

Cormac threw his head back in almost hysterical laughter. "No! No, I didn't," he gasped. "He wasn't that sort of dad. If you must know, I asked Kathryn, Seb's wife. She was going to give it to me." For a split second he wondered what harm would it do to tell him what really happened, show Seb up for the bastard he was, maybe even earn a little sympathy in the process? But pride and what remained of his dignity stopped him, that along with a smidgen of belated loyalty to his sufficiently humiliated brother.

"And what happened there?" Milford asked.

"Seb found out and wouldn't let her give it to me."

"Right," Milford responded, fascinated even more by the surprising little twists and turns this family seemed to take at every turn. He could only imagine the events that must have followed that let-down. "If I can just go back to the day your father died?"

"Sure."

"Yourself and Enya left your parents' house, dropped off the car then went into town to a bar, yes?"

"That's right."

"It's what, maybe a twenty-minute journey between town and your parents?"

"Sounds about right."

"So it's not beyond the realms of possibility that either yourself or your sister could have skipped out and come back here with your alibi intact?"

"I think Enya would've noticed, don't you?" Cormac suggested with a smug grin.

"Maybe you left together to return here? It's possible," he offered in response to Cormac's head-shaking denial. "So, you say both of you left the bar at around six thirty?"

"Yep."

"And you each went your separate ways, alone?"

"That's correct."

"Why?"

Cormac shrugged. "I had work the next day and I knew if Enya came back with me to mine, we'd have opened another bottle of wine and who knows what time we'd have finished up, and frankly I'm in enough trouble at work as it is. I'm supposed to be on good behaviour, you know."

"What was to stop either of you heading over to your parents' house at that point – you had plenty of time."

"Absolutely nothing. But we didn't, or at least I didn't and I'm pretty sure neither did she."

"Yes, but what if you were covering for each other? You said yourself there's no love lost between any of you and your father. You could have planned it that way."

"We could have but we didn't," Cormac replied, not in the least bit amused by the suggestion. "Have you said this to Enya?"

"No, not yet, but we will," Milford told him. "One last thing before we wrap up. Who do *you* think killed your father?" He knew it was a pointless question but asked it anyway, prompting a curiously defensive response.

"Me? Christ, I don't know," Cormac replied, almost appalled by the question and nervous for the first time since they came into his apartment. "How would I? I mean, why would I?"

"So, what do you think?" Milford asked Evans as they strapped into the car.

"I'm not sure. He could have done it, he has the time and motive, but I'm not convinced. He just doesn't seem the type, does he?"

"Hmmm," Milford mused, putting the car in gear. "There never is a type, Evans. That's the problem."

Say nothing. Say nothing. Say nothing, Ciara repeated over and over in her head, nervously facing Milford.

They had arrived, not unexpectedly, at her house about ten minutes previously and, after the usual greetings and pleasantries and the making of tea by Enya, Milford asked to speak to Ciara first, in private.

Her knees quaked, her hands shook and her heart was beating as loud and as hard as a bass drum. The soothing *you'll-be-alright* look from Enya as she closed the door to the living room didn't help much either. She was going to mess this up, she knew it. She always did mess things up.

"Why so nervous, Ciara?" Milford asked her gently.

"You're going to think it was me."

"Ciara, we don't think it was you," said Evans.

"You don't?" she repeated, almost surprised.

"No, we just need to ask you some questions, just to get a better picture of what happened when you got to the house," Evans assured her with a smile.

"Why would we think it was you?" Milford asked with less niceness than his colleague, happy to play bad cop to Evans's good one.

"Well, because I probably have the best reason of all, don't I? Because of who I am and what he did to my mother, my real mother. I'm the one with the real motive, I'm the one who shouted my head off at him and even I'd think it was me if I were you."

"Tell us how you came about your discovery – you know, about your parents," asked Milford.

They listened intently to her as she spoke, like this was the first time they'd heard the story, fascinated on the one hand and disturbed on the other. This wasn't just any man and any secret; this was a public representative selected to govern their country on their behalf. And now they realised this was a man with neither morals nor scruples. This was a man they knew, that the whole country knew and one who should have known better. Secretly, both Evans and Milford were thinking that if she did do it – murder her father – not only did he deserve it but she deserved to get away with it.

"You need to speak to Martha, she really knows more about it than I do," Ciara said when she came to the end of her story. "She got a lot from the home in Ballybeak –

she showed me my mum's letter."

"So you've spoken to Martha then about this?" Evans asked gently.

Milford was glad she was there as the moment called for the sensitivity of a woman and Evans was filling the role pretty well.

"Yes," Ciara smiled, "we've talked a good bit since all this came out. She's pretty messed up too. Rian and her are supposed to be getting married."

"Supposed to be?" Milford inquired, hoping he didn't sound too forced.

"It's all a bit up in the air, to be honest. I don't think either of them wants to rush into anything until this gets sorted."

"Understandable," Milford muttered.

"That's why I went to see my father at the hospital," she told him, conscious it was in fact the last time she saw him alive. "I still have so many questions, but now ..." Her words hung loose in the air, the words shared with the nurse in the corridor coming back once more to haunt her.

"I have to ask this, Ciara," Evans said kindly. "Can you tell me where you were that day, between four thirty and eight?"

"I was at home for the most part of the day. I knew Dad was being discharged from the hospital and that the others were going back to the house to see him but I couldn't bear the idea of being around him so I let Enya go without me. Robert was on call and, well, the walls of the house were closing in on me and I just thought a walk would help me clear my head. So I headed out to Strandhill and walked the length of the beach."

"Did you meet anyone?" Milford asked. "Can anyone confirm that you were there?"

"There were lots of people there but I didn't see anyone I knew – certainly didn't talk to anyone – so no, I suppose not."

"And what time did you get home?"

"Oh God, I don't know – about half seven, maybe eight?"

Milford recorded the times.

"Thanks, Ciara," he said. "I think that's about it for the moment."

Evans stood to walk over and open the door.

The interview was over and Ciara left, relieved and more relaxed than when she had sat down.

Enya almost bounded into the room, delighted, it seemed, to have her say. She oozed a heady combination of confidence mixed with defiance.

"So," she started, expertly hijacking the interview, "I'm just going to say it out straight, put it out there, so to speak."

She looked at both of them, making sure they were ready and listening.

"I didn't like my father very much. He was a bully and a control freak who as good as ruined my life and I am glad he is dead. Now maybe we can get on with our lives, the way we want to and not the way he'd have liked us to." Spectacularly relieved to have that off her chest, she clasped her hands in her lap, prepared to take any questions and face the consequences of her confession.

"Right!" Milford replied, sitting back in the chair as if blown there by her outburst. "That's very honest of you."

"Well, I thought I'd be better to get it out in the open from the get-go. And just so you know, I didn't kill him. I could have, but I didn't."

"How could you have killed him, Ms Bertram?"

"Enya, please," she replied, throwing her eyes to heaven. "I don't mean literally – but figuratively speaking I could have done it. I had a motive, I suppose."

"Why so?"

"That man did his best to control me and interfere with my life for as long as I can remember."

"Maybe he just wanted the best for you?" Milford suggested.

"Best for himself more like. Dad never did anything '*just*' for any of us – everything had to have a reason that served his purpose, no one else's."

"That's a bit harsh, don't you think?"

"No. I don't."

"So, you said you're glad he's dead then."

She didn't hesitate for a moment. "Yes," she told him firmly, "yes, I am. I'm sorry he died *that way* but yes. Yes, I am."

"They're strong words, Enya, so why should I believe you didn't do it?"

"Because I didn't and you'd have to prove I did," she challenged him confidently.

"But you did discover his body,"

"*Ah-ha!* I discovered it but I didn't create it," she said with a cheeky grin.

"So tell me what happened?"

"I told you most of this before."

"I know, just tell me again, to be sure you've left nothing out."

"I got to the house at about five to eight. Cormac and I had had a few drinks and, well, I was a bit pissed and I wanted to give my father a piece of my mind. He'd behaved appallingly earlier to everyone and it was about time someone stood up to him, I thought. I didn't want him to get away with it. He'd got no right."

Nodding as if to agree, Milford encouraged her to continue.

"The cars were there and there was a light on in the living room so I just assumed they were still up. But there was no answer at the door so I used the spare key."

"Where was it?"

"In its usual spot in the fake rock thingy by the pots."

"Go on."

"When I got inside, I called out. But there wasn't a sound."

Despite her bravado and guff he could tell that Enya was upset by her experience. She closed her eyes as she remembered and relived the journey. "I stood in the hall for a while and listened but I couldn't hear a thing. It was so quiet. So, I went straight into the sitting room. I suppose I was kind of expecting a bit of trouble anyway and I was a little tense not to mention a little tipsy." She opened her eyes to look at Milford. "And when I went into the room there he was. Slumped over the table. The lamps weren't on, just the main light. I went to him. I put my hand on his shoulder. But he didn't move. I knew he was dead. I saw the blood, you couldn't miss it – it was everywhere." She shivered. "I think I screamed, I can't remember. I'm not sure. And then I thought, shit, Mum. And I called her name. But she didn't reply. So I ran. I went straight upstairs – I ran up those stairs faster than I've ever done before."

She stopped talking and opened her eyes wide. Taking a deep breath, her tone becoming less emotional and more direct, she continued on the journey.

"I didn't know what to expect, but there she was, unconscious but alive. Thankfully." She gave a nervous laugh. "I wasn't sure if she was actually alive until I took her pulse and realised her state was self-inflicted – she was just pissed. I tried to wake her but she wouldn't open her eyes, so I rang Seb." Enya stopped and shrugged. "I didn't know what else to do."

"What time was that?" Evans asked.

"Oh about eight, I don't know. Seb said he was on his way, not to touch anything and then, well, I think I tried to wake her again."

"Did your brother tell you to call us, the police?" Evans asked.

"Not exactly – he said to call the ambulance but I just wanted her to wake up, she was really drowsy, and when she did kind of come round a little, only then did I call them and they called you."

"What time was that?"

"Oh God, I don't remember for sure." She agonised, closing her eyes in a tight squeeze, pressing herself to recall. "I think about ten past, maybe quarter past eight."

"Okay, that's great. And then?"

"Well, then you arrived first and Seb after that."

"Did Barbara say anything to you when she woke up?"

"No. Nothing and she's still not saying anything. I don't know what's wrong with her. The doctors are saying its post-traumatic stress syndrome or something ridiculous like that."

"You don't seem very sympathetic."

"I'm not!"

"So, bringing you back a little, tell us," he asked, changing direction, "what you did after you left your parents that evening."

"You know! Cormac has already told you, and he also told me what you think, but for what it's worth we left my parents and drove back to Ciara's. Ciara wasn't there and Robert needed his car because he was on call so we took a taxi into town for a bite to eat and a bit of a post mortem about what happened with Dad." She flushed at her unfortunate choice of words.

Ignoring it, Milford enquired formally, "And do you know where Ciara was?"

"Not there anyway!" She laughed at her own flippant remark but, seeing his face turn sour, replied with a little more decorum. "I don't know. Robert said he'd only just got back and she'd gone for a walk."

"So you went into town?"

"Yes. The plan was to get stinking drunk, but it wasn't working."

"How so?"

"Cormac was getting all maudlin and I can't stand that and, anyway, he had work the next day so ..."

"So what time did you stay until?"

"I don't know, about six or so?"

"And where did you go from there?"

"We left the bar and then he went his way and I went mine. I think he got the bus, but I took a taxi."

"Did you keep the receipt?"

"No. Sorry. Anyway I got to Ciara's but no one was home. I managed to work myself up into a right state and made my way back to Mum and Dad's house, and, well, the rest you already know."

The clock ticked loudly on the mantelpiece as Milford took his notes. He purposely let the silence linger longer than was necessary. Let her stew a bit, he thought.

Nervously Enya waited for him to finish, unconsciously wiping her clammy palms on the legs of her trousers, the edge taken off her attitude.

"So tell me about your relationship with your father," Milford eventually asked her.

"I thought I'd made that pretty clear already."

"Well, you clearly don't like him very much, but why?" Milford prodded.

"Seriously?" she demanded. "Look at what's just happened. Look at what he did to me, what he's done to Mum for years, to the lads. The man was a pig."

"And what do you make of Ciara and her situation?" he asked, changing tack.

"It's completely nuts. I mean that poor woman – her birth mother, Lillian – he completely manipulated and ruined a perfectly innocent life, pushed her to suicide." Her face was twisting in a display of disgust.

He wasn't surprised by her outburst and imagined they all felt that way about William.

But Enya wasn't done yet.

"And as for Mother, well, she just doesn't care anymore, does she – hasn't for years – and now we know why. This will mess her up even more. Even dead he's going to continue causing trouble."

"So what do you think happened in the house?" he asked.

"I think his meddling and fooling around just caught up with him. You don't think that Cormac's conduct came from nowhere, do you?" she asked cockily. "My father managed to upset so many people, one too many it would appear." She stopped to look at Milford. "I just think that the only thing you'll find taken from the house was whatever it was Dad was using against someone. I think they came, fought back and defending themselves took whatever it was he had against them and," she shrugged, "it's gone now."

"And what about you? What did he have belonging to you?"

Milford saw her defiant spark flicker and almost vanish.

"For years I blamed him for taking the single most precious thing I had in the world that I can never get back. But now ..." she paused, biting back the tears, refusing to give his memory the pleasure of making her cry, "now I don't think he deserves even that much of my attention."

"I'm sorry, sorry you feel that way," Milford offered, a little embarrassed by his petulance with her.

"What are you sorry for?" She looked at him as if he were stupid. "You did nothing."

"Bloody hell," Evans heaved once they had the house to their backs, "that was a bit intense, wasn't it?" She sighed almost in awe of the audacious young woman as they drove down the dark tree-lined approach to Ciara's house out onto the main road.

A little stirred, Milford didn't quite know what to think. Was Enya challenging him to catch her, he thought, or was she using the truth of her innocence as an outward and petulant display of contempt for the dead man?

Martha and Rian sat hand in hand, but despite the apparent display of affection there was an irrefutable tightness between them.

"It's important you know this," Martha told them, her voice laced with trepidation.

"We *both* feel it's important," Rian stressed, looking at Martha with strained tenderness.

Intrigued, Milford sat back, happy to listen and curious to know more. They had come to the station of their own volition and asked to speak with him. They were next on his interview list, so he was completely prepared.

"As soon as I found out what happened to Lillian," Martha stated, "I promised I'd find him and make him pay."

"Who's *he*?" asked Milford, immediately alert.

"William Bertram," Martha replied, her face flushed as she looked straight into his eyes.

"Should I be recording this?" he asked, acutely aware of what this informal meeting was beginning to sound like.

"Let me explain first. If needs be I'll happily say it twice."

Intuitively he let her go on.

"I set about finding him, and it wasn't hard. He wasn't exactly a shrinking violet." She laughed. "In my mind I had decided that I needed to track him down, observe him for a while and then decide how best to get to him."

Milford felt her pain. He could tell how difficult her confession was to vocalise and appreciated how difficult it must be for Rian to hear her say it.

"Aside from finding him I was of course also eager to see Ciara for myself. I cried the first day I saw her." Her eyes brimmed again, but taking a breath she kept them at bay and recovered her professional tone. "I'll never forget it. It was the day he was re-elected for a second term. There was a press conference and she was there, looking so awkward and glum. They all looked pretty uncomfortable actually, to tell you the truth." She glanced at Rian who smiled, knowing exactly what she meant. "I think I was most surprised by how alike she was to the others . . . that kind of got to me. I wanted her to be different, more like me. Or Lillian if I'm honest, but I couldn't see Lillian in her at all. That was tough." She took a moment to check her composure. "In the beginning I actually thought Enya would be my way in. She looked like the kind of person I could connect easily with, and she is, but then her world kind of fell apart and then, well, it just didn't seem right. She'd been through enough. So I looked at Rian and it sort of changed everything, more by accident than by design really. It wasn't a plan, more of a contingency that morphed into something else completely." In her admission she threw an uneasy glance at her fiancé and clutched his hand tightly. "Getting to know Rian, it was easy to see how Lillian might have fallen for William. He was so utterly charming, so incredibly charismatic. Rian, that is. I found him so empathetic, so attractive. It wasn't anything I'd anticipated and I certainly didn't bank on falling in love with him." She sobbed suddenly. It came from deep inside her, guttural and untamed.

Rian lifted her hand to his lips and kissed it gingerly then dropped his head, unable to look at her.

Her pain was palpable.

"What was your plan?" Milford asked her, sitting

forward to rest his elbows on the table. “What were you going to do?”

“I don’t know,” she sighed. “I hadn’t thought it through that far. All I knew for sure was that I wanted William to suffer like we did. I wanted him to experience our pain. I even thought about how to … to …” she stumbled over the words, humiliated by their implications, past and future, “how to end his life. Just as William, indirectly I know, did to Lillian. But even though it consumed my every waking moment I just couldn’t see beyond the decision: I wanted to, but didn’t know how, or where even to begin.” Her head shook unsteadily on her shoulders as if inebriated by her shame and humiliation. “And then all those poisonous thoughts just kind of stopped, like it didn’t matter anymore, and it became more important to focus my energy on trying to find a solution to how we could overcome who I am, who his father is. It all just changed.” She shrugged. “I knew I’d have to tell Rian this one day. I didn’t plan on keeping it a secret. Not in the end, not once I knew I loved him.” She looked beseechingly at Rian. “And I do. I love you, Rian. You mean the world to me, and I know I can’t fix this but I can’t let this whole thing ruin our lives. I won’t.” Pathetic tears of humiliation rushed down her cheeks as if in a race to reach her chin as she implored him to listen and understand.

Milford blushed, embarrassed to be caught in the middle of such a heartfelt and genuine plea for absolution and acceptance.

The spectacle of the demise of a prominent and respected family was nothing short of an intimate cataclysm in motion. Morally, it wasn’t right that this much pain was being witnessed so publically. For six out of the seven family members it wasn't fair. But for one, these were the consequence of his lifetime of actions.

"Let's take a break," he suggested, getting up from his chair, affording them a moment on their own. "Can I get you some coffee? Water?"

"No, thanks," they replied in unison before slipping into an uncomfortable silence.

Milford indicated to Evans to follow him.

"Oh my God," Evans whispered as the door closed behind them.

They walked back to his office.

"What do you think?" Evans asked.

"I have no idea, but I do think it's a bloody mess."

A knock on the frame of the open door took their attention and turning they were immediately on alert.

Superintendent Lisa Burke stood framed by the open door. Although her face was smiling, Milford had the experience to know that she wasn't smiling inside.

"What's the update on the Bertram case?" she demanded, her tone brisk and direct.

"We're just about done with the interviews now, ma'am."

"Good. Any success?"

Evans looked at Milford, curious to know for herself how he'd respond.

"I think so," he told her to raised eyebrows from both his boss and the young officer.

"Don't waste time, Milford. The media are all over this one. They're after blood here."

"I know, ma'am, I'm hoping for a result shortly."

"Excellent. You can brief me fully in my office in ten," she said, turning as she spoke.

Chapter 31

The letter, when it arrived, was handed to him by the desk sergeant with a sly and seemingly knowing smirk. Only when Milford inspected it further did he understand why. His name, beautifully scripted on the front of the envelope, combined with the distinctly female scent coming from it had all the suggestion and ingredients of a good old-fashioned love letter. Throwing a tired but superior glance at his juvenile colleague, intrigued, he pulled away from his computer and stuck his thumb under the seal at the back to tear it open unceremoniously.

Dear Detective Milford, it began.

Skipping to the end he searched for a signature to see who it was from then, turning back the sheets of vintage and decadently elegant writing paper, he continued to read.

Permit me to begin this letter with an apology: I am sorry to have lied to you. Believe me, it wasn't intentional. It is not in my nature to be deceitful. It came about more by accident than on purpose. Call it an opportunity, so to speak, that I couldn't see wasted.

Allow me to fill you in on recent events and, hopefully, when I'm done you'll understand and forgive me.

I shall start by telling you something that will surprise you: I am almost three weeks sober now, to the day. The evening of William's death the reason Enya couldn't wake me was not because I was drunk, but rather because I was asleep. Not just halfway or partly dozing, I mean really asleep. I don't think I've slept that soundly in years. You hear people compare the two – a sober and a drunken sleep – and it is true, as I have now discovered, there is a significant difference. Combine that with the reprieve of having finally fixed a wrong that has been an irritant for so long, I don't know, like a humming sound in a room that you can't trace. My resulting slumber, having found and silenced that proverbial hum, is out of this world, literally.

I won't lie to you by saying I wasn't tempted by the bottles on the tray and as you know I even went so far as to take one with me that night as I left the sitting room but I have invested too much at this stage to go back and I refuse to give him that pleasure. I have to say I haven't enjoyed myself much. I had forgotten how my mind actually works, how I work. I'm not sure I like myself much, but I deserved a chance to at least try to reacquaint myself with myself if only for a few weeks.

And I'm intrigued by who I have become. It's like I've been driving all these years with the handbrake on: the distance I make is a struggle and it just doesn't feel right. And now, released, I know what I've been doing wrong all these years.

I've written and rewritten this letter a hundred times over trying to eloquently describe what happened that night. But each time I read it back it fails to capture the experience as I believe it warrants to be both documented and remembered.

What I cannot vocalise in words from my mouth I had hoped I would be able to transfer easily to paper, but it's not as easy as it sounds. Remembering isn't coming effortlessly, not from the shame or the disappointment or even the remorse of the events of that night but more from the speed at which they happened. My mind raced. It happened so very quickly. I had hardly time to think.

That evening, when I did finally wake all I saw in Enya's eyes as she looked over me was relief: relief that I was alive, I think. She hugged me so hard. I can't ever remember her, or any of them for that matter, doing that and it felt gorgeous. She struck a chord in my heart and it sounded too beautiful to let go, so I didn't.

Seeing the bottle by my bed she just assumed I'd been drinking, as did you, I believe, and it was easier to let her believe she was correct. She looked flushed but at the same time remarkably calm. I was sorry she had to be the one to find him. She asked me what I'd done and I told her the truth: I told her it was over. I told her I'd finished it. Incredibly she hugged me harder. I didn't want her to let go. Sleep she said, so I did.

And when I woke up again she was still there. They rallied about me then, the children, all of them, in the days that followed. And I loved it. My plan hadn't involved being around this long. But I couldn't leave, not yet. I only wanted to experience their love a little bit longer. It was never, I thought, too much to ask and definitely worth the risk. But I see you now, watching them, interrogating them over their every move. I can see you wondering which one of them is to blame. Just who is the culprit. But I am telling you now that the only thing they are guilty of is protecting me, or trying to. I am telling you now, you can stop looking because I did it. I ended William's life.

"*Evans!*" Milford roared from his office without putting the letter down.

"Yes, sir," she responded at his door almost immediately, still chewing a mouthful of freshly prepared ham-and-cheese toastie.

"See if there's a squad car in the vicinity of the Bertrams' and send it round there *fast* to check on Barbara Bertram. And when you've done that get yourself together and we'll follow. Right? I'll wait for you downstairs. And hurry."

"Yes, sir," she said, gulping down her food.

He was ready and waiting when only minutes later she met him at the entrance, his face flushed and urgent.

"Here," he said, throwing her the keys. "You drive."

Putting the car in gear Evans drove out of the station and with their lights blaring and her foot to the floor she tore up the road to the Bertram family home.

And for Milford his thoughts, intensified by the speed and urgency he was experiencing, started to make some sense. This case was one of his most challenging, mainly, he decided, because it was different. In most crimes there were inconsistencies, little discrepancies that niggled and irritated into the small hours of the morning. Irregularities that couldn't be explained, moments unaccounted for. But not here. With this one it was absolutely seamless, no flaws, no time delays. Their stories matched perfectly. And that was odd. And then there was his instinct, which up until now he could rely on to point him in a direction, any direction, sometimes wrong, sometimes right, but a direction nonetheless. But with this one there was nothing. With the Bertrams, they had stripped all the personality out of their father's murder and he couldn't figure it out. Until now. They had, he now knew, erased its character to protect their mother.

Caught in the moment of his revelation, Milford continued to read.

Why? I suspect you're asking yourself. Well, let me tell you. William was no good, not for himself, not for me and not for the children. I should have stood up to him just as I should have stood up for them but I did neither, and seeing him behave like such a bastard only served to make me feel like an idiot all over again. And while back then, when the children were much younger, I knew no better, I had the excuse of youth to fall back on. However, I am not so lucky now. What is it they say: fool me once shame on you but fool me twice shame on me. Well, shame on me, thinking I could remain with him, after everything he's done. I should have left him then in the past but I had neither the confidence nor the brains to do it. And here I was, only days ago, about to make the same monumental mistake all over again. But watching him rage on like that, listening to the words falling from his mouth, each one nastier and meaner than the last, was thankfully just too much. And I thought to myself: Really? Is this the way I want it to be? It was supposed to be different. I just assumed after his heart attack that he would be different: he certainly seemed so in the hospital. But, as we now know, I am a fool.

"Sorry, sir," Evans interrupted, "but can you fill me in on what's going on?"

"Just drive, Evans," Milford said, anxious to get to the end of both the letter and the journey.

I sat that evening listening to him drone on and on, until I stopped hearing his words. I don't know how long we sat, him in the chair at the bureau ranting to himself but wanting me to hear and me by the fire just staring at the flames flickering. And it caught my eye. It was decent enough size with the butt end of a branch coming out of it. I don't think I thought much about it. I just imagined myself doing it. And then it came to me, an odd but honest question: What if? What if I hadn't called the ambulance then? What if I just hit him now? And then: Why not? Funnily enough, he didn't hear me get up from my chair to rummage in the log basket, nor did he hear me as I approached him. I didn't try to sneak up on him or anything. I suppose I'm just light on my feet, that's all. And lifting it high I brought it down hard on his head and, just like that, he shut up. The noise it made was so peculiar but the silence immediately after was delicious. He didn't fall immediately, just kind of teetered before slipping a little then toppling over, his head first on to the desk. I watched for a minute, rapt by the sight of the blood that trickled from his wound to colour the desk and thicken in his hair. But it didn't stay that exciting for long and bored by it I left. I was making my way upstairs and I'm not sure what came over me – an intense fury perhaps at what I had just done? That burst of anger drove me into the study to rip that room asunder, his room. I swept books off shelves, papers off his desk. I smashed lamps and ornaments: I wanted him and everything to do with him gone. I even emptied the safe. At last I stopped myself and, exhausted by it all, emotionally and physically drained, I surveyed my work and, satisfied, left and went to bed. And that's it.

"That couldn't be it!" Milford shouted at Barbara Bertram's letter. "What about the broken window?"

"Sorry, sir," Evans interjected, running another red light. "What are you talking about?"

"This," he blustered, shaking the letter in his hand, "is apparently Barbara Bertram's confession but she's left us hanging!"

So you see, you can stop looking now. I've told you the important bits, the rest is self-explanatory and really quite superfluous. I've enjoyed the last few days immensely, I've experienced my children as I should have and I think, I pray, I have corrected a great wrong done to Ciara. I know she forgives me and I guess she'll eventually forgive her father, not that I really care but it's not in her nature to hold on to her rancour for long. But I'm done now, and it's my time to go.

"Jesus, Evans, step on it," he urged. "She's in trouble. It's all here. She's telling us."

By the time you get this I will have picked up the end of my original plan and sent myself off to where it is I truly deserve to be: let God be the judge of that. I know I'm being a coward, but I cannot face my future with only myself to entertain me. This is my gesture to Lillian: a lovely innocent child deceived and abused by a monster. I am that monster.

By the time they reached the house the squad car was there. One of the officers had scaled the wall to gain access to the garden and was now knocking hard on the door.

"It's no use knocking, she won't answer!" Milford yelled over the tall timber gate. "Open the gate, use the sensor!" he shouted and minutes later heard the mechanism kick in and the gate slowly draw aside. Dashing in, he ran up the steps.

"Find the key thingy," he told them frantically, searching around the pots of shrubs.

"The what?" the confused Garda asked.

"It's a key holder that looks like a rock," he told them. "Enya said she used it to get in the night William was murdered. I told them to get rid of it, but I'll bet a million to one they didn't listen."

And sure enough it was eventually found behind one of the many plant pots.

Pushing the key into the lock and the door into the hall Milford charged up the stairs while Evans followed, calling out a pointless "*Barbara!*" as he ran.

She was in her room, lying on the bed, on top of the covers, fully dressed and made up as if prepared to go out for lunch at her favourite restaurant with the girls.

"Shit," Milford whispered as he stepped towards the bed, breathless and defeated. Kneeling at her bedside he felt for a pulse. Her make-up looked dense against the pale grey of her lifeless skin. In her hand she clutched an old St. Christopher medal, for her safe passage no doubt, he thought.

"Oh God!" Evans gasped, reaching the room only seconds behind him.

"She's gone," he told her. "Call the ambulance."

She looked at peace, finally, he thought, liking the way

her lips curved round in what he could only describe as a satisfied half smile. Her job was done.

On her bedside table was a neat bundle of letters, one for each of the children explaining, no doubt, what she had done and saying goodbye.

"I'm sorry, ma'am," he told the ever-elegant Superintendent Burke with a disappointed air of defeat, "but I can't fill in the details here."

"But, you have a confession, don't you?" she asked, exasperated by him and his demands for meticulous detail.

"I do, ma'am, but it doesn't –"

"Stop right there," she told him, showing him the palm of her hand. "I've followed this one with you, I've seen what you've seen. You have here a woman so obviously distressed and oppressed that for her the detail *is* the murder, by her own admission and her own hand. So take it. Another solved and closed case under your belt. You know as well as I do sometimes we can't explain –"

"But I feel –" he interrupted.

"Stop!" she cautioned firmly. "I know what you feel, I know what you always feel. But in this instance I'm guiding you to stop and you would do well to take heed of my advice. Unless of course you're telling me you don't believe her? Do you have an alternative theory?"

"No. I believe her, but it's too easy," he ventured defiantly to which she responded with a look sharp enough to cut his argument down.

Chapter 32

The bells tolled at the end of the ceremony and once again from behind they were a unified force, standing tall, shoulder to shoulder, all dressed up for the occasion.

Here they were in familiar territory. This was where they had come as children to pray each week. It was where their parents had married and where they were each christened, all five of them, and now where both parents were buried. However, on this day they were celebrating with tears of joy rather than tears of sorrow.

Hand in hand they walked down the aisle to the joyous carnival of bells that rang out merrily to announce the blessing of their marriage. Martha and Rian smiling at their guests, hugging many, kissing some and touching fingers with others as they passed. Behind them their siblings followed. Enya beside Cormac and Ciara with Seb, walking arm in arm out of the church, into the waiting embrace of the bride and groom.

"Thank you so much," Martha whispered to Seb, looking beautiful in her cloudy-pink silk A-line dress.

Seb held open the door of his beribboned Jaguar.

"It's the least I can do," he replied honestly with a small bow.

"I hope that's because you want to and not because you feel have to," she said, feeling Rian squeeze her hand, not wanting her to upset the perfectly balanced equilibrium of the day.

But he needn't have worried. Seb, blushing brightly, lowered his eyes, knowing she knew that at a previous time not long past he wouldn't have bothered with her. "Have no doubt, it's because I want to," he said.

And once she was settled into the car he leaned in to give her a kiss on the cheek and firmly grasp his brother's hand.

"It's never too late to change," he said and actually meant it.

It was he who had spoken to Rian not long after they buried their mother and convinced him to at least give Martha a second chance. He had, Seb told him, found someone in Martha who genuinely loved him despite all the odds and it was a venture, Seb reasoned in his inimitable way, worth both the investment and the risk. The fact that Seb was even remotely concerned was the deciding factor for Rian. At the time when Seb cornered him while dealing with an overheated barbeque he was tempted to tell him to mind his own damn business, he'd done enough damage. But against his better judgement he listened without speaking, turning over the sausages and drumsticks one by one as Seb made his pitch. In doing so he opened a door to his domestically awkward brother who was doing his best to not necessarily make amends, but to connect. And Rian was glad he did.

Sitting in the luxurious back seat of the Jaguar, holding Martha's hand, he felt an enormous sense of gratitude. He was completely happy.

Through the open window Cormac handed them each a fizzing glass of champagne with a small tray of chocolate-covered strawberries.

"A little something for the journey," he told them before heading round to slip into the front passenger seat, his own glass of bubbly in hand.

"All set?" Seb asked, putting the car in gear and with a long and loud toot of the horn pulled away from the kerb to a whooping hurray from the watching crowd.

"Spill that and you'll be sorry," Seb growled at Cormac with a sideways glance.

"Don't worry, Bro, it won't last that long." And in three gulps it was gone.

Seb threw his eyes to heaven – there were some things that would never change.

From the back seat Martha observed the gesture with a quiet smile.

It had been a long and tricky road to church.

"Do you think you'll ever be able to trust me again?" she had asked Rian on one of their many journeys.

"You just need to give me time," he told her gently, conscious that by right she had more to be forgiving of than him. He still loved her but he was confused by how much. He couldn't fathom why, having been deceived so fundamentally, it didn't seem to matter to his heart. He needed the time to make sure that some possible dormant part of him didn't suddenly wake up one morning to decide 'Nope. Can't do it.'

So they started again.

"Let's keep the ceremony simple," she told Rian when finally it was clear they couldn't be without each other.

The news was met with relief and jubilation from the

girls who had to have the definition of 'simple' explained more than a few times. Although his second, this was her first wedding and while they were to be officially married in the registry office the real ceremony in Martha's eyes would be the blessing in the church.

"I don't want the memory of our day to be posed and false," she told him.

"No problem," he replied with a kiss on her lips. "Whatever you want. No formal photography so."

"But we could stretch to a DJ," she proposed with a grin, knowing how much he hated dancing. Probably because he had no rhythm, she acknowledged to herself, willing to accept him despite this undisputed failing.

"Anything to keep you happy but don't expect me to join you on the dance floor."

But he soon changed his mind and, during a quiet romantic shuffle around the small sprung maple dance floor, she whispered in his ear, "It's been perfect."

And sealing their future with a kiss he was inclined to agree.

Seb watched them from the bar, lifting his whiskey tumbler to take a long large gulp while thinking of his own failed marriage and the prospect that Rian and Martha might actually do something great for each other. Right there and then, in the midst of such apparent adoration, it was impossible not to feel a little bitter but there were positives too. It was fair to say he'd never had much time for Rian, not when they were children and certainly not as they grew older, but the recent events seemed to put things in perspective for him. There now existed between them a clandestine bond that together they were bound to safeguard.

One by one he spotted the rest of his siblings dotted around the room engaged in various acts of entertainment. They appeared almost normal, if that were even or ever possible, as if with the passing of their parents their level of dysfunction had been downgraded. They hadn't changed but their relationship with each other certainly had. Without the manacle of their parents, or parent, forcing them to be something they weren't, they were free to choose and behave as they wished. The pressure had been released.

He watched Cormac at the opposite end of the bar, flirting outrageously with a leggy brunette – he certainly hadn't learnt his lesson. Inevitably Seb thought of Kathryn, imagining her in some fancy New York loft apartment wildly spending his money. He had let her go, money and all. He could have challenged her, forced her to pay it back – she had stolen it from the company after all, not him – but he didn't bother: He didn't have the energy. While he didn't deserve the crude manner in which she left him neither did she deserve his treatment of her in their last days together. Call it guilt money, he supposed, cringing as he remembered how he'd behaved.

It was, most people who knew him well enough seemed compelled to say, time to put himself out there, like it would fix everything that needed to be mended, including his pride. And there were plenty of matchmaking situations to be avoided. While he had unquestionably mellowed over the last number of months, he hadn't gone completely soft. Letting his siblings find his next partner wasn't high on his agenda, but he knew they meant well.

And then there was Ciara. Something inside him had

opened up to her – pity or empathy, he wasn't sure. But looking at her now, laughing loudly at someone else's joke, he didn't feel the same level of irritation as he might have previously. There was a tolerance, which was odd, for him. It was just her and her way. It was sad, she had told him one afternoon shortly after they buried their mother, that between them as siblings there had been only one child and, she acknowledged miserably, she wasn't ever going to be the one to change that number. He felt her pity but in a different way. All Ciara wanted was a child. But she was never going to bear one herself. It was an official diagnosis. It was like the final slight in a year of insults for her.

When Enya first told him of her plan to offer herself as a surrogate he thought she'd finally lost it.

"No, seriously, I've been thinking about it for a while now, almost since the day I got back," she said, remembering her conversation with Ciara right after Joe left. It was just a seed then that had blossomed over the months into a fully mature idea.

"Ciara," Enya pleaded when Ciara balked at the notion after she'd first mooted it, "I'd like to help. I need to help. We have made so many mistakes this is something to make it right. It won't erase what's happened but I hope it will make it easier to cope with."

So that was the plan, for now anyway, Seb scoffed cynically as he watched, not in the least bit surprised by Enya's bored expression as one of Rian's more attractive friends did his very best to electrify her. She was damaged, of that he was sure. She had proclaimed she never wanted to replace Lia but could at least help her sister find that joy. As the patriarch of the family now he felt a responsibility for her. She had been let down by almost every man in her life, including himself, but she was a strong, capable and attractive woman. She'd bounce back, of that he was sure.

After they buried their father he eventually admitted to her what William had done with Tanglewood. But with William's death she would get the house back, there was no question of that. Seb had tried to confess to Enya the night William died. He had called her specifically, but circumstances got in the way. *Circumstances*: an interesting word to describe what had passed. A smile crossed his lips as across the room Enya, unresponsive to his flattery, swatted the eager young man away like an irritating fly. Catching her eye he acknowledged her with a discreet nod of his head. In return she raised her glass to him, their bond strengthened by what happened that night.

He had called her with the intention of exposing their father's scheme but as soon as she answered her phone he could tell something wasn't right. She had returned to the house but much earlier than she'd told Detective Milford, almost a whole two hours in fact.

"Enya, are you alright? What's up? Where are you?"

Her reply was a sob without words.

"Enya,"" he repeated, "what's happened, are you okay?"

"Holy shit, Seb," she whispered tearfully into the phone, "you need to get over here."

"Where are you?"

"Now, Seb, I mean it. *Now*. Mum, she's ..."

"What about Mum?"

"I think she's killed Dad."

Seb's heart missed a beat, immediately feeling like the world had stopped but he was still turning.

"Mum?" he said incredulously. "Alright, Enya – you're at the house, right?"

"I'm at the house, Mum and Dad's, in the hall outside her room," she answered, her breathing fast.

"And where's Dad?"

"He's downstairs. He's covered in blood, Seb, he's not moving," she told him with rising panic in her voice.

"Okay." Thinking fast, looking first at his watch then through the glazed partitions of his office to see who else was in and working. "First, you need to calm down. Take some deep breaths." He walked across his office to take his gym bag out of the closet.

He waited for her to do as he asked, listening to her suck deep gulps of air into her lungs.

"Feel any better?" he asked while unzipping the bag to see what clothes were inside.

"No," she replied honestly with a sniff.

"Did you take his pulse?"

"*Are you insane?*" she almost shrieked. "He's covered in blood for God's sake! I'm not going anywhere near him."

"Jesus," he fumed. "What about Mum?"

"She's asleep. Locked, I think."

"Okay," he said decisively, a plan forming fast in his head. "Stay there. Don't touch anything. I'm on my way."

Enya slipped to the floor in the corridor outside her mother's bedroom door and, holding her hands to her face, waited for Seb to arrive.

Seb checked his watch. It was just after six. John was the only man left in the open-plan office but giving off signs that he was ready to go. Patiently Seb sat at his computer and waited for him to leave with a cheerful wave as he passed. Waving back as casually as he could, despite the almost frantic bobbing of his knee under the desk, Seb didn't move until he was absolutely sure John had left the building. Then he headed to the adjoining bathroom to change.

Slipping out from his office into the hall, making sure he avoided sight of the security camera, he swiftly made his way across to the emergency exit, down the stairs and onto the street.

Pulling his peaked running cap down as far as he could he walked to the taxi rank three blocks away and got into the first one. Giving an address two streets away from his parents' he sat into the back and once past the pleasantries buried his face in his phone. Paying in cash with an unremarkable tip, keeping his head down, he made his way towards his parents'. Avoiding the front gate he headed down the side street and rounded the corner to the rear access and old servants' entrance to the house. Hardly used these days it was overgrown and deserted. Scaling the wall rather than disturbing the rust and dirt on the gate, he flipped over the coping with ease and keeping tight to the wall made his way around to the front door.

With no other option he rang the bell. He felt stupid, standing there, waiting, guessing what was going on behind the door.

Enya, primed for his arrival, opened the door within seconds and immediately threw herself at her brother.

"What are we going to do?" she asked as he peeled her arms from around his neck: even in the face of turmoil he was uncomfortable with such measures of affection.

"How's Mum?"

"Still sleeping."

"Is she hurt? Did she say anything?"

"She's still out for the count."

"Okay, go back upstairs, stay with her and, if she wakes up, I don't know, knock her out again."

Despite the humour Enya nodded eagerly before asking, "What are you going to do?"

"I'm not sure – just go and I'll get you when I'm done."

Waiting till she was out of the way Seb headed straight for the sitting room. Pushing the door open slowly he stepped gingerly into the room. And there he was: William, slumped forward on the desk, his arms hanging loose at his sides. From where he stood he couldn't see his father's face, just the back of his head and a deep burgundy patch standing out against the salt-and-pepper colouring of his hair.

On the floor, not far from his father lay the log his mother had used. He circled it twice, assuming its purpose, then turned back to his father, stepping around to see his face. He certainly looked dead.

Kneeling down and taking a fortifying breath he delicately took hold of his wrist only to drop it almost instantly, sure he felt a faint but definite pulse. With his own heart racing, he checked again. Yes, William was alive and, as if sparked by the magnetic connection of Seb's touch, opened his eyes wide. With a terrified screech Seb jumped back, almost knocking over the lamp on the bureau as he reached out to steady himself.

"Bloody hell!" he exclaimed, clutching his pounding chest.

Composing himself, he stepped in close again even

more cautiously than before to look into his father's dead eyes. But they weren't dead.

They moved slightly but didn't blink, were open but unfocused.

Seb stood up straight and considered the limp and almost lifeless body slumped over the desk in front of him. Out of the corner of his eye the log beckoned him. He resisted both it and the words that were merging to formulate a scheme of his own for as long as he could, until eventually he could ignore them no longer because, quite simply, they were beginning to make sense.

He walked out to the hall to make sure Enya was safely out of the way and, heading back to the living room, picked up the log. *Fair play to her*, he thought, thinking of his mother and the weight of the log in his hands. He stepped forward until he was standing over his father's body, probably in almost the same spot his mother had stood earlier and, sizing up the wound, the position of the log in his hand and the calculated force needed, he aimed. Raising the log slowly above his head he brought it down heavy, fast and precisely onto the back of his father's head. Again. An eerie hiss, like the final expulsion of air from a deflating balloon released from William's lips. Seb watched him for a minute to see if anything else might happen, but there was no more. Slowly William's eyes closed.

Bracing himself, Seb checked William's pulse again. Nothing.

Crossing to the almost extinguished fire Seb took the poker from the hearth to stoke the dying embers. Placing a fire lighter in the middle to reignite the flames he cast the log in and watched as it was quickly engulfed in the thick grey smoke until finally the bark begin to smoulder before igniting itself.

Focusing his mind on the task that still lay ahead, he told himself: it needs to look like someone else did this. Like they were looking for something. Building the motive into the scene, he took the keys to the safe from William's belt and made his way to the study and began the systematic disruption of an ordinarily untidy but organised personal workspace. Ignoring his conscience which tried to remind him of what he had just done, he felt an extraordinary, almost exhilarating delight as he wiped the desk clear of its belongings and imagined his father standing in front of him watching.

"*The pleasure is all mine*," he whispered to the vision in the empty room.

The chime of the grandfather clock in the hall brought him rudely back to his mission. Sitting down in the chair in front of the desk he yanked at the middle drawer and, realising it was locked, plucked the ring of keys from his pocket. But thinking twice, he picked up the letter opener from the floor and drove it hard into the lock. He pushed with all his might until the timber splintered, shattering a little further when the drawer hit the ground. Not even remotely interested in its contents he got up from the chair and stepped over the clutter to walk in the direction of the recessed cupboard. Pulling the doors open, he cast the contents carelessly aside with some spilling out on to the floor, Seb didn't stop till the safe was fully revealed. This was the mystical item of their youth. As old as the house, or so they were told, Seb remembered the fascination of it as a child and his endless imaginings of all sorts of fantastical reasons why the house was built with it at all.

Taking the key from the ring he placed its long thin stem into the hole, turned it and heaved open the heavy cast-iron door. Leaning in he peered into the darkness. There were the usual and expected things inside, jewellery, passports and the like, which he paid no heed to. He was more interested in the bundle of documents on the top shelf. Pulling them out he sat on the floor to see what he had found.

There was something inside for each of them, a reward or consolation prize of sorts he thought mordantly as he opened each of the files. Ciara's original but never-filed birth certificate; Martha's fact file as compiled by McDaid; a letter from Father Sullivan addressed to Rian, an apology, it seemed, crafted from his death bed four years ago; and finally the deeds of Tanglewood for Enya. But for Cormac was the unintended and definitely most hilarious prize of all. In an unassuming white envelope with William's name typed formally on it was a bundle of 10 x 8 colour prints. Seb instinctively knew what they were before he'd even extracted the first picture.

Oh good God, he asked himself almost hysterically. *Is that Judy Hayes? Cormac, the little shit, is going to love this one!* He chuckled, flicking through the intimate pictures. Judy Hayes was the ultimate hustler, everyone knew that, he scoffed, disappointed more by his father's choice of woman than his act of indiscretion. She'd been around forever and for everyone, it seemed. So, it was like father like son, Seb decided, putting the photographs back into the envelope and wondering who had taken them and how much William had paid to keep it quiet. How disappointing.

Seb knew that collectively these individual files would

become William Bertram's legacy to each of them. They were the score-settlers that would set about putting their lives on track and filing away their past.

And for himself, his own prize was at the bottom of the pile. Underneath the rest was the file he had been looking for, the file that would help him put things right. With *Ronson Street* written on its face he didn't need to look inside there – he knew that somewhere within the sheaves of multicoloured papers he would find the evidence needed to properly put right what his father had put wrong.

"Jesus, Seb!" Enya exclaimed, coming into the room. "What on earth have you done?"

"I have created a story," he stated calmly. "That's what I've done."

He stood to survey the room and, satisfied he'd done a good job, fixed his T-shirt over his tracksuit bottoms and, gathering up the files, left the study to head back to the hall and the little cubby under the stairs. Taking a rucksack off a hook he put the files from the safe into it and dropped the bag at the bottom of the stairs. Then making his way to the kitchen and out to the utility room with Enya on his heels he wrapped a towel around his fist and punched the window hard from the outside in, unlocked the window and carefully distributed the glass to look like someone had climbed through. With the scene set he left the way he came with instructions for Enya to wait a full hour before calling him first and the police after.

When she woke and came downstairs Barbara had been confused by what she saw. Supported by Enya who told her to say nothing, at first she actually thought she'd done it. There was no other explanation. And as the police asked question after question she was asking herself the same thing: *What happened here?*

It was much later sitting around Ciara's kitchen table that Seb handed each of them their respective file and explained what he had done, leaving out his role in certifying their father's death. With minute precision together they agreed on their story, keeping it as close to reality as possible, ensuring the least amount of error.

Seb knew Milford didn't believe them, he knew he would always be looking over his shoulder waiting for the day when he or some other overeager investigator would come knocking on his door looking to know what happened or worse still having figured out what happened. But, Seb had already decided, it was a better life to lead than the one decided and dictated by a man with only his own self-serving interests at heart.

Toasting the bride and groom, Seb took the remains of his whisky in one go and got up to leave the party, a very guilty but equally content man.

THE END